GIRL FROM THE BLUE CLOUD NEBULA

GIRL FROM THE BLUE CLOUD NEBULA

B C HOWELL

Cover Design: B C Howell

ISBN–13:
978–1723240751

To: All the people I've known who help others as a way of life and don't realize it's a big deal—thank you.

1

The Sufficiency Test

CONVERGING ON THE GLENWOOD HEIGHTS COMMUNITY of Los Angeles, sirens and helicopters jolted Sunday morning sleepers awake just before dawn. A hot July, the vintage suburban neighborhoods were accustomed to the constant drone of rooftop swamp coolers and distant highway noise, but no one could sleep through this new racket, especially as barking dogs and sleepy children added to the uproar. While some residents rushed outside to look, most turned on local TV stations or went online for answers, but none were available until the first news chopper arrived and began transmitting live.

> "This is Rachel Hughes in Skybird 6 with breaking news.
>
> "As you can see, the Glenwood Heights High School is gone. So are the ballfields, park, roads, and recreation areas. In their place, a huge square expanse of tall grass with a strange three-story house at the center.
>
> "See how roads have been cut clean away at the outer boundaries of the grassy area? Fences, yards, and small buildings that protrude across the boundaries of the area are the same way. Look at that

playset, cut in half! Where did the rest of it go? What could have caused this?

"I'm turning the camera to three police cruisers arriving in front of the house. Two officers are running up onto the front porch while four others run around to the back. More police vehicles are entering the grassy area from surrounding—"

Static interrupted.

"—stopped working so I switched to the stationary tail camera. Whoa! Our pilot just informed me that police helicopters ordered us to move away. Javier, I'll turn it back over to you in the studio until we hear—"

Whomp!

The picture darkened and shook. A man and woman screamed.

The transmission ended.

Dazed with pounding ears and sweating buckets, Detective Lieutenant Tom Patrick sat with his back against the front bumper of an unmarked police sedan. Just beyond his outstretched feet, a thick layer of brownish-orange substance had replaced the mysterious grass. He guessed that it was responsible for the stifling heat. Drawing his legs up and getting to his knees, he "walked" forward on his hands to confirm he was right then slipped and put a palm down when he reached out to it.

Next thing Patrick knew, he was back leaning against the car bumper holding his burned, blistered hand and experiencing a violent onset of nausea. Vaguely, he recalled following two patrol cars toward a big Victorian house when swirling, glowing grit engulfed the way ahead and he stopped just before plunging into it.

Then he spaced out for a while.

Feeling cooler, his thinking was more coherent. He forced his head up to look out across the barren area. The house was there, but he'd worked cases in these stucco neighborhoods for years and never seen the likes of it. Helicopters had been everywhere, too. Where were they?

His cellphone was in his hand. He tried to call for help, reminding him the battery had been dead after the incident. The car's battery, too. That's why he'd gotten out, wasn't it?

A solitary squad car with the front doors wide open set in front of the big house with an officer standing beside it. He didn't seem to know where he was. Patrick wondered how he missed seeing the man and car the first time he looked.

But several patrols had been at the house when the blast, or whatever it was, occurred. He'd heard them on the radio. Where were the other vehicles? The other officers? And where in the hell did the helicopters go?

Reaching with a finger to wipe away a sticky substance blurring one eye, he discovered it was blood. He should have been concerned, but he wasn't.

Patrick closed his eyes and experienced a floating sensation. It wasn't unpleasant, felt good, in fact. But why was he feeling so cold now?

A slight noise pricked his policeman's instinct, demanded attention.

A pretty girl, mid-teens perhaps, wearing a voluminous black calash over honey blond hair that cascaded over the front shoulders of a lacy black dress with cuffed long sleeves, stood just inside the barren area regarding him with concerned brown eyes.

She reminded him of the PBS Victorian dramas his ex-wife had made him watch, the ones he grew to dislike almost as much as her. Then it occurred to him that the girl might be nothing more than his confused mind using the past to play tricks. He looked closer at her clothes, trying to decide whether she was real or not.

Her dress reached to just below the knees with a thick ruffled petticoat underneath that he could plainly see from his low vantage point. Glossy black, high-button shoes wrapped tight around her ankles. Black diamond-patterned leggings emphasized shapely legs, and he felt guilty appreciating them because of her age.

He must have blacked out. His legs were numb, tingly, and so heavy he couldn't move them. He made his eyes open again.

The girl sat face-to-face on his lap, black diamond legs stretched provocatively either side of his hips. Bunched up between them, the rest of the dress and petticoat spread out behind her over his legs. He was underneath them with her, yet felt nothing of her body other than warmth and weight.

She held a big ugly doll with a pinched, misshaped white face pressed against his chest. He wanted to push it away, but couldn't feel his arms, much less raise them. He tried to tell her to stop, but couldn't speak.

Then, in a voice devoid of any expression, the girl said, "No effect shall extend beyond the prescribed area during the test, John Justice."

Behind her, in the exact spot she had stood in the barren area, a pale, slight boy appeared. Younger, but with similar features and Victorian clothing that included tight knee pants, he gave an impression of being excessively prim and proper.

"Criticizing test methodology could be interpreted as interfering, you know," he responded with a toss of his wispy blond hair.

She did not look away from Patrick. "I'm merely pointing out an error. I have a right to demand they correct it."

"A few casualties more or less now won't make any difference to the outcome. You shouldn't be sitting on him that way, either. He will have bad ideas."

"It's so I can administer to his injuries without getting my clothes dirty."

"It's a waste of time helping him, and it looks indecent, Mercy Ann," he responded, making it a sharp rebuke.

She twisted around, giving a hard stare over her shoulder. "No effect shall extend beyond the prescribed area during the test."

"You already said that."

"Yes, because you didn't go tell them to make adjustments after the first time."

"You do it. They won't listen to me."

"Do as I say before I get pissed off. Their ship will be in deep space out of range soon."

Making an exasperated noise, he vanished.

She withdrew the doll from Patrick and felt his cheek with the backs of exceptionally white fingers. "Sorry for your injury."

Then she was gone.

Rob Pike, a brainiac high schooler ready to begin his senior year, lived in a neighborhood adjacent to the school and park. He had worked several jobs to buy a sophisticated drone with a professional HD camera to use for science experiments. At least, that's what he told his mother. The real reason was so he could get naked pictures of Missa MaCaron, whose house was directly behind his and the only two-story on the block.

They had grown up together—bookworm nerds so close her parents installed a gate in the back fence for their convenience. The relationship continued into their second year of high school when she shocked him by trying out for the cheerleader squad. Not that he was surprised they chose her. She had trained and competed in martial arts since preschool and was in tiptop physical condition.

But Missa had never been interested in school social activities until then. Her idea of fun was taking engines apart, building complicated mechanical devices, and understanding their science. Often, she and Rob worked on projects together, competing to impress each other. So it was only natural their parents thought they would become romantically involved at some point. So had Rob, but then Missa's popularity went off the charts as a cheerleader and a new circle of in-crowders closed around her, determined to keep separation from dorky Rob.

Missa began dating a certain Jerry O'Brien, heartthrob football star who drove a hot red convertible. Feeling completely outclassed, Rob doted on her from afar, missing her terribly. He told himself that he didn't want naked pictures for revenge or prurient reasons. He simply wanted something deeply personal that he could hold onto until the pain of losing her to the biggest jerk in school subsided.

To that end, Rob practiced flying the drone until he was expert. His single mother, a second shift emergency room nurse, often did not return home until after midnight. Missa was as far from a morning person as anyone could be and usually bathed after supper rather than before school, so he had many opportunities to spy on her.

Yet, Rob hesitated until near the end of the school year when Jerry and his football buddies corralled him and warned to stay away from Missa during summer break. Then they took his clothes, leaving him to run home in underwear after telling their classmates. The video went viral and he became a laughingstock.

The following night, Rob, with tears in his eyes, flew the drone outside Missa's window and saw her on the monitor gloriously naked before a full-length mirror. Hardly able to breathe, his hands shook as he reached to turn on the camera.

He wimped out. The drone had been exiled to a shelf in his bedroom ever since.

This morning, after the sirens and helicopters woke him and his mother, she decided to go to the hospital emergency room in case the incident caused enough casualties to need extra nurses and give her overtime. Since the car battery and phones were dead, she jumped on Rob's bicycle and took off. To say the least, his mother was anything but average.

When the power came back on, Rob was surprised his cellphone battery showed a charge again. He listened to excited reporters on the news while holding the front door open a crack to watch police and other emergency personnel running door-to-door yelling everyone had to evacuate. There had been fatalities, but no one seemed to know where or how many.

A few minutes later, more police showed up and began herding people away from the disaster area so they could cordon it off. Then trucks and buses began arriving and evacuating people whether they wanted to go or not. It was amazing how fast everything happened and how little anyone seemed to know.

Rob's curiosity was aroused. He locked the door, turned off the TV, and retrieved the drone, not realizing these batteries had been dead before the blackout.

A tall hedge ran along the park side of their backyard wooden fence, so he couldn't see into it the way Missa could from the upstairs of her house. He tried to launch and discovered the battery had run down. Running back into the house hoping the spare had power, he heard pounding on the front door and ignored it. Seconds later, he was back outside.

Missa, hair in tangles, no makeup, and a big untucked men's dress shirt half-buttoned over rumpled, ragged jeans, stood next to the drone. Obviously not wearing a bra, she stretched and yawned mightily.

"What's all the racket?" she wanted to know.

"According to the news, our school and everything around it were blown up or something. People, helicopters, and vehicles are missing. Supposedly, a big house no one has seen before is all that's out there now. Didn't you look out your window?"

She clasped hands over her head and leaned back, stretching again. "That's just nuts. Does your mom have coffee on? My parents left early to show houses."

He had to force his gaze away from her. "She went to the hospital. Something sure as hell is going on. They're evacuating everyone."

"I take it you're planning to fly your quadcopter for a look. I've been waiting for you to offer to let me try it."

Just as if it was his fault, he thought, expelling a deep breath. "If this battery doesn't have a charge, there's no time."

Her thoughts were slow until she had coffee. "They can't make us leave our homes, can they?"

Behind them, a girl's voice. "That is what they're doing."

Very pretty, her black dress and huge bonnet were outrageous. Even stranger, in spite of being too old for dolls, she held a big fancy-dressed one with a creepy face in the crook of one arm.

Rob blurted, "Did mom leave the front gate open?"

The girl ignored his question. "Can your drone stream video?"

Rob glanced at Missa, wondering if she knew her. "Of course it can."

Absurdly resolute, the girl walked to him and thrust out a hand. "Give me the battery for a sec."

Surprised, he handed it to her.

She touched it to her forearm and gave it back. "Fully charged. Hurry. They'll be here in a few minutes." She ran around the corner of the house.

Rob went after her then hurried back to Missa shaking his head. "The gate's locked. I don't see how she could have gotten over an eight foot fence so fast in that getup."

Missa grabbed the battery and put it in the copter. "How'd she know it had a full charge?"

They were struck speechless the moment the craft cleared the fence. Everything was gone except a huge field of tall grass around a big square of orange-brown ground with a three-story yellow house trimmed in green standing at the center. Flying low and fast, Rob guided the drone towards it then sent it straight up about fifty feet.

Standing on the front porch were an old woman and blond boy. Her gray hair was pinned in a bun and she wore a long-sleeved, to-the-ankle dress from a bygone era. The boy had on a black waistcoat and knee breeches.

"Looks like a movie set," Missa commented.

Rob turned the camera to the police car in front of the house. Standing beside it, an officer with a dazed expression seemed stuck repeating the same motion—slowly wadding and unwadding a sheet of paper in both hands. Rob panned the area and discovered another man in a soiled suit trudging toward him.

Sirens sounded just up the street and Rob began bringing the copter back.

Missa said, "Those people at the house were dressed in medieval clothing same as that girl."

"It's Victorian, not medieval," Rob corrected. "So is the house."

"Yeah, whatever," she answered, irritated because he always corrected her about things that didn't matter. "Anyway, the school didn't blow up because there's no rubble, and who are those weird people? Do you have any ideas?"

She'd always given him a hard time for watching TV shows about aliens, so he didn't mention them as the only explanation that came to mind. "Got me."

As the drone came over the fence, Missa thought of something else. "You sent the video to social media already, didn't you?"

"No. I'll just give it to the authorities."

"If you do, they'll probably haul us off to jail for filming the balls-up result of some secret experiment. Might even be on the way to arrest us already."

Although not nearly as paranoid as his mother, Missa shared her beliefs in wild conspiracies and big brother activities when it came to the federal government. Rob laughed.

Reddening, Missa defended herself. "What else can this be? They're evacuating everyone so they can clean up the mess they made. Seriously, I think we should put the video on the internet. Then it won't accomplish anything for them to arrest us."

He picked up the drone. "They're evacuating people for safety reasons. That's all this is."

Without warning, she threw her arms around him. "Promise you won't leave me again."

His knees almost buckled with her hanging on him. "I didn't leave you!"

"Going to make me say it, aren't you? I'm sorry for what that jerk, Jerry, did to you. I just wanted to be sure of my feelings before getting too committed to you. I sure messed things up."

Shouting and heavy pounding came from the front of the house. They bolted through the back gate and ran into Missa's house. She grabbed some clothes off a dirty pile in the laundry room, wrapped them in a towel, and took her mother's SUV keys from a hook as they ran to the garage. Rob, texting his mom they were going to the MaCarons' real estate office, followed on her heels.

Police crashed in the back door as they drove away. The drone was on the floor next to the kitchen table. They called forensics and searched the house.

Rob drove while Missa, in the bucket seat next to him, pulled out a twisted black sports bra and yellow pullover from the towel. She sniffed them then slid down in the seat, unbuttoned the shirt, and pulled it off.

"Keep your eyes on the road," she said, staring up at him.

It was impossible. "Are you crazy?"

She tugged on the bra and top then grinned at his red face. "I could have put them on under the shirt, but didn't think it mattered. We used to bathe together, after all."

"We were little kids."

"We weren't little kids when you saw me naked with the quadcopter. Did you get good pictures?"

It took a few seconds to answer, but there was no point in lying. "Didn't take any. I'm sorry."

"Sorry you peeked in my window or sorry you didn't use the camera?"

His throat constricted. "Mostly that I did it. It was stupid."

"Mostly? Then you wish you'd made yourself a dirty little video of Melissa MaCaron naked, huh? Why would you even think of doing something like that to me?"

Suddenly, without meaning to, words came out. "Because I love you and missed you so much it hurt all the time!"

He couldn't believe he'd told her. Jerry O'Brien was right. He was pathetic.

Missa rested a very warm hand on his arm. "Let's stop and eat. I have to get some coffee or my brain's going to shrivel and die."

The restaurant was crowded but they didn't wait long to order. Then Missa received a call and exchanged a few quick comments before clicking off.

"Mom got a call about us from frigging Homeland Security. I told you."

He was incredulous. "What'd they want?"

"Wouldn't tell her. Dad says to stay away from the house until they find out what the problem is. They'll be with clients until eleven and meet us at the office. I have a key so we can wait for them." She saw the waitress coming with food. "Wow, look at that omelet."

As they ate, Missa kept glancing at him with uncharacteristic blush on her cheeks until he asked, "Going to let me in on the secret?"

"It's a little hard to say."

He was intrigued because she was very hard to embarrass. "You know you're going to tell me."

She leaned close. "Kiss me."

He was the shy one, the one who always looked around the room or hesitated too long, but not today. He kissed her hard on the mouth.

"I don't suppose you have any condoms," she asked, looking at him with softness he'd never before seen in her. "There's a drug store near the office. You can get some there."

"Missa...?"

Two black police vans with flashing lights roared up to the entrance of the restaurant. Six officers in SWAT gear leaped out and ran into the dining room. Forming a phalanx with assault rifles shouldered and sweeping the room, they yelled for everyone to remain seated and keep their hands in sight.

In seconds, they had Rob and Missa corralled in the booth. Big hands grabbed and shoved them to the floor. Turning his head, Rob saw Missa's grimacing face ground into the carpet and reacted, trying to kick her assailant, which earned him an expertly placed knee in the back and twisting of the wrists as zip tie restraints drew tight around them.

Applying painful pressure to their arms, the officers perp-walked the teenagers outside and shoved them into an unmarked black van that pulled up. When it roared away, the SWAT team piled into their vans and left.

Meanwhile, a man in a suit entered the restaurant dining room from the kitchen, held up a badge, and explained that the couple were drug dealers. Then he wished everyone a good day and departed to a smattering of applause and complaints. While he was inside occupying everyone's attention, his partner drove off in the MaCaron's SUV. The entire scenario took less than four minutes.

On the floor of the unmarked van, Rob and Missa had black hoods with drawstrings tied over their heads. Heavier restraints immobilized their ankles, legs, and arms. A man made a call to ask which kind of injection to give them. Seconds later, they were unconscious.

A Division Director from the Department of Homeland Security (DHS) was on a surprise inspection tour in a helicopter headed to Los Angeles with two agents when notified by Washington to go to the disaster site, take charge, and assess the situation.

He surprised local authorities with his quickness to the scene. First thing, he forbade anyone assisting the two police survivors near the big house until he personally surveyed the site, drawing the ire of emergency personnel suiting up in hazmat gear to retrieve them, especially after he and his agents appropriated the gear for themselves.

As they put it on, the Director received a text and announced to the locals, "Federal agents took down the terrorists who flew the drone over the area, so you can stop looking for them."

The mayor had arrived. "You're officially calling this a terrorist attack?"

The Director reacted more officiously than necessary. "For now, we'll say it appears to be a natural disaster but won't rule out the possibility of terrorists until we investigate more fully."

The DHS men had bodycams fitted to the hazmat suits and established secure feeds through the local office to their headquarters in Washington. When the mayor complained, the Director assured he would provide copies of the videos to the city. Both knew it was a lie.

A few minutes later, driving a police SUV slowly across the strange substance blanketing bare ground, they reached the police officers standing next to a squad car. They were Detective Lieutenant Tom Patrick and a uniformed officer, Andy Lawrence, who was too confused to make sense.

Patrick described how he survived the blast and went to help Officer Lawrence, not mentioning his encounter with the girl and boy. The last thing he wanted was a psychological evaluation marring his record. If someone else saw them, then perhaps he'd say something.

The Director noticed something clenched in Lawrence's hand. Patrick worked it free and carefully tugged it open. A hand-printed sheet of paper, the letters were so precise they might be mistaken for commercial printing from a few feet away.

Sufficiency Test Site for Humankind

You must solve the riddle:

This is an alien facility with capabilities vastly superior to yours
Destroy it and pass the test without further evaluation
Each unsuccessful attack doubles the area of devastation and increases chances of failure
As the situation evolves, you must take the most intelligent actions or fail the test

Sufficiency judged at the end of Day 30

Pass — Humankind continues on present course
Fail — Humankind purged from Earth

This is Test Day 1

The Director scowled. "Is this bullshit someone's idea of a sick joke?"

Giving the paper back to Patrick, he ordered him to stay with Lawrence, and the DHS agents went onto the porch. Peering through the thick glass of the big door, they saw a high foyer with a crystal chandelier and an ornate switchback central staircase. To the left was a parlor sitting room with velvet upholstered furniture, shiny wooden tables, and ornate lamps plugged into electric outlets, which looked out of place in this house.

A boy wearing a frilly white dress shirt, black knee pants, and glossy black shoes sat on the stairs staring at them. The men looked at each other because he had not been there a few seconds ago. When they looked back, the boy was gone.

The Director yelled, pounded, and shook the door. “Open up!”

An old woman walked into the parlor from somewhere they couldn’t see. She had on an apron over an ankle-length dress. After waggling a big wooden spoon at them, she turned and went back the way she came.

Angered by defiance to his authority, the Director stepped back to kick in the door. “Homeland Security, open the door now!”

A pretty blond girl peered at him through the glass and mouthed, “Please don’t.”

He kicked the door with all his might.

The second incident disintegrated everything inside a square area two times larger than the first except for the house, the squad car, and two cops next to it—as revealed minutes later when a swirling orange-brown cloud of granules settled gently to the ground.

Missa MaCaron’s parents ditched their clients after hearing news of a second incident and not being able to get their daughter on her cellphone. Driving to the office, a radio station ranted that terrorists had to be responsible. Worried, her mother drove too fast and an unmarked police car roared up behind them, signaling to pull over.

The MaCarons tried to explain their hurry to the police while she rummaged a new purse for the license, which for some stupid reason was not in the wallet where it should be. Then men in suits appeared on both sides of the vehicle with weapons drawn and yelling at them to get out. In short order, they arrested, cuffed, and shoved the couple into the caged backseat of a black SUV. Two men in jeans and sports shirts jumped in and drove off with them. An identical SUV with two women followed close behind.

The hospital emergency room was crazy busy all morning. Ashlyn Pike finally got a short break, shed her bloody operating gown and gloves, and then sprinted down the hall to a staff bathroom while trying to call Rob. When he didn’t answer, she left a voicemail and sent a text to Missa for one of them to contact her.

Seeing someone’s feet waiting outside the bathroom stall wasn’t unusual. Ashlyn hurried out and a tall blond nurse carrying folded hospital blankets blocked the way. A small, youngish nurse standing at a sink turned and jabbed a hypodermic into her thigh.

They carried Ashlyn, wrapped in blankets, out to a gurney in the hall just as Mercy Ann appeared in the bathroom. Hair in a ponytail and wearing shorts, t-shirt, and flip-flops, she listened at the door then followed the nurses to an exit. She walked past while they loaded

Ashlyn into an ambulance with two men inside then stood at the curb looking around as if waiting for someone to pick her up until the ambulance departed. The two nurses followed it in a black SUV.

Mercy Ann appeared in the dining room of the Victorian house.

Crumbling a handful of crackers over a big bowl of tomato soup, John Justice saw how she was dressed and frowned. “Does this mean I can stop wearing these stupid horror movie clothes?”

She did not like the question. “I went somewhere and didn’t want to be noticed, that’s all. Anyway, that suit looks good on you. Stop complaining about it.”

“It’s hot, tight, and uncomfortable, not to mention a hundred years out of fashion.”

“Get used to it,” she snapped. “It’s important everyone remembers seeing us in the beginning.”

“We could wear clown costumes or cute Japanese neko ears if that’s all you want,” he muttered as he began eating.

Hiding how much his words stung, Mercy Ann said, “You were right about authorities picking up those high schoolers and their parents for questioning, but I didn’t see anything sinister about it. Just the usual heavy-handed cop overreaction horseshit. They’ll probably apologize and release them after questioning.”

“Wouldn’t be so sure,” John Justice answered, dabbing his mouth daintily with the corner of a linen napkin. “Many of the arrests were by agents working outside regular government channels. Some were even criminals masquerading as agents. They operate with impunity under the noses of legitimate law enforcement. It’s an unusual situation that’s very well organized.”

“Are you certain?”

As much as he enjoyed telling her things she didn’t know, it annoyed him having his lunch interrupted. “They appear to have a well-defined agenda and be ready to do whatever necessary to carry it out.”

“For what purpose?”

“I don’t know. You don’t want me to waste time finding out, do you?”

She could tell he wanted to get under her skin, but held her temper. “I got those teenagers involved and feel responsible. Please keep tabs on them. In fact, find out what’s going on with the bogus agents. Might be something we can use.”

The order massively annoyed him. “You’re not planning to violate more directives and meddle in this planet’s political affairs, are you?”

“It probably won’t be necessary.”

A non-answer irritated him even more. "Why did you insist we try to help Earth pass the test, anyway? You keep saying that you don't have a clue what to do, other than hang around in hopes something occurs to you. We're just wasting time, and you upset the Guardians for no reason."

As usual, when confronted with arguments citing irrefutable facts or criticism, Mercy Ann became evasive and shifted the subject. "In all our trips to Earth, you've liked the people we've met, haven't you? Do you want all of them to die?"

"Of course not," he replied, aggravated she would even ask such a thing, "but Guardian tests are fair. If Earthlings deserve to survive, they will. What puzzles me is that you always hated this planet and now you want to save everyone. Good grief, nothing you do makes any sense."

Tired of him badgering her, she made up a lie to shut him up. "If you must know, Earth reminds me of the planet where my brother and I grew up. It faced a similar test and failed, so it hurts me having to discuss these matters. Pisses me off, too."

Dumfounded, he stared. She and her brother had always refused to talk about their home system except to say it was far away from the Guardian territory they patrolled. And since her brother died, she pitched fits if anyone asked about him or their home planet, and now he'd made her discuss it with him, of all people.

"I didn't mean to bring back bad memories for you again, Mercy Ann," he said finally.

Then stop the whiny bullshit, she thought, and called out to the kitchen, "Miss Flowers, I want some soup. Bring it to my room, please."

The old woman looked into the dining room to make certain Mercy Ann was gone before speaking. "That girl and her foul mouth. She made all that up to keep you twisted around her little finger. Will you ever learn that you can't believe a thing she says?"

He wouldn't look at her. "She sounded sincere this time."

Miss Flowers returned to the kitchen. "Doesn't she always?"

The Deputy Secretary of DHS addressed Dr. Helen Rogers, the Under Secretary of Intelligence & Analysis, in their Washington headquarters. "How long before you can give us useful data?"

She had two doctorates and resented political hacks such as him, yet answered professionally with pretty much the same response as when they talked privately before the meeting began. "Our teams will be onsite in twenty minutes and provide an initial assessment, assuming it's safe."

"But you don't personally have any idea why there are no bodies or wreckage, do you?"

"We saw everything disintegrating on the helicopter news video," she responded evenly, "which must account for the layers of matter on the ground."

"What could do that?" he demanded.

As he well knew, the answer was nothing on Earth, but she couldn't discuss the existence of otherworldly beings except with people who had the proper clearances, and not even their boss, the DHS Secretary, was on the list. In fact, of all the people in the room, only she and the Deputy Secretary knew the truth about aliens.

She answered as best she could. "Anything I say at this point will only be conjecture."

Shaking his head to show his poor opinion of her, he had videos shown from cameras outside the area destroyed by the second incident.

Aghast, everyone watched as vehicles, houses, and people dissolved in swirling clouds of matter that quickly settled to the ground. Objects and people that straddled the new boundary line of destruction appeared to have parts sliced off because the disintegration occurred so quickly.

Ignoring a man throwing up, the Deputy asked the hushed room if anyone had any comments.

To his aggravation, Dr. Rogers asked that they show the Sufficiency Notice from the site. She pointed out the first incident created a one-eighth mile square of destruction around the house, and the second doubled the size to a perfect one-quarter mile square, exactly as the notice warned. She knew of no weapon or explosive that could so precisely limit damage to a defined area.

The Deputy disliked her so much he had a bad taste in his mouth. She had been a shoo-in to head DHS before the President gave the job to a close friend. Then everyone assumed she would be Deputy and the President appointed him instead. Now she opposed and embarrassed him constantly, and he felt threatened by her.

"I want satellite lasers used to verify your numbers before we announce any findings," he ordered with a sneer.

"Those were satellite measurements," she responded, not hiding her contempt.

The bitch, he thought. It's time to show her who's in charge.

"Then you must believe we should take everything on that scrap of paper literally," he shot back, no matter that she had said no such thing. "If we attack the building, the consequence will be an area of destruction a half mile square. Is that your official position?"

Politically, she thought it better to sound strong and be wrong than to sound weak and be right. "Absolutely!"

"Then you must think we should just sit back and do nothing to combat a dangerous threat in the middle of an American city."

Since she couldn't mention aliens, he had her in a corner, but before he could pounce, a young woman hurried in with a message for the Deputy, forcing him to switch off the microphone while they had an intense whispered exchange.

Finally, he announced, "The terrorist video from the drone flown over the site was put on the internet by hacking into a communications satellite over Africa. We need to determine whether an enemy government was involved, so I'm adjourning so department heads can consult with staffs before we finalize briefing information for the Secretary to present tonight. No one leave the building, please."

After everyone filed out, the Deputy motioned the assistant back. "Tell me the rest."

"The drone operators are students from the missing high school and insist they only wanted to see what all the fuss was about. They claim to have no knowledge how the video got on the internet. Nothing indicates they have contacts outside the United States, or that they communicated with anyone after the incident other than the girl's mother. Nothing about any of the parents is suspicious. Should we release them?"

His stare showed contempt for the question. "We can't have troublemakers blabbing about the incident since they may contradict the facts we decide to present. They could kick up a fuss about how we subjected them to enhanced interrogation, too. That would be most unwelcome since everything we did was with people outside official channels. We have no choice but to make them casualties of the event. Schools are overcrowded anyway."

The assistant forced a smile at his sick joke, not daring show how appalled she was that he could sentence two high schoolers to death so easily. "Yes sir."

But then something else occurred to him. "On second thought, transfer them to our western interrogation facility. They had to be involved with getting that video onto the satellite. Do whatever it takes to find out who worked with them. Gloves off. Is that clear?"

"Yes sir. What about the parents?"

"Keep them on ice for the time being."

After she hurried away, the Deputy placed a call on a secure line and whispered the details of Homeland Security's actions to the man leading a conspiracy to seize control of the government.

Meanwhile, at the White House, the DHS Secretary entered the Oval Office and found the President stressed and troubled. Friends since meeting in a college fraternity, the Secretary knew it was better to wait for the President to discuss matters with him. He began outlining his department's findings.

"The military says aliens from space are responsible for Los Angeles," the President stated suddenly. "Can you believe it?"

The Secretary's surprise was genuine. He did not know what to say.

"They insisted I not tell anyone outside a special group, but screw them, you're in charge of Homeland Security." He took a folder off his desk. "Look at these pictures."

The first showed two oval lights against a black sky. The next was a close-up of a disk-shaped object, the quintessential flying saucer.

The Secretary gasped. "Are these real?"

"So they say, but it's hard for me to believe."

The President and his family had strict fundamentalist religious beliefs so the Secretary understood why he'd be upset. He had trouble believing it, too, but not because of religion. It was simply too extraordinary.

"The light with the circle drawn around it is a UFO over LA the night the school disappeared," the President explained when the Secretary reached the last photo. "What do you think?"

"Doesn't look any different than other lights."

The President nodded and tossed the folder back onto his desk in a dismissive manner. "They say we've been aware of aliens for years, but this is the first time any have been brash enough to land a ship in a major city and commit acts of war."

"There's a ship?"

"Yeah, well, our scientists claim to have data indicating one on the ground where the house is, only we can't see it," the President said, very dubious. "They're making a presentation to the inner circle about these things after the staff meeting this evening. I want you to stay for the second meeting. I'll have them change your security clearance."

The Secretary was astounded. "I thought I already had access to everything."

The President shook his head. "Once we eliminate the menace in LA, we'll announce terrorists were holed up in a tunnel plotting another attack or something. That'll stop the world from panicking about aliens and leave precious beliefs intact. God knows, we have enough to deal with without stirring up something else."

The Secretary mind was awhirl. "Are you certain we have the means to defeat them?"

The President did not sound very sure. "Turns out, we have missiles and other weapons under wraps that is based on alien technology. The military assures me they will do the job. You'll hear more about them tonight."

"You weren't told about aliens and these secret weapons until now?" the Secretary realized suddenly.

"Heads will roll when this is over," the President answered as his face reddened, "but the first order of business has to be moving everyone out of danger and trying to come up with plausible explanations for the missing bodies and everything at the site. I've declared martial law, imposed a no-fly zone, and deployed military to take control of the area. I'll take a beating in the press for being so heavy-handed and answering questions with obvious lies, but I've been assured the matter will be resolved before my chances of reelection are harmed."

Abruptly, the President stood, shook his friend's hand, and pounded him on the back. "Thanks for coming. See you tonight."

The President's personality and behavior had always struck the Secretary as bizarre, but never before to this extent. He stopped for a double whiskey on the way back to the office.

After the meetings that night, the President addressed the nation. His main goal was to be ambiguous yet reassuring.

He spoke movingly about the dead. He said initial findings suggested gasses with extreme corrosive properties escaped from a deep underground fault. Everything pointed to it being a localized occurrence that needed more investigation, but the danger was contained.

At the same time, given world events, they would not rule out terrorism, although it made no sense attacking a residential area when so many high profile targets existed in Los Angeles.

He warned about misguided people creating videos showing strange occurrences and making absurd claims—reprehensible behavior that dishonored the victims of the disaster. He'd ordered the FBI to investigate and charge those responsible. The Justice Department would prosecute to the full extent of the law.

By the time the President finished, he'd said all the expected things, showed the appropriate concerns, and did as well as anyone could under difficult circumstances. Near the end, he announced the deployment of military to secure the area around the site so local authorities could concentrate efforts on evacuations, protecting citizens, and keeping order. He did not use the term martial law that night, nor did he specify how long it would take to resolve the situation.

Afterward, many TV news outlets showed the Governor and city officials giving details for evacuations and refusing to discuss possible causes for the disaster until federal authorities completed a full investigation.

As the first day ended, the incident was of great interest but not a huge concern outside of Los Angeles, giving the government time to concoct a better cover-up story and plan the secret destruction of the aliens.

2

On This Barbaric Planet?

WATCHING THE SUN COME UP OVER A PARKING LOT, Tom Patrick's aggravation grew having to stay in a hospital bed hooked up to so many machines when he felt fine. He'd answered the same questions repeatedly while kept in ignorance about developments at the disaster site, even suffering insinuations that he'd done something wrong because he could not explain why he and Officer Lawrence didn't die with everyone else.

All he remembered of the second incident was the strange boy holding onto his and Lawrence's arms while blowing grit blew by without hitting them. He couldn't explain that any more than the rest of it, although now he thought the boy saved them and the girl was real.

Not that he was about to tell either story. His life was pretty much crap after a painful divorce from a lonely wife pregnant by someone else because he neglected her to pursue an all-consuming career, which was ironic because it was all he had left and he hated it.

Glancing into the hallway, he could not see the cop stationed outside the door but felt his presence. Two FBI agents had told him the extra security was to keep the press from bothering survivors, but he wasn't foolish enough to believe that was the real reason. They wanted to put a lid on this incident, so authorities had to hear everyone's accounts to insure no one spoke out of turn.

Convoys of military vehicles continued streaming into Los Angeles in greater numbers than the public expected. Army and Guard troops seemed to be setting up temporary facilities everywhere to expedite evacuations and reinforce security around the disaster site.

Meanwhile, scientists and security specialists in hazmat suits combed the devastation taking readings and collecting samples. Under strict orders from the site commander not to touch the house, they took thousands of pictures and videos to examine in temporary labs established nearby.

A special team hauled the squad car away for analysis in hopes of discovering why it survived, a mystery they would never solve because Mercy Ann had John Justice shield the police officer holding the Sufficiency Test notice both times. The purpose was to protect the notice, not the man, because she wanted to insure as many people saw it as possible. Simply by luck, Patrick stood close enough to Lawrence during the second event for John Justice to grab both of them. And since he braced against the vehicle each time, his protective "bubble" encompassed and protected it, too.

A scientist, taking pictures of the front of the house, called the site commander and told him that all of the window glass had just turned opaque and somewhat metallic in appearance. Other scientists confirmed it was the same all around it.

Inside a big discount store in Beverly Hills, two women chatted while pushing shopping carts, each with a small boy in the child seat. They noted how attractive a blond boy and girl dressed in elegant nineteenth century clothes were watching the news on a display TV. They especially liked the girl's honey-blond hair, strikingly radiant under the display lights.

One of the women asked if she and the boy were brother and sister.

Not looking away from the TV, the girl delivered a curt, "No."

The other woman, a famous actress in disguise, tried to strike up a conversation. "Are you actors? Is that why you're wearing period costumes?"

The girl leveled a withering stare at her. "Are you making fun of our clothes?"

Irritated, the actress started to leave then reconsidered. She pushed two business cards into the girl's hand.

"Have your parents call if they're interested," she said, moving away.

One of the cards identified the first woman as head of a top Hollywood talent agency. The other showed nothing but the actress' name and a phone number. Realizing who they were, the girl grabbed the boy's hand and hurried to catch them.

Placing the cards in her pocket with a flourish, she curtsied. "I am Mercy Ann. The young gentleman is John Justice." She hissed at him. "Introduce yourself the way I showed you."

He bowed to each with grace and aplomb. "Pleased to make your acquaintances."

Everything about them blew the actress away, even the girl's initial snooty behavior. "Really, be sure to call. With the right agents and good fortune, you have a good chance of getting work. You can never tell where it might take you."

As they walked off, Mercy Ann leaned over to John Justice and whispered excitedly, "How about that? She thinks we have what it takes to be movie stars, too."

Mercy Ann was a complete nutjob when it came to movies and had a way of blowing everything out of proportion. Of course, he knew better than to say so.

"I'm going to have their cards laminated," she declared, holding them up to admire.

"Are you through shopping yet?" he asked, conveying his boredom.

She frowned. "I thought someone would recognize who we were by now. This kind of makes up for it, though."

"Shouldn't we be working to find a way to help Earth?"

"Plenty of time for that later. What say we get a cheeseburger and fries on Santa Monica Pier? Would you like that?"

He loved cheeseburgers, and she'd told him about visiting beaches at Santa Monica but had never taken him. "Won't we be out of place dressed this way? Wouldn't take but a minute to pop back to the house and change."

She turned slowly, modeling her clothes. "This is California, John Justice, so you can wear anything. After burgers and fries, I'll take you for a ride on the Ferris wheel, buy you a hotdog on a stick, and stroll around Venice Beach looking at glistening muscles. Doesn't that sound like fun?"

"Good grief."

She pointed at his skinny upper arm and snickered. "Yeah, I see why you're embarrassed, but you'll enjoy it."

He was used to ignoring her insults. "Should I tell Miss Flowers where we are?"

"Let the old bat stew and worry. She'll call if anything happens, and I assume you're monitoring everything anyway. Right?"

"Of course. Lots more soldiers arriving, but no one is talking about attacking us, yet."

"Good for them," she said, taking his hand and transporting.

A few days later, after seeing pictures of Mercy Ann and John Justice popping up everywhere, the actress and her agent friend told about meeting them in an interview with the FBI. Numerous people reported seeing them the same day in Santa Monica, too. By then, however, so many people came forward with sensational stories and claims that no one paid much attention to the mundane ones, even when they involved famous people.

The owner of a sandwich shop near the evacuation area worked as a long distance truck driver for twenty years, saving, scrimping, and sacrificing until he had enough money to fulfill his dream of buying a franchise business. Then he met a woman on a dating site, they fell in love, and were married. Now they had a baby boy, a tiny dog, and, in their opinion, lived the quintessential American Dream.

The only fly in the ointment was the up-and-coming neighborhood location of his business. Racially mixed with mostly good people, an element of gangbangers were still around, although they seemed to go out of their way to avoid causing trouble in the community. That did nothing to stop the wife from being afraid when either of them worked, however.

With the evacuations causing unrest, police warned of a surge in looters and break-ins. The sandwich shop owner decided to stay in his store a few nights until everything settled down because police were so overwhelmed. In spite of her fears, his wife would not hear of him staying alone, so they left the baby and dog with her mother.

The wife was the organized one, taking lawn furniture cushions to sit on behind the showcase counters, lit at night so police patrols could see inside through the big front windows. She even had cards and board games to play if they tired of watching the dining room television and playing games online.

The husband had a shotgun loaded with birdshot, figuring it would be enough to frighten off anyone breaking in. The last thing he wanted was to hurt misguided, hard-up kids trying to steal a few dollars.

Around midnight, the husband dozed while the wife talked to her mother on a cellphone. The television was off and soft music played on the ceiling speakers.

Without warning, a pickup truck backed over the curb at high speed and crashed through the front windows. The husband jumped up fumbling with the shotgun. A hail of bullets cut him down, shattering showcases and glass shelves on the wall, showering the couple with broken glass.

Hanging out the passenger window of the pickup, the young shooter yelled at the driver. "You hit the wrong store, dumbass!"

Tires squealed, the truck roared back over the curb into the street, reversed, and crashed through the front of the store next door. The building shook violently, causing more glass to fall in the sandwich shop.

The wife's anguished screams went silent when she realized her husband was dead. Pulling up on the metal frame of a showcase, shock stopped her feeling the cuts and embedded glass shards all over her. Nor did she notice her mother yelling her name from the cellphone lost beneath bloody pieces of glass piled around her ankles or comprehend that she could see in the shadowy room because a few display lights had survived in the wreckage.

Falling one piece at a time from the big front window frames, glass fragments made tinkling sounds when they shattered, reminding her of the silver bells her grandmother had played so joyously in church. She'd inherited them and wondered where they were.

Then a surreal sight—a girl with long blond hair high-stepping from the dark storage room holding a rustling black dress hitched above the knees as she passed through the dining room. Glass crunched loudly under her heavy shoes until she stopped suddenly in mid-step, turned, and stared.

Later, the woman would recall the next events with clarity but was never sure any of it actually happened.

The girl carefully cleared glass and debris from around her feet with her heavy shoes then led her to the front to sit on a chair. From under the black dress, the girl ripped a long piece of petticoat and tied it above a gushing cut on her thigh. She pushed a capsule into her mouth with her thumb and had her swallow it.

Then she said, "I called an ambulance. It will be here in a few minutes. Don't worry about the men next door. I won't allow them to harm you anymore."

The attackers were new members of a local gang led by a man named Blake Ferrell. He had a reputation as someone not to cross, but behaved more as a local politician than a strong boss did. He imposed costly rules of behavior such as always paying for everything and not preying on people in the neighborhoods under his control. So the new men had begun recruiting outsiders to eliminate him and take over.

While the Glenwood Heights incident sowed confusion, the men decided to break into a small Asian market on the edge of the gang's area after they shoplifted in front of the owners and they ignored the incident rather than make a fuss. People like that would not stay in a store at night, in spite of rumors they kept a couple of Glocks under the counter. If they left the pistols in the store, they were valuable and easy to sell. There was an ATM they could break loose from its floor anchor and drag away with a vehicle, too. Easy pickings too long ignored, far as the new gang members were concerned.

They stole a truck and smoked pot all evening, which accounted for the driver crashing into the wrong business. If a guy hadn't been inside with a gun, it would have been funny, but an Uzi made short work of him. Whooping and shouting, they backed into the grocery store, knocking the ATM free of its floor mooring.

Alarms went off, but they figured police wouldn't respond very quickly because of the evacuations. While one secured a chain around the ATM, the other searched for the Glocks. While at it, he thought someone moved in one of the dark aisles and fired an Uzi burst. Nothing was there and his friend ribbed him. They couldn't find the pistols, so they jumped into the truck and roared into the street, the ATM making a frightful racket bouncing and crashing behind.

A police car came from a side street, forcing them to stop. The truck's driver jumped out and ran while his partner decided to shoot it out with the Uzi. He died in a hail of return fire.

The driver ran into a sparsely lit, dead end alley thinking it led to the next street over. Panicked, he kept looking back over his shoulder and slammed into dumpster at full speed, knocking himself silly.

The two cops knew the alley went nowhere and took their sweet time. They spotted their man flat on his back moaning and holding his head. Giving a high sign to each other, they pushed their bodycams to the side so they showed nothing but darkness when they entered the alley.

Approaching the man, one officer yelled, "Keep your hands where we can see them, scumbag!"

The other shouted, "Watch out, he's got a gun!"

Fifteen shots echoed in rapid succession.

Hand over his camera, one of them ran and pressed a small pistol into the dead thug's hand. He intended to run back so they could show closing in on a downed armed suspect, but a young girl dressed in a fancy dress stood on top of the dumpster peering down at him. Startled, he aimed his weapon at her.

His partner hurried up and whispered, "What are we going to do?"
He whispered back, "Switch off the cameras. She'll just have to be collateral damage."
"But she's just a kid."
"So was he, you shitheads," the girl accused, pointing at the body.
Her arrogance and insolence was enough justification for the reluctant cop to pull his gun and level it at her, too. "You're right. She'll drop us in it, for sure."
A boy's voice came from behind them. "Leave her alone."
The officers whipped around to find a slender boy in black knee pants confronting them. Faint yellow light shined around him. With guns coming to bear, they laughed at his ridiculous bravado and appearance.
"Stay out of it, John Justice," the girl said. "I just wanted to see if they showed any remorse for murdering that man."
"On this barbaric planet? Are you serious?"
One of the officers fired at him.
Bright yellow flashes lashed out from John Justice, turning them and the gangbanger's body into smoldering black corpses.
Mercy Ann was furious. "I told you to keep defenses set for protection only. Now look what you've done."
Tears welled in his eyes. "I forgot to change it."
"I'm fed up with your stupid mistakes. I'm going home." She disappeared.
Knowing he'd better stay away until she calmed down, he decided to go watch the fires and riots for a while.

The gang leader, Blake Ferrell, had gotten wind of what his two newest men were up to, tailed, and witnessed them crash into the stores. Hearing the Uzi in the sandwich shop, he thought the stoned morons were just shooting up the place. Then, on a police scanner, he heard them dispatching a patrol car. They said no backups were available, so he decided to stick around and watch.
After parking a couple of blocks away, he hid in a doorway and witnessed the shootout in the street. Then he followed the cops going after the other guy.
When they entered the alley, he sprinted, closing the distance, and heard the flurry of gunshots. Darting a quick peek around the corner, he thought someone stood near three bodies, but looking again, no one was there.
Blake did not want to chance being bottled-up in the alley, but really wanted a closer look. He ran to the damnedest sight he'd ever seen.

Three bodies burned beyond recognition. Weapons inexplicably twisted and glowing red-hot, although the pavement showed no evidence of heat whatever. He heard approaching sirens and hurried back up the alley.

Sitting on the curb under a streetlight, he spotted the woman from the sandwich shop, seriously bleeding and crying into her hands. He surmised she and her husband had been watching over their property like so many others in the area. Not having time to go around, he ran past behind her as quietly as possible and watched from his car until the ambulance arrived.

Driving away, he struck the dash with his fist. He'd eaten in that sandwich shop many times. Talked to the woman and her husband. Seen pictures of their baby, the dog, and the wife's mother. He'd allowed worthless hoodlums into the neighborhood, and those nice people paid for his mistake.

Looters set fires and broke into buildings all around the area. Flames engulfed a big auto parts warehouse and spread to a small two-story apartment building before fire trucks arrived. Usually, other emergency vehicles accompanied them, but the riots had everyone stretched thin.

Residents of the building outside said two families had not come out. The upstairs unit belonged to a senior couple while the downstairs apartment had a single mother with three children. Firemen ran inside as hoses went into action. The downstairs apartment was next to the auto parts store and ablaze already. Two firemen found a hysterical mother trying to carry her children, overcome by smoke. They grabbed up the kids and herded her outside.

A third fireman, a big, powerful man who, in spite of the weight of his equipment, bound upstairs three at a time. Smoke was heavy, but he could see the way and wore a breathing apparatus. A section of ceiling had fallen into the living room of the seniors' apartment. Flames raged in the attic above, burning through the roof. He spotted a boy face down on the floor covered in debris. Grabbing him up, he made it out of the building with the boy over his shoulder as the roof pancaked onto the second floor.

The fire was contained. The old couple who lived upstairs had gotten out on their own. The rescued boy had a big bump on the head, but was remarkably well otherwise. None of the residents knew him and his clothes looked foreign. The Captain thought he probably ran into the building to steal and told the big fireman to keep an eye on him until they could take him to a hospital and notify the police.

The fireman did not think someone dressed as nicely as this kid would be stealing. "Going into burning buildings can be a mite hazardous, kid."

"I wanted to see the fire close up."

"That's really dumb."

"Yeah. That describes me pretty good, I guess," the boy said, staring down at his feet.

He sounded so morose, the fireman felt sorry for him. "My name is Rudy."

The boy looked up, black smudges on his face stark against very pale skin. "I'm pleased to make your acquaintance, Mr. Rudy."

"No, my name is Rudy Johnson, but you may call me Rudy."

"I can't get anything right. Sorry."

Rudy had emigrated from Nigeria as a child, which he thought was the reason he felt an almost overpowering affinity with this kid. "Do you have a name?"

"Yes."

A few seconds passed. "Uh, do you mind telling it to me?"

"Oh, sorry. I am John Justice."

"Do they call you John, Johnny?"

"No. I am called John Justice."

"Uh, that's a mouthful. Would it be all right if I called you J.J.?"

"No. I am John Justice."

Rudy smiled. "You aren't from around here, are you?"

"No."

Getting nothing more, he shrugged and took a Heath Bar from a big pocket. After unwrapping, he offered half to the boy. "This will make you feel better than any doctor I know."

He took it. Sniffed it. Turned it over, examining. Everything but eating it.

"What are you doing, John Justice?"

"What kind of medicine is this? Smells like candy."

"Why would you think it is medicine?"

"You said it is an alternative to a doctor."

Rudy guffawed. "Sorry, it is definitely candy."

John Justice took a bite, a smile lit his face, and then a look of consternation replaced it. "May I have the wrapper?"

Rudy pulled it from his pocket and handed it over. "Saving it for later?"

"I will give it to Mercy Ann. She's in a bad mood. This will help."

Rudy pulled another candy bar out and gave it to him. "My last one. Use it to make up with your young lady."

John Justice smiled. "Rudy's last Heath Bar. Thank you very much."

The Fire Captain called across the street. "EMS will be here in a few minutes to take the kid."

Rudy jumped up and turned to help John Justice, but he was gone. It was most mystifying but too much was going on to give it more attention.

Around midnight, a research chemist from UCLA-Berkeley stood in front of an army tent getting a breath of air. He could not believe how fast the government set up field research labs under canvas. Everywhere he looked, people, mostly soldiers, worked furiously. At first glance, it seemed chaotic with everyone at cross-purposes, but he soon realized how tightly organized everything was.

Mostly, it was due to a grizzled sergeant major directing activities with the grace of symphony conductor and the no-nonsense discipline of a warrior used to dealing with life and death situations. An old mongrel dog with one ear chewed half-off followed the sergeant major everywhere, always at a constant three feet behind his heels. When his master stopped, the dog dropped to the ground and waited.

The site commander, a two star major general, came by and said hello to the professor on his way to the sergeant major. After a quick, earnest conversation, they shared a laugh about something and the general moved on. The professor had the impression the two men had long association and were close friends.

The other members of his Berkeley team had gone to eat at a military mess facility nearby. Since they departed, he'd determined the compositions of some of the granules taken from the ground, and the findings were equally incredible and monstrous. Now, he realized why they had them sign Nondisclosure Agreements. Moreover, he thought rumors whispered by the soldiers about aliens might not be so crazy. Shaking his head, he went inside to run more tests.

3

People Falling through Cracks

MERCY ANN RAN OUT OF ANDY LAWRENCE'S HOSPITAL ROOM past a half-asleep cop and went into Detective Tom Patrick's room. The startled guard went after her, but other than the sleeping detective, no one was in the room. Then an alarm went off on the equipment monitoring Lawrence, followed by him yelling for help. Respondents found him rational and able to speak for the first time.

A handful of special agents met with Lawrence in a secured operating room. An encrypted video feed connected them to DHS Headquarters in Washington. Rolled in on a hospital bed, he recounted what happened leading up to the first incident.

He and his sergeant had been in the first patrol car to arrive at the house. Two more police cruisers followed, each with two officers. The sergeant directed them to the back of the house while he and Lawrence went onto the porch.

A notice was on the wall next to the door, which the sergeant glanced at then ripped down, balled-up, and gave to Lawrence. An old woman and boy watched them through glass in the door. The sergeant warned them to come out or be arrested, but received no response. The sergeant broke the door's glass, intending to reach in and unlock it.

The next thing he remembered was the boy standing beside him next to a squad car in front of the house with glowing orange particles blowing around them. Then he woke up in the hospital with a girl holding an ugly doll to his face. He had a mouthful of sweet liquid that he swallowed before yelling for help. He did not see where the girl went.

Tests found no evidence Lawrence had taken any substance not administered by the hospital. They asked him many questions, but nothing added anything important to his original statement.

The DHS Secretary, standing before a packed conference room in Washington, DC, after watching the interview in LA, did not recognize the majority of attendees. Most worked for other agencies or in secret capacities for the government, but all had special clearances and knowledge about aliens for one reason or another.

He had thought having membership in the upper echelons of people possessing the highest state secrets would benefit him, if for no other reason than rubbing shoulders with some of the most powerful people in the world. Instead, he had an executive leadership role in an exclusive club of eccentrics and weirdos pleased to have him between them and a President they held in low esteem because he was ready to go to any lengths to deny and cover up the truth about aliens.

After they discussed Lawrence's statement, he showed a live surveillance feed of the notice on the alien house. "In spite of being removed before the first incident, the notice was back next to the door when our agents arrived before the second incident. The last line inexplicably changes precisely at midnight, Pacific Time, counting off the days to thirty. The notice we took from Officer Lawrence changes, too. Analysis indicates they are hand-printed sheets of paper with nothing unusual about them. Any ideas how that can be done?"

Other than blank stares, he received nothing.

"If that's not disturbing enough," he went on, feeling as though he might as well be in the room alone, "our Science and Technology Division verified the layers of material on the ground are indeed the remains of disintegrated objects and organic matter. No surprise, except that each bead consists of one kind of matter exclusively, something else no one can explain. Any ideas about that?"

Frustrated by their silence, he showed videos of the alien boy and girl at numerous public places in Los Angeles. "Any opinions why they dress in clothes from a different era?"

"To stand out and be noticed," a woman with wild jet-black hair responded as if doing him a favor by participating.

"Any ideas why?"

"That's the same question," a bearded man answered in a bored voice.

"Maybe they're not really children," someone in back called out.

"Maybe they're not human," a disheveled man added. "If they can make a UFO appear as a house, they can probably look any way they want."

The bearded man responded, "Maybe the dinosaurs didn't die out. They're still amongst us, masquerading as people."

"Yeah, they run the government," the disheveled man fired back.

A few people laughed. The rest just sat there, staring.

Tight-jawed, the Secretary said, "Everything is on the table at this point, people, but let's keep it serious. What do they want? Ideas?"

The woman with wild hair stood. "We're the goddamned United States of America, not a namby-pamby, third-rate power. Let's wipe them out and stop fiddle farting around. Strike now with everything we have while the area of damage will be smaller if we're unsuccessful."

Nearly everyone supported the call for swift action.

So did the DHS Secretary, in spite of his low opinion of these people. "Before I take this recommendation to the White House, does anyone give credence to other parts of the message?"

Since Dr. Rogers of DHS Intelligence and Analysis had gone to LA to inspect the site firsthand, no one saw any reason to discuss it.

Sedona, Arizona, famous for towering red bluffs, spectacular foliage, and phenomenal landscapes, is a breathtaking place to visit. Hikers, campers, and tourists flock there from around the world, seasonally jamming luxurious resorts, recreation areas, restaurants, and shopping venues. In addition, artists, writers, and free spirits of every ilk cite it as a mystical, supernatural, and especial location to congregate, create, and commune.

Hidden in a hillside northwest of town, no one suspected an illegal interrogation facility operated by conspirators dedicated to seizing control of the government existed. An innocuous double-gated, chain-link fence topped with the typical three strands of barbed wire enclosed the only approach to a camouflaged entrance. Uncurious signs forbade trespass, citing Department of the Interior designation of the small plot of desert as an aquifer-monitoring site, a bogus claim no one questioned.

Missa MaCaron had no idea she was in Arizona. The tiny room was eight-by-eight feet with no furniture, no bed, and no toilet. The floor and walls were concrete. A steel door provided the only way out. A single harsh light bulb that never turned off hung on a back cord from a high ceiling.

Noise blared when she closed her eyes for more than a few seconds. All she had on were lightweight cotton pants and a short sleeve pullover with no underwear, socks, or shoes. Even with the thin blanket pulled around her, she shivered from the cold.

No one responded to her cries for a toilet, and she had to go in a corner if she couldn't wait until the scheduled times they came for her. She tried not to think who watched, for certainly, someone did.

A big-assed woman came in with a mouthy skinny woman periodically. They slapped and kicked Missa then dragged her down a dirty hall to another room where they made her strip. After a hosing with icy water, she sat naked on a metal chair with hooded lights shining in her face while they shouted accusations and threats.

Missa screamed that she was an underage teenager. They screamed that acts of terrorism made her a legal adult so keep her fucking mouth shut except to answer questions. She yelled about being imprisoned for no reason, demanded a lawyer, and her rights. They called her a treasonous, murdering criminal with no rights who would be in prison the rest of her life unless she answered their questions truthfully.

But they didn't ask any questions, so Missa yelled explanations about the quadcopter and her running from the police, but they slapped her in the face until she shut up. Then they dragged her back to the cell—hosed out while she was gone—and threw her on the wet floor next to a cold, sodden change of clothes.

From books Ashlyn had given her to read, she realized they wanted to establish a routine with sick rules of behavior to keep her at constant disadvantage before listening to anything she said. They probably thought, take a pretty girl, mess her up, and make her cry. She'll pee her pants and tell them anything they want. She did her best to play the part they expected, which wasn't hard considering how afraid she was.

But Missa could tell they were under pressure to deliver fast results, something she might be able to use to advantage. She had something else going for her. They didn't seem to know she competed in taekwondo. It was common knowledge in school amongst people who knew her, although no one had ever seen her fight and did not realize how tough she was.

As Jerry O'Brien discovered when he and his best friend tried to pin her down in the backseat of his car after she broke up with him for attacking Rob. The conceited bastard thought because he was a popular football player and she'd allowed him to put his hands inside her shirt, he could have his way with her. When it was over, she promised to keep silent about whipping their asses in exchange for leaving her and Rob alone. If they didn't, she threatened to do it in public next time.

Jerry and his friend told everyone the bruises, battered faces, and black eyes were because they'd had a manly disagreement and fought each other to a draw. The airhead girls buzzing around them thought they were the coolest things ever.

She felt her swollen face and spat a gob of blood. She'd almost given herself away and taken the skinny bitch out with an elbow for saying she was responsible for her parents dying in the second blast, but forced herself to cry instead. It helped that she didn't believe they were dead because the house showings had been far from the destruction, but it left her uneasy and afraid until she found out for sure.

She thought of Rob often and assumed he was nearby so their interrogators could crosscheck anything they said. She also assumed their parents were raising hell with the government to let them go, and it wouldn't be much longer, which was the main reason she was able to bear this ordeal so far.

For now, though, all she could do was play along until they asked questions and she convinced them to let her go. Sensing it was about time for them to come for her again, she let out a pitiful wail, figuring they would go easier thinking she was breaking down.

Meanwhile, Rob woke up strapped by the legs and forearms to a heavy wooden chair fastened to a concrete floor. His feet rested on a step attached to the chair and he couldn't move them off, making his legs cramp. The only light shined down from above, glaring in his face. He tried to move his head to look around and discovered something prevented it.

A tiny globule of blood on his left forearm near the elbow showed someone had given him a shot, probably to wake him. He had seven pinprick marks in a line, but didn't remember much of anything after they took him and Missa from the restaurant and pulled the bag over his head.

A loud voice from the ceiling asked questions. At first, they were routine, such as his name, school, and so on. Then the questions turned to the incident and the drone. When he said he hadn't given the video to anyone, electricity jolted him. The question and jolts repeated until he lost consciousness.

He came to with another prick on his arm. The voice asked about the strange girl and boy he had mentioned in the first session. He wasn't certain what, if anything, he'd said, and recounted the incident of the girl in his backyard. The voice asked about the boy. He knew nothing about him and said so. Electric current jolted him, but not as severely as when they asked about the video. Unfortunately, that was the next question.

Waking up on the floor of a small damp cell, Rob thought if he just kept telling the truth, they had no choice but to let him go. Besides, their parents were not the kind of people to sit idly by, so he didn't expect this would go on much longer. He had concerns about Missa, but she was tougher than he was by far. The main thing was to keep it together until release and they took these bastards to court.

The four interrogators were contractors who went by aliases for their protection as well as the people who hired them. Three believed the federal government employed them. The fourth worked for the conspiracy and perpetuated the lie to the others.

They knew nothing of the prisoners other than a scant amount of background information and lists of questions that needed answers. It was rare having the go-ahead to use illegal interrogation techniques these days, especially against a pair of white American teenagers. Consequently, the interrogators were both excited and apprehensive dealing with them.

Having a quick supper, they sat at a round table together. Interrogators did not associate with guards except in emergencies, and had their own breakroom.

The thin woman said, "She's very much in control, a hard nut to crack."

A middle-aged man wearing an expensive dress shirt with an open collar could pass for a bank president relaxing at his country club. "The boy's got it together, too. Unusual for someone his age.

The big woman leaned forward and the metal folding chair creaked in protest. "I can't believe they sent high school kids to this place. And what's with all those questions about aliens and UFOs? What do you think, Charlie?"

Charlie was in charge and had the kind of hangdog face that belied a fiery temper and killer instincts. "Just follow instructions and don't ask questions. By the way, I received a text. We're to step it up. They want answers and won't accept excuses."

The big woman made a blowing sound. “Some things never change. Guess we’ll have to show our Prom Queen she ain’t such tough shit tonight then. Glad I’m not her.”

“You could be,” the bank president responded. “People fall through cracks and go missing in this country every day. Never know when your number may come up.”

Charlie stood and threw his lunch in the trash. “Let’s get back to work, people. This will be an all-nighter.”

The President, sitting behind his desk in the Oval Office, was not happy. The opposition party had accused him of being soft dealing with enemies of America until the notion took root and brought his standing in the polls down fifteen points. As if that wasn’t bad enough, he had to deal with an alien encounter, something that would create chaos, riots, and political upheavals all over the world if they couldn’t keep it concealed. Why did all this have to happen during his Presidency?

Watching and waiting for an answer to a proposal he’d made to the President, the Chairman of the Joint Chiefs, one of the most powerful members of the conspiracy, cleared his throat several times to shake the fool out of whatever reverie he’d fallen into this time.

The President looked up. “You’re certain the missiles will hit the target dead-on and destroy it completely without endangering our solders? The press is already on the warpath over this incident. If we have more casualties, they’ll demand my scalp.”

The Chairman exuded confidence from every pore. “The missiles launch into the stratosphere, do a one-eighty, and come straight down on the target, producing a small, concentrated blast pattern comfortably inside the current area of damage. Since we already have a half-mile buffer zone around the entire site, it isn’t even necessary to move soldiers back except for giving them a better view of the fireworks. We get the added benefit of keeping our new coil cannons a secret, too.”

Wiping out the aliens and putting all this behind him was too appealing for the President to pass up. It would allow him to blame terrorists for the incident and claim the government cited natural causes initially to embolden them to attempt another attack. Then it would be a simple matter to say that the ploy worked, but the terrorists were fanatics and refused to give up their corrosive bombs, which we wanted to examine intact. Unfortunately, the missiles destroyed everything.

He was confident he could sell the harebrained story to voters and fend off doubters, allowing him to avoid the subject of aliens completely. "How soon can you get everything set up and ready to go?"

The Chairman had not expected to get a go-ahead so quickly and could hardly contain his glee. "Day after tomorrow, sir!"

The President gave the order and received a cheering ovation.

As the setting sun cast shadows across Camp Pendleton, Ashlyn Pike watched Marines marching past through a barred window. After three sessions of questions about Rob, Missa, and the drone he bought, she was about to explode from anger, aggravation, and impatience. The whole situation was so stupid she could not believe it. What was wrong with these people? They acted as if Rob was Darth Vader, John Dillinger, and Vladimir Putin rolled into one skinny seventeen-year-old body.

Trying to talk sense to them was a waste of breath. They kept trying to turn everything she said into lies. In her opinion, they were self-righteous zealots capable of doing more harm to innocent people than the enemies they imagined everywhere.

One interrogator said too much, so she knew they had Missa's parents, too. Another kept asking how many trips she'd taken to the Middle East and demanded she name other terrorists. When she laughed at them, they'd gotten angry.

"You wouldn't be so flippant if you understood the dire situation we face," the young one with acne insisted.

"Come work a shift with me in the emergency room and I'll show you real terror," she fired back. "Try holding bleeding intestines while a surgeon digs buckshot out of someone's guts."

They'd stormed out finally, going off-post to a steakhouse. She looked down at the plate of slop they'd given her to eat and dumped it in the commode.

Shortly before midnight, Blake Ferrell and five gang members, staying in the shadows of buildings fronting a wide avenue, ran toward a big grocery distribution facility in the next block. Looters were ravaging nearby areas and sirens filled the night, so a patrol car taking a shortcut this way was a real possibility.

Darting down a side street, they went behind the warehouse and climbed onto the cab of an eighteen-wheeler one of them parked there several hours ago. Then they ran on top of the trailer and stopped under a pulldown fire escape ladder. One of them unfolded a children's backyard trampoline and bounced up to grab it, giving them access to the roof and a skylight protected by a steel grate.

The warehouse had a good security system, but it was easy to bypass sensors, cut the grate loose, and lift off the cover. Their inside guy, a shift manager they'd known since childhood, had turned off the motion detectors when the facility closed early due to the riots and left enough lights on to navigate the shadowy aisles. They slid down a rope between towering shelving units.

Three men went to the offices where the security system panels were located to disable alarms to liquor and cigarette cages as well as the loading dock doors. Two others went to break into employee lockers to get company work shirts. Blake went alone to reconnoiter for other valuables to steal. They had until 3 a.m. to accumulate merchandise to load on their truck. They'd accomplish it dressed as employees with music blasting and dock lights ablaze for the benefit of police patrols, if any came by.

Blake jogged down a wide aisle between towering fixtures. He regretted they only had time to roundup enough people for a quick job because this was much easier than he'd thought. But then, as he reached the end of the fixture runs with the building's back wall just ahead, he heard someone. Pistol out, he stuck his head around the corner to look.

Perched on crates directly under a light about ten feet away, he recognized the blond girl in the strange black clothes he'd seen in the news. A jumbled pile of big cardboard boxes loomed behind her.

"Please don't shoot," she said flatly, sounding as unconcerned as she appeared.

Blake stepped out with the gun pointed at her. Some people claimed she was an alien. He thought it was utterly ridiculous. But why was she here and how did she get in?

Slowly, she raised a big doll from her lap with both hands and held it out towards him, a non-threatening gesture under normal circumstances, but now he could see her eyes.

Blake had grown up hard in a hard place to grow up. He had beaten terrible odds to become a formidable force in his small part of the city. Along the way, he'd learned to trust his instincts and they'd saved him many times. So now, although it made no logical sense, when he experienced inexplicable fear and foreboding facing this peculiar girl, he lowered the gun and stepped back.

"You're one of those kids I saw on TV," he said, none too steady.

She lowered the doll. "I am not a child."

Definitely not, he decided, holstering his weapon and holding his hand away. "No offense intended. You're not an alien, are you?"

"Either that, or you're home asleep having a wet dream that's about to become a nightmare."

Her expression was hard as nails or he might have laughed. "How did you get in here?"

She shrugged, showing no emotion, giving nothing away.

"What's in those boxes?"

"They're mine. Leave them alone."

He decided to push a little. "What if I decide to take them?"

She raised the doll. "What if I punish you for killing that poor woman's husband in the sandwich shop last night, asshole?"

It took him a few seconds to recover. "I didn't do it."

"Same as, you lowlife jerkwad hoodlum son of a bitch."

Those words coming out of that pretty mouth were more startling than offensive, especially since she said them in the same emotionless way. "Okay, I'm responsible. Satisfied?"

"That's not good enough."

God, he could feel that stare on his backbone. "I've arranged to help the wife and son financially for however long it takes to get their lives together and plan to buy the business for more than twice what it's worth."

John Justice had told Mercy Ann about Blake's financial arrangements and she was impressed he didn't mention them until forced, but he deserved to squirm. "Unusual, isn't it, that a worthless prick gives a rat's ass what happens to his helpless victims?"

He pointed to the doll. "Is that a weapon?"

"Not as much as I am."

In spite of chills all over, he smiled at her boldness, hoping she might smile back and defuse the situation, but didn't get one. "I'm sorry for what I did. Keep your boxes, and I'll take others. Does that work for you?"

"Yes."

"May I go now?"

"Sure took your sweet-ass time, loser."

He ran along the back of the building. Just before turning at the sidewall, he looked back and stopped, staring in disbelief. The girl and the cases were gone.

Heart pounding like a bass drum, it was all he could do to whisper, "Holy shit."

4

Bonobos and Chimpanzees

MILITARY CONVOYS CONTINUED ARRIVING, delivering soldiers and equipment to fill in gaps on the outer perimeter of the buffer zone. Their reactions to protesting people and disobeying orders to vacate were different from previous days. They detained and transported them to holding areas for twenty-four hours and threatened hefty fines and incarceration for repeated offenses. Meanwhile, military, fire, and law enforcement swept through buffer zone neighborhoods removing stragglers and charging them.

A large no fly zone wreaked havoc with LAX flights but had the desired effect of making it impossible to take aerial photographs, including with drones because the military took them down with blasts of electronic interference, something they denied when news organizations made inquiries.

Meanwhile, the Chairman of the Joint Chiefs had special units comprised of civilian technicians set up new, top-secret weapons called coil cannons inside large tents on the outer edge of the buffer zone in case the missiles didn't to the job. No one outside the conspiracy knew he'd done this except the military at the site, and they had no reason to think the White House was not aware of the action.

A popular DJ on a LA rock radio station summed up the situation:

> "The Glenwood Heights emergency is halfway through day four and authorities still won't tell us what's going on. Growing numbers of people swear aliens are responsible, and I don't mean run-of-the-mill green men from Mars lusting after Earth women. They're a couple of young teenagers who appear and disappear at will, friendly as all get out, and claim they're not responsible for the deaths and destruction.
>
> "Come on, people, pull the other one, why don't you? Some production company is taking advantage of a serious situation to get cheap publicity, and some of you are falling for it, hook, line, and sinker. When we find out who these kids are, the people responsible will have hell to pay. Nuff said.
>
> "Here's the chill-out news item of the day. In what has to be the greatest college prank or worst case of sweet-toothiness of all time, someone made off with thousands of Heath Candy Bars overnight from warehouses. In spite of alarms and security cameras, no one heard or saw a thing. If you ask me, this is one of the greatest marketing stunts ever conceived, or, just maybe...
>
> "Are you thinking what I'm thinking? It's those alien kids. They're like ants, getting into everything. Hey, little aliens, if you drop some candy by the station, maybe I'll forgive you. You can have our women, but leave the candy alone.
>
> "Hang in tight, city. Don't let all the bull-hockey get you down. We'll still have Hollywood, the best beaches, and greatest music on the planet when this mess is over."

Rudy Johnson, wearing his fireman's duty uniform, stood at the threshold of a small house explaining why to a frightened young woman holding a baby why she had to evacuate while her runny-nosed little boy hung onto her coughing.

She begged him to let her wait until her husband came home because they only had one car and she couldn't carry all the stuff they needed. Rudy was on the verge of agreeing when the army captain in charge showed up and warned that she had five minutes to vacate the premises. Then he yelled at Rudy for taking too long.

The woman jammed a few belongings into a vinyl shoulder bag and ran out carrying the baby and dragging the squalling boy to an army truck. Still holding the front door open, Rudy took a deep breath to calm down then went inside to turn off the TV. The house keys were on a table so he took them out to the woman, who cursed him.

When his group showed up in each neighborhood, an official gave them lists of houses with people hiding inside. He'd been mystified how they knew until seeing a handheld device placed against an exterior wall of a residence that showed the outlines of people inside.

Goddamn, Rudy thought, someday soon you'll go to the bathroom with your cellphone and see yourself on social media taking a dump. He couldn't believe something like that was legal, but it was, apparently.

At another house, an elderly woman peeked out lacy window curtains.

"Lady, I'm a fireman on official business," Rudy declared. "Open the door. It's an emergency."

A slide chain and several locks later, the door opened a crack. "You're not going to rape me, are you?"

Scheduled to be doing this past midnight, which was ten hours away, he took a deep breath. "No, ma'am. We will help you relocate to a safe place until the emergency is over."

"Only if I can take my cats."

From the odor, he guessed she had a houseful. They could not go, but he would not tell her until she got some clothes together. Then he would have female officers bring her out.

It sucked treating people this way, but at least he cared and tried to be polite about it, unlike many of the others, who were sick and tired of the abuse they received. Rudy didn't blame them, either. This was an impossible situation, and it kept getting worse.

After hearing about Mercy Ann running into his hospital room and answering questions about Lawrence's account of events, Tom Patrick still did not tell about his encounter with her and the boy. The fact he had not spoken up right away would be an issue, he decided, and he could add nothing to what they already knew.

Just after four, an FBI agent came in and released him. First thing, he called the office. As expected, they were desperately shorthanded. He felt shaky and worn out, but would rather work than be alone at home. They sent a squad car to pick him up.

While he waited, he looked around as much as he could. Soldiers and police patrolled the floors where they hospitalized witnesses to the disaster. Glancing into a couple of rooms, he felt certain the patients would go home if authorities allowed it, making him doubly glad he'd kept his mouth shut.

Telling his gang that he wanted to explore opportunities to steal from houses in the restricted zone as well as the military, Blake and two of his top guys drove around the outer perimeter of the buffer zone making notes and marking everything they saw on maps.

Blake's real reason for nosing around was that he couldn't adequately describe the feelings he experienced since meeting Mercy Ann. Much more than physical attraction or anything else he ever experienced, it was as if meeting her awakened an awareness of a strong bond between them. He could tell when she moved around the area, knew when she came closer to his location and went farther away. At times, he'd almost swear he "heard" fragments of her thoughts and sensed her emotions.

The feelings had started in the warehouse immediately after she left, and were so crazy that he'd tried to dismiss them, but with each passing minute, they grew stronger. Finally, he realized he should be able to find her, which would verify if the feelings were genuine, so here he was, searching for someone who scared the bejesus out of him in a huge, crowded area of the city.

Large tents manned by civilian technicians were on hills at several locations around the buffer zone. Using binoculars, one of Blake's companions, who served two tours in the Middle East, glimpsed technicians assembling a strange weapon. He described it as a huge ray gun with a long, narrow barrel and had never before seen anything like it. Internet searches could not identify it, either.

After a quick stop for lunch, Blake looked down a long avenue as they passed through an intersection and spotted Mercy Ann with John Justice behind shrubbery watching a military checkpoint two blocks away. He had the car pull over and told his men he'd call them to pick him up later.

Mercy Ann and John Justice were gone when Blake backtracked. Cursing under his breath, he hurried past the bushes where they'd been to a cross street. Down the right way, he saw Mercy Ann alone, walking away on a sidewalk. She had a three-block lead.

Closing the distance between them, she seemed remarkably casual and unconcerned, not paying attention to anything. Passing a gray panel van parked at the curb, the rear doors opened slowly and two MPs emerged, taking care to be quiet.

One motioned to Blake to stop, which he did with a wave of acknowledgement. Then the MPs went after Mercy Ann. As one grabbed for her, she ducked under his arms and shoved him away. The other caught her by the shoulders.

Running towards them, Blake expected Mercy Ann might use some sort of weapon or vanish, but she twisted around and kicked her assailant in the shin, the heavy shoe making a loud thud. Then she kicked him in the knee of the other leg, and down he went.

The other MP pulled his pistol. “Freeze!”

Blake crashed into him from behind, pushed the arm with the gun up, and twisted it out of his hand. Then he knocked the man out with a jarring elbow to the face. The first MP jumped up, and Blake sent him back down for good with a right jab.

He faced Mercy Ann. “Walking around in those clothes is like wearing a target on your back.”

Brushing off the black dress with her hands, she had the same unconcerned expression as last night. “No harm done.”

“Where’s your doll?”

“Didn’t need her.”

“Seems like maybe you did.”

“I’m with John Justice.”

“Where is he then?”

“I sent him to check military preparations on the other side of the area.”

“Couldn’t you have called him for help?”

“Yes, but I knew the men were in the van and wanted to see what you would do.”

“How did you know about them, or me, for that matter?”

“You must allow a girl to have a few secrets.” She reached out to him with her palm turned down so he couldn’t see what she had in her hand. “For you.”

He hesitated.

“I won’t bite you.” She revealed a Heath Bar. “John Justice gave me one from his new friend, Rudy. They’re good.”

He didn’t know what he expected, but this wasn’t it. “Thanks. Who’s this Rudy guy?”

“Actually, I haven’t met him. John Justice always makes friends. It’s hard for me.”

“May I be your friend then? My name is Blake.”

“Yes, thank you. I am Mercy Ann.”

“Do you have a last name, Mercy Ann?”

A flicker of annoyance darkened her face. "Once I did, but it caused me problems and I stopped using it."

"What kind of problems?"

"It's not important. Please listen. I want you to leave this area until tomorrow afternoon. Your government is about to attack the site again, and that could result in another disaster, possibly much more widespread."

"Shouldn't you warn the people around the site? Can you stop the attack?"

Her expression showed how much the questions irritated her. "John Justice and I work for the aliens in charge of the territory where Earth is located. They have strict rules about us interfering in this situation. I've done all I can."

"What's to keep me from warning everyone?"

"Be my guest, but no one will listen to someone as reprehensible as you."

"Ouch."

Mercy Ann looked down at one of the MPs waking up. "More military will be here in a minute. Give me your hand, please."

In a blink, she transported them to the parking lot of the fast food place where Blake ate lunch with his guys. "You're right about people recognizing me in these clothes, but it helps not to be noticed when wearing something else, especially if my hair is a different color."

"I'd notice you, regardless."

For the first time, she smiled at him. "Liar. When you had lunch, I was two tables away. One of your men kept flirting and making eye contact. You even glanced my way to see who had his interest. Next time, if you're not too self-absorbed, maybe I won't have to eat alone."

Then she was gone, leaving him wearing an idiotic expression.

The general and sergeant major had served in both Iraq wars and Afghanistan. In addition, the sergeant major was pseudo-dad for many soldiers who still had growing up to do. Both men were intelligent and well educated, yet could be rougher and tougher than any enemy of the United States could when necessary.

Serving together off and on for twenty-seven years, they were close friends. The sergeant major had never married, embracing the military as family, something the general shared after a childless marriage and his wife dying of cancer twelve years ago.

The sergeant major rescued a succession of mongrels over the years. He'd named all Bongo and trained them to serve by his side, something the Army tolerated for the most part. The current Bongo had been half-dead from shrapnel wounds in Afghanistan when the sergeant major found him in a trash can. With a hitching gait and an extremely bad attitude, the dog was devoted to his master. The sergeant major often joked they were related because both were ornery sons of bitches.

Late in the evening, driven in a staff car by a young sergeant with a new lieutenant at shotgun, the general and sergeant major were with Bongo in the backseat visiting units around the devastated area. The general wanted to make certain preparations for their 5 a.m. pullback of troops into the buffer zone proceeded smoothly.

By design, when the general's car pulled up to each location, all doors opened and everyone emerged together. The driver remained next to the vehicle with the four doors open while the others conducted a high energy, whirlwind inspection. Seeing the general, sergeant major, and Bongo at their place of work was great for soldiers' morale.

It was nearly midnight when they sped back to the command post on a brightly lit avenue and the lieutenant shouted, "Watch out!"

The alien girl had appeared in the road too close to avoid hitting, but after skidding to a stop, nothing was evident except a white fast food bag standing in the road behind the car. Opening it carefully with a pen, the general removed four Heath Bars, a dog biscuit, and single sheet of paper hand-printed with small precise letters.

He read aloud:

> "Eons ago, a highly advanced civilization discovered hominid civilizations in various stages of development on numerous planets in the territory of space where Earth is located. They determined the planets were genetic experiments abandoned long ago by scientists of an unknown culture, and they decided to complete them.
>
> "On Earth, which was the least developed of the experiments, they altered the genetics of an ape species to make it more intelligent, stronger, and less passive. When the desired changes manifested, they split the new apes into two groups. One they allowed to evolve naturally and became the Chimpanzees. The other underwent numerous modifications and became mankind.
>
> "They considered the experiments resounding successes until most of the Chimpanzees evolved dangerous, aggressive personalities while a small minority regressed back to the levels of passivity that

existed in apes prior to any modifications. The aggressive apes began attacking and killing the passive ones.

"The scientists separated the two groups by rerouting a river. You now know the regressed group as the Bonobos. The Chimpanzees have continued becoming ever more warlike.

"Mankind underwent the same evolutionary changes in approximately the same proportions of population as the apes. Some scientists theorized higher intelligence would compensate for the over-aggressive nature of the majority. Others argued mankind's future in peril and demanded scrapping the experiment and beginning a new one.

"Eventually, the two groups of scientists compromised, installing an automated system to monitor your progress. It included tests at specified intervals to judge whether you are sufficient to continue or not.

"I can't make it any simpler. Please take heed."

The lieutenant looked up Bonobos on the internet. "Apes living in the Congo. Along with Chimpanzees, they're closest genetically to humans and known for being passive."

The sergeant major scoffed. "What a crock."

The general put the items back in the bag and placed it in the trunk. "Have someone pick it up for forensic examination."

Arriving back at the command post, the general made an offhand comment. "Can't help but wonder if we're making a mistake attacking these aliens without trying harder to talk and negotiate."

Knowing the general so well, the sergeant major realized he planned to call Washington and express that opinion yet again. "You'll just piss them off, sir."

"Yes," the general agreed, "but I'll sleep better."

When he went next door to his tent, a sheet of paper was on his pillow. The printing was identical to the other note.

It read:

"You should move your soldiers outside the boundaries of the buffer zone until after the attack. We have reason to believe the synchronization of the two missiles will be miscalibrated deliberately so the house

> reacts to two strikes rather than one. Traitors in your government seek to double the size of devastation to cause more troop casualties. Their reason is to discredit the President. Please consider this seriously. M. A."

The general's first thought was to wonder how the aliens knew about the missile strike. Then he noted they did not sound concerned for themselves, but why would they care about saving his troops? How would they know if someone planned to sabotage the missiles? Why would anyone do such a thing, anyway? It was too fantastic to take seriously.

He started to take the note to the command post then stopped, folded, and stuck it in his shirt pocket. There was no way in hell his soldiers were leaving the buffer zone, so making this threat known before the strike would only cause them unnecessary concern. Too tired to undress, he stretched out on the bed and turned off the light.

Shortly after midnight, a young sergeant was outside a tent to grab a quick smoke. He could not believe they had a .50 caliber machine gun setup in the middle of a LA neighborhood.

He could not help thinking how laughable the void between generations guarding the site was. Older officers and NCOs went around describing the boy and girl they wanted apprehended with stern warnings how dangerous they were, as if soldiers had not already seen them on the internet chatting with people, giving away candy bars, and posing for pictures.

He and his men were seasoned war veterans used to life and death situations, but this was equal parts spooky and silly without much danger if they left the house alone. Yet, they were preparing to attack it with missiles in the morning. It seemed wrong and crazy to him.

He flipped away the cigarette and lit another. He had been doing his weekend training and would have been home already if not called up for emergency duty. His wife was pissed, but not as much as his boss was. Probably get fired over not returning to work on time.

Someone in the tent yelled for him.

He crushed out the cigarette and walked around the corner. Light from the door flap cast a slice of illumination across the road into the front yard of a house, and there stood the alien, John Justice, big as life. Dashing across the road after him, he shouted for help. The boy turned and ran into the darkness. He went after him.

They searched for a long time before returning to the tent. No one else had seen him, but everyone was glad to have routine interrupted. It gave them a neat story to tell everyone when they went returned home, too.

Five times soldiers had chased John Justice since he left Mercy Ann. She was certainly looking for him by now, but he seldom had the opportunity to be on his own and was making the most of it. Keeping his sensors attuned to detect her, he looked for more soldiers to play his game. The rules were simple. If they got close enough that he had to transport to escape, they won. If he managed to run away and hide, he won. So far, he was up five-zip.

It was great fun until he realized how late it was. Turning up the power of his internal scanning system, he concentrated, searching for Rudy's location. He had to hurry because Mercy Ann could locate him easily using this much power. Fortunately, it only took a few seconds then he transported.

Mercy Ann showed up behind the tent and stomped her feet. "I'm going to give him a good smack for this."

In truth, though, she thought he was playing hide-and-seek and enjoyed it. After all, she could not interfere with the attack without causing a test failure, so all she could do was try to help the fools not kill too many people then continue looking for a way to help them pass. The note about mankind's evolution had been her first attempt to some sort of communication, but it was probably a waste of time. She couldn't believe the government wanted to destroy them and not discuss anything.

On the other hand, the note to the general to move his soldiers was because John Justice had information that conspirators trying to take over the government wanted the missile strike to kill a large number of soldiers and discredit the President. Trying to save lives didn't interfere with the test any way that she could see, and it might possibly establish a rapport with the commanding officer.

Soft chimes sounded in her ear because someone had moved into the alarm perimeter she had set around her. A spatial grid appeared in her right eye with a blue blip representing her and yellow blips soldiers sidling along both sides of the tent. She transported.

Standing under a streetlight, Rudy held a long list of addresses. It was after three and he was just inside the outer perimeter of the buffer zone. Many people violated the evacuation order in this area since authorities hadn't swept through yet. He stretched and looked up at the sky. The rest of his team had gone home. Looking around trying to remember the way to his vehicle, he stopped dead in his tracks.

John Justice stood at the foot of a driveway waving to him.

Rudy had seen him and Mercy Ann on TV. He had not told the officials about it because there was no point and it would freak out his wife. Even before this mess began, she worried herself sick about his job, especially after they discovered their eight-year-old son had leukemia. She wanted Rudy to quit the Fire Department, but good jobs with insurance were scarce.

"I wanted to pay you back," John Justice said, approaching and holding out a bag.

He just couldn't believe this kid was an alien. "I hate to run, but I have to go home now. I hardly see my family these days."

"You have a family, Rudy?" John Justice asked, very concerned suddenly. "I should have realized. What's your address?"

Rudy could not imagine what would happen if his wife opened the door and found John Justice standing there. "Why do you want it?"

John Justice did not understand his reluctance. At the same time, he sensed Mercy Ann not far away, so he grabbed Rudy's arm and jumped to another location.

In the parking lot of a drug store outside the buffer zone, Rudy looked around in confusion. "Oh my God."

John Justice didn't notice. "Ah, I found it. Rudy Johnson, wife Elena, and son Zachary, 18448-B, Mason Ridge Parkway. That is too close to the zone to be completely safe, Rudy."

"What the hell are you?" Rudy blurted, a little frightened and angry.

John Justice still had hold of his arm. Suddenly, they were on a white sandy beach with breaking waves lit by silvery moonlight. Behind them, perched high above the ground, a row of big beach houses with fancy decks.

Frantic, Rudy looked around. "This is Malibu!"

Mercy Ann had a dilemma. It was only a couple of hours before dawn, she had not found John Justice, and Blake had not left the area. Searching again, she discovered John Justice's location but hesitated, thinking she should go after Blake. Then John Justice was gone again.

She pitched a hissy fit, stomping feet and waving arms in the air wildly. She did not have time to take care of all these idiots. She made herself stop and take deep breaths until she decided what to do.

Handcuffed in the backseat cage of a police vehicle, Blake had been a passenger in a car pulled over for rolling through a stop sign. Checking everyone's identification, the cops said they wanted him for questioning about an open case. They jumped him when he asked questions and charged him with resisting arrest.

Blake punched the officer now driving him to jail several times during the altercation. He and his partner had the other gang members picked up while keeping Blake with them. They planned to administer a little personal justice before taking him to the station.

Lieutenant Patrick showed up before they got a chance. Now, his partner followed in the detective's car and he had the lieutenant in the seat next to him. Making matters worse, Blake smirked every time he looked at him in the rearview mirror.

Seething, the officer glanced in the mirror again. Rather than Blake, he saw a girl staring back. He recognized her from the picture on a small clipboard hanging from the dash. Before he could sort his confused thoughts, her hand darted through a hole she burned in the metal cage and grabbed Patrick's shoulder.

Staring back over his shoulder at the empty prisoner cage, the officer rear-ended a parked car.

Mercy Ann located two homes in the Hollywood Hills with owners away. Both had spectacular views of downtown Los Angeles and a patio with a pool. It would be a while before the two men woke up, but she wanted them apart in case she couldn't get back in time. It wouldn't do for one to kill the other.

Next to an infinity pool, she deposited Tom Patrick and Blake Ferrell on chaise lounges. Making her palm glow, she searched Patrick's pockets and found his keys. None of them fit Blake's cuffs, so she cut through them with a narrow beam emanating from her forearm. She burned one of his wrists.

"Tough guy like you shouldn't mind another scar," Mercy Ann muttered. "If I have time later, I'll heal it."

Then she transported Blake to the second house and deposited him on a poolside couch. In spite of being in a hurry, she studied his face for several minutes then shrugged. Must be my imagination, she thought, and transported back to her house.

5

Mercy Ann Sleeps Around

BEFORE DAYLIGHT in communities of the sprawling Los Angeles metroplex, thousands of people leaving for long, arduous commutes can't help but wake neighbors with conversation, slamming car doors, and other noises. Then highways, already overburdened twenty-four hours a day, become a nightmare of stop-and-go traffic, filling the sky with noxious clouds of yellow-gray smog that filters out the vaunted California sunshine and casts a sickly pallor over everything.

Such was the case on day five of the Sufficiency Test, a Thursday with the traffic mess made worse by authorities detouring vehicles off highways around Glenwood Heights. Chemical spills were the official reason, which was impossible to dispute with no other information available.

The no-fly zone kept aircraft away so they could not see the accident scenes were empty trucks parked on highways with emergency vehicles staged around them. Highway traffic cameras on those stretches of road malfunctioned. Cellphone signals were inexplicably weak and intermittent.

Thousands of frustrated commuters milled around outside vehicles in monumental traffic jams when they witnessed two missiles drop out of the smog layer at 9 a.m. Bedlam ensued with people screaming, praying, shouting, kissing goodbye, taking cover, running, and sharing an expectation of death in an apocalyptic event.

Reality was a subdued boom followed by a smallish, brown-orange cloud over Glenwood Heights that dissipated in minutes. Hundreds of videos of the incident and angry diatribes against whoever was responsible for putting so many people in danger would be all over the internet as soon as authorities stopped throttling wireless communications.

The incident was much more dramatic at the disaster site.

The explosion woke up Bongo, sprawled across the sergeant major's boots inside a temporary command post located in the buffer zone. Then his master jerked his feet out from under him and hurried to the general, studying videos of the missile strike taken by surveillance cameras.

An ashen-faced captain reported, "The house was not destroyed. Sensors indicate the area of damage around it expanded to a half-mile square following impact of the first missile. We lost contact with the second missile, but it did not detonate or the devastation would be a one mile square, killing everyone in the buffer zone, including us."

The general and sergeant major, followed by Bongo, hurried outside. The airborne matter settled so fast they could already make out the big house in the distance.

The sergeant major said, "The second missile must have disintegrated without exploding when the house reacted to the first one, but I can't understand why they didn't strike together. Everything showed all systems functioning correctly."

Tight-jawed, the general nodded. "Soon as the ground cools, we'll look around."

A sergeant ran from the tent. "Sir, the goddamned aliens are on the front steps of the house eating candy!"

The sergeant major lost his composure. "Someone get me a rifle!"

"Everyone calm down," the general ordered, feeling Mercy Ann's note in his shirt pocket. "Notify all units that no one is to take any action except by my order. Move! Get it done!"

In the Oval Office, the President yelled at the Chairman of the Joint Chiefs. "You certainly made a mess of this! What am I supposed to tell the country now?"

"I'm sorry, sir," he replied as though it wasn't a big deal. "A glitch in the firing mechanism of the second missile occurred. Unfortunate, but we can still tell the country we took action to take terrorists out."

Too furious to speak, the President glared at his staff.

The Secretary of Defense tried to reassure him. "We'll come up with a scenario that works, sir. Long as we don't mention aliens, everything will be fine."

The Secretary of State had an ax to grind. "The military needs to stop screwing around and catch an alien so we can determine what they are."

Defense fired back, "They disappear and relocate at will. How the hell do we catch something like that?"

The Chairman of the Joint Chiefs demanded, "Give our soldiers permission to shoot and we'll get you the next best thing—two specimens to dissect. We need to stop pussyfooting around."

The Secretary of DHS warned, "If you shoot one of them, who can say they won't destroy the whole city or half of California?"

"Then let's try inviting them to talk again," the Secretary of State suggested. "They certainly don't hesitate to have conversations with every Tom, Dick, and Harry they encounter. Maybe we can end this thing peacefully."

Defense responded angrily. "They initiated aggressive actions against America and killed our people for no reason. I'm coming around to the Chairman's way of thinking. We need to consider shooting on sight."

The Chairman tried to bring the discussion back to the conclusion he wanted. "If the missiles had struck together, the entire matter would be resolved already. I say hit them again with everything we've got, take out the whole shebang, and be done with it!"

The President leaned back, rubbing his temples. "Do you want the city evacuated before you blow it up, Mr. Chairman, or do you consider a few million dead, a collapsed American economy, and Los Angeles destroyed as acceptable losses?"

The Chairman wanted to yell that the President was a weak moron unfit for the job who would be overthrown soon but was under orders from Handley to appease him until the conspiracy was ready to strike. Even so, it was difficult to be civil.

He took a deep breath and forced a smile. "I'm only giving the military perspective, sir. Decisive action is the best answer."

Fed up with the lot of them, the President was close to losing his composure, too. "I do agree that we have no choice now but to announce terrorists were responsible for the attacks and come up with reasons to keep the site off-limits. If we can't resolve this satisfactorily and soon, the truth will get out. Must I remind you that most of our personnel at the site are aware of the true nature of the attackers? Rumors are spreading. We can't keep denying forever."

The Chairman declared, "We've put the fear of God in our people and can deal with leaks as long as this doesn't stretch out too long, which is why we need to act now. Then we'll push our version of events and go after anyone who violates the security agreements they signed. If we remain aggressive, the LA incident will go the way of Roswell."

After the meeting, the White House announced that the President would hold a televised news conference that evening to explain why a missile strike had been necessary, which caused the expected uproar. They would spend the rest of the day gauging media reaction and preparing answers for the President based on issues they raised.

Ashlyn Pike felt disoriented since having her status redesignated, the government's officious name for releasing her conditionally yesterday afternoon because they ran out of room to hold all the people arrested in LA.

She signed an agreement to stay in the city of Oceanside at government expense and to check in at the base every morning until they finished investigating her son. She also signed documents to keep silent about the incident because she didn't think they would stand a stink test if she kicked up a ruckus, which she planned to do if they didn't release Rob and Missa in the next few days. She had no intention to remain in Oceanside, either. Something about this whole thing didn't smell right to her.

Two MPs drove her off post then disobeyed orders to deposit her at a seedy motel downtown, taking her instead to a nicer place near the beach. They were guards in the detainment facility and resented the arrogant civilians who questioned and bullied everyone even more than she did.

After pondering whether to check into the hotel before going into hiding, she decided it would be a useful ploy to throw them off her trail. The desk clerk mentioned a convenience shuttle into town once an hour, so she hurried to the room to cover her tracks.

Stripping to underwear, she climbed into bed, kicked covers loose, and rolled around. Used the toilet, pulled out hair, and tossed it in the tub; followed by liquid soap, shampoo, and conditioner. Turned on the shower and deflected water onto the shower curtain and walls. Wet a couple of towels and a washcloth, and threw them on the floor.

For a few dollars, the shuttle driver dropped her near a strip shopping center with a branch of her bank. It was much easier cashing a large check than hassling with limited amount ATMs. She bought toiletries and a box of black garbage bags using a credit card then asked another shopper if a thrift store was nearby.

Carefully avoiding surveillance cameras, Ashlyn walked the opposite direction of the store, ducked down an alley behind houses, pulled the credit cards and cash out of her purse, and stuffed them in her pocket. She jabbed her hand with a small pair of scissors, took out her cellphone, and smashed it. After smearing blood on the purse and phone, she ran a block down the alley, dropped them in a trashcan, and ran back the opposite way to a cross street that would take her to the thrift store.

Worn jeans, a man's shirt two sizes too large, and a pair of sandals, together with an assortment of cheap hats, caps, and sunglasses, were perfect for getaway disguises. Changing clothes behind a dumpster, she stuffed her belongings into her shirt and cut up the credit cards. Then she walked to the bus station hunched over with a pronounced hitch in her gait.

Arriving in Los Angeles, it was dark when a grisly old man inside a seedy hotel security cage told Ashlyn how lucky she was to find a room with all the nearby evacuations. He said it as if the place wasn't a dump filled with druggies, whores, and predators coming and going around the clock because of cheap rooms rented by the hour.

But that also meant the guy didn't care that she carried her belongings in garbage bags and had a twelve pack of cold beer under her arm when she paid for two nights with cash. Sliding a sticky key to her through a slot, he issued a warning to mind her own business.

Ashlyn watched cable news on a small TV chained and alarmed into the wee hours because the Camp Pendleton interrogators had asked so many questions about Mercy Ann and John Justice that she formed a half-baked idea of trying to find them since they must know something about Rob and Missa. It had seemed a reasonable plan inside the small cell, but back in the hustle and bustle of LA, not so much. Yet, it was all she had.

She woke up from a fitful sleep in a chair with the TV droning in front of her. Bleary-eyed, it took a while to get oriented. Eventually, she realized newscasters and politicians were going crazy about the White House allowing a missile strike in the city.

She dumped water and a packet of rotgut coffee into the basket of a smelly coffeemaker then took a shower. She'd left all her makeup in the discarded purse and looked like crap. Drinking the gag-worthy coffee made her stomach roil. Close to retching, she left to do some shopping.

Chaos reigned in the cut-rate discount store she found. Crowds of evacuees competed for cheap, poorly made clothes and necessities. Ashlyn joined in, elbowing and glaring her way to everything on her list except an inexpensive pair of running shoes in the right size. Fortunately, she was able to grab what she needed from a woman's cart when she looked away. Then she picked up the biggest school backpack they had, stuffed her acquisitions in it, and left the store without paying.

A track star in high school, Ashlyn ran regularly to control the stress that came with working in the emergency room, raising a teenage boy, and dealing with all the bad decisions she made. Consequently, she knew the streets, alleys, and shortcuts for miles around their Glenwood Heights neighborhood. Which was a good thing since she wanted to search for Mercy Ann and John Justice in the restricted area, assuming she could get past patrols without too much trouble.

Later, when the drugs her questioners had secretly administered wore off, Ashlyn would look back on her actions in amazement. Sure, she mistrusted the government and didn't believe half of what they said, but the idea that she would consider sneaking into a secure area guarded by the military staggered her.

Jogging close to the curb of a wide street skirting the buffer zone, Ashlyn steered clear of sentries and guard posts. Reaching an overgrown utility alley she used often in the past, she took a narrow walkway off it that ran through a neighborhood play area to the next street, which was inside the buffer zone. It was almost too easy.

The houses were empty and a little spooky. Making her way through backyards, over fences, and around houses, she moved towards big tents in the distance, surmising they must be the temporary command post TV newscasters mentioned. In her confused state of mind, she thought that was where the aliens would go to spy on military activities, not considering it was the place with the most soldiers and surveillance.

Progress was difficult. She had to hide from several patrols. Two hours passed. She was exhausted.

Ashlyn ran across a street and scrambled over a fence into a backyard. The tents were on the other side of the fence behind it. She heard a hubbub of voices, but could make nothing out clearly.

Despairing, she rested her head against the fence as she realized how stupid this was. The odds of her finding John Justice and Mercy Ann this way were worse than finding a needle in a haystack. She tried to think of something else to do, but had nothing. She turned to retrace her steps.

Mercy Ann stood about ten feet away.

Stricken by how pretty she was, Ashlyn thought the girl exuded confidence almost to the point of arrogance, yet sensed vulnerability, a softness about her.

Finally, Ashlyn spoke. "I've been looking for you."

Mercy Ann gave no indication she heard.

"They took my son. I have nowhere else to turn. Can you help me?"

Still receiving nothing back, Ashlyn fumbled over words. "Rob is really smart, but does incredibly dumb stuff sometimes. I get terribly angry with him, but no matter what, I love him."

Mercy Ann nodded. "Yeah, I have someone like that, too."

"They think he flew a drone over the devastation and put a video on the internet. They arrested him."

"Yes, I know."

"They arrested me, too, but I ran away. Now I'm a fugitive."

"I know. The Marines had you in Oceanside."

Ashlyn was hysterical, crying, not comprehending what Mercy Ann said. "I'm his mother. I don't know where he is. They won't tell me anything. Can you do anything to help?"

Mercy Ann walked to her holding out a handkerchief, but when Ashlyn took it, they were standing in the small neighborhood play area she had passed through.

"The military has listening devices and heard us," Mercy Ann explained. "We have to go. Where are you staying?"

Ashlyn told her.

In a heartbeat, they were in the hotel room.

As Ashlyn tried to get her bearings, Mercy Ann said, "We're trying to find your son and his girlfriend already."

Ashlyn wrapped her in a bear hug. "Thank you, but how do you know about Missa?"

Mercy Ann did not want to explain she was responsible for this mess. "What is Missa's last name?"

"Actually, her name is Melissa MaCaron. Everyone calls her Missa."

"John Justice, I need you," Mercy Ann said.

He appeared sitting cross-legged on the bed. "I'm busy."

Mercy Ann introduced Ashlyn and asked, "Have you had any luck finding them?"

"Not yet, and I have to take care of Rudy and his family, too."

"If you'll give Rob and Missa priority, I'll help Rudy if you'll tell me what you want to do."

They conferred a few minutes then John Justice was gone. Mercy Ann told the wide-eyed Ashlyn not to worry. She'd contact her soon as they found out something. Then she vanished.

Ashlyn called down to the desk for the nearest place to buy a bottle of whisky. She needed more than beer.

Rudy Johnson came awake thinking how much he loved his expensive king-sized, gel foam mattress. His wife had insisted they buy it while he recovered from a fall at work. He felt her warmth near him and smiled. Then he heard waves, breathed ocean air, and realized that ten feet above, sunlight shined between the rough planks of someone's patio deck.

Sitting up, he gasped. His wife slept next to him in loose mom jeans and a ragged sweatshirt she wore around the house. On the other side of her, Zach was fast asleep in Spiderman PJs. Curled up next to him, one arm around the ugly doll he'd seen on the internet and the other curled under her head, Mercy Ann stared with the softest brown eyes he'd ever seen. She pushed herself up.

She had an extreme case of bed hair with strands stuck to her lips and face. Running fingers through it, she managed to get most of it behind her, but it was still a tangled mess. She smoothed the rumpled dress and tried to straighten the twisted leggings.

"Sorry," she muttered, looking up with genuine concern, "I'm not usually this big a mess."

In spite of the absurdity of the situation, he stammered, "No, you look fine. Really."

"John Justice said you were nice. Thank you for the candy. I liked it very much."

He gave her a big smile. "I assumed that when it disappeared everywhere."

She blushed. "I got a little carried away."

"You and John Justice have a strong resemblance."

She was still waking up or would not have said it. "They restructured his body to resemble me more than he did originally. Pissed me off, but I couldn't say anything because they meant well and everything was my fault."

He looked bewildered as he tried to find a reply.

"Sorry," she said. "I tend to babble nonsense sometimes. Did John Justice explain why he brought you here?"

"He said it was to protect us."

"Yes. He wants you to find somewhere outside the city for your family to stay until the test concludes."

"What test?"

"Sorry, more babbling," she answered, annoyed with herself. "Oh. I should introduce myself properly. I am Mercy Ann. Pleased to meet you."

The needless introduction caught him by surprise, and she very much seemed to be waiting for him to reciprocate. "Uh, I'm Rudy Johnson. It is nice to meet you, Mercy Ann."

"Does this mean we're friends?"

"Yes, if you would like."

She looked pleased. "John Justice told me your son had a defect."

It took him a few seconds. "Do you mean the leukemia?"

"Yes. I made alterations to its composition."

Rudy was jarred. "What do you mean?"

"John Justice was concerned."

"What do you mean, you altered it? How?"

She held up the doll. "This is Hanna Beatrice, but I nicknamed her Honey Bee because she's small and has a mean sting. She's in semi-hibernation, but remains fully functional when she's with me. She helped."

"I'm not sure I understand what...?"

"Honey Bee is pleased to meet you, Rudy."

He took a deep breath, tried to calm down. "Uh, yeah, okay."

Seconds ticked by as Mercy Ann stared, expecting more. "Aren't you glad to meet her?"

This is nuts, he thought. "Uh, it's nice to meet you, uh, Honey Bee."

Mercy Ann sat Honey Bee in her lap. "I will send you home before your wife and son wake up. John Justice understands your occupation requires you to be in danger, but no need to endanger them unnecessarily. Please, have them stay outside the city. John Justice is no good to me worrying and upset."

"Just tell me what you did to Zach!" he demanded.

"I fixed him."

"What exactly did you do? If you hurt..."

"Just move your family outside the city, Rudy," she said, louder and more insistent. "Promise me, please."

"Okay, I will, but what did you...?"

Rudy, his family, and his gel-foam bed were in their master bedroom.

Tom Patrick woke up in bright sunlight soaked in sweat. Before him was a beautiful pool, beyond which stretched the hazy LA cityscape. Before he had a chance to wonder how he got there, he realized someone lay next to him. It was Mercy Ann, asleep with the doll in her arms. He jumped up on the other side of the chaise, shaky legs almost causing him to stumble into the pool.

"What the hell is going on?" he shouted.

"Your face is a little sunburned," she replied, yawning and getting up slowly. "Sorry I left you so long."

He knelt, splashed water on his face, and stood back up, glaring. "What happened to my prisoner?"

"I have him."

"I remember being in a police vehicle with him then waking up here. Did we have an accident or something?"

"I transported into the backseat of the car and removed you and Blake."

"That's not possible."

She wondered why everyone seemed determined to piss her off lately. "You're in Hollywood Hills. How do you think you got here?"

He knew where he was but shouted, "Stop the bullshit!"

She grabbed his arm.

The change was instantaneous. Pulsing music pounded their ears. In pitch darkness, they sat squeezed together shoulder-to-shoulder, hip-to-hip on a low-backed, hard seat inside a tight compartment. Disorienting strobes and colored lights flashed, illuminating a narrow tubular passageway and showing they teetered on the fulcrum of a precipice above a deep pit of blackness. Booming voices counted down to zero. They plunged, whipped around a turn, throwing Patrick against Mercy Ann, who squealed and put her arms up over her head.

Not until then did Patrick come to his senses. "This is a rollercoaster!"

They were back on the patio with Mercy Ann in a chair next to Patrick, stretched out on the chaise again.

"What do you think now?" she asked, laughing.

"Must be nice not to have to stand in line for rides," he responded sourly.

She liked his answer. "Indeed."

"What happened to your doll? Did you leave it on the coaster?"

"She gets sick on amusement rides so I sent her home. If you knew her better, you'd realize how strange that is."

Referring to the doll as if it was alive was silly and irritating, reminding him that he was a police detective who didn't stand for childish nonsense, no matter how fantastic the circumstances.

"Why did you kidnap me?"

"I came for Blake and found you, so I decided to check your health. It's good as can be expected so far."

"The hospital said all my x-rays are normal."

"I know."

"But you think there's something else?"

"Yes."

"What?"

"We'll discuss it later, but don't worry, we'll find a solution. Why did you arrest Blake?"

He realized she was not going to answer his question, so he didn't answer hers. "What's he to you?"

"I owed him a favor."

"He's a thug."

"Yes, but he's very intelligent and values life, too. An odd combination, don't you think?"

"It's dangerous for a naïve young girl to be around someone like him. Stay away."

"He won't hurt me."

"Why would you think that?"

"He finds me interesting, but more than that, he's afraid of me."

A seasoned interrogator, he ignored everything except the words he wanted to use against her. "If you really think Blake's afraid of you, you're a fool. He'll chew you up and spit you out."

She had enough. "I'd take you home but you're pissing me off. Go wait in front of the house and someone from your office will pick you up in about thirty minutes, depending on traffic."

He wouldn't leave it alone. "How do you know that?"

This is as bad as talking to John Justice, she thought. "They just answered a text I sent from your phone. Read it for yourself."

He put a hand on the phone in his pocket. "That's not possible. I have my phone."

She lost her temper. "Seriously, think about what it takes to transport people in and out of fast moving objects over long distances then decide if something as asinine as hacking a goddamn cellphone or protecting myself would be a problem. I travel between stars on a spaceship, so use your head for something more than a place to display a bad haircut and stop acting like a frigging jerk."

She vanished.

The President sounded and appeared strong, decisive, and confidant as he told lie after lie in the news conference. The government realized terrorists were responsible for the LA attacks from the beginning. Operating out of a house in Glenwood Heights, one of their bombs went off accidently, destroying the high school and the area around it, alerting authorities to their presence. They set more bombs to avoid capture and went into hiding inside the restricted area.

This morning, they discovered the hiding place. The terrorists threatened to set off more devices if we closed in. The military used new missiles recently added to our arsenal because they were the safest, most efficient way to destroy an enemy with minimal collateral damage.

To be certain the terrorists did not leave other devices in the restricted area, they would increase the size of the buffer zone temporarily and search everything thoroughly. He regretted the further inconvenience of more evacuations, but when they finished, life in Los Angeles would return to normal. If everyone cooperated and vacated the new buffer area by midnight tomorrow, they could finish in three weeks.

While he understood the press' fascination with the subject of time traveling aliens that appear and disappear at will, mysterious haunted houses, and all the other ridiculous videos and stories on the internet, they were huge distractions to authorities trying to deal with a difficult situation.

Then the President deflected and defused criticism with self-deprecating humor, wry witticisms, cutting sarcasm, and more lies, resulting in the vast majority of Americans, especially outside California, discrediting and criticizing any notion of aliens. At the same time, he acted magnanimous towards the citizens of Los Angeles and first responders for their bravery, sacrifices, and perseverance.

His staff agreed that it was his finest performance, leaving most of the country feeling the matter would be over soon; or, as the President's Chief of Staff summed up: "Mission accomplished."

The hotel made Ashlyn feel dirty, so she finished her third shower of the day and came out of the bathroom around midnight with a towel wrapped around her to find Mercy Ann stretched out on the couch watching TV news about the news conference and sipping the last of a full whiskey and Coke.

Ashlyn took the glass from her. "I made this for me, young lady."

Mercy Ann was drunk. "I drank that one. This one, I made for me."

"You're too young for alcohol."

"I'm older than you, kiddo."

Ashlyn was more amused than upset, although she tried to hide it. "Sure you are. Anyway, it's not good for you."

"You drink it."

"It's okay for adults, long as they don't drink too much. Understand?"

Mercy Ann yawned, started to reply, and then closed her eyes, fast asleep.

Ashlyn gulped down the drink. "Tonight, I need too much."

Later, Ashlyn woke up in bed with Mercy Ann's leg and arm over her. She'd taken off the girl's clothes, leaving her in a loose camisole and old-fashioned bloomers that reached half down her thighs. She could only imagine how uncomfortable wearing so many clothes was.

More importantly, if anything about Mercy Ann was different from an Earth human, Ashlyn did not find it with a quick examination. Being a nurse, she was not shy about conducting one, either, but she did notice other things.

Mercy Ann's temperature was definitely higher than normal for Earthlings. Occasional soft whirring noises came from her while asleep, sounding mechanical in nature. Then, as day dawned, she reached over to push Mercy Ann's heavy hair off her face and discovered three hard protrusions sticking out on the back of her head. She touched one with a finger. It felt exactly like a din jack plug on the back of a stereo.

Mercy Ann's eyes popped open, staring straight into hers. "Don't fiddle with that."

Ashlyn moved her hand. "Sorry."

"What time is it?"

"Around five."

She sat up. "I have a headache. Never could drink hard stuff."

Ashlyn gave her a couple of aspirins and a soft drink. "Gulp them down fast. It'll make you belch and feel better."

While Ashlyn made coffee, Mercy Ann turned on the TV and sat on the couch burping. "I must apologize. I planned to tell you last night that John Justice discovered that Rob and Missa were taken to Sedona, Arizona, initially, but they moved them before he arrived."

"They took them to Arizona? Why?"

John Justice's message explained the purpose of the secret facility, but he'd made so many mistakes recently she did not want to tell

Ashlyn yet. “I’m not sure. He’s looking for where they were taken, but it may take a few days.”

Disappointed, she nodded. “Okay.”

TV news people were discussing the missile attack.

Mercy Ann muttered, “Four more and it’s a failure.”

“What are you talking about?” Ashlyn asked.

Mercy Ann had not meant her to hear. “Just thinking about something I forgot to do.”

“All that stuff about terrorists is lies, isn’t it?” Ashlyn asked. “Those missiles were fired at you.”

“Yes, but don’t be concerned. We’ll find Rob and Missa.”

“What’s this all about? Why are you here?”

Mercy Ann got up, went to the bedroom, and came back with the Sufficiency Test notice she always carried.

Ashlyn read it. “Why hasn’t the government told us about this?”

“They have a secret weapon they think will destroy us. Then they won’t have to tell the world the truth about aliens because it’ll plunge the world into chaos.”

“Do you think we would react like that?”

“Most definitely, but it’s better than failing the test. Your government is too stupid to realize that.”

“So you really would destroy us?”

“John Justice and I belong to a militia that protects Earth for the beings conducting the test. They gave permission for us to help you pass but imposed so many restrictions that it’s very difficult.”

“The people trying to destroy us sent you to help us? That doesn’t make sense.”

Mercy Ann took the notice back. “I know. Sorry. For now, though, you should leave the city and hide. John Justice just sent a message that agents are looking for you in Oceanside. They’ll figure you returned to LA. I’ll contact you soon as we know something.”

“How will you find me?”

“I inserted a tracking device in one of your orifices last night after you molested me.”

Ashlyn gasped. “Where did you put it?”

“Relax, it was a joke. John Justice will track you no matter where you go. Do you have enough cash?”

“I withdrew as much as I could. It won’t last long.”

“Be right back.”

She reappeared a few minutes later with bundles of cash in her arms that she dropped onto the bed. "They're used bills that won't cause problems."

"Where did you get all this?"

"Judging by the way they reacted to a girl in her underwear taking their money, I think they were either bankers or drug dealers." She cocked her head, listening. "John Justice says this area will be evacuated in two hours. You must leave before the authorities come. They will be here looking for you in LA by then. Do you need assistance disguising yourself and hiding your tracks?"

"No. You're really serious that everyone on Earth could be killed, aren't you?"

Mercy Ann was lonely and needed to talk to someone, but realized she should not have told Ashlyn about the notice. "John Justice will find Rob and Missa. In the meantime, don't lose faith. If you're in danger of capture, don't do anything too drastic. One of us will come rescue you."

Mercy Ann walked into the bedroom, gathered up her clothes, and disappeared.

6

No Mess, No Fuss, No Bother

DEPRESSED, BLAKE FERRELL MADE HIS WAY through alleys and backstreets slowly. He'd called his attorney and found out the cops had not filed an arrest report after he escaped yesterday but still had orders to pick him up for the other case. He didn't understand why Detective Patrick didn't use that against him, but still couldn't hang with the guys and frequent places he liked, which aggravated him no end.

As much as those things concerned him, the way he'd behaved with Mercy Ann bothered him more. He'd acted like a jerk and discovered the hard way that she could take care of herself. She'd almost killed him, and he didn't blame her.

When she woke him up in Hollywood Hills, he resented feeling so vulnerable and helpless, even though she only wanted to help him. When she offered to treat the burn on his wrist, he told her to leave it alone. Then he proposed that she help him rob the house and kept insisting, just to give her a hard time.

Mercy Ann tolerated his idiocy, treating it as a joke, until he said, "They may have some decent clothes to replace that ugly getup you wear. If not, I'll take you shopping so you can get dolled up right and proper."

Instantly, her anger flared. "I'm not some cheap whore you can buy, asshole!"

Blake hadn't meant it the way she took it, but knew he'd gone too far and needed to apologize. He did not get the chance.

She slapped his face, and he found himself standing on the hood of a luxury SUV moving through a carwash with water jets, soap spray, and spinning brushes battering him. Knocked to the concrete floor, his right hip struck the chain rail and he banged his head. One of the front wheels nearly ran over his legs. He managed to crawl away intact, but it was close.

Now he had bruises all over, moved as a decrepit old man might, and deserved it. Then he caught himself wishing her and Mercy Ann were closer in age, as if someone as intelligent as her would consider friendship with a loser like him, much less anything else.

The President had begun investigating rumors of illegal arrests and interrogations. The conspirators found out. Not sure how much he knew, they ordered all detainees released or eliminated except for a few special cases they decided to send outside the country. Then they convened an emergency meeting at a Maryland estate belonging to the leader of the conspiracy, Jared Handley.

He introduced the CEO of one of his conglomerates that operated legitimate private prisons as well as the conspirators' clandestine facilities around the world.

"This is a video from Sedona we put together from surveillance cameras at the interrogation site," the CEO introduced. "As you can see, the alien known as John Justice appeared in the entry hallway, which activated body scanners. If you look closely, you can make out circuitry and numerous small devices inside him."

The picture changed to another room. "This shows him in the cell where we held one of the teenagers from LA. Next, he's in the cell of the other one. Fortunately, both had been relocated already."

The DHS Deputy Secretary commented, "Jared, leave it to you to downplay such an extraordinary event.

Handley, sipping hot tea, smiled. "It's not as if we didn't know aliens existed."

A member of the NSA spoke up. "If we can capture this boy and extract the technology, no telling what we could do with it."

The Chairman of the Joint Chiefs was less impressive in a civilian suit than a military uniform. "Jared and I believe the aliens may track the prisoners to the Middle East and attempt a rescue. We're setting up equipment to disrupt their internal systems. If that doesn't work, al-Bensi soldiers will attack them with new weapons developed by Handley Industries."

The FBI Director asked, "Mightn't the high schoolers be aliens, too?"

"We scanned them," Handley answered, surprised he thought of that. "They're perfectly normal humans. The interrogations will unearth what their connections to the aliens are."

"What about the parents of the prisoners?" the NSA member asked. "Won't they kick up a fuss?"

A bit too smug, the FBI Director bragged, "The boy's mother thinks she signed National Security forms when we released her. We're trying to get the girl's parents to do the same, but they're proving obstinate. It's only a matter of time before they cave, however."

The Chairman asked, "Why not lose the parents?"

"We can't kill everyone," the Director snapped.

The Chairman pressed. "With respect, anyone we send to the Death Valley Prison won't be coming back. Security agreements won't keep them quiet if their children aren't returned."

The Director realized he'd made a mistake but didn't want to admit it in front of Handley. "Teenagers fall in love and run away. Happens every day. With all the excitement in LA, no one is going to pay attention to missing love-struck kids."

Handley frowned. "No one knows we picked the kids up except the parents. Dispose of them and doctor records to show they went missing in the LA incident. That way, there will be no mess, no fuss, no bother."

Ashlyn Pike left the hotel in LA much less confident that Mercy Ann and John Justice could save Rob and Missa. The whole thing seemed so fantastic and overwhelming in the sunshine amongst bustling people going about daily business. They would say she was nuts if she told them the world could end in three weeks. So, why did she believe it?

Crossing the parking lot with her stuff in the backpack, a sense of helplessness overcame her. Someone honked for her to get out of the way.

She yelled, "Blow it out your ass!"

A rugged old fart with a ZZ Top beard, prison face tattoos, and a Willie Nelson bandana on his head pointed a pistol as he rolled slowly by, but the only thing that blasted her was thirty-year-old death metal rock. Then he squealed tires turning onto the road.

The incident was a slap in the face. If the world ended, there wasn't a damned thing she could do about it. For now, she'd follow Mercy Ann's instructions and hope everything worked out the way she said. The first order of business was to get serious and go into hiding.

Speaking enough Spanish to get by, a must in the emergency room, Ashlyn stopped in a Latino market then went to a restaurant in an old service station to eat tacos. On the way out, she ducked into the restroom, stuffed her cheeks with gauze pads, and lightly smeared cheap mascara around the eyes. Using a pair of school scissors and a razor blade, she cut her hair, making it a jagged mess. Quickly cleaning up, she pulled a Boonie Hat down to her eyebrows and departed, not looking at anyone.

Passing a charitable thrift store, she pulled a flower-print dress from a drop off bin and tugged it on over her jeans and shirt. She headed to the bus station.

On the way, she used one of the burner phones from the market to call an old high school classmate she ran into occasionally over the years. He was a wealthy surgeon and lived in Laguna Beach. One night over drinks at a seminar about emergency room procedures, he'd hit on her and mentioned he had a condo in Palm Springs if ever she wanted to borrow it.

The call surprised him, but he was pleased she asked, probably because of illusions she would sleep with him when next they met. She smiled, wondering what he would say if he could see her now.

Ashlyn wasn't a big fan of the desert, but it was the perfect place to hide in summer if you had a place to hole up. When she bought the ticket, she twisted her lip and faked a tic. The gauze pads made it difficult to speak clearly, causing people to look away, not wanting to stare at someone afflicted.

Just use what you know, she thought. Just use what you know.

To people shopping Rodeo Drive that day, the boy and girl had the right mix of aloofness and attitude for children born into the Beverly Hills wealthy elite. After all, children such as these had bank accounts, credit cards, and were ready to satisfy every whim with Daddy and Mommy's delicious money, which came in every flavor known to the world.

Perfect beach tans, realistically applied at an exclusive spa, suggested days spent at mansion pools and surfing. His jet-black hair had the sweep, drama, and sideburns of a young Elvis. Her perfectly applied makeup, highlighted by outrageous ruby red lips, were just right for a young teenage girl harboring twenty-one-year-old starlet ambitions.

And then, there were the clothes.

Graceful in movement and elegant in concept, the boy wore a top designer's flowing, calf-cropped black pants with legs wide to the extreme. Paired perfectly, a custom-tailored, red silk dress shirt with black onyx buttons. Accessories included a black and red-checked neck scarf, matching socks, and eye-catching, red leather Buscemi high-top sneakers.

In jarring contrast, the girl wore a pair of thousand dollar skinny jeans with legs outrageously cut-off ragged, frayed, and uneven at mid-thigh. A patched and faded black Rolling Stones 94/95 Voodoo Lounge Tour t-shirt swayed from her slim shoulders, decorated by a heart-shaped diamond broach pinned through the Stones' logo red tongue. Tied around her waist instead of a belt, a weathered piece of nautical rope with a big knot hung down out of the shirt, bouncing and swinging between her legs as she clomped-clomped in authentic Jordan basketball shoes, stuffed with socks to keep her feet from sliding overmuch. The Jordans had bright pink shoestrings, which went with nothing either wore, the ideal fashion counterpoint.

Rich, famous shoppers ogled them, trying to guess their pedigrees. Store personnel, adept at recognizing wealthy clientele and estimating net worth at a glance, could not run outside to show windows fast enough to ask if they needed assistance.

As a disappointed clerk went back into a store, John Justice turned to Mercy Ann. "This wig is hot."

She was tired of his complaining. "I keep telling you, it's a disguise. You look fabulous. Every female on the street is drooling. Men are, too, lover boy. You ought to take some of them home with you."

"Ha-ha," he answered dully. "Why wouldn't you let them spray my hair same as yours?"

She had a much darker shade of honey blond, and it made her look older. "I already told you that it's easier to get a wig over your hair than mine. We shouldn't look too much alike, either."

"It has been two hours since we left the spa. How much longer are we doing this?"

Refusing to be irritated, she pointed in a window at a platinum watch with emeralds. "Isn't that gorgeous?"

"It is a primitive timepiece."

"Yes, but look at the green sparklys on the face. Just think how great it would look on my wrist."

"I guess, long as you don't care about function."

Annoyed, she led to the next store thinking she would buy his patience with a present, but it had windows full of Gucci bags and purses. Hurrying past, she realized John Justice had stopped, peering intently at something.

She went back, followed his gaze. "Bright diamante leather messenger bag. You like it?"

"It's for females."

"Men carry them, usually in grays and browns, but you can have burnt orange if you want. It doesn't match your shoes exactly, but close enough with that shirt exuding causal island flair and those super-hot, bitchin' Cossack pants showing off your tight little butt. I'm surprised someone hasn't tried to run away with it already. I mean, come on."

Reddening, he looked at her curiously. "You've been watching those stupid fashion shows on TV again, haven't you? These wide-leg pants look like I'm wearing a dress. A Gucci purse would make me over-the-top effeminate."

"So what? It's a good look. I haven't been watching TV fashions shows, either. You don't have to know anything about fashion to persuade people you do. Just make wild-ass pretentious statements and look down your nose at the same time. Go ahead. Try it. It's fun."

"You just brought me along to make me look ridiculous, didn't you?"

"No, John Justice. I thought we should have a special day out before everyone starts trying to kill us. After today, we will most definitely keep a low profile and work behind the scenes. We discussed it. Remember?"

He sighed. "You still don't have a plan, do you?"

She was determined not to let him upset her. "Not yet, but I have determination and confidence."

"You're unbelievable."

She went into the store, paid in cash, and had the bag giftwrapped in fancy gold and silver paper with a big, black bow. She came out and presented it to him with both hands.

A group of pretty, young women watched nearby. One of them, with a big smile, asked, "Is there an occasion?"

"It is his thirteenth birthday," Mercy Ann replied without missing a beat.

The women burst into a loud birthday song with Mercy Ann shouting "John-Boy" when they paused for a name. Other people stopped to listen. Everyone applauded. John Justice, eyes glued to the box, bowed his appreciation all around.

It was a perfect moment until one of the women pointed to Mercy Ann's outlandish basketball shoes and tried to make a joke at her expense. "Couldn't you find a bigger size?"

In her best deadpan way, she did a perfect California girl imitation with exaggerated hand gestures. "I realize my footwear is a bit skimpy on size. When in Cannes last season, actress acquaintances wore humongous vintage sports shoes to the after-event parties. Well, I thought, O-M-G! How absurd! How fricking sensational! I simply must have some. But then I discovered shoes worn by big name sports stars are hard to come by, not to mention way-way expensive. So I keep my collection of rare ones in our vault room at the bank. I only take them out for special occasions, and never for shopping in places with nosy tourists from the Midwest. Where does your tour stop next—the Wax Museum?"

Pulling John Justice away, Mercy Ann whispered, "Thought about stomping her ugly feet, but was afraid I'd do something even nastier if I lifted my leg that high."

He laughed. "Don't talk dirty, Mercy Ann."

"I do have to admit these shoes are a bit ridiculous and awkward. On the other hand, I may have just started a new fashion trend."

"You're so crazy."

"Yeah, I guess, but it is fun."

She sounded like old times before the accident, and he was touched. "Why did you buy me a birthday present?"

"Because, John Justice, you're my best friend."

"But I don't have birthdays."

"Well, that's true, but for today only, I hereby declare you are thirteen, same as me."

"But you're not thirteen, are you?"

"Yes! How many times do I have to tell you? But tomorrow, you'll be twelve again. Then next year, we'll have a cake and celebrate your thirteenth birthday all over again. We'll make it a tradition. How's that sound?"

"Thank you, Mercy Ann."

"You are very welcome, John Justice."

"Am I really your best friend?"

"Of course you are. No one else will have anything to do with me."

He laughed again. "You have a point."

"Don't be mean."

She bought him a salad and pizza for an early dinner. She ordered wine, too, but they would not give it to them, even after she offered a shocked waiter five hundred dollars.

Seated at an outside table, they people-watched as the sun went down and made small talk as each waited for the other to bring up the subject most on their minds.

Finally, John Justice asked, "You're worried, aren't you?"

She nodded. "I assumed the government would be more intelligent about the riddle and we could nudge them in the right directions. Can't believe they acted based on one line and disregarded the rest. How dumb is that?"

"Well, you did say the way the Guardians worded it was too vague."

"Yeah, they wouldn't let me change it. They sure made this difficult."

"You still don't have any ideas?"

She stared then brightened. "Let's try Chaos Theory! Do wild, unexpected things that keep them flummoxed, making mistakes, and giving us opportunities to act."

He wasn't sure whether she was joking or serious with this latest crackpot idea. "Strictly speaking, that's not Chaos Theory."

"Yeah, but it could work and make everything easy-peasy."

"If you say so. Uh, I'm having trouble locating the high school students."

"You'll find them, so stop worrying."

"Conditions at the Sedona facility were pretty bad. Did you tell Ashlyn Pike what to expect?"

"No. She's already worried sick."

"I'll have to show you some of the stuff she did to avoid the authorities. She's pretty amazing."

"Yeah, I like her."

Then he slipped up and said the worst thing possible. "If something bad happened to them, promise that you won't go out of control again."

Her friendly demeanor turned sour. "I keep telling you that won't happen again. Sheesh."

He had messed up the best day they'd had together in years and wanted to make it up. "If you can you spare me a couple of days, I will try tracking them physically."

Mercy Ann mulled it over. "Well, it's not as if you can't come back right away if I send a summons. Are you sure you'll be all right on your own?"

That question irritated him. "I suspect they took them to a military base in Phoenix and flew them somewhere, so I'll go look at their records. Load weights and other flight data will offer clues even if they didn't use their names. I'll find them."

"Do not attempt a rescue on your own," she warned. "I'll do it. Okay?"

Instantly angry, he stood. "I am not helpless, Mercy Ann. I'll let you know what I find."

"Wait, don't leave from here."

It was too late. He was gone.

He'd said her name too loud, drawing attention before transporting. Everyone on the terrace stared at Mercy Ann, including the actress who'd given her the business card. She was a few tables away, gaping in surprise as she recognized her.

Mercy Ann took a last bite of pizza, waggled her fingers goodbye, and vanished.

Missa had no idea how much time had passed since Skinny Bitch burst into the cell, gave her an injection, and taunted how she was going to the worst place on Earth. Ever since, she had drifted in and out of consciousness with a blackout bag over her head and wrists bound painfully behind her. She remembered several aircraft and thought they must have left the United States, a terrifying thought.

Currently, the sound of propellers roared through the cabin, shaking the plane. The seat was small and hard, making her butt hurt. Her captors seemed less concerned about administering knockout shots and she thought they might be close to their destination. She continued being careful not to vary her steady breathing or move much, allowing her to hear them. Everyone spoke a Middle Eastern language now with occasional English words now. That was how she knew Rob was on the same plane.

Someone kicked her in the ankle and jerked off her head when she cried out. A burley soldier in a brown uniform peered into her face, his strong tobacco breath making her wince. He fondled her breasts, and made loud comments that brought jeers, laughs, and comments from others around her. He pulled the bag back over her head and tightened it around her neck so she could hardly breathe. She felt a needle jab her arm.

Those were her last memories of planes.

"Well," the anthropologist responded to the White House staffer's question, "to explain the Bonobos' significance to evolution, one must discuss three species: humans, Chimpanzees, and Bonobos. Chimps and humans derived from a common African ancestor approximately six million years ago. Around one and a half million years ago, the Congo River permanently separated the Chimpanzee population into two groups. Those on the north side evolved into modern day Chimps, while those to the south became Bonobos. The two groups developed distinct physical and behavioral differences, but both species still share

98.7% the same genetics as humans and 99.6% the same as each other."

The staffer handed her a single typed sheet of paper titled, *Bonobos vs. Chimpanzees*. "Your account is a little different from this one."

The anthropologist read and handed it back. "I don't know who wrote this, but someone is living in a fantasy world."

"Remember that this is a matter of national security not to be discussed with anyone. I was told to consult the Smithsonian for information and prepare a briefing paper for the White House Chief of Staff about Bonobo monkeys."

"They're great apes, not monkeys," the anthropologist corrected. "Probably what they want are the evolutionary differences in behavior between Bonobos and Chimpanzees. Bonobos are reluctant to fight and known as the peaceful apes. The females have more dominant societal roles than males, the exact opposite of Chimpanzees, which are led by alpha males that subjugate females."

"Same as the men in Washington," the female staffer replied.

The anthropologist smiled. "Bonobo males tend to retain strong bonds with their mothers for life, to the extent that mothers often pick mates for their sons. Bonobos have prolific amounts of sex, too. They'd rather have an orgy with strangers than fight, especially the females, which are very promiscuous."

The staffer sighed. "So, Bonobos are the hippies of the ape world."

"It has been remarked many times that mankind would benefit by being more Bonobo and less Chimpanzee."

The staffer summed it up with words the President would remember after the Chief of Staff briefed him. "In other words, make love, not war."

Missa MaCaron's parents were in every way good Americans. Growing up in a proud blue-collar family, her father and his brother listened to their parents, studied hard in public schools, and worked their ways through good colleges. Her father became a real estate agent in a big firm where he met and married another agent with a similar background and work ethic.

Around the time they had their one and only child, Melissa, they decided to open a small agency of their own. It was hard going, put a strain on the marriage, and bumps in the road to a future together, but they kept at it, becoming reasonably successful. They built personal and business reputations as honest, reliable people known for strong religious convictions and not overly concerned about accumulating wealth.

Her father loved the Lakers and went to as many games as possible. His dream was to have season tickets, but work and money did not make that feasible. Otherwise, he was a passionate backyard grill master who studied and experimented enthusiastically with recipes that he used to compete in state competitions. His biggest flaws were impatience and a tendency not to think matters through, traits that kept them from being more successful.

Her mother, on the other hand, was a tireless volunteer in church, helping plan and organize activities, especially for the elderly and unfortunate. She had begun martial arts as a way to lose weight and gotten Missa involved, initially because children's lessons were cheaper than daycare. She was the one who made certain the American flag was in the holder next to the front door on holidays and worried about family finances. She was fast to express dissenting opinions to her husband then give in to him just as quickly.

They believed in their country and rights as American citizens, exactly as they should have. So when the bogus authorities put them together in a cell so the wife could talk her husband into signing a National Security Agreement, he not only refused but also convinced his wife back to his side. Then together they told their captors to shove it up their asses and give their daughter back.

A short time later, an agent came to tell them orders for release had come through and agents would take them to pick up their daughter, remanded to their custody pending completion of the investigation. Unable to leave well enough alone, her father told them it was about damned time and that after his lawyers finished suing, they'd be lucky to have jobs.

The big SUV departed a federal detainment facility located near Lompoc with the MaCarons seated in the middle row of seats. Two women rode in front and two men in the rear. Rather than taking the coastal highway to LA, they turned onto a narrow dirt road running through fields of beautiful flowers basking under luscious California sunlight. By then, the MaCarons were dead from lethal injections.

A funeral home with crime ties cremated the bodies. Conspirators added them, Missa, Rob, and his mother to lists of casualties in the LA incident.

The FBI Director sent an encrypted message to Jared Handley that ended with a promise to have the nurse picked up in Oceanside and eliminated. He did not know that she had gone into hiding.

Elena Johnson cried after they took Zach to his doctor, who confirmed the leukemia was gone. She could tell her husband was holding something back and bombarded him with questions until he said that he had prayed until an angel told him in a dream the boy was cured. The explanation was too preposterous for words, but she was too thankful to make a fuss about it. After all, Rudy always had good reasons for what he did.

But then, on the way home, he told her that she and Zach had to go stay at his brother's house in Redlands until the crisis in LA ended. She didn't like that he would only be with her when he could get away from the job, but she had been a nervous wreck since the whole thing started. She did not think the government was telling them everything, but also thought the stories about aliens were just plain crazy. Then she realized Rudy was driving to Redlands already and complained.

Rudy used the easy grin that usually melted her resolve. "The suitcases are in the trunk. I'll spend the night with you at Thomas' house. Anything I missed, I'll bring in a few days."

Much as Elena didn't want separation from Rudy, she was relieved to leave the LA mess. "Just don't take unnecessary chances."

"I do my job and keep my head down. Besides, I'm too ornery to be abducted by bug-eyed aliens."

"Don't joke about that! It's bad luck."

He looked in the back seat at Zach sleeping. "It's hard for me to think about bad luck after this miracle. We've been blessed, for sure."

She leaned across the console and rested her head against his shoulder.

The general enjoyed smoking a cigar and having a quiet walk to mull over the day's events after dinner. Passing through an older upscale area, the street had the extra serenity of palm trees lining the way. The yards were decent sizes, too.

He wondered if anyone had read the recommendations he'd sent up the chain of command with the note they'd found. He'd invited the wrath of the Army by sending an unofficial copy with a note to an old West Point football teammate who worked at the State Department. He'd asked him to pass it along to someone at the White House, if possible.

He'd spent today setting up a new perimeter a mile beyond the current one, one and a half miles from the house at the center of destruction. The President would go on the air in a couple of hours to tell the country more lies about the incident. He didn't see how they could keep everyone finding out the truth about the aliens much longer, even though nearly everyone outside Los Angeles still thought that aspect was some kind of hoax.

They'd established more checkpoints on major thoroughfares to scare away looters and troublemakers flooding into the city. Policing such a large area was next to impossible, even with law enforcement working around the clock and a thousand more soldiers assigned to help. They'd even assigned a one-star general, allowing him to focus fully on the devastated area.

Technicians had shown him how much power the new coil cannons generated, and he didn't think anything could survive against them. As a military professional, he should feel excited about seeing them in operation, but had strong qualms about attacking the young aliens with them.

Other than reports of the aliens shopping at Rodeo Drive, there were no sightings today, which was very different from previous days.

He had orders to keep the notice on the house covered at all costs beginning today. He'd pointed out that everyone at the site already knew about it, but it not matter. He had a feeling the whole situation would spin out of control if someone didn't do something soon.

A somber DJ summed up the day's events in the city:

> "Arguments continue to rage about whether John Justice and Mercy Ann are the cutest aliens in the universe or simply talented actors. I grew up looking at that big Hollywood sign every single day of my life, so I think they're a sham. I have to admit it is genius marketing, though. Hey, producers, give a lonely DJ a piece of the action.
>
> "Not that other people aren't jumping on the bandwagon. Tapes, videos, and websites with different alien kids are popping up everywhere. Give us a break, people!
>
> "When the first reports came in about Heath Bars disappearing from stores, one of our DJs asked the aliens to bring some to the studio. A few hours later, a boy wearing a blond wig walked into our lobby and gave a bag full to the receptionist. She took a selfie with him. Wasn't the John Justice we're used to, but he did have a good sense of humor.
>
> "Now, for some serious news. The President announced more evacuations to provide a bigger buffer zone around the Glenwood Heights disaster. Don't be like the guy who fired shots at city workers.

> Does no good to end up dead. Nobody likes this, but authorities say it will be over soon. I'm sleeping on a cot at the station, so don't call me bitching about it, either. My back hurts too much to listen.
>
> "And if any of you outlaws out there think you can find easy pickings in the evacuated areas, think again. Those long military convoys that keep rolling into the city mean more armed patrols. If you try to steal someone's television, you're likely to get a bullet in the butt, so everybody be cool. Soon we can party and tell tales about how we fought off an alien invasion by having orgies in tent cities and sleeping alone in radio stations.
>
> "Back to the music. Turn up the volume! Let them hear it in space!"

At 2 a.m. on the seventh day, bedlam broke out in the Army command tent when Mercy Ann walked out and sat down on the front steps of the house. She wore a white nightgown that reached to the ankles and socks so big they bunched around her ankles rather than staying up on the calves. Ignoring the spotlights, she rested her head on her knees and remained that way until dawn. Then she got up, stretched, and removed the military's cover from the Sufficiency Test notice before going back into the house.

7

Mercy Ann and the General

NO MORE ALIEN SIGHTINGS OCCURRED until 2 a.m. on day eight when Mercy Ann came out of the house dressed same as the night before, sat on the steps with her head on her knees, and slept until dawn, when she got up and ripped down the cover placed over the Sufficiency Notice yesterday. Then a difference—she stared in the direction of the military command post for long seconds before going inside.

Some authorities in Washington wanted the military to attempt sneaking up and capturing Mercy Ann. Others wanted snipers to wound or kill her outright. They all had the same ultimate goal of obtaining the aliens' technology, which they insisted to the President should be his first priority.

When the Chairman of the Joint Chiefs pointed out that it would assure him an honored place on a short list of great Americans, the President cut him off and declared once again that he opposed any action that could lead to the public finding out about the aliens. Arguments continued off and on all day into the night. Even the President's staff thought he placed his personal beliefs ahead of what was best for the country, but his determination outlasted them.

No other alien sightings occurred until Mercy Ann came out and sat on the steps at precisely 2 a.m. on day nine. She knew the White House had ordered everyone to leave her alone until the President gave the word to execute an attack. Tonight, she stared in the direction of the command post before sitting down on the steps and resting her head on her lap.

"Watching her is getting kind of like watching a cuckoo clock," the sergeant major said, looking up at the big monitor.

The general opined, "I think she has a problem and wants our help."

The sergeant major stared in surprise. "Surely, she doesn't expect to get it."

"My gut says I should go talk to her."

The sergeant major had learned not to second-guess the general's intuition but thought he was wrong this time. "She and the boy always go inside when anyone approaches the house, not to mention you could be disintegrated."

"I think it'll be fine," he said, setting down the coffee.

"With all due respect, sir, we were ordered to stay away from the house except for keeping the notice covered. Are you going to tell Washington what you're planning?"

He stood and stretched. "I'm not planning anything. I'm going outside to smoke a cigar. If our neighbor invites me to sit a spell, then maybe I will. If I were you, I'd roust the colonel. The Pentagon will call soon as they see me near the house, and they always feel better having a high-ranking officer to chew on. No offense."

The sergeant major ordered someone to wake the colonel then said, "I'll let the sentries know you're outside. Don't want you getting shot in the ass again."

The general laughed. "Yeah, that was a mite embarrassing."

A few minutes later, Mercy Ann lifted her head from her knees and called out, "Good evening, sir. Care to join me?"

Still in darkness behind the big spotlights, the general wondered how she knew he was there. "Good evening, young lady. Don't mind if I do."

As he moved out of darkness, he crushed the cigar on the ground and held up a walkie-talkie. "I don't have any weapons."

She stood as he reached the porch steps. "I'll get some chairs and refreshments for us."

The general came from an old Southern family steeped in tradition, military service, and genteel manners, so his reply came automatically without regard to how absurd it was under the circumstances. "May I help you with anything?"

She stared for long seconds then opened and held the door for him. "Yes, thank you."

Inside the command post, it would be accurate to say that everyone went nuts. In Washington, panic ensued and phones rang all over the city.

The general and Miss Flowers carried out two wooden chairs with seat cushions, followed by Mercy Ann with a small round table. Then Miss Flowers hurried back inside and returned with a pitcher of lemonade, two glasses, and white linen napkins.

After she went inside, Mercy Ann filled the glasses. "None of your surveillance equipment can hear us and our mouths will be blurred on videos, so these discussions are private. Thank you for coming."

"You're welcome, but you must realize that I'll report everything to my superiors."

"I just ask that you give me a fair hearing then decide what to tell them."

"I'm listening."

"First off," she said, "the Sufficiency Test is an automated program John Justice and I have no control over. We want to help you pass, but can't tell you what to do directly without triggering a failure. I know this sounds crazy and raises endless questions, but I thought I should say it before asking a favor. I need your help to locate John Justice."

"That's a lot to take in. Even if I believed you, why would you think I'd help?"

"I want to make a trade. The people who tampered with your missile strike have him. They're members of a conspiracy working to seize control of your government. I know you find it hard to believer, but I can provide ample evidence."

"What kind of evidence?"

"We have the ability to monitor any Earth communications, whether they are personal conversations or the most sophisticated electronic transmissions with the highest levels of encryption."

The general tensed. "That's impossible."

Miss Flowers came out of the house, handed a computer tablet to the general, and went back inside.

Mercy Ann explained, "The names on the screen are the inner circle of the conspiracy. Jared Handley runs it. Next in line is your Chairman of the Joint Chiefs. Even your three-star boss at the Pentagon is a major player, although he is not in the top echelon. Unfortunately,

John Justice hasn't finished compiling all the members, so you have no way of knowing whom to trust. Because of that, I suggest you keep this to yourself for a few days. Otherwise, they'll kill you."

Incredulous, the general touched Handley's name on the tablet and pages of dozens of numbered files appeared. He opened one and a video ran. It was a meeting in Jared Handley's home in Denver. The Chairman and several men he didn't recognize attended. They discussed funding and carrying out assassinations of people in the government. Tight-jawed, the general stopped the video and put the tablet down.

Sizing him up, Mercy Ann said, "Communications, computer systems, and ship operations are John Justice's forte. If he was here, he could show you tons more stuff than I can without breaking a sweat, but I think you get the idea."

"How could you have video from Handley's house? He's notoriously security conscious."

"I can't explain right now."

The general hesitated. "What do you know about John Justice's disappearance?"

In a few short sentences, she told him about false government agents taking the two high schoolers who made a drone video of the site to a secret interrogation facility in Arizona then sending them out of the country to keep real government agents from discovering the conspiracy's illegal activities.

Appalled, the general asked, "Can you prove all that?"

"Knowing John Justice, we probably have all their communications recorded one way or another. I can access them, but it'd take me weeks to locate and extract specific files. He can do it in minutes."

"You think he has all their communications?"

"He's very thorough."

"The conspirators operate secret facilities?"

"John Justice said they have an extensive network of operations countrywide. He thought they have a better than even chance of overthrowing your government, too. It is not far-fetched considering how many conspirators hold key positions in business and government."

The general shook his head. "All we see here are two children and an elderly woman in an old house. No one has an inkling what your capabilities are. If they did, they might take this threat more seriously. Can't you do something about it?"

"That's an interesting idea. It might be possible to—"

Mercy Ann cried out and pitched forward suddenly. Her knee struck the table, sending the tray and contents tumbling down the steps as she fell.

The general caught her arm and pulled her back into the chair. “What’s wrong?”

She had both hands pressed to her side, breathing hard. “A soldier shot me. If he’d hit the house, the reaction would have killed everyone a mile around. You didn’t order that, did you?”

“No, of course not. How bad is it? Do you need medical assistance?”

“I’m okay, but my defenses are turned down. Please tell your soldiers to stop pointing weapons in this direction or they’re going to cause an enormous catastrophe.”

The general called the command post. The sergeant major had posted the snipers for his protection. The general ordered them to stand down immediately. The sergeant major confirmed it accomplished.

Mercy Ann shook her head. “Private Larry Stanton is still in a prone firing position seventy-three feet beyond the leftmost spotlight. He’s the one who fired the shot.”

“Are you certain?”

She presented him an annoyed stare.

The general switched frequencies, yelled into the radio for Stanton to lower his weapon and return to the command post.

He nodded to her. “Well?”

“He aimed at you before obeying. You should remove him from duty. His current girlfriend is one of your soldiers. In texts with her sister back home, she says he deals drugs and abuses her. She’s afraid to breakup with him. If you’ll protect her, she’ll sell him down the river.”

“How do you know all that?”

“Everyone puts too much information on social media these days. We have internal high-speed data processing systems that can access communications systems, internet, and so on. Enhanced systems are necessary for advanced humanoid civilizations performing deep space travel, so please don’t think I’m a freak or anything special. As I already explained, John Justice is the expert in these kinds of skills.”

“That makes sense and explains a lot, actually. What are your special skills?”

Mercy Ann hesitated, wondering whether to tell the truth. “Currently, I’m the primary offensive deterrent against enemies of the territory.”

It took him a few seconds. "I don't understand exactly what that means, but it sounds as if you're a soldier, same as me? Looking at you, I can't believe that's true."

She shrugged. "Yeah, I've heard that before. If you don't mind, let's get back to John Justice, shall we? For some reason, he walked into a trap, or at least that is what I presume since his system readings went inactive suddenly. His last message said the high schoolers departed Arizona on a plane leaving from an Air Force base in Phoenix. Do you know someone who can figure out where they went without creating trouble for yourself?"

"Forgive me for asking, but how do you know he's still alive?"

"In the event of an unauthorized breach of his internal security system, a recognizable seismic event will occur."

"An explosion?"

"Yes."

"Do you realize how amazing all this is for me?"

"Yes."

He expelled a deep breath. "I'll look into it."

"I'll get back in touch with you, if that's okay. I have to go now."

"May I help take the chairs in?"

Mercy Ann smiled. "They go inside on their own when the ship completes the next scheduled scan of the house. From your perspective, it will look as if they disappeared." She noted his expression. "We're aware your scientists detected our ship. It was unexpected. Goodnight."

He waited until she closed the door behind her then slowly walked back to the command post.

Detective Tom Patrick tossed and turned in bed all night. Whenever he fell asleep, he dreamed of Mercy Ann and the ugly doll with the devastation spread around them. Then he would wake up with crawling sensations in his chest.

He'd gone back to the hospital twice and insisted they take x-rays. Nothing out of the ordinary, everything normal, both times.

He got up, changed the sweat-damp sheets, and took more sleeping pills in spite of dawn not far off. He dozed until he tried to draw his knees up to roll onto his side.

"Lie still!" Mercy Ann ordered.

Sitting on his legs, she had on a white nightgown. He looked down at the doll. A tube ran from its chest up into his right nostril. He did not feel anything, but reached up to pull it out reflexively. Before he reached it, his whole body went limp. It seemed a long time passed before he felt the tube pulled from deep inside him.

Then Mercy Ann was gone, but her warmth remained on the sheet that had been between them.

Charlie the interrogator did not like his situation one bit, but at least he was alive. The team that showed up in Sedona to take the prisoners away shot his three coworkers in the head then the man in charge dropped a capsule in his coffee and told him to drink. Assuming that if they wanted him dead, he would be on the floor with the others, he gulped it down.

He'd come to in a sling seat on a cargo jet. A burly Arab soldier came and sat across from him. He recognized the uniform and his blood ran cold.

The soldier was brutish, but spoke educated English. “We're taking over interrogations of five prisoners, including the young man and woman your team handled. Your new role will be as liaison with your organization. Do you have any questions?”

“Did they say where I go when we're done?”

He looked amused. “Since you asked so politely if you get to live, I will answer honestly. They haven't said.”

Charlie nodded. “I suppose the job doesn't pay that well, either.”

The man did not see the humor in the comment. He got up and went to the front of the plane. Charlie was hungry but no one offered food and he knew better than to ask.

They flew low over desert terrain for half an hour then banked sharply into a deep valley full of military dug around a high-walled fortress complex with watchtowers and gun emplacements protected from attack by sandbags and curved steel roofs. Rising out of the valley, they circled an airport next to a small city.

Charlie experienced a sick, sinking feeling. By reputation, he knew no way existed out of this place except by death or consent of Dictator General Abd al-Bensi's forces. He had not realized the conspirators had ties to him, which was knowledge that might be his death sentence. He hid his dismay and tried to act as if he belonged after they landed.

Shiny modern hotels of steel and glass and expensive designer brand stores lined a main avenue. Otherwise, buildings were squalid, slapdash, and crowded along narrow winding streets and alleyways except for the occasional garish mansion and numerous mosques.

Cars, trucks, carts, motorbikes, and pedestrians competed for the right away. Honking horns and roaring engines were a loud constant. Small impromptu cafes and shisha smokers crowded walks next to the street. More people were in military garb than civilian clothes, but nearly everyone had automatic weapons.

Charlie was glad when the truck left town. The six soldiers who had been on the plane sat silently in back with him. They'd piled the five unconscious prisoners on the floor, leaving nowhere to put their feet but on them.

This was no place for anyone not worthy of a bullet in the head. Charlie felt a little sorry for the two teenagers, but he had himself to worry about, which meant nothing else mattered now.

Suddenly, the front of the truck pitched forward steeply and the prisoners slid to the back of the driver's compartment, almost dragging the riders off the bench seats on either side. Soon they would arrive at the fortress known by mercenaries and covert operatives as the other Death Valley, but this one received its name from a prison few people departed, not the sweltering heat.

The Palm Springs condominium was a luxurious two-bedroom unit on a golf course and had a patio pool and spa. Ashlyn used a golf cart she'd found in the garage to scoot around on short trips. A Subaru Outback was there, too, but Ashlyn didn't plan using it.

Before this incident, she would have thought herself paranoid changing her hair so often. She cut most of it off, dyed the short crop that remained reddish brown, and tinged her eyebrows to match.

Then she lost track of time sitting by the pool, watching TV, and drinking up the doctor's considerable bar supply until a news report from LA about an off duty policeman shooting the outraged father of two children jarred her out of a drunken stupor.

The father had dropped his kids off at a restaurant for a birthday-costume party and gone to park the car. The kids wore cheap blond wigs and black clothes, pretending to be the aliens on TV news. A police officer in civilian clothes, leaving the restaurant with his wife, whipped out a gun and demanded IDs from the kids. Of course, they weren't carrying any.

The father saw a man waving a gun at his children and ran at the assailant cursing and yelling. Shot three times in the chest, he was at the hospital in critical condition.

Officer Andrew Lawrence had been on convalescent leave from the Glenwood Heights disaster. He'd been incoherent at the scene and taken away with his wife, who collapsed in shock. They were still waiting for a statement from the police.

The story made Ashlyn cry and feel that she should not be hiding out and leaving everything up to Mercy Ann. Who did those bastards think they were, treating people like this, anyway? It took more drinks before she calmed down enough to stay put and give Mercy Ann time to help.

The President did not assign any significance to the idea that the evolution of apes had anything to do with the LA situation, but the Chairman had sprung the news that the coil cannons were at the site and recommended using them for the next attack. The President could see no reason to employ an experimental weapon if another missile strike would do the job, but received such acrimonious disagreement that he decided to sit back, bide his time, and let the factions argue about apes, mankind, and alien experiments. It amazed him how fast everyone became entrenched in his and her positions.

Meanwhile, the situation in LA had become more stable as evacuees adjusted to new daily routines. The only downside to delaying the strike against the site was allowing rumors about aliens to spread, but it wasn't so bad that a few more days should matter. At least, that's what he thought at the time.

Keep arguing about nothing, people, the President thought, looking around the room. A few days of this will wear down your resolve then I'll give the order for a missile strike and take all the credit for dealing with the terrorist threat.

Blake leased a small apartment he used as a safe house when he needed to lay low. Located in an area popular with young professionals, he went there to unwind and think when facing tough challenges. No one knew about it.

His lawyer thought someone in the gang had implicated him in an armed robbery. That was why Detective Patrick was after him. He hadn't been involved, so wasn't overly concerned about beating the charge, but that was not the problem. Given the turmoil in the area, he couldn't afford to be in jail for a single night until everything returned to normal.

He had not planned to stay the night but changed his mind as he drank a beer and began to relax for the first time in days. He rummaged through the fridge and cabinets for anything quick to prepare for supper and came up with half a dozen eggs, a chunk of cheddar cheese, two cans of chili, and half a package of bacon.

While the beans heated, he fried bacon and scrambled all the eggs since they were close to the use date. Listening to news on the TV in the other room, he watched out the window as evening activities increased on the street below. A restaurant and bar a few doors down provided interesting flows of people on the street. He had never been inside, but frequently promised himself that he would one day.

Yeah, he thought, it'd be nice to act the same as a normal person.

He sat at the small dining table in the living room eating and watching commentators speculate about the President's chances in next year's election.

Groaning, he complained aloud, "Nobody wants to hear that crap. Tell us what's going on with the aliens."

"One of them is having dinner with you," Mercy Ann said, walking out of the kitchen with a plate of his food and dressed in shorts, sleeveless blouse, and sandals. "Do you have any tea?"

It took him a few seconds to answer. "No."

She set the plate down across from him. "I didn't see any pepper or hot sauce, either."

"Sorry."

She reached into her pocket, took out a rubber band, and pulled her hair back through it into a ponytail. "Excuse me a minute."

He began counting. When he reached fourteen, she reappeared. In one hand, she had a tall glass of iced tea. In the other, a bottle of pepper sauce and a full pepper mill. She sat down, took a sip of tea, and made a face.

"I don't have any sugar, either," Blake said.

She reached into her shirt pocket and pulled out sugar packets. "I figured."

"Where did you get that stuff?"

"In the restaurant downstairs."

"I don't suppose you paid for it?"

"I left money on a table."

"No you didn't."

"Don't be a pain." She began eating.

"I apologize for being a jackass."

"Was that the first time ever that you've been a jackass?"

"No."

Reaching back and pulling the rubber band off the ponytail, she shook her hair out. "Maybe it's a habit, then."

"You almost killed me, you know."

"It seems to have had the desired effect. Your manners have improved."

Smiling, he pointed to the right corner of her mouth. "You've a little egg."

She wiped it off. "Just so there's no misunderstandings, I don't want you thinking I'm here to jump your bones."

"You don't sugarcoat things, do you?"

She shrugged. "Do you always talk to the TV like a crazy person? If you want to know anything about aliens, you can ask me."

"Okay," he answered, not missing a beat. "Something's been bothering me. Did you have anything to do with the deaths of two cops in an alley near the sandwich shop? It was strange, to say the least."

If the question surprised her, she didn't show it. "Finish eating, then we'll talk."

Blake took the dirty dishes to the kitchen and put them in the dishwasher. When he returned, two large desserts were on the table—key lime pie and chocolate cake with strawberries.

"Which do you prefer?" she asked.

"I'll have the cake."

She handed him a fancy fork. "We'll share because that's my favorite, too."

"Couldn't you get another one?"

"If you'll go oink-oink like a big fat pig, I'll do it."

He laughed. "Yeah, it is a lot of cake."

When they finished, Mercy Ann sat back in the chair and folded her arms. "I witnessed the policemen kill your guy, who was unarmed and hurt on the ground. They thought they had to kill me, too. John Justice interfered and they fired at him. We have internal defenses. He had his set too high. They died."

Blake hesitated. "John Justice makes lots of mistakes, doesn't he?"

Mercy Ann expected questions about internal systems and weapons, not John Justice's shortcomings. "Why do you think that?"

"I haven't the slightest idea," he answered, mystified. "I just do."

She unfolded a copy of the Sufficiency Test notice and slid it across the table. "This is posted on the front of our house. Your government decided to keep it secret. Tell me what you think."

He read it. "This is what's going on?"

"Yes."

"Then we shouldn't be attacking you."

"You sound awfully sure of yourself."

"It says plain as day that it's a riddle. Then it says you're vastly superior. Those two facts should keep us from thinking we can destroy you, especially after failing a few times. If we leave you alone, at the end of thirty days we'll pass the test. Is that right?"

She said nothing. She showed nothing.

Watching closely, he commented, “You should play poker.”

“I used to, a lot.”

He could tell she told the truth but didn’t understand how or why. “Where did you play?”

“Places along the Mississippi River and Gulf Coast mostly.”

“They let you play at your age?”

“It wasn’t an issue. I won, too.”

Something made him ask, “When was this?”

Again, exactly the right question, Mercy Ann thought. “Your feelings that John Justice is a screwup are accurate. He messed up and they captured him. Now, I must go retrieve him soon as I pinpoint the location. But first, I want your advice about something.”

She was one surprise after another. “I’ll help anyway I can.”

Instantly, she became all business. “Have you ever faced a strong rival that didn’t take you seriously as a threat? I require a quick solution that avoids prolonged conflict.”

He tried to respond accordingly. “Identify the enemy’s strengths and weaknesses then make a plan to achieve the desired outcome with minimum risks to your side.”

“That is a simplistic version of Sun Tzu war philosophy,” she observed with sharp coolness. “It could as easily apply to an ad campaign to sell burgers.”

“You’re familiar Sun Tzu?”

She frowned. “Stop screwing around and tell me the real answer.”

From the way she looked at him, he felt foolish thinking he needed to protect her. He had been reluctant to describe grim violence to a young girl, not taking into account she was alien and struck fear in him.

“It’s not complicated,” he replied with a shrug. “Strike hard without warning and make certain to leave bodies horrible beyond recognition. You must give enemy survivors nightmares. Then you offer a generous alliance. If they refuse, you must strike again with even more brutality. Repeat the offer for alliance. Two times usually does it. Once they accept, you have the option of taking them into your organization or betraying the agreement and killing them. Just depends on what’s best for your side.”

She showed disappointment. “I hoped you’d know a better way. Commit too many atrocities, and you’re the one suffering nightmares and screaming. By any chance, have you experienced any of that, yet?”

Blake could hardly breathe as shocking visions of grotesque dead creatures, blown apart and strewn across a burning landscape beneath a pale pink sky, filled his thoughts. He knew the images were from her memories. They were terrifying. He started to ask about it.

Flustered, Mercy Ann stood up quickly. "Thanks for dinner. Please remain near a TV for the next few hours. I want you to see something."

He replied to an empty apartment, but had a hunch she heard. "Whatever you're planning, be careful, Mercy Ann."

Overbearing government agents questioned the general about Mercy Ann and the house, but he did not tell them what she said about John Justice and the conspiracy. The last thing he wanted was tipping off the people holding the teenagers that Mercy Ann was coming, and that was before he discovered where they were.

A cargo jet had departed the air base in Phoenix carrying a top-secret cargo to Iraq. An old CIA drinking buddy of the general's nosed around and found out that an hour after the plane arrived, a small group of special prisoners left Bagdad for Death Valley in Syria on an Iraqi military aircraft as part of a hush-hush deal with Dictator-General Abd al-Bensi.

Mercy Ann did not show up last night nor been seen anywhere. The general thought she may have gone to search for John Justice already and surprised himself by how concerned he felt for her. After working a second long day well past midnight, he ordered the command post to wake him if they saw her.

His tent had plywood walls inside a canvas exterior, air conditioning, and decent furnishings. At a small bar, he poured a glass of bourbon and drank it while undressing. He needed a shower, but was too tired. Flopping down on the bed, he reached to switch off the light and someone took hold of his wrist.

Mercy Ann, decked out in her Victorian regalia, asked, "Did you find them?"

The general, struck by a sense of unreality seeing her in the shadowy light, replied, "The prisoners were taken to a Syrian prison in an area called Death Valley. I'm sorry."

"Why are you sorry?"

"Ten thousand soldiers guard the valley, not counting the ones in a nearby city and high desert camps. They're fierce, seasoned fighters loyal to a cutthroat dictator named Abd al-Bensi. He has a sizable air force, too."

"Oh, I see. I didn't realize a rescue would cause so many casualties."

It took a few seconds for her meaning to sink in. "What on Earth do you intend to do, use spacecraft?"

"No, it will just be me, alone. I could just snatch them away, but I've decided to fight the army and show the battle to your government. Perhaps then, they'll give the first line of the riddle the attention it deserves. John Justice needs to know I can hold up in a major ground battle, too. Once he realizes, everything will be better with us. I call it my two birds with one stone plan. Catchy, huh?"

He did not know what to say.

"I'll arrange for you to see the battle, too. I'd explain more, but I have to hurry. In a few hours, it will be dark on the other side of the world, and I don't want to waste energy lighting a battlefield. You'll probably hate and fear me afterward, which will make me sad, because I like you. It can't be helped, though."

He wanted to say so many things, but she was gone.

8

The Death Valley Prison

CHARLIE THE INTERROGATOR HAD BEEN DISMAYED when a hundred western personnel in nondescript desert fatigues arrived to set up tons of equipment inside the prison, but other than a warning to stay out of the way, they had nothing to do with him and the prisoners. When they departed, they left behind a team of twenty hardscrabble mercenary-technicians. He hoped his death was not part of their mission.

It was early in the morning when yelling, gunfire, and two explosions awakened him. The entire prison complex shook and vibrated as though experiencing a major earthquake. Running to go outside, one of the mercenaries tripped and clubbed him. He came to on the floor of his room with a throbbing headache. Prison routine was back to normal.

Two days later, he still did not know what happened. The mercenaries said the cell area where the prisoners were was off-limits for the time being. When he argued that he had a job to do, three al-Bensi prison guards with automatic weapons warned him away.

At lunch, the educated military man from the plane sat down across from him. Prior to this, everyone ignored him, so he knew something was up.

Quietly, the man asked if Charlie knew anything about the western boy who somehow had gotten inside the prison and been captured.

Surprised that he didn't, the man told him about a surgeon and team of scientists arriving this morning to examine the boy.

Charlie asked about the boy's appearance and realized who he was, but kept it to himself unless they could make a deal. "I'm certain my people plan to kill me. I can pay well if you help me get out of here."

Aware his men watched them, the man laughed then whispered behind his hand. "My position is as bad as yours. I can't depend on my soldiers any longer. Their loyalties are with those who pay us."

Charlie laughed, too. "If that's the case, what would you say to working with an infidel?"

"Necessity creates strange bedfellows. Any ideas?"

Charlie told him that the blond boy was one of the aliens from LA and the two teenagers he'd interrogated worked with them, which was why they were here.

The man scoffed. "Aliens blowing up Hollywood sounds like a bad movie to me. I assumed your government made up that stupid story to distract from how long they're taking to catch domestic terrorists."

Charlie insisted the aliens were genuine. He thought his employers must have set a trap and snared the boy, which explained why the surgeon and scientists were here. He must have something inside him they wanted.

The man's eyes grew wider. "These are amazing times, indeed."

"Yes, but think what they'd pay if we could get our hands on him."

"I like what I hear, but considering what's happened in Los Angeles, he must be dangerous."

"Yes, but he came here after my teenage prisoners. If we have them, our first priority will be making him help us get away. Then, with a little luck, maybe we can capture him, but if that's not possible, at least we'll be alive."

The man chuckled. "Sounds crazy enough to work."

The sun blazed down though a dust-filled sky as constant streams of military vehicles moved up and down roads connecting the city and lower reaches of Death Valley.

Atop a guard tower on the valley's desert rim across from the city, a bored soldier picked up a pair of binoculars and looked around. Fiddling with the focus, the details of someone standing on a rocky outcrop between two of the busiest roads sharpened into the alien girl with blond hair he'd seen on the internet. Warnings had been given that she might show up, but he refocused and looked three times before he believed his eyes.

He called the sergeant of the guard and reported.

Alarms sounded everywhere the valley. Inside the prison, security sprang into action, closing passageways and manning machineguns between areas. The mercenaries turned on the huge generators powering the electromagnetic equipment that disabled the other alien.

Rob—stretched out on a bare wooden table retching from a bout of waterboarding—watched his interrogators running from the room, leaving the door open. Vaguely, he wondered if the shrill alarms were a new torture. He tried to get off the table but could not.

Farther down the same hallway, Missa—battered, bruised, and chained by the wrists to hooks in the ceiling that kept her in a constant standing position on tiptoes—raised her head slightly.

Gunshots came from the hall. The door flew open. Charlie, accompanied by the big Arab soldier, ran in.

TVs and communications devices of top US government and military officials involved with the LA incident had come to life, showing video feeds of Mercy Ann in Death Valley. Then they came on for Jared Handley and the inner circle of his conspiracy, for the general in charge of the LA disaster site, and for Blake Ferrell, still ensconced in his secret apartment.

The video showed close-ups of weapons emplacements around the big prison, lingering on cannons having enormously long barrels with glass coils around them. Energy began pulsing up and down the barrels. Then the picture went back to Mercy Ann.

A White House staffer in the Oval Office exclaimed, "Those were the secret beam weapons developed by Jared Handley Industries. How come Abd al-Bensi has them?"

The President was furious. He yelled that he wanted Handley brought to the White House to explain.

Another staffer stopped everything. "The alien girl vanished!"

The surgeon had insisted they open the dead boy's chest without further delay. He began drawing lines down his sternum and across his torso for incisions. The chief scientist argued they should first hook up scanners to determine whether the devices and circuitry inside him retained charges that could cause damage to them or the alien technology. They argued until another team member sent a message asking for guidance.

The reply was swift. How to proceed was up to them, but if they damaged the boy's internal equipment unnecessarily, punishment would be severe. The surgeon agreed to wait for the scans.

As best they could tell, there was no danger. The surgeon did not pass up the opportunity to point out they had confirmed what he knew all along, which was that the boy and his equipment were dead as doornails. The chief scientist went for him. The others pulled them apart. Peace restored, the surgeon picked up the scalpel to make the first incision.

Alarms, gunfire, and artillery fire came from outside the prison. Then alarms began going off. Announcements from speakers in the hall echoed and were unintelligible. The surgeon wanted to leave and take shelter in an underground bunker.

The chief scientist, who had rank in this matter, ordered, "The military is always making fusses of some kind. Just do your job!"

Suddenly, John Justice threw off the sheet covering his nakedness, sat up, and shrieked, "She's coming! She'll kill everyone!"

The team moved away from the table, astonished and afraid.

Again, John Justice shrieked, "No! She's here! Help me!"

Two scientists drew pistols as the others grabbed whatever they could use to fight. In a semi-circle, they faced the heavy door into the room.

Appearing on the stainless steel examining table standing between John Justice's legs, Mercy Ann stared down at the astonished surgeon and scientists.

One pointed a pistol at John Justice's head. "I'll shoot the little freak unless—"

A swarm of pink specks engulfed the man and he literally exploded, bloody viscous matter splattering everything in the room except Mercy Ann and John Justice. Another scientist fired pointblank at Mercy Ann and suffered the same fate. The others ran from the room, screaming.

Mercy Ann knelt and hugged John Justice. "I told you I wouldn't lose control again, and I haven't."

It took him a few seconds. "Why would you use that kind of weapon for close combat?"

"I want them to fear our capabilities."

He looked up at the dripping ceiling. "Glad I was able to get my shield to activate or I'd be covered in that mess."

"How much damage have you sustained?"

"Internal monitors and auto-response systems shutdown so I went into hibernation mode. That jolt of power you used to reactivate me hurt."

"It was the fastest way to locate you."

"You'll have to take me back for repair. My transport circuits burned out."

Annoyed, she wondered what else was wrong with him. "Do you have enough manual function to locate and protect Rob and Missa while I finish outside?"

He'd assumed they would simply leave. "What are you planning to do?"

"Defeat the army around the prison. I created video feeds of the battlefield so the knuckleheads in Washington can watch. I plan to make it so gross that the images will be stuck in their minds forever. You shouldn't watch. You'll get upset."

"I'm not the one we need to worry about, Mercy Ann. And don't you think this will be construed as interference by the test monitors?"

"The first line of the notice says we have capabilities superior to Earth's, so it's not like I'm doing anything the Guardians didn't tell them. I feel stupid for not thinking of it already."

"The monitors may not agree."

"Screw the monitors! The Guardians have to allow us a little wiggle room."

"I think you're overreaching."

"And I think you were stupid and careless when you came here. Why were your shields down?"

He teared up. "I'm sorry."

"Did you destroy the equipment they used to disable you?"

"No."

"Did you at least take out some of the people operating it?"

He began crying.

"Do you want me to do it for you? I can save Rob and Missa, too, if I must. Then I'll go defeat the army by myself. I don't need your help. I was just being nice asking so you wouldn't feel left out and cry, and here you are, crying anyway!"

"You don't be such a bitch, Mercy Ann," he said, wiping his eyes. "I admitted that I was careless. You go fight outside. I'll take care of things inside."

Glaring, she said nothing.

"That's what you wanted, isn't it? Answer me, please."

She gave a curt nod.

"Then stop being so pissy. I'm just concerned about you having another breakdown. You haven't been in a big ground battle since the incident. Are you certain you can handle it?"

She didn't answer.

"You know that I still love you, don't you? Well, don't you? Talk to me, Mercy Ann."

She did not want to give that stupid assurance again, but knew he would get upset if she didn't. However, saying it sent little jerks of revulsion through her body. "Yes."

"Are you planning to destroy the army in the same manner as these men?"

"Yes."

"What if you freak out again? Shouldn't you have brought Honey Bee, just in case?"

Would he ever stop asking her that? "I don't need her. I don't have time to keep repeating everything to you, either."

He exhaled loudly. "Okay. How many enemy are outside?"

"Nine thousand eight hundred and eighty-four."

He grimaced. "Really, you should reconsider this, Mercy Ann."

"Their deaths will save everyone else on Earth."

"But they are humans like us."

"I'll just kill enough to make the others give up."

"Yes, but...but...oh, never mind!"

He pulled his legs up and swung around off the table. You gave me enough power for the job, so I'll rescue Rob and Missa then wait for you to transport us out of here."

She made a face. "Please put some clothes on. They're in the corner with your Gucci. Want me to send it home for you?"

He walked over, snatched up the bag, and slung it over his slight white shoulder. "Instead of a soldier of fortune, I'll be a soldier of fashion. What do you think?"

In spite of everything, she laughed. "Fine, but cover up your thingy before you leave the room or some idiot will put your picture on the internet and get rich."

When John Justice stepped into the long hall, soldiers opened fire with a machine gun behind sandbags. The bullets disintegrated when they struck the faint yellow aura around him. He would have ignored the attack, except for it being the way he wanted to go.

Pulsing light flew from him, reducing everything in the intersection to a powdery material that settled to the floor by the time he reached it.

Interfacing with the prison's surveillance system, John Justice located Missa and Rob together in a room. She sat slumped in a wheelchair while two men lifted Rob into another one. From computer files he'd copied at the Sedona facility, his system identified one of the men as an interrogator with the code name Charlie. His partner was bigger and wore an al-Bensi military uniform.

Soldiers kept popping out of rooms to shoot. Wishing he had Mercy Ann's specialized weaponry to clear out all of the rooms at the same time, he kept firing his disintegrator at low power and relying on defensive systems, which still used a lot of energy. When the electromagnetic force field hit him this time, he was ready, deflecting the waves of energy Scanning, he located the generating equipment and sent a powerful pulse down the long hall into the prison's entry foyer, where it blew out the walls, causing the upper floors to collapse, destroying the power generating equipment and people manning it.

The whole time, John Justice monitored the room with Rob and Missa. When he neared its open doorway, Charlie motioned the big soldier to crouch and lean against Rob. Then he leaned against Missa. Apparently, he knew the disintegration weapon killed anyone in contact with a target. He stopped to think before going in.

At one time, John Justice had been a highly skilled fighter and fearless in combat, but those times were long since gone. Unsure what to do, he worried Mercy Ann would not forgive him if the hostages were harmed, so he hesitated.

On the video feed, he saw Charlie inexplicably shoot the big man, who sagged down on Rob's lap. That made no sense to him. No matter, he couldn't wait any longer.

He entered the room and had to say something. "You're Charlie, I believe."

The man had a smarmy smile while he pointed the gun at Missa's face. "My friend was more interested in martyrdom than getting out of here alive, so I killed him for you. Transport me and the girl somewhere safe and I'll let the prisoners go."

John Justice thought how Mercy Ann would stare and say nothing in hopeless situations. He didn't know what else to do.

"I'll kill her!" Charlie yelled.

John Justice hoped his face showed no expression.

"Kid, I'm not joking. It's your decision."

In an impasse, Mercy Ann would change the subject and wait for odds to shift more in her favor. "How did you know to stay in contact with someone so I couldn't strike without killing them, too?"

Charlie sneered and pointed to a laptop. "You're not the only one watching surveillance cameras."

John Justice became aware of a new problem. Missa's muscles were tensing, indicating she was feigning unconsciousness and about to try something. He wanted to stop her, but it was too late.

Missa threw her body sideways, twisting the wheelchair to face Rob and knocking Charlie off balance. Grabbing the gun from him, the heel of her other hand drove up into his nose, crushing cartilage and sending him sprawling backwards.

The big soldier on Rob's lap raised up and lunged for her. She fired three shots into his chest and he went down.

John Justice's yellow light disintegrated Charlie, reaching to grab hold of Missa again.

Staring at the shower of glowing particles, she dropped the gun. "Good riddance."

John Justice moved around the wheelchairs to face her. "You surprised me."

Although bruised and battered, angry defiance reigned. "He faked shooting the big guy. They wanted to catch you off-guard."

"I could tell he was not hurt, but couldn't do anything until you and Rob were clear. It doesn't sound as though killing them bothers you."

The comment caused her confusion. "No. I don't know. Later, maybe it will. I never fired a gun before." She looked down at the floor. "I guess you really are an alien."

"I was born somewhere other than Earth, but I'm human, same as you."

He realized her eyes were on the Gucci bag hanging from his shoulder. He took out a candy bar, took off the wrapper, and placed it in her swollen hand.

Missa was ravenous, but had more to say. "They kept asking about Mercy Ann. I met her in Rob's backyard, but never told them. That seems such a long time ago."

John Justice nodded and looked down at Rob. "If he's as strong as you, he'll be fine."

Suddenly, the building rattled and shook from enormous explosions outside. Then everything blurred around them.

Missa yelled, "What's happening?"

Mercy Ann had reappeared on the main road between the city and the prison. Infantry swarmed in her direction, firing weapons. Artillery bombarded her. Jet fighters streaked down, launching rockets. The beam cannons released charges, engulfing her in a huge white-hot ball of crackling energy. Then came an enormous explosion. Billowing smoke and raging fire shot more than a mile into the sky.

The barely visible image of Mercy Ann, a silvery silhouette trying to escape an inferno of hellish proportions, melted away to nothingness. Yet, the beam cannons continued firing for several minutes more before disengaging.

The fires burned out quickly, revealing a gaping crater. No evidence of Mercy Ann's existence remained.

Watchers in the White House whooped and cheered. Blake Ferrell, watching at the table where he and Mercy Ann had eaten, felt so sick to his stomach that he threw up. The general bent down to scratch Bongo behind the ears to hide wet eyes from others in the command post.

In the White House, the Chairman of the Joint Chiefs made himself heard over the din. "Mr. President, allow me to explain how our new weapons came to be in Death Valley. After we learned of the two teenagers' alliance with the aliens, we decided to use them as bait to tempt the aliens into a rescue. We needed someplace off the grid and lured them to an unused storage facility in Arizona before deciding it wasn't remote enough."

The President was livid. "What does this have to do with our weapons being in the hands of Abd al-Bensi?"

The Chairman could not have been more sequacious. "We negotiated with al-Bensi for the prisoners to be interrogated by our people in Death Valley Prison because it was the perfect place to set a trap for the aliens. The weapons were completely under our control at all times and will be on planes back to the good ole USA in a couple of hours."

"How did you get al-Bensi to agree to this?" the President demanded.

"The old fashioned way. Money, lots of it."

"That smacks of treason," the President declared.

"No sir," the Chairman replied. "It makes perfect sense. We wanted to be certain our weapons would destroy the aliens before using them in Los Angeles, and now we know for certain."

The President thundered, "Why wasn't I told about this scheme of yours? Last time I checked, I'm the Commander-in-Chief!"

The FBI Director spoke up. "Several of us are on your calendar next hour to brief about this matter. We didn't expect the aliens to show up at the prison so fast. It was an extremely fast-moving situation, Mr. President. I add my apology for springing it on you this way."

The NSA conspirator wore the biggest smile in the room. "We mustn't overlook the fact that you can clean up the mess in LA with the cannons anytime you want, Mr. President, success one hundred percent guaranteed!"

The President swallowed his anger because they had given him the solution to his biggest problem, but he was also a petty man who resented others telling him what to do. He said he would reserve judgment about their insubordination until they resolved the LA incident, which he decided to drag out long as possible just to watch them squirm. Besides, it would be foolish not to publicly predict success and claim all the credit.

As he left the room, the conspirators exchanged knowing glances and nods. The President, who Jared Handley called Mr. Huff and Puff, had acted exactly as predicted.

John Justice stood at the kitchen counter staring at nothing and shaking violently. Mercy Ann's final message still reverberated in his ears: "Please save Earth for me, John Justice."

Disoriented, Missa stared at him. A few seconds ago, they were in the prison listening to a battle raging so ferociously that she thought they were about to die. Rob was still in the wheelchair next to her, unconscious. Then an old woman rushed in from a side doorway, Missa recognized her, and realized with amazement where they were.

"Miss Flowers," John Justice said, "somehow Mercy Ann transported us all the way back in one jump without physical contact."

She replied in a language unlike any Missa had ever heard. She had a lot to say.

John Justice gestured with both hands, stopping her. "We didn't expect them to have alien beam weapons, but Mercy Ann was strong enough to withstand them. I don't understand what happened."

Miss Flowers responded quietly.

"No, the test isn't going well, but she felt certain she'd find a way to save them. This is nothing at all like the other time when she tried to kill herself. I was there. You weren't."

She responded sharply.

He nodded. "Okay. I'll watch the battle video then decide."

Missa didn't realize she had asked a question at first. "Did you say Mercy Ann tried to kill herself?"

John Justice came to her. "It was a long time ago when I was commander and Mercy Ann..."

Miss Flowers cut him off.

He shouted, "I don't care!"

Then John Justice told his story:

"I was commander of the fleet that protected the territory for beings we call the Guardians when they brought Mercy Ann and her brother to us as new members. At first, all her duties were medical in nature and soon she ran our infirmary on the flagship.

"Then they determined she could use advanced Guardian technology and wanted to give her powerful new weapons no one else could handle. She objected, insisting she didn't want to kill anyone. They understood her concerns, but warned that new enemies were about to attack us, they were stretched too thin to help, and the enemy could only be stopped with the weapons.

"Mercy Ann's brother and I convinced her to accept the changes since we had no other choice. She understood, but was still reluctant.

"Mercy Ann decimated enemies in several small skirmishes. Everyone treated her as a hero. We did not notice how seldom she spoke except to carry out missions or answer questions posed to her, however.

"The powerful new enemy that raised the Guardians' concerns bided their time until they could set up an ambush in a remote part of the territory. They caught Mercy Ann's unit on the ground in a small town and concentrated firepower on them while their fleet attacked our squadron's ships, in orbit around the planet. I was in one of them when the battle started.

"The enemy decimated us and began mopping up. I had survived a crash and rallied survivors to join with remnants of Mercy Ann's unit. Not until then did I find out that Mercy Ann ran away and abandoned them.

"I had reinforcements coming, but holding out was hopeless. The enemy critically wounded her brother and he screamed for her on all frequencies. She didn't answer and everyone thought she must be dead already.

"Suddenly, Mercy Ann appeared in the middle of the battle. Hysterical, she kept screaming and firing salvos with weapons that we'd never seen in use. She destroyed everything and everybody she encountered, whether friend or foe, including all the ships and crews. In a terrifyingly short time, hardly anyone was alive but her and me, and still, she kept screaming and firing.

"I thought she had recognized and spared me. I had to stop her attacking our reinforcements, due to arrive any moment. I approached, called out to her. I discovered my survival to that point was just dumb luck. She attacked me.

"But then she realized who I was and turned the weapon on herself because she couldn't stop it firing. They found us on the ground together, all but burned to death.

"While we underwent reconstruction, Mercy Ann broke free from restraints and self-administered drugs to kill herself, unaware her defense mechanisms would purge most of them. Even so, she fell into a deep coma that lasted more than a month. After she came out of it and they finished the surgeries, they sent us to rehabilitate and recover together. We've remained together ever since."

"I thought you were her brother because you look so much alike," Missa said.

He answered as though the response wasn't the most horrific of all the things he said. "The Guardians used her brother's body for my repairs. Not much remained of mine, and they thought her brother's likeness would please and facilitate Mercy Ann's recovery. They meant well, but tend to get things with other species terribly wrong sometimes."

"They put you inside her brother's body?" she stammered. "That's terrible."

"Yeah, especially for us at the time. I was in love with her before the accident and thought she felt the same way. Afterward, it took years before she could look directly at me again."

That was Missa's last recollection of the conversation other than seeing Mercy Ann's doll in Rob's lap and wondering where it came from.

After making certain the visitors were unconscious, Miss Flowers said, "You should not have told her all that."

"I know."

"I guess it doesn't matter now. How soon do you want to leave Earth?"

"I will stay and try to save it for Mercy Ann," John Justice declared with bravado he did not feel one bit.

She stared, mouth agape. "You fought with her about coming here. We can rejoin the fleet and let the test run its course. That was what you wanted, wasn't it?"

"I'll understand if you go."

"You're still lovesick over her after all this time? Men are so crazy."

"That's not the reason, Miss Flowers," he answered quietly. "Or maybe it is. I don't know. Do you want me to have the flagship send a shuttle for you? I want to keep ours."

"No. If you stay, I stay. What about Honey Bee?"

"If it's for Mercy Ann, she'll remain here. How much longer will she be in hibernation?"

"Anytime now. But to be honest with you, my biggest regret is not kicking Mercy Ann's butt when I had the chance. She was the most aggravating person I ever met. I never wished her dead, though."

"I know that."

"I'll transport our guests upstairs and prepare rooms. We'll talk more about this later."

Alone finally, he whispered, "Each of us will have to deal with Mercy Ann's death in our own way, Miss Flowers."

9

Doldrums, Killers, and True Love

DURING THE HEYDAY OF SAILING SHIPS, windless zones known as the Doldrums left many of them stranded near the Equator. Subsequently, the term came to mean a period of inactivity or inertia. Such was the case in Los Angeles during the next week, inasmuch as no one did anything to destroy the aliens due to the President's machinations. Meanwhile, many people involved in the incident failed to realize how inexorably intertwined their lives were becoming with the aliens.

Two of the phony agents that killed Rob's parents were a pair of female assassins known in the underworld by the codename Cowboy. Calling themselves Brandi and Sheri Collins, they masqueraded as Texas sisters who grew up on a small ranch somewhere between Abilene and El Paso, which intentionally covered a tremendous expanse of territory.

Sheri had an amazing memory and high intelligence, allowing her to quick-study complex subjects. Brandi could bluff her way through most situations using spectacular looks, an outgoing personality, and flawless intuition. Experts at altering their appearances using makeup, wigs, and customized padded clothing, they could portray well-educated professionals, business people, or anything else employers required.

Neither knew much of her partner's life before teaming up and made it a point not to ask.

So Sheri didn't know Brandi was from Ukraine, a farmer's daughter who passed for much older when she was young. With looks that belied incredible physical strength and endurance, she worked as a waitress, escort, prostitute, and soldier whose marksmanship earned her a coveted apprenticeship on an elite team of government-backed assassins before her sixteenth birthday.

Then she hit a rough patch during a period of political upheaval, ending up on the losing side of a struggle between factions vying for power. The only one in her group to survive, she fled the country.

Working as a model and companion-bodyguard in Italy, Spain, and France, she used a variety of guises and identities to freelance discreetly as an assassin specializing in tough, dangerous jobs. Very quickly, she developed a system to remain anonymous by contracting through intermediaries who knew her by reputation and phone numbers only.

Her success attracted the attention of the French National Police, which networked with other European countries trying to locate and determine who she was. But as they closed in, rumors spread that she died when a yacht exploded near Marseilles during a botched hit. Police found several unidentifiable bodies but suspected the incident was a ruse by the killer. Nonetheless, leads evaporated into thin air and they had to close the case.

Nor did Brandi know Sheri's history, although occasionally she let slip a comment about her childhood in the Netherlands. The fact Sheri spoke Dutch gave it credence, but she was actually from northern California. Her mother, from Rotterdam originally, was an abusive alcoholic with a serious drug habit when twelve-year-old Sheri committed her first murder and ran away from home.

Raped twice and threatened to silence in her bedroom by one of her mother's boyfriends, Sheri stabbed him in the heart the third time with a sharpened screwdriver. Her mother was out cold when it happened and wouldn't remember who brought her home, something she counted on.

An extremely methodical, practical young girl who had learned the hard way to feel very little, Sheri did nothing important without thinking it through first.

She'd "acquired" a roll of thick poly plastic, latex gloves, and duct tape from a home supply store to cover her mattress under the sheet, making it easy to roll up and seal away the bloody body and bedcovers.

She slid the bundle outside and pulled it up into the back of the guy's clunker pickup using a rope and makeshift ramp fashioned from heavy cardboard taped around an aluminum ladder.

She'd never driven before, but it was an automatic and easy except for sitting on the edge of the seat stretching to reach woodblocks she'd taped to the pedals. After driving to a wilderness area seven miles from town, she unwrapped and dumped the body in a deep wooded ravine. Then she returned to town, disposed of the plastic in a grocery store dumpster, and parked a few blocks from a bar the guy frequented. She removed the woodblocks and wiped fingerprints with an oily rag.

Sheri sat in her room crying and reading until mid-morning when her mother yelled for coffee. She went in and picked an argument until her mother slammed her into a wall. Yelling and cursing that she was leaving and never coming back, Sheri left. None of this was unusual, except this time Sheri did not return.

Her mother did not report her missing. Eventually, someone from the school called and her mother's new boyfriend told them she had gone to live with an aunt in Alaska. He even provided them his cousin's address in Fairbanks. They never called, and no one else noticed or cared the small girl who kept to herself reading all the time was gone.

When a small carnival packed up and departed town the night Sheri ran away, she was with them, the new guilty secret of a seedy man in charge of arcade games. She pretended to be his niece until four months later when he began beating her. She left him buried in the Wisconsin Dells then told the carnival's owner, a kindly man with a nice wife, that her uncle had started drinking again and ran off with a woman he'd met in a bar. The couple took her in, and for nearly two years, she learned the carnival business and self-schooled herself before striking out on her own with another new name and a job with a circus that mainly toured rural Mexico.

When Brandi teamed with Sheri for a one-off job, she did not think much of a small partner who seemed to be a chattering airhead until three men ambushed them going into an abandoned building. Tased from behind, Brandi writhed on the floor while Sheri dealt with the attackers.

Tumbling away, small knives flew from both Sheri's hands, precisely striking two attackers in the throats. Pirouetting and dodging the third man with the grace of a professional dancer, she whipped a machete from a sheath on her back and cut his head half off. It all happened breathtakingly fast.

Several days would pass before Brandi realized the pounding in her chest was her first encounter with love that she wanted returned. Then she discovered Sheri felt the same way about her. It wasn't a marriage made in heaven, exactly, but it worked for them.

Each provided something missing from the life of the other. They decided to stay together as a couple and business partners, but those decisions brought many challenges.

They had to kill the mutual acquaintance who paired them. He knew too much about their pasts and would sell them out in a heartbeat. Well-connected in the underworld, removing him required taking care of several other loose ends in order to cover their tracks thoroughly.

Then they spent six months scrubbing old identities and setting up new ones, including several that were male. Bills piled up and more people died before they were satisfied.

In all their preparations, only one point of contention remained, and it was minor. Brandi habitually ate peppermint, especially when she went on jobs. It had replaced the cigarettes she stopped smoking because they stained her teeth. She swore eating it had the same calming effect.

"So now you're trying to rot your teeth out," Sheri answered after Brandi explained.

It was a real concern. Brandi's peppermint breath might prick someone's memory of a past encounter that no disguise could hide. Brandi saw her point and agreed to stop finally, but continued sneaking a few pieces when Sheri wasn't around.

The new team known as Cowboy moved into the upper ranks of killers for hire, but not without creating animosity and powerful enemies. It came with the profession, but they were at a disadvantage because they were independent, not part of a larger organization.

While celebrating their seventh anniversary together in Rio, they cut it short to take work from a West Coast broker that used them frequently. The employer wanted to remain anonymous but paid $100,000 plus expenses for a couple of weeks of small jobs as backup to another team.

First, they sat in an SUV while teams impersonating federal agents arrested a couple of young hoodlums in a restaurant. Then they kidnapped a nurse and handed her over to the primary team, which took all of an hour. Finally, they went with the primary team to pick up a married couple from a federal prison because one of them was female, which required at least one female agent. Then they helped dispose of them.

For professionals with their skill levels, it was easy money until the nurse vanished without a trace and the employer tapped them to find and kill her for an extra $10,000 each. They expected it would go quickly then hit nothing but dead ends trying to find her.

People from the hospital where she worked had scattered all over the city due to it being in the evacuation zone. The second blast at the disaster site destroyed her house and vehicle, sources for clues to her whereabouts. City records were unavailable because of shutdowns and general turmoil.

Sheri paid an underground group of hackers to locate her on the internet and discovered she and her son were on the casualty lists for the LA incident. They called the broker and told him she was already dead. He sent word that a representative from the employer would meet with them.

In a city park, a stately man in an expensive suit sat across a table from them. He explained the couple they picked up at the Lompoc prison had a daughter who was involved with the nurse's son. They were students at the high school that disappeared in the disaster. Their employer had the high schoolers and nurse added to the disaster casualty lists prematurely. They were still alive.

He stopped talking, sized them up. "In order to do this job, I must share some information. If you repeat any of this, we'll kill you. Understood?"

This type of stipulation wasn't unusual in their profession, but what he said next was.

"The government is doing backflips to hide the fact that aliens are behind the LA disaster," he stated with no particular drama. "We think the teenagers are holed up with them in the big house at the site. The nurse is probably somewhere nearby looking for them."

Brandi asked, "The President said that house was part of a hoax video or something, didn't he?"

"That's where the aliens are," the man growled. "The President is lying."

Taken aback, Sheri said, "Just to be sure we're on the same page, you are saying creatures from outer space caused the disaster in LA and probably have the high school couple. Really?"

"If you can't get your heads around the situation, we can't use you."

"Okay," Sheri said. "It's aliens."

"Are they the John Justice and Mercy Ann everyone talks about?" Brandi asked.

"You know what I know. If you get your hands on the nurse, you might be able to coax the teens out of hiding. If you manage to kill or capture all three, we'll triple the final payment."

They had more questions, but he repeated he had nothing more to say and left.

"Do you believe what he said about aliens?" Sheri asked.

Brandi was more pragmatic about the situation. "Whether it's true or not doesn't matter. Did you recognize that guy?"

"Yeah. His organization eliminates lose ends after big jobs, including outside contractors they hire."

They discussed the situation and decided they had no choice but to keep working and hope a chance to make a clean getaway presented itself.

So Brandi canvassed city hospitals and clinics looking for the nurse while Sheri, who could pass as a teenager in the right clothes and makeup, visited temporary shelters looking for high school students who knew Melissa MaCaron, Rob Pike, or his mother, Ashlyn.

Detective Tom Patrick had a long frustrating morning. He had rounded up some of Blake Ferrell's gang members, feeling certain he could squeeze them enough to implicate Blake in a series of burglaries, but they covered for him. Aggravated, he decided to go have lunch.

He liked a small, out-of-the-way Mexican place. Normally it was quiet, but today people working in the Glenwood Heights disaster area crowded it. When he received his order, the only vacant seat was at a small sidewalk table with a city fireman. He asked if he could join him.

The fireman surprised him, reaching across the table to shake hands. "Rudy Johnson."

Tom felt good engaging in idle conversation with someone who was not a cop or crook for a change. After they exchanged the usual inane pleasantries, the conversation turned inevitably to the disaster.

Everyone was under strict orders not to discuss details of their work with strangers, but worry, insomnia, and searching for Mercy Ann had worn Tom down. "Don't suppose you've had an encounter with those alien kids?"

Surprised to have the subject broached so directly, Rudy laughed to cover his discomfort. "If I had, I'd still be running."

For a seasoned detective, Rudy's face was an open book, so Tom decided to confide in him and hope he told what he obviously knew. "I was a survivor of the first incident, only a few feet outside the perimeter. Mercy Ann treated my injuries. You'll never guess what she used."

Rudy eyed him for long seconds then lowered his voice. "We're not supposed to talk about this stuff."

Tom decided to level. "The doctors gave me a clean bill of health, but last time I saw her, she said I required daily treatments to live. Now, she's disappeared, and I don't know what to do. Do you know anything that might help me find her?"

Rudy took out a piece of paper, scribbled with a pen, and placed his hand over it. "I wrote down what I saw her use to treat someone's illness. If you know what it is, we'll talk."

"A big doll she calls Honey Bee."

Rudy described how Mercy Ann cured his son's leukemia.

After a short discussion about it, Tom said, "Wish I knew someone in the military who could tell me what's going on with the aliens."

Rudy shook his head. "I talk to lots of them, including the general in charge, but they won't discuss those kinds of things. They'll be locked up if they do."

"How on Earth did you get close enough to the general to talk to him?"

Rudy explained his late night patrols and running into the general. "Mainly, we talk about fishing."

"Do you think he'd talk to me?"

"Please, man, I can't help you with that."

Tom pleaded with him, even describing how Mercy Ann transported him and a prisoner from a moving police car to Hollywood Hills and took him for a ride on a rollercoaster.

Rudy could see that the detective had a rapport with Mercy Ann and gave in finally, but warned not to get his hopes up that the general would be helpful.

John Justice wanted to end an argument with Rob and tried to change the subject. "Miss Flowers says I have to accept that Mercy Ann is gone."

Sitting across the dining table from him, Rob wouldn't let it go. "You should have let me tell Missa about her parents' deaths instead of just blurting it out. After all, you're to blame."

"We aren't responsible for the Sufficiency Test," John Justice insisted.

"So you keep saying, but I don't see anyone else here."

"Taking lives is a serious matter. When I do it, I own up to it."

It was such a curious statement that Rob asked, "Exactly how many people have you killed?"

"I don't know."

"How can you not know something like that?"

John Justice expelled a long breath. "It's so many that it's impossible to calculate."

Rob's mouth dropped open. "Are you serious?"

"Earth is in a very desirable territory surrounded by a very hostile area of space. Expansionist regimes, marauding renegades, and species collectors are numerous. Sometimes, it's necessary for us to track and counterstrike where attackers originated, be it planet, moon, or mothership. Since we fight most battles with ships, we don't know the numbers of dead and wounded. Often we don't even know the species of our enemies."

"That sounds like *Star Wars*!" Rob cried, flabbergasted.

"An accurate assessment, but reality is far more complicated. Battles resemble your computer games more than traditional combat on your planet. Technology makes it possible to kill while sitting in a comfortable chair on your butt. It is much more barbaric way to kill, if you stop and think about it."

He sounded more the tired old soldier than the pale young boy staring at Rob with a morose expression did. "Just how old are you, John Justice?"

He hesitated, the answer depending on whether he counted the considerable time he lived before the incident with Mercy Ann. Then he decided he didn't want to explain his age, regardless. "Mercy Ann said that I will always be twelve."

"I don't understand."

Miss Flowers hurried into the room and told John Justice something Rob could not understand. He reacted angrily and transported away.

Miss Flowers motioned Rob to tilt his head sideways. She dropped something into his ear. Then, for the first time, he understood her.

"John Justice is the only one who can locate your mother," she said, "so it's best not to squabble with him too much. He's sensitive and sometimes it affects his behavior."

"Yeah, whatever." He got up and started from the room.

"Aren't you going to ask what I put in your ear?" she called after him.

"It's obvious."

She went and placed a tiny silver bead in his hand. "Put it in Missa's ear. Until John Justice gets over Mercy Ann's loss, we'll need to communicate. Meanwhile, try not to upset him, please."

"When are you going to let us out of here?"

"Dangerous people are hunting you. For now, you must stay here."

He didn't like it but knew she was right. "My mother's name is on the lists of people killed at the site with Missa's parents, but John Justice says she's alive."

"Then she is. As I said, he's the only one who can find her."

"Are you in charge here?"

"Mercy Ann was in charge, and now John Justice is. Mercy Ann was the most headstrong, self-centered, pain in the ass I've ever encountered, yet John Justice depended on her for everything. If you and Missa will be friends with him, it'd help him regain his confidence."

More than a little confused, Rob agreed. "That won't be a problem. We like him."

"He's upstairs in Missa's room. Give me your hand and I'll transport you."

Appearing outside the bedroom door, Rob heard John Justice speaking. "Do you ever feel something's happening inside you that you can't explain?"

"I'm a girl," Missa answered. "I feel like that most of the time."

"I'm certain that I began changing when Mercy Ann died."

"In what way?"

"My thinking, the way I feel, pretty much everything."

Rob walked in. Missa and John Justice sat on the bed facing each other. He joined them.

Blake met five key members of his gang in an empty apartment in a big complex several miles from their neighborhood. Just before dark, it surprised them to find him in a fluffy bathrobe and bedroom slippers.

He laughed at their stares. "I've been relocating so often that I'm beat. I have a sleeping bag in the bedroom."

As they munched pizza and drank beer off the kitchen counter, he explained that he'd decided to stay out of sight for a month or two. Meanwhile, they were on their own.

One of them asked, "What if something comes up and we need to get in touch?"

"I trust you guys to hold down the fort. Long as you take care of the neighborhood, I won't criticize."

After discussing a few pressing matters, Blake ushered them out and sprang into action.

Whipping off the robe, he kicked the slippers across the room. He had on the uniform from the security company that patrolled the apartments.

He'd chosen this apartment because it was on the top floor and had attic storage. He already had a ladder in place inside the bedroom closet. Pulling it up after him, he slid the ceiling panel back over the opening, stepped into his shoes, pulled on a cap, and climbed up through a hole he'd cut in the roof. Sprinting the length of the building, he climbed down another ladder into a furnished unit belonging to a sometimes girlfriend who was a flight attendant and away.

When police swarmed the building and cut off escape from the apartment where he met his guys, he was two blocks away in a busy shopping district, sitting on a bench at a bus stop.

A minivan swung to the curb. A woman got out, opened the sliding side door, and removed two shopping bags. The driver, one of the gang members from the meeting, leaned back over the front seat as if to speak to the woman.

"You were right about who tipped the cops. I'll take care of it."

Keeping the cap pulled down to hide his face, Blake disappeared into a shadowy area between stores. When he reached the next street, he took the first bus. He'd wanted the gang in the dark about his plans, which was the reason no one picked him up. If his break with them became permanent, it was better this way.

He planned to find John Justice to tell him Mercy Ann had not died. He realized approaching him with nothing but feelings to back up the claim might be dangerous, but he felt compelled to try.

For years, the general had heard rumors about a group of scientists and industrialists reverse engineering recovered alien technology to make weapons and aircraft. He'd thought it was a bunch of hooey until this incident. They'd given him a special clearance and disclosed that aliens were responsible of the incident in LA. Getting rid of them was only half of his job. He also had to do everything possible to help the government keep it a secret.

The technicians who set up the beam cannons bragged they were the invention of a group of young genius scientists whose identities were secret. He didn't know if they really believed that, not that it changed anything.

He wished he'd warned Mercy Ann about the new cannons, but with the kind of access to information the aliens had, he couldn't imagine her not knowing already. Yet, it appeared they'd caught her by surprise. He could think of no other explanation for her death.

He glanced up at the clock in the operations tent then at the big monitor showing the front of the alien house. Now, the empty porch and steps made him think of Mercy Ann's death, not having tea together and speaking for the first time. He looked at the sergeant major, half-asleep in his chair.

"Go get some shuteye," he whispered. "I'm going for a walk then to bed."

Many of the houses in the evacuated neighborhoods had lights on inside and out, and streetlights burned as usual, but the empty silence gave him the creeps tonight. He sat down on the wide steps of someone's front porch and smoked a cigar, but it did nothing to help him relax. So when he spotted the big, unmistakable silhouette of Rudy Johnson ambling towards him, he was glad.

Sitting next to him, Rudy explained how the device he carried showed people in houses then expressed how much he resented it, even though it saved lives.

The general liked Rudy. He could inject humor into subjects where none should exist and was genuine with no agendas. That's why he'd asked Rudy to call him by his first name when they were alone.

"I have a little story to tell, if you have time, Harry," Rudy said. "Promise it won't take long."

"I'm all ears."

He related his conversation with Tom Patrick then added, "I wouldn't feel right misleading you, so thought I'd just tell you outright that he needs Mercy Ann to continue treating his injuries."

The general couldn't tell anyone she was dead. "I'm dubious she can treat serious medical problems our medical facilities can't. He probably should go back to the hospital."

Rudy explained how Mercy Ann cured his son's leukemia. "I haven't told my wife. She'd freak out."

The general crushed out his cigar. "I keep thinking I can't be more amazed by these aliens then it happens again. I never expected you'd know Mercy Ann so well."

"Actually," Rudy answered, "I know John Justice better. I rescued him from a burning building right after all this started. I gave him a Heath Bar, and the next day they began disappearing all over the city. Mercy Ann said she took them."

"Good lord," the general answered, "you're that Rudy. I should have realized."

"That is my one claim to fame, and I want to keep it secret."

The general thought the video of Mercy Ann's death would make it onto the internet soon. "I can tell you a couple of things. There were credible sightings of John Justice this afternoon at a discount story in Sacramento. People took cellphone videos showing him with a cart full of merchandise. Nothing at all about Mercy Ann, though. I suggest telling Tom to keep an eye on social media.

They parted ways, troubled shadows moving different directions.

Ashlyn Pike became more undone by the hour. Stuck in a cycle of drinking and sleeping it off, her mouth tasted putrid and her head boomed when she awoke. Rolling onto her back, she tugged off the smelly sweat suit, stumbled out the open patio door, and let herself fall into the pool. Hanging on the side, she vomited.

After a cold shower, she staggered to a fast food joint, stuffed herself with dollar cheeseburgers, fries, and a sickening-sweet vanilla shake. Then she threw up on the sidewalk in front of an angry mom with a brood of loud children.

Ashlyn stumbled to another fast food joint and punished herself with pasty bean burritos, greasy tacos awash in hot sauce, and stale unsweetened tea out of a plastic dispenser that gave it an aftertaste. As she gripped the table struggling against a protesting stomach, three young men caught her attention.

Excited about a video on a smartphone, one waved the phone in the air and commented how it was a shame he couldn't bang Mercy Ann now that she was dead.

Ashlyn came out of the chair, snatched the phone from the guy, and watched a scene straight out of a war movie. She couldn't tell what it had to do with Mercy Ann, though.

She waved the phone in front of their faces. "What is this?"

The owner stammered that it was a video of the alien girl's death in the Middle East.

Ashlyn slapped the phone back in his hand and demanded he run it from the beginning for her. He was afraid not to do it.

Back at the condo, Ashlyn put on shorts, jogged onto the golf course, and ran under the moon and stars until she could think about the image of Mercy Ann being torn apart without screaming as she had in the burger place. They called the police.

She'd gotten away. Cleaning up, she tried to force some semblance of order to her hair. It was futile.

After hitching a ride to a Palm Desert truck stop, Ashlyn told a hard luck story to big rig drivers about how her dead end husband in Ohio abused her for twenty years then left her flat for a barfly floosy. She'd headed for Los Angeles to start a new life and help her poor mother, forced from her house by the evacuations, only to have her old car give up the ghost to the desert heat. Now she was stuck here, down to her last twenty dollars.

She arrived in Los Angeles at noon in an 18-wheeler operated by a nice couple from Tennessee. They let her out at an exit not far from Glenwood Heights.

She felt bad accepting their forty dollars and blessings because she had nearly all the money Mercy Ann had given her. Nor did she believe God looked after anyone, but reckoned their beliefs made them feel good.

As the big rig pulled away, she hurried down the exit ramp with her garbage bag full of stuff, worried cops might come by and hassle her.

Sheri did not like the crowded, smelly buildings crammed with displaced people, preferring the huge tent and trailer cities in parks, school grounds, and parking lots.

But it was easier to roam and ask questions in buildings than tents and trailers laid out in orderly grids, because a sense of neighborhood made people territorial against strangers. By studying emergency websites and paying attention to posted notices around the disaster area, she quickly learned how everything worked and pinpointed where most of the people from the first evacuations had gone.

Wearing a smock with a Los Angeles County Department of Health Services Inspector badge that she took from another shelter, Sheri walked in the front door of a high school complex closed for the summer and down a wide, crowded hall until she found the emergency administrative offices. Choosing a woman at the back of the room who was obviously in charge and not busy, she asked for help locating the MaCarons and Pikes.

The woman was annoyed, but Sheri's badge had authority. After entering the names into a computer, she advised none were in the city shelters, but many classmates were here and might know their whereabouts. Families with teens from the missing high school were in tents on the athletic fields behind the gym building.

Sheri found a couple of girls who had been on the cheering squad with Missa. One called her an ingrate for quitting. The other declared she was crazy for breaking up with Jerry, a hunky, dreamboat football hero.

Sheri despised prima donnas who never found enough bad things to say about other people. She'd picked up a clipboard with forms and documents to add to her officious persona, so she flipped through a few pages.

"Oh, sorry," she said. "She's on the list of people killed in the disaster."

Instantly, the one who called her an ingrate was grief-stricken. "How awful."

Sheri did not bat an eye. "Did you know Rob Pike?"

"What a loser," the girl responded, making a face.

Wandering through rows of tents, Sheri heard someone shout the name, Jerry. A tall, good-looking young man leaned against a flashy car holding court with a group of fawning, giggling girls. It had to be him.

Sheri took off the smock, threw it in an empty tent, mussed her hair, and made a beeline for them. Intending to bring up the subject of Rob and Missa, she changed her mind when Jerry stared her up and down as if she was a piece of candy he wanted to lick. Stepping through the admirers, she stood close in front of him and looked up into his eyes.

With a honey voice, she asked, "Hey, big guy, give a girl a ride?"

He leered. "How far do you want to go?"

"Far as you can take me if you answer a question. Seen Missa around?"

He grabbed Sheri by the shoulders. "Who the hell are you?"

Caught by surprise, she kneed him in the groin.

He went down and rolled up around his hands, holding his balls.

Sheri looked at the gaping gaggle of girls. "Better keep your legs together. Six months after graduation, this guy will be a has-been loser with a bad drug habit. Last thing you want is a baby with him."

One girl was braver than the others were—or maybe it was love. "He has a football scholarship and will be a lawyer someday, you bitch!"

She reminded Sheri of herself. "You don't get eyes like his overnight. Really, better run while you still can."

As she walked away, the girl shouted, "You won't come back if you know what's good for you! Go to hell!"

Before going into the building, Sheri stopped and looked back. Kneeling over her hero, the girl stared after the other girls, walking away.

"Or maybe you'll get lucky," she muttered, "but I doubt it."

10

Dangling Conversations

THE CHAIRMAN OF THE JOINT CHIEFS turned to answer their host, the FBI Director, who had walked to the bar to refill Jared Handley's ice tea. "You don't need to be concerned. The weapons are in place and ready. Jared's specialists will program the firing sequence instead of the site commander's soldiers. We'll get the number of casualties we want this time."

The DHS Deputy Secretary crowed, "The President will be impeached for sure."

"Are you certain our strikes will be precise, Jared?" the FBI Director asked, giving him the tea. "The loss of life will be catastrophic if the area expands more than once."

Handley chuckled. "True, true, but then again, the greater the casualties, the worse it will be for the President."

"We can't kill that many innocent people!" the FBI Director replied, overexcited.

Handley smiled in spite of thinking he might have to eliminate this nincompoop sooner rather than later. "It was a joke."

The Chairman summed up their discussion. "Then we'll stick to the plan. I'll order the general not to pull back his soldiers, hit the house with an artillery round, and fire the coil cannons two seconds later. That will expand the devastation, kill enough soldiers to bring down the President, and wipe out the aliens as well."

The FBI Director sat down heavily, shaking his head.

Handley had enough of his insipid behavior but still needed him. "Soldiers consider it a sacred duty to make the ultimate sacrifice in service to our great country. I'll insure they are revered and celebrated amongst the greatest heroes in history. Hell, I'll even fund a memorial monument in the National Mall to insure the country remembers them forever. What do you say to that?"

Hiding his disgust, the FBI Director nodded and forced a smile because even he realized his life was likely forfeit if he did otherwise.

The Chairman, Handley's choice to replace the President, wanted to keep it that way. "I ordered the site commander to remain near the strike with his troops. That way, we can blame him for the losses and not worry about him saying otherwise. It will also discredit the President for leaving him in charge since he overruled my decision to replace him."

Handley stood. "I have a surprise for you guys. I instructed Abd al-Bensi to attack Iraq immediately. The President will delay sending troops to stop him until he gets rid of the aliens because he'll have more support. That will give us a head start taking over the Middle East."

The FBI Director opened a bottle of champagne. They toasted and praised Handley for recognizing an opportunity and seizing it.

John Justice told Missa and Rob how Mercy Ann had been crazy about movie musicals before she caused the battle incident. Then the Guardians sent them to Earth to recuperate, and she became obsessed with horror movies, especially the old black and white ones.

"She began making up her own scripts and acting out scenes, doing all the parts," he explained, very much enjoying the memory. "She was incredibly funny and smart with voices. The plots were insane, the endings never what was expected, and yet everything made sense in a crazy kind of way. She'd laugh until she cried. It was the only time she acted like her old self before the incident."

Missa said, "I really like old horror movies, too. Did she have a favorite?"

He rolled his eyes. "The original *Village of the Damned* was the one that hooked her. She went to the premier in London then made me go back with her to see it again. That's where she got the idea for us to wear Victorian clothes for the Sufficiency Test. She thought it added a sinister aspect that would make authorities take us more seriously. I thought it was ridiculous."

"Didn't that movie came out in the late 1950s?" Missa asked quietly.

John Justice stared, sheepish. "1960."

"1960?" Rob questioned. "How can that..."

Miss Flowers walked in from the kitchen. "John Justice, you're telling them everything."

He shrugged. "They can't leave here until the test concludes. In fact, I was about to tell them more about the Sufficiency Test. Do you have any objections?"

She stared for a moment. "No, I guess not."

John Justice had a viewing monitor appear on the wall and showed them today's Sufficiency Test notice:

Sufficiency Test Site for Humankind

You must solve the riddle:

This is an alien facility with capabilities vastly superior to yours
Destroy it and pass the test without further evaluation
Each unsuccessful attack doubles the area of devastation and increases chances of failure
As the situation evolves, you must take the most intelligent actions or fail the test

Sufficiency judged at the end of Day 30

Pass — Humankind continues on present course
Fail — Humankind purged from Earth

This is Test Day 15

He explained the automatic nature of the test. Then he told how Mercy Ann pitched fits to help Earth pass until given permission.

Rob kept interrupting and demanding details and answers John Justice didn't have.

Finally, he had enough. "Mankind would have been wiped out long ago without the fleet protecting it. And now we've lost Mercy Ann and the Guardians have broken off contact, so I don't know if we can still do it. Even so, we'll try, but first, you must pass the test."

"We can fight for ourselves!" Rob insisted.

Shaking his head, John Justice ordered silence and listened to an intercepted communication. "A FBI conspirator just called someone named Brandi Collins that Rob's mother arranged to meet a friend in a Glendale mall. Brandi contacted someone named Sheri to come help her. I have to go."

When Rob stopped complaining about John Justice not taking him, too, Missa asked Miss Flowers, "What did he mean by calling that FBI person a conspirator?"

Miss Flowers explained the conspiracy to overthrow their government they had discovered. At this point, she figured nothing she told them could be worse than what John Justice had already said.

Sitting on a plastic bench in a wide hallway opening into the mall food court, Ashlyn sipped a giant-sized soft drink and wondered what her friend would think of her appearance. She'd probably freak out and think she had gone off the deep end.

She'd shaved her head smooth as a baby's butt and wore a bandana tied over it. Even more startling, she used skin-darkening crème on her whole body. An elastic body wrap flattened her breasts. Worn jeans, a Laguna Beach t-shirt, and battered work boots finished her transformation into a man with a decidedly rough, ethic appearance. In fact, she was so authentic that she worried immigration might stop her and ask for identification.

She'd end up in a rubber room if she kept acting this way, she thought, making her laugh aloud, causing a woman walking by with a little boy to hurry away.

An unruly group of teens chaperoned by two women carrying Bibles went by and scattered to different food counters to order. They made the food court much noisier.

Ashlyn had called her friend from the food court so she could watch for anyone that might be after her. It was a typical Monday morning, an hour before lunch. A few store workers and early shoppers were eating already.

Her friend arrived, bought a gyro, and sat where Ashlyn instructed. Only two people in the area seemed suspicious. One was a well-dressed, middle-aged man carrying a small satchel that reminded her of the interrogators at the military base. The other was a casually dressed blond woman who seemed familiar for some reason.

Then she remembered and cursed under her breath for how long it took to recognize the nurse with the blankets in the hospital restroom. She looked for someone who might be the other nurse, but hadn't gotten good enough look to be certain.

Meanwhile, the blond picked at her food, looking around the dining room in a careful methodical way. A group of sales associates from a department store gathered around her male suspect, and he said something that made them laugh. Obviously, he was legit, so maybe the blond was the only one, not that it mattered. All she could do now was leave.

The Bible teens sat at four tables near Ashlyn. Their chaperons sat across the food court where they could see them without being disturbed by the racket they made. More people streamed in, too many to scrutinize.

Disappointed, Ashlyn got up to go and collided with a young woman wearing a department store shirt and slacks. She started to apologize then felt something sharp pressed against her stomach. It was a knife.

Sheri smiled and had a sweet, girlish voice. "Make a sound I don't like, I'll gut you. If you're friendly and do as I say, I'll let you live. Up to you."

The blond woman joined them. "Shit. Is that really her?"

Sheri laughed as if they were friends discussing weekend plans. "If she hadn't been goose-necking you so hard, I wouldn't have given her a second look. Even then, I almost dismissed her as some horny toad fantasizing about getting into your pants. That's a good disguise, nurse lady. Can't fault you that."

Brandi spoke with a reassuring voice. "You have nothing to worry about, Ashlyn. We're government agents. Answer a few questions and you're free to go."

"If that's true, why has this little bitch got a knife out ready to kill me?" she demanded. "Is the government out of guns and badges?"

Brandi glanced down. "Oops, didn't see that, but no matter. Keep your mouth shut until we get outside, answer a couple of questions, and you can be on your merry way."

"What if I just start yelling my head off?"

"We have ID's and badges," Sherry explained. "Cause a fuss, we'll knock you senseless, cuff you, and carry your ass out of here."

Ashlyn nodded and the knife disappeared up Sheri's sleeve. One at each elbow, they turned Ashlyn to leave just as a running boy in a baseball cap plowed into Sheri, separating her from the others.

She vanished.

Brandi stared dumfounded as she recognized John Justice, reaching for her. She dodged and jumped back. He grabbed Ashlyn.

They vanished.

As Brandi gawked, people shouted John Justice's name and looked around for others quick enough to get pictures and videos they might be willing to share. At the center of so much attention, Brandi fled the mall.

While Ashlyn, Rob, and Missa had a reunion, John Justice told Miss Flowers about intercepting more calls from the conspirators.

The FBI Director, breathless with anxiety, had told his wife that Jared Handley was going ahead with the plan to kill soldiers at the site with no regard for his objections. His wife threatened to leave him if he allowed it to happen.

The Chairman of the Joint Chiefs called the general at the site to order troops not to relocate to safer areas before the attack. They argued hotly, ending with the Chairman shouting and the general agreeing to obey.

"You should warn the general their intentions," Miss Flowers said.

"What's the point if he's going to keep attacking us?"

"One minute you're determined to save everyone, the next you're blaming them for Mercy Ann's death. If you can't make up your mind, let's return to the fleet now."

He said nothing.

"Go discuss it with your new friends then. See what they say."

"It is not their responsibility. It is mine."

She grabbed and shook him. "What's wrong with you?"

Instantly, he became a frightened young boy again. "I don't know! One minute I understand everything and know what to do. The next, nothing makes sense to me."

"Are you thinking of ignoring directives and recruiting Earthlings?" she asked with no warning.

John Justice swallowed hard. "Well, Rob and Missa are exceptional. I never understood why the Guardians and advanced societies in the territory opposed Earthlings in the fleet so much."

"Right now, we need to survive in the present," Miss Flowers replied. "If Earthlings can help, so be it. The other systems will have to live with it. I suggest you allow the ship's systems to begin evaluating the suitability of anyone you want in case we have to leave on short notice."

"What if the Guardians return? What will we do then?"

"If we don't do it, we probably won't be alive when that occurs. In the meantime, I suggest you invite the others to a meeting to help decide what to do next. That will help gauge their potential.

His smile returned. "That's what we'll do then."

At first, Rob, Missa, and Ashlyn just listened to John Justice and Miss Flowers, but Rob and Missa were not the kind of people to sit idly by if they had ideas.

Missa expressed the opinion that Mercy Ann's idea to use her battle prowess to demonstrate how difficult it would be to destroy the alien facility was a good one, which prompted Rob to ask why a demonstration had to be in the form of warfare.

John Justice said they had never considered anything else.

Missa warmed to Rob's idea. "It could be any mind-boggling event that doesn't hurt anyone. Maybe you could destroy uninhabited islands or mountains in Antarctica."

"Can't we come up with something that doesn't involve blowing things up?" Rob insisted. "Since all the media in the world is in Los Angeles, it should be here, too. Something so outrageous that it will force everyone to recognize that only aliens could do it."

John Justice disagreed. "That would turn your world upside down overnight."

"If the Sufficiency Test is real, mankind is fifteen days from being wiped out," Rob responded. "It's now or never."

Missa and Ashlyn agreed, but John Justice remained unconvinced. Miss Flowers suggested he go tell the general how the conspirators planned to kill his men since he needed time to move them to safety. Then they could finish this discussion.

This time he didn't argue.

The general, propped up on his bed reading a book about ancient Egypt, did not show surprise when he looked up and saw John Justice sitting in his recliner. "My condolences for your loss. Mercy Ann's death was a terrible event."

John Justice didn't know what he expected from the general, but it wasn't that. It surprised him so much that he said something asinine. "I see you like reading about Egypt. Me, too."

"Yes," the general answered. "I've always been fascinated by their accomplishments."

John Justice seemed at a loss for anything else to say.

The general helped him out. "I'm relieved you were able to escape Death Valley. Did you get the two teens out, too?"

"Rob and Missa are at the house, recovering. Rob's mother, too."

The general gave him a genuine smile. "When Mercy Ann asked me into your home, I was left with an impression of warmth and hospitality. I'm sure they'll find a stay with you healthful."

Astounded, John Justice sat up straighter. "She allowed you inside the house?"

"I helped take chairs out for lemonade on the porch."

"Miss Flowers didn't tell me about that," was all he could think to say.

"Mercy Ann told me you have access to all Earth communications, even those with sophisticated encryption. That's amazing."

John Justice's mind raced, trying to figure out why she told him so much.

"She came to see me the night she left for Death Valley and seemed remarkably unconcerned at the prospect of facing an entire al-Bensi army. I think the new weapons must have caught her by surprise. I feel bad I didn't tell her about them."

He wondered why the commander of the force trying to destroy them would feel bad about not warning her. "We don't understand what happened. Did she tell you about the conspiracy to overthrow your government?"

"Yes. She even showed me evidence you've gathered."

John Justice took a deep breath. "I came to warn that Jared Handley wants to cause an expansion of the devastated area in order to kill a large number of your soldiers then wipe us out with the coil cannons. By doing so, he thinks the President will lose most of his support, making it easy for Handley to take over."

"Those people are despicable."

"I have the phone call Handley made to the Chairman about keeping your troops in place if you need it later."

"Thank you," the general replied. "I may have to take you up on that offer."

John Justice, who had been glum since arriving, brightened suddenly. "You've given me an idea that might make them postpone the attack, but you'd better move everyone, anyway. I may not have time to discuss it again."

The general did not have time to do anything after John Justice disappeared other than hurry to the operations tent as he pulled on his clothes and gave orders to evacuate.

11

Brazen Acts

A DJ summarized the situation in LA:

"Do you remember those smiling soldiers and first responders helping everyone when the Glenwood Heights mess began sixteen days ago? Well, that has become a thing of the past. Same for those cute alien kids everyone claimed to see all over the city. No one feels much like joking about this situation anymore. Probably why their agent, or whoever was responsible, has them under wraps now.

"A new order went out to evacuate an additional half mile around the site by six this evening, no exceptions. They posted the exact boundaries, along with new highway closings and alternate routes.

"Unlike the other evacuations, this one is temporary, giving credence to rumors that they located the terrorists and gave an ultimatum to surrender or face consequences tomorrow.

"Don't get your hopes up too much, but tomorrow night we may be reporting the end of this nightmare, so if you're stuck in a traffic jam, get out of your

vehicle and shake your butt to this next one. We still
live in the funkiest city on the planet, people."

The President announced to the staff that evening he had ordered the military to destroy the aliens at 9 a.m., California time. A few feigned surprise even though new evacuations gave it away. They had expected he would cave and use the new cannons as the Chairman argued, too.

Recognizing the President's disappointment at the lack of reaction, the White House Chief of Staff tried to cheer him up. "Perfect timing, sir. In spite of the female alien's death leaked to the internet, you managed to cover up the true nature of the threat. After our strike in the morning and life goes back to normal in California, you'll ride a tidal wave of support to a historic wins in the next election."

The President clasped his hands and gave them a victorious shake to acknowledge the applause. This was the best he had felt in weeks.

In the wee hours of the next morning, a scientist climbed onto the empty trailer of a parked Army flatbed truck, made his way to the cab, and climbed up on top. Sitting with his legs resting against the windshield, he admired the city lights. Views here were spectacular because it was one of the highest hills in the buffer zone around the area of devastation.

The scientist heard someone else in the truck bed and assumed the biologist from a downtown research lab he'd met on site had arrived. Both had enrolled on various dating sites, but never the same ones at the same time. Both were workaholics, and more interested in research and teaching than dating and socializing. Forming instant bonds, they couldn't believe their good fortune meeting here, of all places.

He turned around and reached down into the darkness to help her climb up, but the hand that grasped his was calloused and rough. The man was instantly likable, however.

"Hi, I'm Blake. From the look on your face, I think you might be waiting for someone else."

The scientist laughed. "Yeah, but you're very welcome. I'm Pete, a soil specialist, amongst other things. You must be one of the guys from the big tent the army set up a few days ago. A lot of activity over there this evening. Is something about to happen?"

"If I told you, I'd have to kill you," Blake answered with an easy smile.

"Actually, we wondered if you guys ever left the tent. I'm outside most of the time, and you're the first person I've met."

“We’ve been busy. Thought this might be a good time to get some fresh air.” He held up binoculars. “Hoped to catch sight of one of the aliens, but the view is too messed up.”

“A military guy assigned to us claims he chased John Justice right after this mess began, but who knows if it’s true. Sightings have pretty much stopped, so you may be out of luck.”

“Mercy Ann’s the one I want to see,” Blake responded with just the right amount of suggestiveness.

“Don’t we all?”

“My bad luck. Guess I might as well get back to work. Hope things work out with your friend.”

As Blake reached the end of the truck, he found a woman with a small flashlight trying to negotiate a shaky stepladder up into the high bed. To put her at ease, he told her he’d just left Pete before offering a helping hand. He couldn’t see her very well, but was inclined to like her for no other reason than she had the foresight to bring a ladder and flashlight to the rendezvous rather stand in the dark calling for help.

Blake found it easier leaving through the cordon of special guards in this area than it had been entering. He’d paid a small fortune for an ID with sensors that identified him as a civilian security specialist with access everywhere in the buffer zone, but it wasn’t helping him find John Justice. All he could do was wander and talk to people in hopes of catching a break.

A fast moving truck turned onto the street towards him. Rather than answer questions again, he dived behind shrubbery next to the sidewalk thinking it would go past, but it stopped at the house next door. Two people got out. The truck roared away.

Blake heard them talking plain as day. “This gizmo allows me to see through walls and tell if anyone is inside.”

The other man whistled. “The department has some of those on order. I don’t know how many times I’ve had to go blind into a building after someone. Man, that thing is going to save lives and give assholes their just due.”

The first man was much less enthusiastic. “Yeah, but you know damn well organizations will abuse its use, Tom.”

“Hell yeah. I can think of lots of instances where we could do without search warrants and not have to wade through endless rules that only protect bad guys.”

They came down the street towards Blake. “People got a right to privacy in their homes. I don’t want some pervert using one of these things to look through walls at my wife and kids taking baths.”

"How much detail can you see with it, Rudy?"

"Just shows outlines, but I suspect it has been dumbed-down same as airport body scanners. Probably can show everything, and you know every government agency is going to come up with justifications to do it. Talk about Big Brother. Shit, man."

Holding his breath, Blake scooted around the bush as they walked past. Rudy was a fireman. Then he recognized Detective Patrick and couldn't believe his bad luck.

"Guess we're just going to have to agree to disagree," Patrick said. "Do you really think John Justice might seek you out?"

"If he realizes I'm nearby, I'm certain of it," Rudy answered. "I'm interested hearing why he and Mercy Ann dropped out of sight. They're good kids."

Then Tom staggered and stopped, holding a hand to his chest. Rudy grabbed onto him until he recovered.

"That one hurt like hell," Patrick said. "God, this is driving me crazy."

"Come on," Rudy said, "let's keep looking."

Blake had resolved to leave quickly as possible, but that was before he heard the fireman talking about finding John Justice. Keeping a good distance, he followed.

John Justice appeared in the dining room wearing shiny, skintight metallic shorts and a matching collarless pullover without sleeves.

Agitated, Miss Flowers asked. "Are you certain you can do this on your own?"

"I have Urlak moving the flagship into Earth vicinity and standing by for instructions."

"How did you get Esmé to agree?"

"I told Urlak that Mercy Ann didn't want her to know."

Miss Flowers shook her head and said nothing.

"Who is Esmé?" Ashlyn asked.

"Vice Commander of the fleet," John Justice answered. "We can't tell her about Mercy Ann's death until the test is over. She was against trying to save Earth and will order us to leave."

"You were against it, too," Miss Flowers pointed out drily. "She'll strip your rank when she finds out about this."

"I'm carrying out Mercy Ann's last wish. Did you wake Honey Bee up?"

"Yes, but she's angry about it. She's in the operations room."

"Are you referring to the doll?" Rob asked.

"She's a lifeform, a member of the crew," John Justice said. "Later, we'll introduce you. Miss Flowers, I'll connect in the battle room rather than dealing with Honey Bee now. We'll have our new friends assist."

Miss Flowers was thrilled. He sounded like the commander from before the accident, something she had given up hope of hearing ever again.

"We'll walk rather than transporting so our guests will understand the relationship between the house and ship better," John Justice continued. "Follow me, everyone."

They went through the kitchen and parlor into the foyer, then down the hall beside the staircase where John Justice opened a hidden door, revealing a passageway under the stairs. It led to a wide gray corridor of gray metal illuminated by dim light from no apparent source.

After a short distance, a section of wall opened and they entered a big, empty circular room. The opening closed behind them.

John Justice stood in the center of the room with his arms straight out to the sides. A loud whoosh sounded and a pedestal with cables dangling from the top came out of the floor and locked into place.

Taking Ashlyn to his right side, Miss Flowers sent Rob and Missa to the left. She pressed John Justice's inner wrist with her thumb and a small sliding door opened, revealing a blue shiny square with tiny holes. She plugged a blue cable from the pedestal into it.

"Everything is color-coded," she explained. "Open the right wrist and connect the red plug."

Under John Justice's hair on the back of his head were six small circular ports. After inserting matching cables, Miss Flowers told them the remaining twelve cables on the pedestal were for other tasks. They would find out later that two were for John Justice's internal weapons. The remaining ten had been for Mercy Ann.

Miss Flowers led their guests to an area behind John Justice and a semi-circle of padded chairs came out of the floor. After they sat, she pressed her chair arm and restraints came out of seatbacks around them.

Meanwhile, a domed ceiling formed, replacing the flat one. All room surfaces became luminous.

John Justice's voice was all around them. "No one talk to me unless I ask something. You may speak to each other, but do it quietly."

The floors, walls, and ceiling became transparent. The ship was hundreds of feet high in a night sky directly over the site, the city lights spectacular around them. John Justice and the pedestal appeared to float in thin air.

Miss Flowers whispered that if anyone suffered vertigo, to close his or her eyes.

Six yellow disks flying in a circle materialized above the ship. They moved ever faster, forming a continuous yellow line. Below them, seen by some kind of night vision, a violent vortex of wind spread, whipping dust and debris through this part of the city.

John Justice spoke suddenly. “Three civilians are in a buffer zone neighborhood on the edge of the storm area. I’ve sent Honey Bee to help them. More people are inside the devastated area near the command post, but I can’t get an accurate reading on the exact location yet.”

A stern female voice boomed in the room. “Mercy Ann, why are you airborne? Is there an emergency?”

John Justice answered, “Esmé, Mercy Ann is on a special mission. We have serious subsidence under the site creating unstable conditions. She ordered me to do whatever necessary to repair it. I require the assistance of the flagship.”

“Your ship can take care of such a simple matter, can’t it? Besides, the flagship is too far away to reach you until tomorrow evening.”

“I had Urlak move into close Earth vicinity already. I imposed radio silence to keep enemies in the area from tracking his ship. Soon as we finish, I’ll release him back to you.”

Esmé reacted with anger. “Why didn’t you call me before countermanding my orders to the flagship, John Justice?”

“Mercy Ann told me not to bother because you were on a routine patrol in a safe area and having the flagship two days farther away wouldn’t make any difference.”

Esmé did not care for having words such as routine and safe applied to her missions. “Our scans do not show a problem with the ground at your location.”

“False readings occur from so far away, Esmé.”

“Send me your data to analyze and I will consider giving approval to your request.”

“It is not my request, Esmé. It is Mercy Ann’s order.”

“No offense, but I can’t believe Mercy Ann left a big operation in your hands, John Justice. Her mission must really be important. Tell me what it is.”

His face reddened. “It has to do with the Guardians breaking off contact. She told me not to ask more questions about it.”

“I am Vice Commander, and I want to discuss this with her, not you. Give me the emergency contact information.”

"Honey Bee just informed me that Mercy Ann has been monitoring our communications and wants me on a private line. Please standby."

John Justice killed time checking data scrolling across his screen and measuring the density of swirling dust clouds that now churned around the ship.

He reestablished contact. "Esmé, Mercy Ann said you will either stand down or face discipline when she returns. She will apologize to you later if she misunderstood your need for the flagship."

"Did you tell her I wanted to talk?"

John Justice made no response.

Long seconds ticked by. "Esmé relinquishing flagship command to Commander John Justice for a special project. Ending transmission."

A rectangular screen appeared in front of John Justice showing instruments and readings. As he scanned them, Miss Flowers was so proud that she had tears in her eyes.

Then to the others, she whispered, "He wrested control of our most powerful ship from our toughest officer without batting an eye. Unbelievable."

"Why does Esmé have the flagship instead of Mercy Ann?" Rob asked.

"Using the flagship allowed enemies to track Mercy Ann's whereabouts too easily," Miss Flowers explained. "By using battle cruisers, she kept her location secret until powering up weapons. It gave us the added advantage of having Mercy Ann and our most powerful attack craft patrolling different areas, which gave us two fronts in battles."

A deep male voice called, "John Justice, I overheard your conversation with Esmé. Tell Mercy Ann the flagship crew will buy you dinner next time we have rest and recreation together."

"Urlak, greetings," John Justice responded. "My calculations show that you will be at the load site in eleven minutes."

"Yes, but it seems odd that you want to use that to fill in a collapsed area."

"Actually, there isn't one."

Urlak chuckled. "I already scanned your site. What's Mercy Ann up to this time?"

John Justice, in spite of his bravado using Mercy Ann to put Esmé in her place, felt guilty hearing their friend Urlak speaking as if she was alive. He struggled to keep his composure.

"John Justice, are you reading me?"

"Mercy Ann wants the load relocated to the Sufficiency Test site intact. I'm not certain what she has planned and she pitched a snit fit when I asked. She and Esmé drive me crazy with their wild ideas and constant bickering."

"Yeah, me, too," Urlak agreed. "I'll enclose the load inside a force field and verify the weight and stress numbers. Holding this big a load together during transport takes finesse. Take a look at how I propose doing it and see if you agree."

John Justice examined the diagrams and numbers on the screen. "Will you have enough power to keep the field rigid under the load without it sagging?"

"It depends on total weight so I'm probing to determine how deep I have to go. You'll see the numbers in a minute."

"Soon as I get them," John Justice advised, "I'll prepare the ground for a perfect fit. Orientation to the planet's poles will be the same as the original. The load will intrude into surrounding neighborhoods in a few places, but can't be helped."

"It will be tricky, but I've been doing operations like this since long before you were born. I look forward to Mercy Ann's explanations to the Guardians when they reestablish contact. Tell her I'll be at your location in forty minutes with the load."

John Justice looked back at the others then a small viewing screen appeared in front of each of them. "Use controls on the arms to scan the area for the people near the command post I detected. I'll see anyone you locate, so please remain silent until I finish site preparation."

In a restaurant just outside the new buffer zone, Brandi shaded her bleary eyes from harsh fluorescent light. It would be daylight soon and she needed sleep instead of watching her druggy partner scarfing down greasy eggs and pancakes swimming in butter. She glanced at her own double order of dry toast, cold for a long time already. Picking up a piece, she nibbled off some of the crust and followed it with a jolt of hot, black coffee. The bitterness made her stomach grumble.

A TV over the bakery counter held the attention of diners as excited commentators ranted about Dictator General Abd al-Bensi' armies attacking Iraq. A well-dressed woman with an expensive perm, sat in a booth with a fat husband and two young men wearing university t-shirts. She commented loudly that the President had better get off his ass and commit the military to protect American interests.

Brandi responded just as loudly. "If none of you served in the military, shut your yap, lady."

The sons half-stood to give warning looks that changed to concern they were about to get their butts kicked by a woman when Brandi rose from her chair with a menacing glare to give them the finger. Suddenly, they had important matters to discuss and didn't look her way again.

Sheri was oblivious to everything except food. She asked a passing waitress if she could get a scoop of vanilla ice cream with strawberries and whipped cream to go with her blueberry pancakes. The waitress didn't answer and Brandi thought she realized Sheri was stoned out of her head since she still wore a hospital robe and PJs. Then she brought the order anyway.

When surfers and lifeguards pulled Sheri from under Huntington Beach Pier, she had banged her head on the pilings and a jagged bone stuck out of her left arm, broken in two places. Thinking she had fallen or jumped off the pier, they rushed her to the hospital, where they found a small amount of money and Brandi's cellphone number on a plastic card. She had no other identification.

Brandi had to drive through heavy traffic to reach her while the incident at the mall kept playing in her mind. Never had anything frightened her so much, and people around them had cellphones out, recording them.

If someone back home recognized her and blabbed online, it would put the family she left behind in danger. Not that she loved or liked them particularly, but they didn't deserve the kind of people who would come looking for her.

She found Sheri in a recovery room out of her head on painkillers. A big sling held the braced arm strapped to her chest with useless black and blue fingers sticking out just below her chin. Brandi had known there would be questions since Sheri never went anywhere without an assortment of hidden weapons strapped to her.

Fortunately, she'd only had custom-made plastic knives around her waist and a small pistol in her pocket. A sheath for a big knife on her back was empty, probably lost in the surf. Fighting back tears, Brandi explained to a cop that her a gang of young hoodlums brutally raped her sister on vacation in Mexico a few years ago. Then she showed him Sheri's registration for the tiny pistol.

The cop pressed about the odd assortment of plastic knives. Without missing a beat, Brandi recounted how she made Sheri stop carrying real ones by convincing her the plastic ones she found on the internet would protect her just fine.

He felt a blade. "You could kill someone with this."

"Yeah, I was surprised how well-made they were," Brandi answered. "I almost didn't give them to her, but the kitchen knives in her underwear set off alarms everywhere, not to mention cutting her. You can ask the nurse who just examined her. Poor thing has scars all over. Goddamn those immigrant greasers who did that to her. She was the sweetest, kindest girl and they...they..."

The tears and Brandi clinging tightly to him were too much for the cop to withstand. He had her sign a form then hurried outside where ambulances were in line with casualties from a gang brawl.

The hospital wanted Sheri to check-in for observation until Brandi said they had no insurance or cash to cover additional bills. They discharged her with a week's supply of pain pills, prescriptions for refills, and lists of doctors with whom she could make appointments.

Brandi had lost track of time and was surprised it was past 2 a.m. when they departed the hospital. All Brandi wanted to do was sleep and regroup, but Sheri wanted to eat.

Brandi pulled in at an all-night place near the buffer zone. It was crowded, but the staff was sympathetic to Sheri's condition and gave them a table in a closed-off area. Brandi had paid for the hospital gown, robe, and slippers rather than go out to buy her clothes.

The food kept coming until wind roared so ferociously that a man entering the restaurant had the door ripped from his hand, breaking out the glass almost at the same instant a flying metal trashcan smashed one of the front windows. Howling wind sent menus and other objects flying off the hostess stand and tables. People covered their heads and ducked under tables as dirt and debris blew in.

Even with street and porchlights, Blake had a hard time keeping Rudy and Tom in sight. They walked fast and passing military vehicles did not give them a second look but stopped and check his ID if they saw him because he was dressed as a civilian technician. It was faster to hide until they went by, but after a long convoy, they were out of sight when he jumped up.

Reaching the intersection where he last saw them, he took potluck and turned right. There were fewer streetlights and darker this way. Rather than chance blundering into them, he ran along the shadowy side of the house on the corner to get past the corner streetlights. He stepped in a deep hole and fell, striking his head.

Blake sat up and spat dirt out of his mouth. Electricity had gone off while he was out. Feeling around, he determined he was in a shallow hole with piles of dirt and cinderblocks next to it. Judging from the lump on his forehead, it could have been much worse. He stood up. The batteries in his flashlight and burner phone were dead.

"What the hell?"

Stumbling to the dark street, he listened for vehicles, but it was eerily quiet. A couple of blocks away, a solitary flickering light was next to the road.

He pulled binoculars from his small pack. The light was a candle standing on the curb. Beside it, Rudy crouched over Patrick, stretched out on the ground. He hurried to them.

Rudy jumped up, shook hands, and introduced himself when Blake offered to help. He explained Patrick was a police detective. He had trouble breathing and passed out. CPR did no good. Blake offered to help carry him.

Just as they started to pick him up, wind roared around them, filling the air with dust and debris. Overhead, six disk-shaped lights flew in a circle above the devastated area.

Rudy was past being afraid. "Flying saucers."

Blake did not contradict, but thought they were just lights, not that there was an explanation for that, either.

As they discussed the best way to go, Blake glanced down at Tom and gasped. Honey Bee was face down on the detective's chest.

Rudy was just as astounded. "My Lord, where did that come from?"

Overhead, the lights whirled faster, becoming a solid line and widening the storm simultaneously. Wind velocity increased. Trees and shrubs whipped violently, losing leaves and small limbs. A deep roaring noise came from the sky.

Later, Rudy remembered lightning arcing through dark clouds while Blake recalled jagged electricity generated from the sides of a black disk barely discernable in the clouds.

A shriek called their attention back to the ground. Honey Bee, glowing red, jumped up and down on Patrick's chest gesturing with short arms for them to pick him up.

Carrying the detective by the arms and legs with Honey Bee standing on him frantically pointing directions, they ran to the back of a house. Blake kicked in the door. As the building shook and broke apart, Honey Bee had them take refuge in a small bathroom without a window.

Propped against a wall, Rudy sat under Tom's legs. Half-crouched, Blake had his back pushed against the shaking bathroom door. Roof studs crashed down on the ceiling above them. It began giving way.

Standing on Patrick, Honey Bee reached a stubby arm out to touch Blake as the room collapsed.

Meanwhile, the general and sergeant major, with Bongo on the ground between them, knelt in front of the empty command post with hands cupped around their eyes, looking at the most amazing sight either ever experienced. A flying saucer, all but enshrouded in swirling clouds of lightning, debris, and dust was directly above them.

Then the Victorian house literally flew across the devastated area ten feet off the ground and set down gently nearby. A green beam came from the bottom of the flying saucer, sweeping back and forth across the area, stirring up so much more particulate matter that visibility became zero in seconds.

The sergeant major picked up Bongo and crawled into the command post, following the general. The ground began rumbling and shaking violently. Huddled in a corner, debris fell on them as roaring wind tore the tent apart.

John Justice looked back over his shoulder. "Three lifeforms have taken refuge under the remains of the command post. Honey Bee is busy. Missa, are you willing to retrieve them? It will be dangerous."

Rob said, "I'll go."

"Missa is the best choice," John Justice said.

"What do I have to do?" she asked.

Rob wanted to argue. "I'll do it."

John Justice ignored him. "Miss Flowers, give Missa a light and retrieval device from the console."

It only took her a few seconds. "They're on her arm."

John Justice explained, "You'll arrive in front of the command post wreckage. You'll probably have to crawl inside. Use your own judgment how long to keep searching. When you want to come back hold down the big button. If you find them, make certain you have physical contact with everyone before you return. Now, stand up and put a hand over your eyes."

Grit pelted Missa as wind spun her to the ground. Visibility was zilch, but she made out the sound of canvas flapping. Crawling on her belly, she worked her way into the pile of debris and used the light to find ways forward. After experiencing several dead ends, she felt something wet, soft, and warm when she stretched forward with her hand. She "burrowed" to it then did a semi-pushup, lifting the wreckage.

Bongo licked her nose and whimpered.

Reaching along his back, she found an arm. Using every ounce of strength, she pulled her knees up under her and lifted again with all her might. Using the light, she saw three uniformed legs, pushed forward onto them, and held down the button on her arm with her chin.

Instantly, Missa was on the floor of the ship's battle room with the general, sergeant major, and Bongo. She rolled onto her back and let out a whoop.

Then Honey Bee appeared with Rudy, Blake, and Patrick. She communicated that the building collapsed on them and she had no time to consider other locations to transport.

Wide-eyed, Rudy stared down at the roiling clouds and lightning under him while feeling the floor franticly with his hands.

Blake stood up and looked around. "Someone want to tell me where we are?"

"Sit down and shut up," John Justice ordered.

Blake glanced down at Honey Bee, staring up at him and glowing red. Giving her a nod, he sat back down.

Urlak communicated, "I'm directly over you, John Justice."

"The site is ready. I will keep it obscured until you're gone, so time is important. Is the load ready to lower?"

"Yes. Aren't you receiving my information?"

"I'm overloaded with Earth communications and our ship operations at the moment."

"How do you want to do this?"

"I have to remain over the site, so my ship is directly above Mercy Ann's house which is now located at the very edge of the area. You'll have to bring the load down beside us. It'll be tight."

"You never make things easy. Ready."

"Execute."

Urlak set the load in place in just under five minutes. "Anything else?"

"That was remarkable," John Justice answered. "Please inform Esmé that Mercy Ann is grateful for her help."

Urlak laughed. "Hi to Mercy Ann. See you soon. You owe us dinner and drinks."

As the windstorm continued on the ground, John Justice brought the module with the house back inside the ship.

Suddenly, sparks and smoke shot out of his right wrist plug. The ship listed to the right. Struggling mightily, he brought it back into position, but it appeared he might lose control any second.

Blake and Missa started towards him.

Miss Flowers yelled at them. “No! Touching him will kill you!” She pointed to Rudy. “You might be able to help him. The ship reports a 65 percent probability you’re fully compatible, but without tests, it’s impossible to know conclusively. When you met, did you experience unexplained feelings of kinship, an affinity, a close personal bond?”

Rudy got up from the floor. “As if I found another son. How can I help?”

John Justice spoke through clenched teeth. “Full compatibility is extremely rare. Don’t risk your life, Rudy. You have a family.”

“Simply touching him will be enough,” Miss Flowers said, “but only do it if you believe that closeness truly exists. Even then, the risks are great.”

“I do believe,” Rudy said, going to John Justice. “Don’t forget, I owe Mercy Ann for saving my son’s life, too.”

Rudy draped his body around John Justice. Energy sparked for a few seconds then a bright glow enveloped them. The ship jolted sharply as John Justice reasserted control.

Missa, rooted in place since Miss Flowers yelled not to touch John Justice, lost her balance and stumbled towards him. Blake sprang forward, wrapped his arms around her, and rolled away.

After landing, the others lifted the exhausted Rudy off John Justice. Honey Bee sent the general, sergeant major, and Bongo back to a spot near the command post so they would not realize they’d been on the ship.

When the others commended Rudy for bravery, he didn’t feel it was anything special because he never felt at risk. Nor had he ever been more certain of anything in his life than his ability to help John Justice. He didn’t understand why, but he definitely had known it.

On the floor behind overturned tables and chairs with other restaurant patrons, Brandi heard people talking about microbursts, tornadoes, and other weather phenomena, but nothing about this storm seemed natural to her.

Sheri, stoned out of her mind on painkillers, curled up on the floor with her head resting in Brandi’s lap. She had liked the strawberry taste of the pills and somehow left the hospital with a handful in the robe pocket that she kept popping until Brandi caught her and took them away.

The wind had stopped suddenly, almost as if someone hit an off switch. Power came back on, dangerous as downed powerlines sparked and danced in the parking lot. People spoke in hushed tones and began going outside to see the damage.

Brandi decided to give Sheri time to sober up. The roads would be impassable, and they'd have to walk about five miles to the hotel. She didn't want to carry her the whole way. She went into the kitchen and filled a pot with coffee from a big vat. She forced Sheri to drink, hoping she'd throw up.

It was well past daylight when Brandi helped Sheri stand. Everyone had left except a young manager keeping an eye on the place until his boss returned with building materials to secure it.

What a crap job, Brandi thought, feeling sorry for the young man. He was nice, too, helping her lead Sheri around glass shards and other junk that could cut her feet through the slippers, not that she would have noticed if a spear went through her.

Halfway to the front entrance, Sheri stopped and looked around as if seeing the wreckage for the first time. "Are we in Beirut? Did someone set off another bomb?"

The manager thought it was funny.

Out of patience, Brandi yelled in her face. "We're in goddamned LA!"

"Oh yeah, goddamned LA," Sheri repeated, giggling. "Did we kill the nurse? I don't remember."

The manager leaned closer to Brandi. "Got anymore of the stuff she took? I could use something after all this."

Brandi gave him some painkillers.

"Thanks," he said, popping them into his mouth. "Are you girls from around here?"

Sheri shouted, "We're hell-raising heifers from West Texas. Yip-yip-yippee-ki-yay!"

Walking backwards, Brandi pulled Sheri by both hands to the entrance, hoping she would not say something that forced her to kill the restaurant guy.

Without warning, Sheri dug in her heels and pointed with wide-eyed glee. "You little liar! We're in goddamned Egypt!"

Brandi looked back over her shoulder and gasped.

Soaring into the California sunshine out of clouds of settling dust, the Giza Pyramids were magnificent.

12

It's Official. Aliens Exist.

ACTIVITIES IN LOS ANGELES WERE AT A STANDSTILL. Internet servers and wireless networks crashed from the volume of calls, texts, and social media. Nearly everyone was outside, looking for the best vantage points to see the pyramids.

But soon astonishment and confusion turned to fear and anger as people realized the federal government, the military, and the President had lied to them about terrorists being responsible for the LA incident. Even so, many refused to consider beings from other worlds were real, insisting more rational explanations must exist without knowing any, exasperating people who believed only aliens could be responsible.

Many people ridiculed the beliefs of others and discounted facts. Discussions became arguments. Fights broke out and escalated into mobs facing off. Gunfire and sirens came from all over the city as riots and pandemonium spread.

The President of the United States sat at the conference table wondering whether he might be cracking up. Before him were pictures of the Sphinx and pyramids in LA and the empty Giza Plateau in Egypt. He couldn't think straight, stunned that events had spun so far out of control.

The Chairman of the Joint Chiefs and his supporters insisted they should to go ahead with the attack as soon as they could reposition the coil cannons to locations with clear shots at the alien house, now situated between the two biggest pyramids. Others wanted to postpone the attack and reassess options because military assets at the site sustained severe storm damage and the aliens were more powerful than anyone had supposed. One fool argued an attack might damage the Giza monuments and that it would upset the Muslim world. Several people agreed with her.

The President wanted to scream at all of them. Wasn't it a given that aliens who could travel through space would be powerful? And it wasn't as if the pyramids hadn't been around for thousands of years and become little more than dilapidated tourist attractions wasting away because of Cairo's pollution and encroachment. What possible difference would a little more damage make? And what did ancient Egyptian monuments have to do with Muslims?

Then his thoughts spiraled farther down the rabbit hole of absurdity.

What if this turned out to be delinquent alien kids perpetrating pranks on guileless Earthlings? Wouldn't that be a hoot? We destroy LA then their parents show up, give them a spanking, and apologize for the trouble. Hadn't he seen a cartoon with that plot when he was growing up? Yes, he was certain of it. He laughed aloud and looked up, finally noticing everyone staring at him.

He was not so far gone that he didn't know he had to say something that sounded rational. The last thing he needed was rumors about his mental well-being.

He firmed his voice before speaking. "I have no choice but to announce extra-terrestrials are behind the mess in LA, but I need solid reasons why we said it was terrorists."

Jared Handley had foreseen this would be the President's main and the Chairman of the Joint Chiefs was ready to push his agenda.

"We announce an alien ship crashed," he said, acting as if he had not rehearsed it. "When we investigated, they attacked us. Their damaged weapons had limited range, so we contained them at the site inside the ship, which somehow they hide behind the façade of a house. They know we can destroy them at any time, yet refuse all offers of assistance and negotiation."

The FBI Director continued the scenario. "So we had no choice but to demand surrender. Their response was to use up most of their remaining power to move the pyramids to the site. While that was an incredible feat, we don't understand the point, and they refuse to explain."

A NSA conspirator added, “We kept the nature of the enemy under wraps to prevent the kind of panic and hysteria now occurring. We had hopes of reaching a peaceful resolution before making the historic announcement that the people of Earth are not alone in the universe, but these aliens come from a militaristic society that prefers war over peace and death over surrender.”

The Chairman presented the finale. “Mr. President, we suggest you stick to that scenario and cite national security concerns to avoid providing more information at present. One last thing: you must claim that while we do not know the true appearance of the aliens, they’re definitely not children. Those seem to be some kind of holographic images, the same as the house, which explains how they appear and disappear at will.”

The President liked what he heard, but expressed a concern. “I thought we’d determined they really are young teens.”

The Chairman wished the man wasn’t so stupid. “Children don’t fit a scenario of militaristic zealots, nor do we want to plant an image of you killing children in the minds of voters.”

The conspirators felt certain they were going to get approval for attacking right away until the President’s Chief of Staff suggested they might be moving to a decision too fast, causing the President to hesitate.

The Chairman overreacted and pushed back too hard. A vain man, the President felt his authority challenged and made an arbitrary decision to postpone action for two or three days to give the military time to recover from the storm. For once, the other conspirators didn’t envy the Chairman his position closest to Jared Handley, who was not going to be pleased.

Then they discussed Abd al-Bensi’s attack on Iraq. On this matter, the conspirators got their way, persuading the President to wait until after he wiped out the aliens before deciding about a military response. It was more than enough time for al-Bensi to get a stranglehold on the country and would be too late for America to interfere, which was exactly what Handley wanted.

The Chairman was all smiles again. That would make up for postponing action against the aliens.

Blackout curtains made the hotel room dark as night except for light shining under the bathroom door, closed to muffle the shower running. In the scant light, it appeared one person was asleep in the king bed, verified by quiet snoring sounds.

The room door opened just wide enough for two shadows to slip in sideways one after another from the bright hallway then clicked closed. They waited silently about thirty seconds for their eyes to acclimate to the darkness then the first shadow pointed to the bed and started toward the bathroom door.

Two silenced shots struck the shadow moving to the bed, and it crumpled to the floor. Three more hit the other one, diving for the floor too late.

Brandi, underneath a combination table-desk, scooted out with a penlight held away from her body in one hand and pistol in the other. She shot both men in the head for insurance then checked pockets for car keys. Not finding any, she cursed under her breath because it meant someone else had them and she had to take chances.

Several hotel cleaning people jabbered coming down the hallway, so she didn't think anyone with a weapon waited outside the room, which was a good thing because they were on the fourth floor. She checked Sheri, snoring on the closet floor, and as much as she didn't want to leave her alone with nothing protecting her but a Do Not Disturb sign on the door, she had to move fast.

Dashing into the bathroom, she turned off the shower, wrapped a towel around the pistol, and opened the door to the hall, looking both ways with a small mirror. The cleaning people were between her and the elevator, which didn't matter because she wanted to go down the emergency stairs in the other direction.

She sprinted, watching for room doors not closed fully. Reaching the stairwell, she pressed against the wall. If she had run this operation, a backup would be on the other side of the door watching with the latch jammed open since most professionals would not use the elevator to escape.

Taking a deep breath, she flung the door open, ran down the stairs to the switchback, and spun around ready to fire at anyone coming down behind her. God, she thought, seeing no one, these guys sure were cocky bastards. They must have figured a hit on two women didn't require planning.

Reaching the ground floor, she hurried down the long hall past the elevators to the lobby. Other than a young woman seated and working on something behind the counter, no one was around except two families in the complimentary pig-out breakfast room. Then, through the glass doors of the hotel's main entrance, she spotted a familiar black SUV waiting at the curb, engine running.

The driver, a young punk, had parked with his side closest to the hotel, a no-no since it made him more vulnerable to trouble coming out of the building. It was much easier to fire across a vehicle's interior than out the side where you sat, especially wedged under a steering wheel.

His dark window was all the way down, too. He had a cigarette. Two more smoldering butts were on the sidewalk. He kept checking his watch, the rearview mirrors, and the hotel entrance.

A rookie, green as grass, and ready for the mower, she thought. No wonder they had him wait.

Mentally, she measured distances from different points in the lobby and through the front doors to the SUV. She had a nagging feeling she had forgotten something, but other than witnesses showing up and taking care of videos from security cameras, what else was there? She had not slept much and her thinking was anything but sharp.

Then she whispered, "Oh, shit."

Their employers used professional cleaners to insure no evidence left behind, which was a good thing when you did jobs for them, but now it meant a team nearby waiting for a call. They must be concerned about the time by now and would contact the SUV driver soon. From that point, she'd have around ten minutes to get away, which didn't give enough time to take care of security videos unless she could do it before they called.

The office door behind the girl at the counter stood open. She could see the top of a man's head inside. In an economy motel chain such as this, video recorders were usually in a locked closet inside the office. She went into action, experience making all her decisions.

Walking fast toward the counter, she checked the pig-stuffing room again. Those people wouldn't look up for a while with all that garbage piled in front of them. From another hallway, she heard swimming pool noises, but did not see anyone. Outside, the rookie continued fidgeting and smoking.

Removing the towel from the pistol as she reached the counter, Brandi saw an open textbook had the girl's attention. A college student, she thought, reaching across the counter and hitting her hard enough with the pistol barrel to insure she was out of action for a long time.

She vaulted the counter, landed as quietly as a cat, and reached the guy in the office in three strides. Her fist broke his jaw and knocked him out of the chair. They had disconnected the alarm button under the desk, probably because legs bumped where they located it.

She heard the keys on the guy's belt when he fell, but didn't need them. Two digital recorders were in plain sight inside an open closet. It was faster to take the entire units, so she jerked them free and dropped them into a garbage bag she took from a trashcan.

Back in the lobby, she saw the rookie on a cellphone and not happy with the call. She set the garbage bag down, grabbed a newspaper from a table, and checked the time on a big clock over the counter.

The rookie switched off the phone and tossed it onto the passenger seat. He glanced at his watch, the hotel entrance, and rearview mirrors. Then he reached to take another cigarette from his shirt pocket.

Brandi anticipated the sliding doors would not open fast enough at a full run and went through sideways. The rookie was lighting the cigarette when he glimpsed her. He died with two bullets in the head.

Brandi pushed into the driver's seat with him, closed the dark window, and switched off the SUV. Then she jumped out, locked the vehicle, and blew a kiss to confuse anyone who might be watching from rooms above. Details mattered.

Back inside, she grabbed the garbage bag and verified no one had noticed anything. Pushing a rolling luggage cart, she ran to the elevators. Anyone would think she'd overslept and had to hurry.

She put Sheri on the cart and covered her with a blanket, her small size making it easy even with two Kevlar vests strapped around her. They never had more than a single change of clothes in a hotel room when working unless necessary for the job. Sheri's small suitcase of weapons was the only other thing.

Brandi had not been asleep long when John Justice called her cellphone and said their employer had a hit team on the way to the hotel to kill them. When she asked how he knew, the little prick hung up.

She'd wiped the room for prints before setting up the ambush and hadn't left prints anywhere since. That was to keep the cleaning crew from leaving their prints since she hadn't checked out. As a final gesture, she thought of folding a pair of panties on the bed, but decided she'd best not provoke them anymore.

Twelve minutes after starting the countdown in the lobby, Brandi was a block from the hotel when two black SUVs barreled by from the other direction. Using one of her burner phones, she called 911 to report a group of Middle Eastern men running into her hotel lobby carrying automatic weapons. Then she screamed and smashed the phone.

She looked back over her shoulder at Sheri, still out cold on the back seat. "You're going to get a big kick out of all this if you ever wake up, honey. God, how many of those damned pills did you take?"

Standing next to the Sphinx, the general gazed at the sunset then watched the new command post going up on the site of the old one, all the while thinking about recent events.

No one had realized he was conscious during the rescue and on the alien ship. Nor was it lost on him that Missa, a high school girl, risked her life to save him, the sergeant major, and Bongo. Seeing Rudy onboard and witnessing his heroics with John Justice had been even more amazing.

He assumed the unconscious man on the floor with Rudy was Detective Patrick. He had no idea about the identity of the man who grabbed Missa when she fell or the woman sitting with Miss Flowers. Perhaps the aliens brought them on board to save their lives, too.

The general did not tell the sergeant major any of it. He made up a story about escaping into the neighborhood after the command post collapsed. He would tell him the truth eventually, but did not want to explain why he didn't report any of it to Washington until this was over. If they sent two high school students to that hellhole in Syria, they wouldn't hesitate to come after him and the sergeant major.

John Justice had relocated the Victorian house between the two largest pyramids, facing it towards the Sphinx, forcing his troops to find new firing sites for the coil cannons. The task proved to be extremely difficult since they also needed to be on high ground to fire over trees and buildings. Obviously, John Justice had figured all that out beforehand, which showed impressive planning.

Two hours ago, the President went on TV and told the world that aliens existed and were behind the situation in Los Angeles. Then he told a new pack of lies, including that the aliens' appearances were projections of false images to make authorities hesitate taking decision actions against them.

The general exhaled an angry plume of cigar smoke up towards the face of the Sphinx. So here he sat, preparing to attack the aliens that warned him after his bosses set him and his soldiers up as sacrifices to their sick cause.

Because he had gone against orders and evacuated his troops anyway, they'd been able to take cover and suffered no casualties from the storm, either. He'd expected to catch hell, but the media heralded him as a hero and his bosses heaped praise on him publicly. Privately, they let him know they would have his ass if he disobeyed orders again.

To emphasize that point, his immediate boss, a lieutenant general high up in the conspiracy, would arrive with a group of politicians to tour the site in the morning. He was to participate in a meet and greet, then his boss would take care of hosting while he concentrated on storm recovery. John Justice told him the conspirators were afraid he would tell someone what he really thought if asked his opinion.

He gazed up at the enigmatic face of the Sphinx. The lines between loyalty, duty, and doing the right thing were no longer clear. In his long, outstanding military career, this kind of situation had never before occurred. He was deeply troubled.

From the moment they met, John Justice did not like Blake Ferrell, who introduced himself as a friend of Mercy Ann then kept insisting she was alive.

They sat directly across the dining room table from each other. Missa, Rob, and Ashlyn were on Blake's side. Miss Flowers sat next to John Justice.

Tom Patrick was in the ship's infirmary with Honey Bee running tests. Rudy was back with his family in Redlands.

To Blake's wild claims about Mercy Ann, Miss Flowers replied, "You're wrong. The ship reported all her systems shutdown, which can only have one meaning."

Blake refused to be convinced.

Missa thought he was a bullheaded jerk to keep going on about Mercy Ann when the subject upset John Justice so much, so she changed the subject. "I never thanked you for saving me."

Blake had a direct manner that unnerved her. "You didn't need my help. I apologize for underestimating you."

He was right, but she couldn't understand how he would know and said so.

"I realized your athleticism and physical conditioning after I grabbed hold of you. The way you hit the floor to avoid injury was textbook perfect. It made me curious, so I checked you out closer."

Blushing, she demanded, "What do you mean, you checked me out?"

"Muscle development, damage to hands over the years, callouses, balance, and movements indicate extensive martial arts training. Unusual to see that level of development on someone so young. How old are you, anyway?"

The red on her face deepened. "I'd guess you're around forty-five. Am I close?"

He had an easy laugh. "I'm twenty-nine, but it feels more like fifty these days."

Recognizing Missa's growing interest in him, Rob interrupted, "How come you notice those kinds of things, Blake?"

He held up his hands. They showed the same kind of wear and tear Missa's did. "Did a little fighting when I was younger. Nowadays, I lead a band of merry men, take from the rich, and give to the poor—after deducting expenses and our cut, of course."

"You're a crook?" Missa asked with raised eyebrows.

"I prefer to call myself a community organizer."

"But you came here with Detective Patrick," she said. "We thought you were a cop."

He laughed. "Think of Tom Patrick as my Sheriff of Nottingham. His mission in life is to lock me up."

"What's your full name?" John Justice demanded.

"William Blake Ferrell."

It only took him a few seconds. "Detective Patrick leads an investigation into crimes committed by you and your gang."

"Innocent until proven guilty," Blake answered.

"Only because they've never been able to prove anything," John Justice accused.

"Such is life where I grew up."

"That's no excuse," John Justice responded harshly.

"I'm simply telling the truth," Blake said, surprised to find himself under attack. "Don't forget that I met Mercy Ann in a grocery distribution center stealing cases of merchandise. She threatened me when I joked I might take one."

"She told me about encountering an arrogant thug the first night she foraged for Rudy's Heath Bars.

"You call what she was doing foraging? I did the same thing and you call it stealing."

"Because you're a criminal," John Justice retorted.

"She didn't pay for any of that stuff, did she?"

He became even more self-righteous. "It's different for us. We're outside your financial infrastructure and must be careful not to cause an imbalance in your economic inflows and outflows. If we inject large amounts of money suddenly, it will knock the entire system out of whack and create another Great Depression."

Blake kept a straight face. "I assume she taught you that."

"Just the basics," he answered with obvious pride. "She said it takes years to understand fully."

He didn't want to upset John Justice further. "So it does, but that brings us back to where we were before Missa changed the subject. I don't think she's dead because I felt sudden confusion and anger coming from her just before she disappeared. At first, I thought the feelings vanished, too. Then I realized I still felt them, only much weaker. I still feel them. That's why I'm sure she's alive."

John Justice gaped as he realized something. "She showed the battle to you? That means you saw her again after the warehouse. You did, didn't you?"

The amount of emotion he showed surprised Blake. "The night she left to rescue you, we had dinner at my apartment."

"She went with you to your home?"

Blake felt idiotic not recognizing the cause of John Justice's hostility until now. "No, no, you have the wrong idea. Out of nowhere, Mercy Ann came out of my kitchen and acted as if she owned the place. She was sick with worry about you and wanted to talk to someone, that's all."

"Well, you're wrong thinking you shared a bond with her," John Justice insisted.

Miss Flowers said, "Even though he's wrong about Mercy Ann's death, his compatibility quotient might be high enough to use some of her weaponry, John Justice."

He gaped at her, incredulous. "He's a criminal."

She reached to reassure with a hand on the arm. "We don't have to resolve this now."

He jerked away and jumped up. "I want him out of here. I'll transport him to the police and they can lock him up."

Miss Flowers tried to stop him going around the table after Blake. He pulled away again.

She blocked the way and slapped him, a stinging smack on the cheek. "Stop acting like a jealous, lovesick brat. It's petty, embarrassing, and stupid. As commander, you must put the mission first. Blake might be important for us."

Tears welling in his eyes, he went to his room. Embarrassed, Ashlyn, Missa, and Rob made excuses and left.

Quietly, Blake asked, "What makes you think I'd consider joining you, Miss Flowers?"

"You hate your life here," she replied, "but keep in mind that it is John Justice's decision to make."

Blake tried to act nonchalant. "I didn't how he felt about Mercy Ann."

"Now that she's gone, he'll get over it, but you'd do well to remember that nearly everyone who met her came under her spell at one time or another."

Around midnight, John Justice was in the dark parlor alone staring up at the jagged side of the Great Pyramid, illuminated by the military's repositioned spotlights. Soldiers continued working, doing their best to eliminate shadowy areas around the house.

A loud TV from the dining room bugged him. He craved solitude and silence for his self-pity, not news people spouting nonsense about how aliens might really look. He thought this must be the stupidest planet ever.

Rob walked in and sat on the other end of the couch. "Girls are hard to understand, aren't they?"

John Justice just wanted him to go away. "Blake seems interested in Missa. They're together in the upstairs study. You shouldn't leave her alone with him."

"When we were eight," Rob answered, very nonchalant, "Missa's parents gave her a fancy box of imported chocolate truffles. Almost too excited to talk, she ran over to my house to share it. I'll never forget how she took out the first piece and examined the intricate decorations, trying to guess the flavor before biting off half and giving me the rest. It was the best candy we ever tasted."

He didn't say anything else until John Justice looked at him.

"And so it went, until the fifth piece," Rob continued, "which upset Missa because it was the same flavor as the first. Turns out, there were only four flavors in a box of twenty, and she refused to eat anymore."

Another long silence until John Justice asked, "Why?"

"Because she'd experienced everything the box had to offer. When I pointed out that we ate bags with one kind of candy all the time, she said you knew that when you bought them. This expensive box of truffles, on the other hand, raised expectations much higher than it delivered. She gave the box to mom to share with the nurses. What do you think of that?"

"What does it have to do with Blake and Missa?" John Justice asked.

"It describes Missa's personality. She meets very few people she finds interesting, becomes bored with them quickly, and moves on. For me to have a long-term relationship with her, I must keep developing expertise in things that interest her while respecting her needs to experience other people. In essence, I'm saying that one person will never be enough for her."

"Are you strong enough to live that way? At times you'll hate her as much as you love her."

Rob stared, surprised. "It sounds as though you speak from experience."

"Since you used a box of chocolates to describe Missa, I'll tell you that over time I became Mercy Ann's Forrest Gump. If you don't mind me asking, what sort of interests does Missa have that will keep her coming back?"

"You'll probably laugh, but mostly, its physics, math, and science. We also enjoy customizing cars and trucks, and building robots. There's lots more, but you get the idea."

They sat in silence, neither speaking again until Rob asked, "Do you have any idea why people on Earth always depict aliens as creatures called the Greys? Do you know what I mean?"

"Their image became ingrained in your minds because they visited Earth so often in the past. They're from a system in the territory and an ally of ours."

"No shit?"

John Justice leaned across the couch and whispered, "Take a close look at Honey Bee then imagine longer legs, a more symmetrical face, and big eyes. She was a stereotypical Grey, but suffered injuries requiring reconstruction. Her name sounded similar to Hanna Beatrice in English and that was what we called her until Mercy Ann gave her the nickname Honey Bee."

"Do you feel as though you are part of the ship when you plug in?" Rob asked.

"That is an apt description."

Rob looked out at the Great Pyramid. "I will never forget watching it come down out of the sky."

"Yes, it was quite a sight."

"Do you consider yourself a nerd, the same as Missa and me?"

John Justice smiled. "Well, I do have twelve computers inside me."

"Twelve? That many? Do they bother you physically?"

"No. Our internal system components are minuscule, for the most part."

Rob jabbed him in the shoulder. "I think we're going to be good friends."

John Justice jabbed him back. "No shit!"

The late night DJ came on with the news:

"We are one minute into the eighteenth day of the world's first official alien encounter. Yesterday, the President made the momentous announcement confirming the extraordinary claims many in LA voiced from the beginning—the incident in Glenwood Heights is a standoff with otherworldly beings.

"If you want to hear discussions about the historic nature of the event, the speech in its entirety and in-depth analyses are all you'll find on TV tonight. As for us, we'll cover a few salient points then get back to the music.

"Aliens crashed landed in our city, are hostile, and holed up in their ship. They pose no danger outside the area cordoned off. They refuse to negotiate. They have three days to surrender or we'll destroy them.

"The so-called alien children known as John Justice and Mercy Ann are either a publicity stunt or holographic images created by the aliens. Take your pick.

"As to reports of an alien test to determine whether mankind should be allowed to continue existence on Earth, the President asked everyone to refrain from repeating cockamamie rumors. Those stories originated when someone at the site put up a sign as a joke. They've yet to find the culprit.

"The aliens inexplicably relocated the Giza Pyramids to Los Angeles. No one has any idea how they accomplished something so incredible, nor do we know why.

"Meanwhile, riots erupted in cities all over the world. Places of worship are packed. Protests against how our government handled the crisis will take place across America tomorrow. Calls for impeachment of the President are widespread.

"Scientists, religious leaders, and academia want a deputation of experts to spearhead efforts to reach peaceful resolution with the aliens. Many groups condemned American's threats to destroy them. Threats to organize protests at the site brought warnings of strong resistance from the military and arrests without exception.

“In the same vein, world powers, including Russia, China, France, Germany, and Great Britain, demanded all information the United States has about the alien situation and want to participate in decisions about them. The White House refused those demands since the aliens attacked a major American city and we must defend ourselves.

“Otherwise, the situation in Iraq continues deteriorating. The President warned Dictator-General Abd al-Bensi to withdraw his forces but did not say how the United States will respond if they refuse.

“That’s it for now. Go to bed if you can sleep. If not, stay tuned here and boogie the night away.”

13

Getting Sorted

SHERI WOKE UP WITH SOMEONE PULLING HER BY THE LEGS, causing severe pain in her left arm. Not knowing where she was, she kicked one leg free then kicked again, catching the assailant in the face with her heel and breaking the hold on the other leg. Bringing her legs down hard, she intended to spring up and attack, but was too weak and sagged back down, throwing up and choking.

Leaning over her, blood gushing from her nose, Brandi glared. "I swear to God, keep this shit up and I'm going to kill your ass. Do you understand?"

She turned Sheri onto her side and pounded her back until she coughed and cleared her windpipe. Then she muscled her onto her back again and shoved two pillows under her head.

Scared by Brandi's anger, Sheri asked, "Where are we?"

"You've been unconscious since yesterday morning, you pill-popping nitwit. You've been wetting the bed, pooping, and throwing up all over everything. I even risked my life saving your sorry ass from a hit team our employers sent after us, and now, you kicked me in the face. I swear to God, I've had it."

"So we're in hiding, huh?" She looked down at her throbbing, immobilized arm. "How did I get hurt?"

Making an exasperated noise, Brandi went to the bathroom and returned holding a wet washcloth to her nose. "Do you remember being under the Huntington Beach Pier?"

Sheri's eyes widened. "That was real? Last thing I remember was the mall with you and the nurse."

"Do you remember the alien boy? He transported you to the pier."

"Transported? Like, beam me up, Scotty?"

"Yeah, exactly like that."

"Wow. Wish I could remember. Why'd he do it?"

"He was after the nurse, too."

Sheri misunderstood. "Couldn't he have killed her without hitting me with a goddamned pier? I mean, come on."

Brandi took a deep breath and let it out. "He was there to rescue her. After he transported you, he disappeared with her."

She thought about it then became indignant. "What were you doing? Why didn't you stop him?"

"Why don't you kiss my ass? I had half of LA taking cellphone pictures after the woman I love vanished into thin air. I thought you were dead."

Sheri grinned. "You still love me, huh?"

"It's not easy."

"Sounds like you've had your hands full. I'm sorry I caused you so much trouble."

"Forget it. I made you an appointment with a specialist this evening to make sure the arm is healing okay."

"Thanks. Where are we?"

"Anaheim. Figured we'd be less noticeable away from Glenwood Heights. Rooms are cheap here with the amusement parks closed. What are you doing?"

Sheri kept sniffing the air. "I think I need a bath. Could you run some water in the tub and help me in?"

"I'll be happy to, believe me."

When Brandi returned to help her undress, Sheri asked, "I assume you didn't have any problems handling the hit team."

"One was so useless they left him outside in the vehicle and the two who came to the room weren't much better."

"They sent three people? That's insulting if they were that bad."

"They sneaked into a dark room and didn't have the sense to bring flashlights. The only problem was getting your drugged ass out of the hotel ahead of the cleaning team. But I have something else you need to know. We'd be dead if the alien boy hadn't called and warned they were on the way to the hotel. I can't figure how he knew about them, where we were holed up, or why he helped us."

Sheri was unusually contrite. "Sorry for being so much trouble. I owe you big time."

The President listened to a hastily prepared briefing from the CIA Director concerning a huge object discovered under the Egyptian site of the Great Pyramid. The Egyptian government had sent soldiers to chase archaeologists away until their antiquities ministry examined it. The Director passed small slabs of an igneous rocked called Labradorite around the room.

"One of the archaeologists who discovered the object said the surface was similar to these rocks in appearance," he explained. "But striking it with pickaxes did not even leave a scratch."

The President wondered why anyone thought he cared about this. "Do they think the object is man-made?"

The Director corrected politely. "It's an alien construct, most likely."

A member of the NSA said, "If ancient aliens left a secret structure under the Great Pyramid, who knows what technology and treasures it may contain? We must get control of the site without delay."

A science advisor warned, "We mustn't overreact. It may not be a structure. If aliens constructed the pyramids, it might be nothing more than part of the foundation."

The NSA member retorted, "Until we know for certain, we can't allow another country to explore it."

The President, in spite of declaring to the world that aliens existed, did not give credence that aliens built structures on Earth during ancient times for no reason other than he didn't want to believe it.

"Anything else?" he asked in a brusque manner that indicated he wanted the answer to be no.

But the NSA member was tenacious. "We must find reasons to seize control of the site, Mr. President. We can't allow unstable governments in that part of the world to have advanced technology."

The President realized most of his people would agree, but such a rash act would likely mean war with more countries in the Middle East. He felt his headache getting worse.

After rummaging in the kitchen and finding very little except junk food and snacks, Ashlyn asked where they kept the real food. Miss Flowers explained that John Justice and Mercy Ann had been in the habit of picking up takeout at fast food restaurants.

Ashlyn insisted they go to a grocery store. John Justice said it was too dangerous. Rob suggested he transport them to another state and disguise himself. So John Justice found himself in Tempe, Arizona, staring down a long grocery store aisle at Missa and Ashlyn comparing vegetables when someone tapped him on the shoulder.

Two girls, a few years older than him, gawked nervously before one stammered, "Has anyone ever said that you look exactly like John Justice, the alien?"

Rob had instructed him to laugh off situations such as this and claim he attended a nearby middle school. With his ability to access the internet, he could provide enough local information to convince anyone, but shopping bored him and the girls were attractive, so he simply stared and didn't say anything to see what they would do.

The other girl snapped a cellphone picture. "I think it's really him."

Rob came down the aisle behind John Justice and mussed his hair. "You must be a couple of Paul's little classmates. Bet you're excited starting Middle School this year. It's all he talks about."

The girl with the phone was indignant. "I'll have you know that we start high school this year."

Rob looked them up and down. "Gosh, sorry. Don't worry about being late bloomers. You're overdue for a growth spurt."

The girls wheeled around and stormed away.

Rob asked, "What did you do with your cap?"

"It was hot. I must have left it somewhere."

Rob handed it to him. "Keep that hair covered, please. You might as well wear a sign with your name on it."

"Sorry."

Rob gave him a little shove. "Don't act naïve with me. You like the attention."

Missa and Ashlyn disappeared around the corner. John Justice and Rob walked slowly in that direction. Suddenly, John Justice stopped, listening intently for most of a minute before explaining to Rob.

"I just heard the FBI Director on the phone with the President," he said, very concerned. "He's providing information about the conspiracy, but I can't tell whether he's double-crossing the conspirators or setting the President up as part of another conspiracy scheme. Perhaps, it's a little of both. I'll monitor him more closely until I know for certain."

Typically, the technology interested Rob more than the information. "How do you sort and pick out a single item to hear?"

"Data processing modules augment brain functions and call my attention to subjects or people I've earmarked.

"That's amazing."

John Justice hesitated. "I want to discuss something, but you must not repeat it to anyone, including Missa."

"You have my word."

"Much about Blake reminds me of Mercy Ann."

Rob was very surprised. "How so?"

"He is very intelligent and assesses everything, no matter how trivial. Exhibits edgy, aggressive behavior. Self-centered with a gloomy personality and skewed sense of humor. Wants and needs emotional attachments but doesn't trust anyone enough to commit. Makes fast decisions without mistakes, the only difference being that Mercy Ann could never explain her decisions and Blake won't shut up about them."

"You think more highly of him than I thought."

John Justice nodded. "Yet, I had strong feelings for Mercy Ann and can't stand the sight of him."

"Maybe it has to do with the fact she's a girl," Rob suggested. "That can make a big difference."

"No, I'm sure that's not it."

Missa and Ashlyn hurried around the corner with a full cart looking back over their shoulders.

Ashlyn warned, "People at the cash registers are worked up about aliens in the store. A couple have guns out. Can you believe it?"

In the northern Iraqi oil city of Kirkuk, overrun the night before by Dictator-General Abd al-Bensi's armies, soldiers combed through neighborhoods plundering and deciding who lived or died. The circumstances that resulted in one group of soldiers sparing a household often led to its execution by another.

For instance, the daughters of one family did not scream and fight when soldiers dragged them into a back bedroom after threatening the parents' lives. A different group of soldiers executed the entire family and burned the house after accusing the girls of being whores when they tried to save their father and mother from brutal beatings by offering themselves again.

A few blocks away, a small unit of soldiers took a break and gathered around the group leader, Aasim, next to a packed dirt street. They took pictures of each other celebrating another easy victory, bragged about decisions to leave homes, families, and countries to join the cause of Abd al-Bensi, and ridiculed friends and family left behind for choosing cowardly, conventional lives. Proud of their status as warriors in a holy cause that no force on Earth could stop, they felt ready to defeat anyone foolish enough to stand against their might.

Outside the city to the south, sounds of al-Bensi fighter-bombers attacking retreating government forces echoed through the streets, and Aasim led his group's cheers. It was a small air force, but commanded Iraq's skies since America and its allies pulled out of the region.

Aasim spotted his commander's jeep approaching, hustled his men into a line, and stood at attention when he passed. It wasn't a requirement, but he was on his good side and wanted to keep it that way. When the vehicle disappeared around the corner, he ordered the men into the next neighborhood. It would not be wise to be here if the commander came by again.

Tom Patrick woke up in a strange bedroom with an old woman sitting on the edge of the bed watching him. She had on a big apron over the kind of dress that reminded him of PBS dramas again.

"Where am I?" he asked, perplexed.

She got up and left the room.

Then he noticed a man standing on the other side of the bed and nearly choked.

Blake offered him a glass of water. "You've been unconscious a long time."

Patrick was thirsty but refused to take it from this thug.

"I came across you and Rudy after you passed out," Blake explained. "Then all hell broke loose. Luckily, Honey Bee showed up. We'd been killed without her help."

"Who's Honey Bee?"

"She's under the covers with you."

Patrick's face twisted as he recognized Mercy Ann's doll. He flung her across the room. Although appearing soft and pliable, she made hard noises striking the wall and wood plank floor.

Blake ran and scooped her up. "Why'd you do that, you idiot?"

Patrick sat up. "What's your game, Blake?"

He placed Honey Bee on the bed gingerly. "She has a lump on her head and the neck feels as if it might be broken. Miss Flowers!"

The old woman appeared in the doorway and laughed. "That's enough, Honey Bee. Show them you're okay." When she didn't respond, Miss Flowers chided Tom. "If you know what's good for you, you'll apologize. You might want to give her back a little massage, too."

He looked at her as if she was crazy.

Miss Flowers gave shrugged. “Blake, let me know if you need help cleaning up the room if she decides to attack him. I’ll be downstairs until this is resolved.”

“You have to make friends with her,” Blake insisted.

“This is the alien house, isn’t it?”

“They brought you here to save your stupid life.”

“Where’s Mercy Ann? She’s the one I need.”

“Everyone except me believes she’s dead. Regardless who’s right, she’s not here.”

The news shook Patrick. He sagged forward, all fight gone.

“Honey Bee has been treating you. For God’s sake, make a friendly gesture to her. ”

After a long hesitation, Patrick edged his hand toward her, but stopped short and looked up at Blake. “This is nuts.”

The noise was sudden, loud, and electric. *Zzzt!*

Patrick jerked his hand back. “Ow! That stung all the way to my shoulder!”

Blake couldn’t stop laughing.

Honey Bee got to her feet, jumped onto Patrick’s lap, and stared up at him. Then she tried to climb the covers up to his chest, but kept slipping back.

Blake said, “It’s your life. Either help her up or die.”

Patrick moved his arm under her, laid back on the pillows, and closed his eyes

Honey Bee nodded to Blake.

The delegation of high-level visitors departed the disaster site for lunch at a swanky hotel before returning to Washington. They didn’t invite the general, so he decided to check the progress of relocating the coil cannons.

He asked the sergeant major to drive the staff car and rode in front because he could tell his friend had something important on his mind that he wanted to discuss. He knew better than to hurry him, but hoped he would take this opportunity to open up.

As they left a unit situating coil cannons into a hillside, the sergeant major said, “I’ve been thinking about the flying saucer.”

“Yeah, it’s hard not to.”

The sergeant major looked at him sidelong. “What do you know about the young woman who rescued us from the tent?”

“I thought you were unconscious the whole time.”

“I feared you might lie about it, so I put off asking rather than getting pissed off at you.”

"Do you remember anything else?"

"Quite a bit. What about you?"

"We're both too old for this shit," the general replied with a laugh. "Right after the girl showed up, we were onboard the flying saucer. Do you remember any of that?"

"Yes, but it's kind of fuzzy. Was our rescuer an alien?"

"No, but these matters not only concern aliens but a major conspiracy to overthrow our government. I know you're not afraid, but this stuff can get you killed. What do you want me to do?"

The sergeant major turned the car onto a side street and stopped. "What say we go sit on a porch and watch the sun set over the pyramids? You can smoke a cigar and tell me everything over cold beers."

"Sounds great, but where do we get beer?"

"I stuck the big cooler in the trunk."

"This is Esmé calling Mercy Ann. Esmé calling Mercy Ann."

John Justice, eating spaghetti with meat sauce Ashlyn made for dinner, dropped a forkful of pasta in his lap, leaving a trail of sauce down the front of his favorite sports shirt. Then he just sat there shaking and staring down at the mess.

"John Justice, take deep breaths and calm down," Miss Flowers ordered. "Blake, run up to his room and get a clean shirt. Everyone else, help him clean up until he snaps out of it."

Ashlyn unbuttoned his shirt and pulled it off. Missa wiped his face, neck, and chest, finishing just as Blake dashed in with a shirt on a hanger.

John Justice stood up suddenly. "I can't wear that shirt with these shorts."

Blake looked as if he might twist the shirt around John Justice's neck and choke him, but then he held it up. "This is good-looking."

Missa agreed, "Wow, it is!"

"Vice Commander Esmé calling with an emergency. Mercy Ann, I know you're receiving this. Stop playing games! Emergency!"

John Justice came out of his funk suddenly. He looked around as if gathering facts to explain the situation then allowed Missa to help him on with the shirt. He motioned for silence.

"Esmé, can you hear me now?" he said firmly.

The reply was sarcastic. "You had your communications muted, John Justice."

"We've experienced glitches in the system lately and I've been running maintenance checklists trying to isolate the problem. Can't believe it was something so trivial that..."

"There is an emergency! Put Mercy Ann on."

"She will not return from her mission until tomorrow."

"Then put me in contact with her. Emergency!"

"She ordered communications silence. What's wrong?"

"I can't wait to hear her story this time. It will be creative, I'm sure."

John Justice did not comment.

"Have it your way then. Inform her that Gargle ships are headed towards Earth."

"How many?"

"Two."

John Justice waited, growing annoyed. "Where are they, Esmé? What is the heading? What kind of ships?"

Finally, she answered. "Well, they're at the limits of our scanners, so the readings are a bit iffy, except they are definitely on a general course towards Earth. I wanted to give Mercy Ann as much warning as possible. That's why I called."

John Justice smirked. "They're probably probes to pinpoint her location. They haven't done that in a while."

"I just wanted to give advance notice because you're so far away on your own, but with Mercy Ann, that should have no problem. Esmé out."

Missa asked, "Are the aliens' name spelled same as the word for gargling your throat?"

Miss Flowers snorted. "Mercy Ann called them that because of how their language sounds. The real name is unpronounceable."

"Shouldn't you tell Esmé about Mercy Ann's death so she can provide help if we need it?" Rob asked.

John Justice shook his head. "I keep telling you that if she knew Mercy Ann was dead, she'd order us to leave Earth. The two ships she sighted aren't anywhere close to being a threat. She just wanted to talk to Mercy Ann."

Missa was curious. "Were they friends?"

John Justice shrugged. "Sometimes."

14

Pills, Burgers, and a Grenade

On day nineteen of the Sufficiency Test, the President of the United States took his seat in the White House conference room at 5 a.m. Many of the attendees had not slept for more than twenty-four hours. Impatience and irritation simmered and boiled as people presented bleary-eyed assessments and championed recommendations their departments and agencies deemed best for the country and themselves.

The conspirators, led by the Chairman of the Joint Chiefs, proposed justifications for military action to seize Egypt's Giza Plateau for America. Although expecting arguments, the fierceness of the opposition caught them by surprise.

Finally, the Chairman, realizing they didn't have enough support to sway the President, brought up another matter the conspirators wanted adopted—leaving soldiers in place when they destroyed the alien site in LA. He pointed out that the coil cannons only destroyed the target, not the surroundings.

The President refused. "I want everyone outside the buffer zone when we attack."

The Chairman forced a smile. "Outside it? Why?"

"Why not?" the President responded. "If something goes wrong again, our people will be well out of harm's way."

The smile stayed on the Chairman's face, but he smelled a rat. Had the President found out details of the conspiracy's plan somehow? It wouldn't be surprising given the number of people involved, but if someone had leaked information, it might force them to seize control of the government by force rather than pushing the President out of office by legitimate means. Soon as this meeting ended, he'd contact Handley and find out how he wanted to proceed.

The discussion turned to Abd al-Bensi's incursion into Iraq. The President expressed concern that the attackers were doing so well he might have to send in US forces sooner than he wanted.

The Chairman, watching reactions of people in the room, thought it might be time for al-Bensi to suffer a few minor setbacks to get the President to calm down. He'd have to talk to Handley about that, too.

The President unexpectedly returned to the subject of the Giza Plateau with an announcement that the German archaeologists who discovered the object in the ground had been detained "for their protection" by American intelligence. Meanwhile, the Egyptian military and citizen mobs continued fighting for control of the site because of rumors about treasure. No one other than the United States suspected the structure was of alien origin. Consequently, we would continue monitoring the situation and not interfere unless circumstances changed.

"By then, it will be too late," the Chairman warned, glad for the chance to resume the argument. "Who knows what kind of weapons or technology they may find?"

"We're talking about something constructed thousands of years ago," the President responded, aggravated to keep hearing the same argument. "Why would intelligent beings leave technology behind for primitive people to discover?"

The Chairman lost his cool. "We're not primitive, damn it!"

The President had set him up. "I meant civilizations at the time, not modern man, general. Please remember who your boss is."

The Chairman backpedaled. "My apology, sir. It was a long night."

Tight-jawed, the President told everyone to get back to work and left the room briskly.

Tasked with scouring the internet for pictures and videos of John Justice and Mercy Ann that might suggest a new story angle, a college intern working in the offices of a cable news show for the summer realized they just wanted him out of the way. The show's host had made it clear how much she disliked him.

In a cubicle using the computer of one of the show's researchers, he clicked on a program titled *Advanced Face, Eye, and Body Match Tool.* Even he knew programs of this type were highly unreliable though widely used, but had no other ideas to try.

He dropped in a head shot of John Justice and hit the match button. Then he went to the bathroom, stopped by the breakroom to grab a soft drink, and finished it before the results came up. Realizing he should have limited the search to the last month and specified gender, he started to delete everything then looked up at the clock and realized he had two long hours to go.

Just for the hell of it, he sorted the pictures oldest to newest and scanned through them, stopping occasionally to laugh or check out a pretty girl long since dead. He was losing interest reaching the mid-1960s.

The hair and clothes were a riot. Group shots of wild-looking bands were especially fascinating. Alone in the office, he hit links and listened to samples of songs, blown away by how great some of them were.

The phone on the desk buzzed. An associate producer wanted the researcher. When the intern said everyone was with the show's host, the man switched off rudely. He slammed the phone down and grabbed the mouse to close the program. A full color picture, sharper and brighter than others on the page, caught his eye and stopped his hand.

A young boy, the spitting image of John Justice except for longer hair, stood on a crowded sidewalk in front of an old building making a peace sign with his fingers. He wore a tie-dyed t-shirt, bellbottom jeans, and suede boots.

"It can't be him," the intern said, although his eyes argued otherwise.

A pretty girl stood not far away, part of her face obscured by the arm of a gesturing passerby. She seemed to be staring at something down the street. Her long, braided blond hair hung in front of one shoulder, identical to many of Mercy Ann's pictures. Her sandals, ragged jeans embroidered with flowers, and faded denim jacket with sleeves over the hands so only fingertips showed, did nothing to identify her.

He enlarged the photo, surprised by its resolution. A caption stamped on the bottom right hand corner stated, Hippies, Haight-Ashbury, 1967. He guessed the smudged second line with the image of a bird next to it was a photographer or studio name. The researchers might be able to identify it. If so, there could be other pictures or a whole series.

But all that could wait. He saved a copy to file then printed one at the highest resolution the office printer could handle. Grabbing it coming out, he ran to interrupt the meeting with the host. She might not like him, but with this, she might have a major scoop and offer him a permanent job.

Sheri wanted a pain pill.

Brandi told her to wait two more hours.

Sheri complained her arm hurt too much.

Brandi warned if she didn't stop the theatrics, she'd push her out of the car and have lunch alone.

Sheri snapped back that she was not speaking to her for the rest of the day.

Brandi told her she couldn't be quiet five minutes, much less a whole day.

Sheri made no reply.

After a couple of minutes, Brandi asked, "How did you get your legs up under you like that?"

Other than a sullen glare, Sheri didn't answer.

"Really, how'd you get in that position with the seatbelt tight around you?"

Sheri gave her the finger.

"Never mind. It's a relief having you quiet for a change."

That's all it took. "I can get my legs under me because I'm slim and in good shape. Repeat after me: thunder thighs."

"What are you, six years old?"

"My arm has a heart of its own, going throb...throb...throb. How about a little sympathy? How about one little pill?"

"You'll get regular dosages, so shut up about it."

"God, I hate you!"

Brandi swerved to the curb and stopped. "Do you want to walk the rest of the way?"

She put on her pouty little girl face. "Please, don't make Sheri walk, Brandi."

The car squealed from the curb, roared down the block, and turned too fast into a mostly empty restaurant parking lot, scaring a family climbing into a minivan as they barreled by. Skidding into a parking place, they stopped scant inches from the car in front of them.

Dad from the minivan was a big guy. He stomped over to their vehicle and yelled in Brandi's face. Then he stomped back to his waiting family, where he received a hero's greeting. He gunned the minivan as they left the lot, but the engine was so underpowered that it was comical.

Sheri giggled. "Can't believe you just sat there and took all that from a bozo bully."

"Can't blame him for being upset since he had kids. Come on, let's go eat."

"Can't."

"Why not? What's wrong?"

"My legs are asleep. Can't feel them at all. Come help me get out, please."

Cursing, Brandi slammed the door and went around to the passenger side. But then, as she leaned in pulling Sheri's legs from under her, she felt a pistol barrel against the back of her head and froze.

A man reached around, pulled up her loose shirt, and removed a pistol from its holster. At the same time, a big man opened the driver's door, slid into the seat, and jammed a gun into Sheri's ribs.

"Sharpshooters have beads on you," Brandi's assailant said, "so if we wanted to kill you, you'd be dead already. We have a business offer to discuss. Interested?"

Brandi recognized his voice as their contact go-between. "Nothing we'd rather do."

"In that case," Sheri said with a little giggle, "I have a gun to surrender and don't want to surprise a jumpy sniper or the guy next to me. How should I give it to you, sir?"

The go-between tensed. "The shooters can hear every word we're saying. Just take it out slowly and hand it over."

Sheri grinned up past Brandi at him. "Uh, it's in my hand about two inches from your nuts."

He leaned back, looked down, and saw her reaching through Brandi's legs holding a tiny pistol. "They're surrendering the gun, so no one shoot," he ordered. "Now, just drop it, girly."

"You'd better take it," Sheri replied sweetly. "I call her Little Bitch because of a hair-trigger that goes off if someone breathes on it too hard, and being called girly makes me twitchy. You'd better take it, but be careful."

Gingerly, he reached down, took the pistol, and put the safety on. "Why in the hell carry a piece of crap like this?"

"I have a cute scar on my left breast," Sheri answered with a shrug. "Little Bitch put a hole in his eye before he got off a second shot off. Hey, if you're interested, maybe you and I could hookup some night. I'll show you all my scars if you buy me an expensive dinner."

He handed her the pistol back. "Just shut up and put this toy away."

She laid the pistol on the console. "Goes up my sleeve, but can't fit it back in the holder without my other hand. Imagine you're curious how I got the drop on you. Used to work south of the border as a magician's assistant hiding rabbits in hats between gigs as a knife thrower's assistant. Of course, my real goal back then was to become a standup comic. That's why I can show you some real neat sleight of hand when we go out, if you get my meaning. I'll tell you great dirty jokes at the same time, if that's your thing. What do you say?"

The man pulled Brandi backwards out of the car. "Does she ever shut up?"

"This is quiet for her. How do you want to do this?"

"You sit in the driver's seat and we'll get in back. If either of you moves a wrong way, the shooters will take you out."

Once situated, he asked, "Have you had encounters with the aliens other than when the boy took the nurse from you in the mall?"

Brandi wasn't surprised he knew about it since it was all over the internet. "No."

He addressed the next question to Sheri. "What happened when you disappeared? Give me all the details from when the boy grabbed you in the mall. Don't leave anything out."

She gave a big, exaggerated nod. "A pale blond boy ran into me then I was in the sea underneath Huntington Beach Pier. A sexy surfer with long black hair caught my eye, allowing a vicious wave to catch me unawares. Slammed into wood pilings, my arm broke in three places, but it was worth it. Even now, when I close my eyes, I see that tall, erect surfer and imagine how it would be going out with you. What if we...?"

The man snarled, "Stop the bullshit! How long did it take to get to the beach from the mall? Keep the answers short or I'm going to put a bullet in you."

"Less than a blink of the eye."

"Did you feel any different?"

"I was dry then I was wet."

Glaring, the man turned his attention to Brandi. "How do you put up with her?"

"She has her moments."

"They must be spectacular," he responded sharply. "Anyway, the big boss wants you working for us exclusively after the way you dealt with our people at the hotel and seeing you with the alien boy. He wants you to infiltrate the site and find out everything you can about him. Pay is a hundred grand upfront with future payments based on what you find out. What do you say?"

Brandi glanced at Sheri as though wanting to find out what she thought, but the real purpose was to see what weapon she had fished out of the brace during her gabfest since neither of them had used the code word to stand down.

It was a hand grenade. Held tightly between her legs. With a finger ready to jerk out the pin.

Sheri said, "Let me get this straight. Instead of killing us for failing to get the nurse and taking out your hit team, your boss wants to give us money to gather information about the alien. After the way the kid made fools of us at the mall, why would he do that?"

The man chuckled. "There's more. Anyone who delivers an alien dead or alive will get a million dollar bonus."

Brandi whistled. "How do we get into the restricted area?"

"We'll provide military uniforms, IDs, and badges for full access."

"It's a deal," Brandi said.

The man's phone dinged. "The money is your account."

After the men left, Brandi helped Sheri out of the car. "It could have been an interesting negotiation if things went bad."

Sheri shrugged. "If you got to go, might as well go out with a bang."

"Yeah, it was a good call. You agree that this new deal is bullshit and they still plan to kill us when the job is finished, right?"

"Yeah," Sheri answered thoughtfully. "They had to know this was our destination when we left the hotel, too. Either our room or the car is bugged."

Brandi nodded. "I don't know how they found us, but guess it doesn't matter. They may have bugs planted in the restaurant, too. We'll have to have to ask for a different place than the one they offer or watch what we say."

Sheri sighed. "Take what they give us. I'll continue the blabbering idiot act. Wouldn't do for them to realize I have all the brains in this outfit."

Brandi held the door and smacked her rear as she went in. "Your brain is getting flabby from eating too many pancakes, honeybunch."

Sitting on a folding chair eating supper off a camp table in the shade of the Sphinx, the general watched Bongo gulping down dog food. "That dog has it better than we do."

The sergeant major agreed, "Yeah, he's pretty content."

The general stared out at the tall house between the pyramids and thought about Mercy Ann going halfway around the world to prove a point only to end up dying. "Did you know the man who came to see me this morning?"

"No, but the captain said he was a brigadier general assigned to NATO. Figured you'd tell me if I needed to know more."

The general lit a cigar stub, leaned back, and closed his eyes. "I attended West Point with him. He was athletic, brilliant, and ambitious. Everyone expected him to rise straight to the top, but he always came up short of expectations and fell behind over the years. We weren't close friends, nor have we ever served together. Yet, out of the blue, he showed up here to pass along a warning that if I don't toe the line and do as told, I'll suffer consequences."

"He threatened you?"

"Same as. He promised that I'll be promoted next cycle and receive a Vice Presidency in a big corporation when I retire. The deal includes enough stock to make me rich. Even offered a lifetime membership in a highfalutin country club that doesn't admit riffraff like you and me normally."

The sergeant major mulled it over. "Was that when the ruckus started?"

"Yeah. I kept knocking him down until he stopped trying to get up."

"Some of the men said he made nasty threats."

"He lost it and let slip the conspirators have another way to destroy the aliens. When he realized what he'd said, he couldn't get out of here fast enough."

"Do you believe him?"

"I did some checking," the general replied, very grim. "They sent six additional coil cannons to Los Angeles with the ones Handley Industries delivered to us. I suspect they're set up outside the buffer zone ready to attack."

"If that's the case, they'll have the same problems we did getting a clear line of sight between the pyramids, which means they had to relocate. Hiding weapons that large will be easier in tall buildings than outside on hills. We can narrow it down and find them. Then we'll take them out."

The general shook his head. "I can't send soldiers into downtown for a military operation without coordinating with local authorities and headquarters. The conspirators are bound to hear about it and attack the site before we get to them."

"What'll we do then?"

The general hesitated. "What if I ask John Justice for help? Do you have objections?"

"Don't tell me you have a way to contact him."

"Yes, but I haven't tried it. John Justice, can you hear me?"

The boy's voice came from thin air. "Yes sir. Is something wrong?"

After the general explained the dilemma, he apologized and said he couldn't interfere if Handley's people intended to attack the house with the cannons, but some of the people he'd given temporary sanctuary might be able to help. He'd send them to the general's quarters for a meeting.

Dubious this odd collection of people could help, the general explained what they needed then began changing his mind when Blake asked, "Were the cannons transported to the site intact?"

"They arrived in big wooden crates," he answered, puzzled by the question. "Technicians assembled them onsite."

"Were they transported by military trucks, by the company that made them, or a commercial trucking firm?" Blake asked.

"Straight from the factory on Handley trucks," the sergeant major replied. "That probably makes it impossible to get more information."

Undeterred, Blake asked, "Was special equipment or manpower required to offload them?"

The sergeant major explained that the crates required special heavy-duty forklifts with people trained to operate them. Handley technicians unpacked them after the temporary help departed.

After going outside to make calls, Blake reported, "They used the same forklifts and personnel to deliver more crates to two locations downtown. Yesterday, they relocated them. As soon as the owner returns to the office, we'll have addresses. Should be within the hour."

"Is everything that easy for you?" Tom Patrick asked.

"Getting all that with a couple of calls was sheer luck," Blake answered. "I know people who served in the Middle East who are proficient with this kind of operation, but they don't come cheap."

"John Justice showed me a room full of money in the ship that belonged to Mercy Ann," Rob said. "He probably won't mind us using it."

Missa said she and Rob would go, too.

"Meaning no offense," Blake replied, "but this requires professionals."

Reddening, Missa demanded to know why Blake thought he had the right to decide everything.

The sergeant major pointed out that this would be a commando type operation against mercenaries and criminals, and no place for amateurs.

Realizing the sergeant major intended to participate, the general said, "The shit will hit the fan if anyone recognizes you."

"I'll cover my face and wear gloves," he responded. "If I'm a casualty, the others will have to get my body out."

For the first time, everyone realized the seriousness of the mission.

Rob asked, "Can't it be done without hurting people?"

"No," Blake answered. "This will be for keeps."

"I served in the Rangers during the Iraq War," Tom said, "so I'll go. I know some of the men Blake means, too. They're perfect, assuming they haven't hired out to the other side already."

"Just like that?" Blake asked, surprised he didn't object.

Tom shrugged. "I think the sergeant major should be in charge."

Everyone agreed.

Missa still wanted to go. "What if the cannons are located at several sites? You'll need someone with knowledge of their operations at every location."

"You don't need an expert to smash and blow things up," Blake replied.

She shook her head. "Once they begin charging, you'll get a blowback of energy sufficient to level a city block if you don't know what you're doing."

The sergeant major asked how she could possibly know that.

"I heard the cannons revving up and firing in Death Valley. When I saw the videos of Mercy Ann in the battle, I realized they load enormous amounts of energy on the coils then release it at a target. The potential for explosions if the process is interrupted is obvious."

"Everything she said is exactly correct," the sergeant major confirmed, impressed by her.

"Which proves Rob and I are needed," Missa replied, a little too pleased with herself.

Blake turned to Ashlyn and asked what she thought about them going.

"They're older than their years and can decide for themselves. Just promise you'll watch out for them."

"I don't want Blake thinking he needs to babysit me!" Missa responded sharply.

"No worry there," Blake answered with a grin. "I'm afraid to get close to you."

Rudy Johnson flipped sizzling burger patties on the grill, plopped on cheddar cheese, and stepped out of the charcoal smoke while it melted. Seventies funk played on the patio porch speakers and he swayed and shuffled his feet in time, not quite dancing.

Rudy's son, Zach, sat in the shallow end of the pool with his wife. His brother, Thomas, slept in a chaise on the covered patio, half a bottle of beer clutched upright in one hand on his stomach. It had been the last in the cooler and his wife had gone to buy more.

Rudy announced it was time to eat and Zach protested getting out of the pool, bringing a quick warning from his mother. Thomas sat up, automatically raised the bottle to his lips, and drained it before he was awake fully.

Then he called to Rudy, "Isn't Juanita back yet?"

"No man, she just left."

He got up and stretched. "I'll go take the lid off the crockpot and put the potato salad out. We can zap a burger in the microwave for Juanita when she gets back."

Rudy felt obliged to wait. "I can keep them hot on the grill. Shouldn't be more than ten minutes or so."

"Nah, they'll dry out," Thomas answered, going into the kitchen.

They had just begun eating when Juanita called because someone rear-ended her at a stoplight. Rudy offered to go with his brother, but no one was hurt and the cops were already there, so he said to stay and eat.

Rudy waited until he heard his brother pull out of the drive. "You sure you're okay staying here, Elena?"

She glanced to make certain Zach wasn't paying attention. "Juanita's sweet as can be and Thomas wouldn't notice an elephant sleeping in the family room long as it isn't in his recliner. Not that I'm criticizing, mind you."

"No need to explain," Rudy said, shaking his head. "Thomas lives in his own world. Wonder sometimes how Juanita puts up with him."

A short time later, Elena answered a polite knock on the patio door. A boy she didn't know stared up at her, yet he looked familiar for some reason. He carried a small canvas backpack slung over one shoulder. His clothes—baseball cap, t-shirt, and shorts—were just right for Southern California, but his pale skin was not.

"What can I do for you?" she asked, irritated to be disturbed at mealtime.

"May I please speak with your husband, ma'am?"

Elena thought it odd a boy addressed her as an adult salesperson would. "You must want my brother-in-law, whose house this is. Are you raising money for something?"

"I want Rudy, not Thomas."

Raised to believe children should not call adults by first names, Elena made certain her son followed the rule and never hesitated to correct other children. Yet, something about this boy made her hesitate and take a quick look to see if Zach knew him, only to find her son gaping with a mouth full of food.

"Zachariah Johnson," she declared, "close your mouth when eating. What's gotten into you?"

As a rule, Zach obeyed his mother immediately, but this was an emergency. He spat the food out into his hand.

"Momma," he cried excitedly, "he's John Justice, the alien!"

Elena only half-heard as she charged the table to correct her son's audacious lapse of manners.

Wide-eyed, Zach dropped the wad of food on the table, grabbed his tablet, and tapped the screen. As she reached for him, he held it up.

"Look, Momma!" he yelled frantically. "John Justice! Look!"

She grabbed it from his hands then whipped around to face Rudy, shouting her name. He was in the doorway, staring wide-eyed at the strange boy.

She realized at once that Rudy knew him. "What's going on?"

"I'll explain in a minute. John Justice, is something wrong?"

He did not take his eyes from Elena. "We should speak in private, Rudy."

She did not like that one bit. Nor did she believe her son's assertion this slight boy could be one of the horrible aliens that had the world in turmoil. Furthermore, she came from a long line of women who could shake a house with their voice.

"Young man," she scolded, pointing a forefinger at John Justice, "if you can interrupt my family during dinner, you can speak your business in front of me!"

Rarely did Rudy speak sharply to his wife. "Elena, sit down and allow me to find out what John Justice wants. It must be important for him to come here this way."

Astounded that her husband spoke forcefully and knew an alien to boot, she sat and crossed her arms, an indication that he had better have good reasons for all this.

Seated across the table from Rudy and his family, John Justice reached into the backpack and lifted out Honey Bee, but hesitated giving her to Zach, holding his arms out across the table for her.

"I apologize for showing up with no warning," he said, avoiding eye contact with Elena, "but this may be the only opportunity to give Zach a follow up exam. Our situation in Los Angeles has become very complicated of late."

Elena demanded of her husband, "Exam? What's he mean?"

"The aliens cured Zach's leukemia," he responded sheepishly.

She looked back and forth between him and John Justice, unable to say more.

John Justice handed Honey Bee across the table to Zach, who carried her to the sofa and stretched out, hugging her to his chest. Then he was asleep.

Hurrying to him, Elena checked that he was all right then whipped around and pointed at Honey Bee. "That thing moved!"

"I should have introduced Honey Bee," John Justice answered, nervousness making his voice quaver. "She's struggling to adjust to Mercy Ann's death, but insisted coming to do Zach's checkup."

Elena recognized John Justice's grief and difficulty speaking to her. "Please accept my condolences for your loss. I know how hard it can be."

John Justice looked her in the eyes finally. "Thank you."

Rudy asked, "You have another reason for being here, don't you, John Justice?"

"The military plans to attack us tomorrow. You shouldn't go to work."

"What about other people in harm's way?" Rudy asked.

"We'll do all we can, but we can't protect everyone if it's a worst case scenario."

Conversation was awkward after that until John Justice said, "Honey Bee has finished. She says Zach's illness will not return."

A loud sob escaped Elena.

John Justice walked around the table and patted her shoulder. "Rudy and Zach are lucky to have someone so charming in their lives. It has been a real pleasure meeting you."

Elena stared dumfounded at the empty space where John Justice disappeared until finding her voice finally. "How old is that boy?"

Rudy knew he had to tell Elena about compatibility and all that transpired with aliens, but decided to wait and allow her to savor the miracle of her son's cure today. "He says twelve, but I think he's much older."

"I'm sure you're right. Wow."

Tom Patrick's bedroom door was open, but Miss Flowers waited for him to ask her in. She carried a small tray with a teapot, cups on saucers, and a plate of little cakes.

With a slight smile, she said, "If it is convenient, I need to discuss something with you."

Surprised because they'd hardly spoken, he jumped to his feet and asked her to sit on the settee that shared a small coffee table with his chair. "Tea was thoughtful."

Pouring, she seemed more reserved and mannered than downstairs. "It's green, so it won't keep you awake. How do you feel?"

"The best since the incident occurred."

"John Justice wants me to explain the nature of your illness and offer choices, but keep in mind that medicine is not an area of expertise for either of us. Honey Bee can explain in more detail if you wish, but Mercy Ann was the one who diagnosed your injuries and prescribed treatment."

"Surely someone so young wasn't a doctor?"

"Mercy Ann's aptitude for medical functions was unusually elevated and her primary job in the fleet initially. Later, when they discovered she could use advanced systems and weaponry, she would not agree to them unless she could keep the medical modules. It complicated her conversion to combat status, but she got her way as usual. Do my explanations make sense?"

"Systems are installed based on an individual's abilities without regard to age."

Hiding her amusement that perceived age concerned him so much, she wondered if it was because he had been interested in Mercy Ann for a relationship or because Earthlings equated abilities, wisdom, and intelligence with physical aging. Most unenhanced humanoid civilizations she encountered made that mistake because their lifespans were so short, so she didn't fault them.

"The point is," she explained, "Mercy Ann was topnotch in the field of medicine, even after conversion to combat."

"Please, just tell me what's wrong with me."

She chose the words carefully. "The Sufficiency Test's containment area experienced minor fluctuations when it reacted to the first attack, allowing miniscule matter disintegrators to stray outside the prescribed boundaries, enter your body, and harm you. They are undetectable by your science."

"I don't understand."

She tried again. "The house reacts to attacks by releasing machines so small that they're invisible to your science. In the first reaction, a few strayed outside the defined area and found their way into your body. Since their primary purpose is to disintegrate matter, they're causing internal damage."

He blanched. "Okay, please go on."

"They're not supposed to remain intact inside an organism, yet they're still operating. Honey Bee says she never encountered an instance such as this before."

"Is that causing the jabbing pains and crawling sensations?"

His self-control impressed her. "Not directly. Mercy Ann had Honey Bee inject parasites to consume dead tissue and attack foreign matter. She hoped they would destroy the disintegrators, but they've proven too durable. They also create so much dead tissue that the parasites engorge beyond their maximum rate of defecation, which causes them to become bloated and blow apart. That process accounts for the pain and crawling sensations."

He understood but didn't want to think about it. "Can anything else be done?"

"Honey Bee uses the medical machines to stop the disintegrators from migrating to parts of the body that will kill you and keeps adding parasites to replace the dead ones. She's keeping you alive, but it isn't a long-term solution. You have to leave Earth with us and have surgery at our next destination or remain behind and wait to die. She estimates you won't last a year."

Tom had always considered himself a no-nonsense, stick to the facts kind of guy, but he was nothing compared to Miss Flowers. "If I have the surgery, can I come back to Earth to live?"

"No. They'll replace parts of your body, which means you'll have a plethora of alien technology inside. We'll help you establish a new life somewhere else since we're responsible."

"This is grim news."

"Yes, but on the bright side, it may not matter because you could be killed when you go on the mission in town." She cackled.

In spite of the dire circumstances, he couldn't help liking the ornery old woman. "You've got a warped sense of humor, Miss Flowers."

The night DJ gave the news in a hushed monotone:

> "World leaders today continued trying to cope with riots and mass hysteria after the announcement by the President that aliens are behind recent events in Glenwood Heights.
>
> "At the same time, complaints continue that the US has not allowed other countries access to the site or

provided information beyond promising disclosure after the threat is eradicated. The President of Russia accused the US of stalling so we can secure alien technology and secure military advantage over other countries, a suspicion expressed by others.

"Meanwhile, the forces of Dictator-General Abd al-Bensi moved to attack the Iraqi towns of Mosul and Erbil amidst reports of mass slaughters in oil rich Kirkuk. Al-Bensi will control the entire northern area of the country in a few days unless America intervenes, an action the President is reluctant to order because the American people strongly oppose involvement. Many in the Congress hold the opposite view, renewing warnings that al-Bensi will continue aggression into other countries if we don't stop him soon, which the White House labeled as hysteria and warmongering.

"In local news, outbreaks of looting and protests continue in California cities, though not to the extent seen in other places around the globe. The governor called for patience and activated more National Guard troops to help police keep order.

"Day twenty of the alien standoff begins in an hour. If you have someone to love nearby, time to get started. If not, DIY. Sleep tight, Los Angeles."

15

John Justice Takes Charge

ALONE IN THE QUIET KITCHEN BEFORE DAWN making a cup of tea, John Justice thought of Mercy Ann and pent-up emotions overwhelmed him. His distress was so great that he grabbed onto the counter to keep from falling to his knees. Hanging his head down between his arms, his breath came in gasps.

One of the internal alarms he had set buzzed for attention. He listened to an encrypted phone call to Jared Handley from a woman with a Japanese accent. She told him that the FBI Director and his wife had died in a staged robbery made to look as if they came home, surprised a burglar, and all three died in a shootout. Then she said another team had given the DHS Secretary an experimental drug that caused a fatal heart attack. It was undetectable in his system and no one would be too surprised, given his medical history.

Handley was very pleased hearing the news. Losing his closest friend in government would devastate the President, and having the Deputy Secretary move up to run DHS cleared the last hurdle for the conspiracy to carry out his plans. He told the woman how much he appreciated her work.

She thanked him, said she loved him, and hung up.

Still hanging onto the counter, John Justice did not have time to think about the incongruity of the woman's last statement because he received an interstellar communication just as it ended.

"Esmé calling Mercy Ann. Emergency."

Forcing himself to stand, he made a labored response. "Go ahead, Esmé."

"You do not sound well, John Justice."

"I just completed a jogging exercise to improve stamina."

Her response took several seconds. "I see what you mean from definitions on the translator, but it is not necessary for you to waste time with those kinds of things, is it?"

He'd just made it up and stifled a laugh. How absurd that a call from Esmé lifted his spirits, he thought. He asked about the emergency.

She surprised him by not demanding to speak to Mercy Ann. "We've detected more Gargle ships approaching your system from various directions. They're much closer and the courses indicate a rendezvous near Earth's moon. I sent the information to you."

So much for feeling better. "How many?"

"Five pairs."

John Justice pulled up the data and studied it.

Suddenly, Esmé said, "If you have the chance, tell Mercy Ann that I'm sorry if I did something to upset her. End transmission."

John Justice didn't think the ships would come closer to Earth than the Moon unless they detected his ship, which was unlikely if it remained on the ground at low power. He turned his attention to a contentious meeting raging in the White House Situation Room.

The President had instructed no one to notify the Chairman of the Joint Chiefs or Deputy Secretary of DHS about the early morning meeting he convened because the FBI Director had told him yesterday they were top echelon members of the conspiracy. Somehow, they found out and attended anyway.

Since the President couldn't accuse them without the evidence the FBI Director promised to provide, he had concocted a plan to find his own upon hearing of his death. He had a list of lesser conspirators and ordered them picked up. Security people loyal to him felt certain someone would turn against the conspiracy leaders once subjected to hard questioning. All they needed was two or three days.

At the same time, the President felt certain the media would give the Chairman of the Joint Chiefs credit for wiping out the aliens if he went ahead with the attack as planned, so he'd decided to chance postponing it until he had proof the Chairman was a traitor. Then he'd take the conspiracy down, destroy the aliens, and take all the credit in one fell swoop. That was why he hadn't wanted the Chairman and DHS Deputy in the meeting this morning.

Sure enough, the Chairman rallied opposition against the President, who didn't have any new reasons for delaying the attack again. Very quickly, the situation spun out of the President's control.

John Justice had an idea. He transported to the ship's operations room.

Minutes later, as dawn brightened on Los Angeles, John Justice was back at the table dipping a donut in a fresh cup of tea when President stopped the meeting to take a call. Then he announced the aliens had placed messages on the pyramids in LA and adjourned the meeting to give everyone a chance to evaluate the meanings. He left the Chairman fuming.

John Justice went to the sink and stared out the window. Zooming his vision, he watched soldiers dismantling equipment and loading trucks at the command post. He admired how they worked hard while laughing and joking so casually. He wanted to hear them and activated micro machines in the air around them.

Mostly, the conversations consisted of explicit threats about what they would do if they caught the freak alien boy and even coarser comments about Mercy Ann. Sickened, John Justice switched them off.

Rob came up through a hatch on a warehouse roof in an industrial area near downtown and looked through binoculars at the pyramids, awash in early morning sunshine.

Blake, who arranged for them to use the building, was on the roof familiarizing himself with the roads in and out of the area. "Did something happen?"

"John Justice wrote messages on the two big pyramids to give the President a reason to delay the attack. One says, 'Chimps = War, Bonobos = Peace.' The other says, 'Mankind = ?'"

"Why would that stop them?" Blake asked, skeptical.

"Got me, but John Justice said the President was desperate for any excuse."

"John Justice may be as good a leader as Mercy Ann was," Blake replied thoughtfully.

Rob looked at him with surprise. "That's the first time you've spoken of her in the past tense."

"Slip of the tongue, that's all. She's not dead."

There was no point arguing. "By the way, John Justice said the two women who went after my mother will be with the people guarding the cannons."

"Then they'll probably be killed."

"You'd shoot a woman?" Rob asked self-righteously.

"That's a strange question. Are you thinking you might want to have children with them?"

The ridiculous comment surprised Rob. "That has nothing to do with killing them!"

"What is it then? I imagine you espouse equality between the sexes or Missa wouldn't be your girlfriend. Male or female, they're professional killers. If you can't understand that, you have no business in a fight. Is that clear?"

His fierceness shook Rob and all he could manage was a nod, although he didn't know if he could kill anyone, whether it be man or woman.

Blake could tell. "We'd better go down. The sergeant major wants to put us through a couple of dry runs."

Miss Flowers came into the kitchen, turned on a viewing screen, and watched soldiers evacuating the buffer zone. Eyeing her, John Justice took a long sip from his fifth cup of tea, told her about Esmé's call, and explained why he didn't think they had any choice but to sit tight.

"Something else is bothering you. What is it?"

She could always tell. "Do you think I should stop the assassins I told you about from guarding the cannons?"

"If you want to recruit them, you have no choice, do you?"

"A problem has arisen that complicates matters."

She sighed. "What did you find out about them?"

"They were involved in the deaths of Missa's parents."

"You said her parents were casualties of the Sufficiency Test."

"I discovered the conspirators included them on the lists to cover-up their murders. I don't know if Brandi and Sheri did the actual killing, though. If not, maybe it won't be that big of deal."

"Don't be ridiculous, John Justice. You can't have them on a ship with Missa, Rob, and Ashlyn. They'll try to kill each other if the truth comes out. Moreover, it'd be immoral of us not to tell them about something so important."

"Skilled people who meet our all our requirements are difficult to find," he answered, although it sounded half-hearted. "If we're to have any chance at all of holding out without Mercy Ann, we need more ships and crews."

"Even so, you can't hide this from Missa. We're better than that, aren't we?"

He stared then nodded. "Yes."

"Have you ranked everyone in the order of importance to you? Do you think anyone will decline to join?"

He surprised her. "I want Sheri, Brandi, Missa, Rob, and Ashlyn, in that order, but each one has unique talents. The ship's program predicts all of them will choose to go."

"How about Blake?" she asked, expecting an argument.

Distaste clouded his face. "I didn't rank him because he far exceeds the others in potential, and that's assuming he doesn't have any of Mercy Ann's abilities. He's exceptional in all regards, except for his character."

She was not about to cut him any slack. "You don't fault your Brandi and Sheri assassins for murdering people. They're worse than Blake."

He gave her a sly smile. "Yes, but have you seen how they look? I mean, come on."

She laughed. "You're incorrigible, commander. Do you think Blake will join once he accepts that Mercy Ann is dead?"

"Yes."

She regarded him thoughtfully. "Do you realize how much more mature and sharper your thinking has become since she left us?"

"I don't think that has anything to do with it, at least not directly."

"From the day she showed up, that girl did everything possible to make you interested in her. She thought if she could win over the fleet commander, no one would stand in her way for promotions and assignments. Later, after your status changed, she blew you off and made you dependent on her for every little thing. It was her way or no way. Surely, you realize that now."

Speaking of these matters troubled John Justice. "Without helping each other, neither of us would have survived the accident."

Miss Flowers started to point out that without Mercy Ann no accident would have occurred, but thought she had best drop the subject and take points already made. She asked what he thought of Tom.

"Solid, reliable. A good man in every way. If his health is restored, he'll be in the middle of the list."

"Have you considered the general and sergeant major? Neither has personal attachments, and they are experts at war."

"They're too old."

She pointed out that, comparatively, she had been much older when recruited. Then she insisted he consider Rudy because of his compatibility, which made him an extremely rare asset.

"I can't ask him to leave his family."

"Invite his wife and son to go with us. Many in the fleet have families."

John Justice had scant memories of his parents "Families cause endless problems with staffing missions. Better Rudy stay here."

"You must put our needs first. Explain to Rudy and his family that we need them. If they say no, convince them. You've never said what you thought of Rudy's wife."

"Strong-willed, intelligent, and leadership qualities."

"The boy?"

"I don't know, but Honey Bee will have an opinion after treating him. I expect it will be good, considering the parents. I'll think about it more. Okay?"

She got up from the table. "I'm sorry if I upset you about Mercy Ann. I'm going to the control room to help Honey Bee scan for intruders."

When she was gone, he whispered, "You're the only family I have now that Mercy Ann is gone. I just wish you'd done more to get along with her. Our lives together would have been so much better."

One of John Justice's internal alarms went off. He heard a man on a phone asking the front desk of a Los Angeles hotel for Brandi Norris.

When she answered, the man said, "The new Spencer-Jenkins building. Use the construction entrance in the fence along the front sidewalk at noon. Take personal hand tools with noise suppression. They'll provide other tools as required. Identify yourselves as the Cowboy Team. You may have to slap some of them around to prove your identity because they don't know you're women, but I'm sure you'll manage just fine."

Sheri was in the bathtub using a comb to push a washcloth under the armbrace when John Justice walked in carrying the folded change of clothes she left on the bed.

"What the hell are you doing here?" she demanded, glancing at the pistol on the closed toilet seat beside the tub.

"I want you and Brandi to help protect Earth and other planets from invaders," he answered as if it wasn't a fantastic statement. "It will be dangerous and require some travel, but when you get down to it, it isn't much different from the lives you lead now."

She gawked. "Are you crazy?"

He held out the clothes and watched carefully as she pulled her free hand from under the brace to accept them. "I don't believe you would miss Earth very much, but we come back here to visit occasionally. Uh, I didn't mean for you to arrive under the pier and get hurt. I'll have someone repair your injuries when we get the chance."

While he talked, she felt the clothes for the knives that should be there, but only found a wad of money.

Glaring, she held it up. "What's this?"

"Buy whatever you need, but don't try calling your bosses. Communications with them will be blocked."

"What are you talking about? Hey, where's Brandi?"

He shrugged. "You know, Sheri, I can't help noticing you're an exceptionally pretty young woman sitting in that tub of warm soapy water."

Surprised and careless for a second, she glanced down at her naked chest then back up as he touched her shoulder.

She was back at Huntington Beach in waist-high water next to Brandi. The pier was not far away. Surfers sat on boards farther out. Families and young people getting in max beach time before another year of school crowded the shore, playing games and sunbathing.

As a big swell lifted them up, Brandi said, "I'm in my goddamned underwear. When I see that little son of a bitch again, I'm going skin him alive."

"Could be worse," Sheri answered, laughing. "He gave me clothes and enough money to buy you some, as well as get back to LA, but maybe we should get a couple of bathing suits and just enjoy ourselves before we return to all the shit. What do you say?"

"What's wrong with you? We need to call our employer and explain why we're not at the job. They'll sure as hell come after us if we don't."

"John Justice said we wouldn't be able to get through to them, no matter what we try."

"Then we better make a run for it."

Kicking to float on her back, Sheri held the clothes over her chest. "Just listen a minute, sweetie. The kid wants us to leave Earth with him and fight badasses in space. Don't know how much it pays, but sounds right up your alley."

"What?"

John Justice appeared in the general's quarters just as he sat on the toilet. "They're on the way downtown to destroy the cannons, sir. I feel bad not helping."

"Just leave it to the troops, my boy. They know what they're doing."

"I saw your soldiers moving to the outer perimeter of the buffer zone. Did you disable your cannons?"

"The sergeant major fixed them so the controller unit will short out the entire system if anyone charges one of them."

"Are you going to the perimeter, too?"

"Bugging out in a few minutes unless something requires me to stay behind."

"You mustn't take so many chances."

"Being in charge requires it sometimes, but don't worry. No one will be within a mile of here in an hour."

Someone outside slapped the side of the tent. "Sir, the President just issued orders to stand down the attack until further notice."

"There you go," the general said. "Now all we have to do is wait for word that the cannons in town have been destroyed."

"I've got to get back to the ship," John Justice replied with a tired smile. "See you later."

John Justice sat in the dining room checking internal computer feeds. News from the Middle East was especially grim with unedited video showing the al-Bensi forces slaughtering people in Iraq. Disgusted, he shut them off and watched reports of unrest from around the world. It was difficult telling them apart, no matter the location, so he searched for something less gut wrenching. Fifty-year-old photographs of him and Mercy Ann in San Francisco were on several news wire services.

"I looked good with my hair long, but the clothes were atrocious," he observed aloud. Then he lost himself in the past for a few minutes before commenting, "That was one of the good times with Mercy Ann."

Feeling a little better, John Justice sat back trying to reason what the conspirators would do next. He decided that whether the attack on the cannons in LA succeeded or failed, they could no longer wait for the public and members of the government to remove the President from office now that the FBI Director betrayed them. They had no way to know what information he gave him. Handley had to act now against the President.

He gave feeds to Handley and the Chairman of the Joint Chiefs priority and set search parameters to learn the daily schedules of the President, his family, and all the people close to him.

The new hotel-office skyscraper in downtown Los Angeles would be one of the tallest buildings in the city when construction completed. Rising into the sky from an area of busy hotels, upscale office buildings, and trendy restaurants, no one questioned why no construction took place on this typical Friday workday.

Traffic was heavy as people rushed into the area to have lunch before lines became too long. A panel van stopped at the curb in front of the construction site and three men in hardhats jumped out, hurried through an opening in the high safety fence, and exchanged words with a security guard. He directed them to a plywood construction door.

Inside, two burley men pointed automatic rifles with silencers at them. They did not say anything, leaving the visitors to speak first.

Blake said, “We’re Cowboy. Where do you want us?”

The man in charge handed him a clip-on comm device and pointed to a big construction elevator. “Go up to floor sixty and flip the toggle on the control panel to cut power to the elevator. Stay there and make sure no one goes up or down until I call with an all clear. Then you’ll go up to the sixty-fifth floor, help the men pack equipment, and bring it down. Questions?”

Blake pointed to their rifles. “Got any more of those around? I feel a mite underdressed for this party with just a pistol.”

“Two rifles and ammunition are next to the elevator on sixty. They’re the last we have so one of you will have to make do with what you’re carrying. Intruders have to go through us before they get to you, so it shouldn’t be a problem.”

“In that case,” Blake offered, “I can send the rifles down on the elevator if you need them for others reporting in.”

Blake’s easy smile and friendly manner convinced the men to let their guard down. One said the Cowboy team was the last to the party. Blake’s men killed them. Blake ran back to the man outside and said the boss wanted him.

The sergeant major, Tom, and four more of Blake’s men came through the fence from the sidewalk. One took over the watchman’s job.

They hid the bodies of the three guards. The sergeant major reckoned more guards would be at the rear of the building at the loading docks and sent men to take care of them. They were back in less than five minutes.

The sergeant major had building materials and tools piled around the outside of the big construction elevator platform to protect them from lateral gunfire but that left the problem of guards above looking down and seeing who was onboard, so they stretched sheets of canvas over the loads to hide under. Armed with the automatic rifles from the guards, they had an enormous amount of firepower.

One problem remained. Someone had to stay on guard in the lobby. Blake said it should be him or Tom because he did not have military experience and the detective had an injury, but he left it for Tom to decide, and he wanted to go.

The big elevator went up quickly with the sergeant major and Tom the only ones visible from above. The finished exterior walls changed to protective canvas then had nothing blocking the view of dramatic cityscape and bright sky. They reached the upper levels consisting of steel beams and occasional temporary platforms piled with construction materials.

Slowing to a crawl as they reached floor sixty, they observed the two rifles leaning against stacks of boxes and two large platforms off to one side with big generators running. Heavy cables connected them to platforms five floors above.

The sergeant major spoke loud enough for the men under the canvas to hear. “Cables indicate the controller and all the cannons are here.”

Above them, a man leaned over the shaft with a rifle. “Stop the elevator, or I’ll open fire.”

The sergeant major halted the elevator and shouted, “The radios aren’t working. Someone decided you needed a couple more guys to help. Can’t believe they expected ten people to handle six cannons and a sequence controller. What were they thinking?”

“Are you checked out on controller phasing and sight leveling?” the man yelled back.

The sergeant major laughed. “We can do the phasing, but never heard of sight leveling. I hope a right response means you’re not going to shoot us.”

The man set the rifle down. “We’re ready to begin powering up and can damn well use help. Thanks.”

The sergeant major pressed the lift button and informed his men all targets were on the left side. Then he commenced counting down from ten.

The crews with the cannons were well armed and skilled in combat, but did not have a chance. A hail of bullets cut everyone down except for one man who fell to his death on the sixtieth floor.

After smashing the firing mechanisms, the sergeant major had all the coils broken then reversed wires on the controller and turned it on. Sparks and smoke spewed from it. Then he called Blake and the general to report success.

Meanwhile, Rob and Missa stood in front of a restaurant waiting for calls if they were needed. They were disappointed when one of the vans pulled up to take them back to the warehouse.

When the others returned to the house, John Justice asked them not to discuss their success with him, Honey Bee, or Miss Flowers. “I’ve chanced triggering an interference decision from the Sufficiency Test monitor too much already, but I don't know what else to do."

Then he excused himself, explaining he had work to do with Honey Bee in the ship's operations room and that it would take all night. He refused to explain, even to Miss Flowers, who was even more mystified when he turned down an offer for her to bring him dinner later.

16

The White House Tour

Everyone expected a motion to impeach the President to pass in the House of Representatives this morning because so many members of his party indicated they would support it after he delayed ending the alien threat in LA yet again. Then the Senate would support the House action by a wide margin, clearing the way for the Vice President, a conspirator, to assume the Presidency.

The Vice President didn't know Jared Handley already planned for him not to run for reelection next year. Handley wanted the Chairman of the Joint Chiefs in the job because he needed someone willing to carry out ruthless acts to seize control of the country, and that person was definitely not the Vice President, a weak-in-the-knees ninny cut from the same cloth as the current President.

Sitting alone in the Oval Office after ordering the office staff not to disturb him except for a crisis, the President had stared at the handwritten list of the top conspirators the FBI Director had jotted down for some time. He put it down and wiped away tears.

He'd show the bastards, he thought. Enough House members had lied about voting against him to defeat the impeachment vote. It cost him and his donors a fortune in donations and favors, but they'd get it all back if everything worked out.

Once some of the conspirators accused the ringleaders, he'd have time to gather evidence against the rest while removing and replacing as many as possible with new people loyal to him, forcing Jared Handley's conspiracy to its knees. At the same time, he'd crisscross the country campaigning and taking bows for prevailing against the alien threat.

Smiling for the first time that morning, the President sat up straighter, imagining Handley's reaction to him winning the impeachment vote. Yeah, he thought, starting tomorrow, I'll to teach him what it means to play in the big leagues of politics. I'll crush his ass.

But the President had never given Jared Handley enough credit. Handley already knew House members lied about their intentions to vote for impeachment. He'd even considered competing to buy their loyalty then decided to stop screwing around and have the President assassinated instead.

He'd gone to great lengths to have top security personnel in the White House recruited into the conspiracy or replaced by people who were. So while the President thought tomorrow was soon enough to begin actions to save himself, Handley had a bold plan ready to kill him tonight.

The President's secretary broke into his reverie with an urgent summons from the Secretary of Defense to join him in the Situation Room.

When the President took his seat at the conference table, the Secretary advised that three unexplained flashes occurred in space near the Moon. They had redirected one of the big orbiting telescopes to determine the cause. A screen on the wall flashed on, showing a ragged V-formation of flying saucers in such high definition that it appeared to be from a scene in a movie.

A colonel, standing at the podium, took over, using a laser pointer for emphasis. "Sir, seven UFOs. Note the three gaps in the formation. We think the flashes were ships lost in a battle. Note the streaks of light in front them. We believe they indicate weapons firing, but we've been unable to find an adversary so far."

The President showed a remarkable lack of interest in the bombshell news and got to his feet. "Let me know when you figure it out."

As everyone jumped up to attention, the red-faced Secretary of Defense stammered, "Sir, we're not finished."

The President remained standing. "I'm listening."

The colonel continued the briefing. "The UFOs maneuver, change speeds, and courses frequently, but they're approaching Earth at a steady pace. If nothing changes, they'll reach here mid-morning tomorrow. If they were to fly a direct course, they could be here tonight."

The Secretary of Defense added, "Given that we have aliens on the ground in LA, shouldn't we plan for the possibility this is related to them somehow?"

The President slumped back down in the chair. "Go on."

The colonel wore an earpiece giving updates. "Sir, another picture just came in that proves they're in a battle."

It showed the lead UFO exploding.

The President's face showed plainly that he still thought these incredible events a distraction from more important concerns. "Why can't we see who they're fighting?"

"We're working on it, sir," the Secretary answered.

The President stood again, albeit more slowly than before. "Begin preparations to go on full alert if it appears they intend to enter our atmosphere. Otherwise, keep this on a need-to-know basis and provide my office hourly reports."

Shortly before the others returned from destroying the coil cannons the evening before, John Justice overheard Jared Handley discussing his assassination plan with the Chairman of the Joint Chiefs. Then he spent the night with Honey Bee finding out all he could about the details and developing ways to thwart Handley's plan.

Honey Bee made it clear she disagreed with them interfering. Then, this morning, when he told Miss Flowers what he intended, she sided with Honey Bee and renewed the argument. He refused to listen to them and declared the matter settled.

Later, John Justice, Miss Flowers, and Honey Bee listened in when the President learned about the UFOs approaching Earth. By the time he walked out of the Situation Room, Honey Bee had their scanners trying to locate the enemy destroying the Gargle ships. Having no more luck than the American military, she looked back and shrugged.

Seated in a chair beside the one John Justice stood behind, Miss Flowers said, "Honey Bee advises the object fighting them is also invisible to our scanners, but data indicates it has less mass than a Trigite Stinger, which means it is very small."

Puzzled, John Justice asked, "Why isn't she speaking to me directly?"

"She says you don't listen."

He groaned. "I don't know what a Trigite Stinger is."

"They're roughly the size of a small Earth car," Miss Flowers relayed. "She has never come across cloaking such this before, but thinks she will find a way to see it soon."

"As if we didn't already have enough to worry about," John Justice complained. "Now we have two forces with superior capabilities approaching Earth. Honey Bee, can you tell anything about the weapons the phantom ship employs?"

Again, she addressed the answer to Miss Flowers, who said, "She detects no weapon or propulsion signatures, but by extrapolating data from the maneuvers and speeds of the pursuing Gargle ships, the enemy ship is much faster."

"We'll just monitor this until they're closer," John Justice said. "Now we need to work on my plan to rescue the President and his family."

True to nature, Miss Flowers resumed arguing against it. "Protecting two children out of the numbers killed on this planet every day is ludicrous, but if you're determined, save them and leave the President to his fate. No telling what the effect of saving a leader will have on future events."

"Children need their parents," John Justice insisted.

She threw up her hands. "Then go tell the general and let him warn the White House. We should stay out of it."

"With the layers of people between him and the President," John Justice answered solemnly, "he'll be targeted by the conspirators within minutes of telling anyone."

Miss Flowers stared for a long interval. "I hadn't thought of that. Yes, you're right."

It was unusual for Miss Flowers to give up so easily, so he studied her more closely. "You're blushing. You like the general, don't you? That's why you keep watching activities at the site so closely."

Now, she was flustered. "Don't be ridiculous."

He took a deep breath. "I apologize for upsetting you and Honey Bee. I'll explain why I want to do this, but it may not make sense to you. In my last conversation with Mercy Ann, she said we needed to create chaos and turmoil to keep the Earthlings confused and making mistakes that give us opportunities to help them pass the Sufficiency Test."

Honey Bee spoke finally. "That doesn't make sense."

John Justice tried to clarify. "My rescue plan will create confusion in the government as well as the conspiracy. They will lose confidence and make rash decisions. We will take advantage of them."

Honey Bee asked Miss Flowers, "Do you understand this?"

"It's my fault," John Justice said. "I know what Mercy Ann meant, but I can't explain it. Sorry."

"Very well," Honey Bee answered. "If this is what she wanted, I will support you."

"I don't understand it, either," Miss Flowers said, "but just tell me what to do."

Jared Handley was on his lush private jet flying to his home in Denver. Seated in overstuffed chairs across from him, the Chairman of the Joint Chiefs and a Deputy Attorney General from Los Angeles were apprehensive because the great man had told them when they boarded in DC to remain silent until he was ready to deal with them.

A door opened at the rear of the cabin and a Japanese woman dressed in a tailored attendant's uniform emerged. Covering the distance to Handley's chair with precise small steps, she gracefully removed a crystal highball glass half-filled with his favorite Scotch from a small silver tray and presented it gently to his hand. Then she backed away, turned, and exited, the only sound marring a perfect performance, the click made by the galley door closing.

A large TV screen on the wall came to life showing the news. General Abd al-Bensi made a speech declaring the people of Saudi Arabia had worn the yoke of royal oppression too long and should support his army when it came to liberate them after they finished in Iraq. Commentators argued whether al-Bensi would dare carry out the threat because the United States had an agreement to support Saudi Arabia against aggression.

Handley smiled. He'd smuggled a group of al-Bensi terrorists into the United States. They would martyr themselves tonight after killing the President in the White House. Identification of the bodies would reveal many ties to the Saudi royal family, including two officers from the king's palace guard—kidnapped and brought into the country against their wills. No, the American people would not object when the new President reneged on the treaties to protect Saudi Arabia.

Handley turned down the TV volume and made business calls until a special about the situation in Los Angeles came on, which he watched with interest. He finished his drink, and the Japanese woman reappeared with another. Meanwhile, the Chairman and the California attorney never took their eyes from Handley, but were careful not to look at him directly, either.

They were over Kansas when finally he turned and spoke to his guests. He told them flatly that he had not made up his mind whether to blame them personally for the problems in LA or not.

Fixing a hard stare upon the California attorney, he said, "My cannons were destroyed. My best technicians and West Coast operatives are missing or dead. Were you able to get everything cleaned up at the construction site and keep the authorities out of it, or did you screw that up too?"

The man blanched but answered with a firm voice. "The site was cleaned and no one noticed anything out of the ordinary. The construction crews are back at work."

"Any ideas who attacked us, or do all your people have their heads up their asses?"

The man made excuses. "The bodies of two of our men known by the code name Cowboy were not found at the site. They must have been involved. It's only a matter of time before we find them."

"The Cowboy team is two women," Handley corrected.

Unnerved, the man stammered, "My mistake, but they had to be involved. My people will have them soon."

Handley's attention went to the Chairman. "Is your general in LA still dragging his feet and not following orders to get rid of the alien problem?"

It was much more complex, but the Chairman agreed. "Yes sir."

"I listened to you and sent my last four coil cannons to al-Bensi so I don't any available after this LA fiasco. I assume it would cause too many problems to get them back?"

It had been Handley's idea to send the cannons to al-Bensi, but the Chairman accepted the blame. "Yes sir."

Glaring, Handley went to his luxurious bathroom in a back corner of the room. The Chairman and the attorney very much needed to use the other toilet at the front, but neither dared get out of his chair or so much as speak until Handley passed judgment.

Handley read and did not acknowledge them again until the plane landed in Denver, where it received priority over waiting airlines to taxi to a private VIP area. The female attendant appeared from the back with Handley's briefcase and a hot towel. Placing the briefcase next to him, she waited until he finished with the towel then returned to the galley.

A man in a suit emerged from the pilot's cabin, opened the front passenger door, and waited for the stairs to move into place.

Handley spoke to the Chairman. “How fast can you replace your general at the alien site?”

“I can appoint his three star boss and have him report for duty tomorrow morning,” he responded, not at all certain he could do it that fast. “I’ll have him deal with the aliens the minute he arrives.”

Telling the two men to remain seated, Handley stood and beckoned to the man at the door. “Did you hear everything we discussed during the flight?”

“Yes sir.”

“You will take over the LA operations today. We suffered a large setback because of your predecessor’s carelessness, so set an example when you tell him. I’ll leave it to you to investigate and decide the Cowboy team’s fate. Then arrange an accident for the outgoing site commander soon as he’s relieved from duty. Make it nasty.”

The man picked up the briefcase, followed Handley to the open doorway, and handed it off to another man waiting on the stairs.

Handley called to his two guests before leaving. “You can relax now, guys.”

When the door closed, the new LA boss disappeared into the front cabin without a word and the Deputy Attorney General bolted to the small bathroom. Not until the plane was in the air did the Chairman go, after which he and the other man, who had not met before this flight, sat silently watching cable news until the attendant came out with two Scotches and waited while they tasted and said the drinks were satisfactory.

The Chairman, a real lady’s man, had many conquests over the years, especially when wearing a dress Army uniform adorned with medals. He often bragged they snagged more women than fishing lures caught seafood. He eyed the woman boldly. No longer the demure, mannered servant she had been previously, she smiled back at him.

Already wondering how large the galley was, he glanced over to see if his companion noticed the affect he had on her, his need for the admiration of another man stronger than his desire for any woman would ever be. But then, he could only stare, aghast.

The man’s eyes were unfocused, his face twisted, and mouth hung open. The half-empty glass tumbled out of his hand. He clawed his throat as if it could stop him dying. He slumped to the floor.

The woman knelt, put two fingers to his neck. “Grab his arms and help move him out of the way. I’ll have the new boss dispose of the body when we land. There’s no record of either of you on the flight, so have no concern.”

The Chairman realized who this woman was and almost lost his composure. Why hadn't it occurred to him she might be Handley's assistant, closest business confidant, and girlfriend—the infamous Miss Noto? They'd never met, but he'd talked on the phone to her many times. And to think, he was about to hit on her.

Motioning him back to his seat, she sat in the attorney's chair. "Many people will die over the next few days, but Jared says no one will notice after the President's assassination. Think I'll have a beer. Can I get you another drink or glass of champagne, perhaps?"

The Chairman glanced down at the body and tried to hide the shivers running through him. "I'll just nurse this one, thank you."

The smile she gave him was one of the loveliest he'd ever seen.

Aasim was angry the commander chose his group to train as a crew for the new cannons from America. Of course, when told, he praised Allah, Abd al-Bensi, and his commander for their faith in him, but it meant he and his men could no longer plunder and loot, a huge loss of income. It was especially hurtful because he did not have enough money set aside to have the prosperous secure he foresaw when he joined al-Bensi's army.

Nor were his men careful to keep dangerous opinions about losing the money to themselves. He had to beat two of them until they stopped complaining. Then he berated everyone for being selfish while thinking furiously about whether he should stay in the service of al-Bensi and hope a new opportunity to steal presented itself or sneak away with the money he already had.

A little later, the youngest member of his group, a boy actually, asked Aasim if he could take his picture to send his best friend at home who was on the verge of joining the cause. Everyone wanted Aasim's picture because he was handsome and looked so fierce with ammunition belts crossed on his chest over an al-Bensi uniform that he'd tailored himself. Smiling, he crouched with an automatic rifle gripped, ready to fire.

Afterward, Aasim was so pleased with the boy's gushing praise that he decided to stick it out a while longer. He would just have to trust something presented itself to change the situation.

Soon, a truck would carry them back to the last town they passed through because the cannons would arrive there in the morning. Seeing his men's disheartened faces when he told them, he gave a speech about duty to al-Bensi and the cause in spite of feeling angry about it himself. Then he pointed out that while soldiers had picked over the town already, there would still be women willing to raise their spirits, and that helped morale a little.

Someone tapped Aasim on the shoulder, and he whipped around. It was his commander, who had been watching and listening. With a big smile, he explained that he told all his group leaders about reassignment to the new weapons, and Aasim was the only one who had not complained and did his duty. Then, on the spot, he promoted Aasim to sergeant and guaranteed his unit would remain with the infantry during the attack on Bagdad, which had the potential to make all of them rich as long as they gave their commander his fair share, of course.

With the men cheering, it was all Aasim could do not to drop to his knees to give thanks to Allah for making his commander such a wise, fair man and al-Bensi such a great general.

Brandi was a sharp soldier in crisp, creased US Army fatigues, emphasized by boot heels making authoritative thuds striking the pavement.

Sheri's appearance was that of a young girl stuffed into a large, shapeless laundry bag with her head sticking out the opening. Her oversized cap kept sliding down on her forehead, sometimes covering the eyebrows. Her boots scraped the pavement when she walked.

Brandi looked at her sidelong. "You're too much."

"How can anyone fight wearing all this stuff?" she grumbled.

"Can't you at least stand up straight?"

"That strap you put around my neck to hold the arm brace is too tight. Whoever heard of an injured soldier patrolling, anyway? God, this is uncomfortable."

"No one has given you a second look, have they? By the way, when we go back to the hotel, I want to get a picture of you in that getup. Promise I'll cherish it always."

"Bite me."

"Here? Now? You want to give the US Army a bad name?"

Sheri showed her cutest face and surprised Brandi with a question about her past, something they seldom did. "How many years did you serve as a soldier?"

Brandi didn't mind telling her. "Two years in uniform and two in a special unit."

Sheri pushed the cap up from her eyes. "God, did you enlist instead of going to preschool?"

"No one questioned my age because I was tall and had big tits early."

"Was the army responsible for turning you into a musclebound badass or were you were born that way?"

"I'm going to boot your tiny butt thirty yards down the street if you keep this up."

"That's my big strong Brandi talking her Amazon shit," Sheri said, somehow making it sound endearing.

Brandi raised the big binoculars around her neck and examined a hill in the distance. "Some sort of fancy cannon up there with soldiers everywhere. Let's go back the other way."

Sheri could not remain quiet when she was bored and began singing off key to the cadence of Brandi's boot heels. "Burger, cola, hot fries! Mustard, ketchup, fruit pies!"

Brandi snapped, "What are you, six years old?"

That was when they saw John Justice standing in the middle of the road in the next block.

Instantly, Sheri was all business. "What do you want to do?"

Before Brandi could answer, John Justice was standing ten feet in front of them with Honey Bee in the crook his arm.

"Yes, Brandi," he asked with a smile, "what do you want to do?"

Sheri said, "A doll is not something I expected a young man to have, in spite of you being so pretty."

"Honey Bee's a lifeform, not a doll," John Justice answered with a slight smile. "Allow her to hold onto your brace while we talk, and she'll fix the injury."

Sheri glanced at Brandi, who shrugged. "Either you believe it or you don't."

Sheri moved close to John Justice, Honey Bee grabbed onto her arm brace, and pulled tight against it. Brandi and Sheri didn't try hiding their surprise.

Finally, Brandi turned to John Justice. "Sheri said you want us to join you."

"Yes, but we'll have to talk about that later. You have a new boss in LA. He killed the old one and took over this morning. He ordered his men to dispose of you."

"Do you know his name?" Brandi asked, showing no concern.

John Justice showed them a picture on his phone.

Sheri knew him. "Jerry Kaminski, out of Atlanta. Has quite a rep. Wonder who all these guys work for?"

John Justice told them it was Jared Handley.

Sheri whistled. "He owns half the world. Surely he's not involved with these scumbags."

Brandi surprised her. “Years back, a broker offered me a small fortune for a one-off job in the Middle East. Turned out Handley was the client. He had an employee problem and insisted on going with me. I thought he’d just get in the way, but he proved to be ruthless as they come. The employee was Abd al-Bensi, by the way. Handley forgave him and the rest is history, so to speak.”

Before Sheri could ask questions, John Justice broke in. “I don’t have much time. Handley’s people plan to attack the White House tonight to assassinate the President and his family. I want you to help me save them.”

Brandi stammered, “The White House?”

At the same time Sheri exclaimed, “Is this a joke?”

John Justice found it ironic they would consider leaving Earth to fight in space yet be astounded by something as commonplace as a political assassination, especially given their backgrounds.

“Honey Bee and some people I know will help,” he explained, “so it should not be too difficult.”

Brandi sputtered, “No offense, but alien or not, you’re still just a kid, and it is the White House.”

“I have a sound plan, but need two more people.

“Can’t you call more aliens?” Sheri asked.

His anguish was obvious. “Mercy Ann died, so now there’s only Honey Bee and Miss Flowers, who takes care of the house.”

“We saw a video on the internet,” Sheri said quietly, “but didn’t know it was real. What happened?”

“I went to rescue someone in the Death Valley Prison and was careless. Mercy Ann died getting us out. It was my fault.”

Sheri shook her head. “Sometimes things go wrong. All you can do is learn from your mistakes and move on.”

Brandi told something else about her past. “I was held in Death Valley Prison for a few months until a ransom came through. Tell you what, kid. If Sheri doesn’t object, we’ll help.”

Surprised, Sheri felt that she’d learned too much about Brandi’s past recently to ask more questions, so she said, “Always wanted to take a White House tour.”

“I will return in a little while and go over the plan,” John Justice said, taking Honey Bee from Sheri.

Wide-eyed, she unfastened the brace and removed it after handing Brandi the grenade that dropped out. “God, that feels good. Sorry if we offended you, Honey Bee. You’re beautiful. If anyone says different, tell me. I’ll take care of them for you.”

John Justice nodded. “She says because you’re so nice, I should tell you that she fused the firing mechanism on the grenade. It won’t work anymore.”

Then they were gone.

In the White House, the President tossed and turned in fitful sleep, unaware his wife had given up getting any rest with him and gone to share the bed with their eight-year-old daughter.

Beginning at two, a violent thunderstorm lashed the city, waking the First Lady, who went to check on their young son because he was afraid of storms. Consequently, she was back in her daughter’s bed with both children when twenty dark clad al-Bensi terrorists came over the fence and ran across the north lawn.

Pressure sensors, motion detectors, and other safeguards were off. Security personnel in the conspiracy had killed the other guards and dogs and had control of the two security monitoring stations inside the White House.

The terrorists entered the building through the unlocked north portico door. Two guards lay dead on the floor, killed by the same kind of automatic rifle the terrorists carried. It was on the floor nearby. They took it.

The plan was simple. Do as much damage to the White House as possible with grenades, automatic weapons, and bombs after they killed the First Family. Then set off the suicide vests they wore and martyr themselves.

Reaching the Grand Hall running the length of the building, they passed more dead bodies and split into two teams, half going to the Grand Staircase, half to the smaller west stairwell that was usually closed off and secured, but not tonight.

After verifying power to the President’s secret escape elevator was off, the leader gave thumbs up to his men. All that remained between them and the President of the United States was a door at the top of the stairs, and they had the secret code to open it.

Meanwhile, the other team ran up the Grand Staircase to the landing, shoved four dead guards out of the way, and took firing positions to stop anyone passing by them. They were to wait until hearing their brothers inside the residence before blasting through the front entrance.

Eyes shining with pride and excitement, the men in the small stairwell hurried up the stairs, ready to go down in history as the greatest martyrs who ever lived.

John Justice, Brandi, and Sheri materialized in the big upstairs oval room that served as a formal gathering place. Four cadavers—a family with a boy and girl the approximate ages of the President's children that had burned to death in a Canadian cabin fire—were on the floor. Honey Bee, with the help of Tom and Blake, had brought them here.

Sheri looked down at them. "Oh gross."

John Justice had already explained they needed the bodies to keep the conspirators from realizing the First Family had escaped. Looking around, he wondered what was taking Honey Bee so long just as she appeared.

He took Sheri's hand and the two of them were next to the snoring President's bed.

Sheri put her rifle on the floor, pulled a pistol from the shoulder holster, and nodded. John Justice shook the President.

Sitting bolt upright, he looked around the room then addressed Sheri as though John Justice, standing closest, did not exist. "Who are you people? Where's my wife?"

John Justice answered, "Asleep in your daughter's room with your son. They're safe."

"What do you want?"

"Handley's conspiracy has control of White House security," John Justice replied. "A team of Abd al-Bensi terrorists are in the building downstairs and will be here in a few minutes. We're here to help you get away."

He looked around again, demeanor anything but cooperative. "I recognize you. You're that so-called alien."

John Justice removed a computer tablet from a canvas bag and thrust it into the President's hands. "Look for yourself. Al-Bensi soldiers are coming up the stairways."

The President hit John Justice with the tablet and jumped out of bed. "I've got to get to my wife and family."

Sheri grabbed hold of the President's wrist, twisted, and forced him to his knees. Picking up the rifle with the other hand, she nodded to John Justice.

He touched the President, and they were in the bedroom with his frightened wife and children, sitting up in bed.

Brandi, holding a rifle, stood from a chair and put a hand on Sheri's shoulder. "Relax, Mr. President. Take your wife's hand and John Justice will take us to a safe place."

Terrorists opened the door from the small stairwell and ran through the dining room into an ornate sitting room. The President's bedroom was on the other side. Three men charged in with weapons blazing on full automatic.

No one was there. Angry, the leader directed the others to search the rest of the rooms while he remained in the big hall to watch for anyone running from a hiding place. Then an explosion blew open the main entrance door at the far end of the hall and the second team charged inside the quarters.

"Where are they?" one of them shouted.

"Hiding," the leader yelled back. "Search the rooms."

A man called from the big oval room that he had found bodies.

The leader ran and examined them. "This makes no sense."

"It has to be them, doesn't it?" the man asked.

"These are not fresh." He shoved the man from the room and returned to check the corpses more thoroughly.

Outside the building, sirens and alarms blared as lines of vehicles streamed toward the White House from every direction. The roar of descending helicopters became deafening. Headlights and spotlights shining through driving rainfall made seeing out of the building impossible. The terrorists became evermore frantic and confused.

A near-blinding red light appeared in the big hall near the oval room. The terrorists opened fire from both ends. The leader, carefully avoiding the hail of bullets, looked into the hall just in time to see Honey Bee, standing beneath a big, red pulsing globe, vanish.

No longer protected by her from the gunfire, the globe shattered. A shockwave shook the city for miles around.

17

Girl from the Blue Cloud Nebula

MERCY ANN'S ANGER HAD BOILED OVER when the Guardians transported her from the Death Valley battle to their ship and insisted she leave Earth with them. Arguing that putting the planet's future in the fumbling hands of John Justice guaranteed failure of the Sufficiency Test, she refused to go.

Then a Guardian had the audacity to say, "You shouldn't blame your crewmember for shortcomings you caused in him."

Another was even worse. "The planet's failure was inevitable, regardless."

Usually, she ignored their callous, hateful remarks, but not this time. "Goddamn you! I demand that you send me back to the battle! Now!"

Her next memory was waking up with glowing bird-like Guardians disconnecting hoses and cables that sustained her during something they called spatial travel, which meant she had just concluded a very long trip. Thinking they'd doomed mankind by taking her away, she pitched a fit.

At first, they gave rambling, incomplete explanations about the necessity of bringing her to the Guardian home system of planets. Then they became agitated when she refused to look at their home planet on a monitor they'd made especially for her. Anger replaced agitation when she told them it was a shame they didn't have assholes for her to shove the monitor up.

A Guardian got in her face and insisted she needed essential enhancements to her biological and weapons systems, so she should be grateful and understanding.

A different Guardian responded that she was a savage from a third rate system so they should expect this type of behavior and make allowances.

She screamed more insults and threats until they did something that caused time and reality to become a blur for her. She followed a Guardian in the form of a glowing ball of energy through countless corridors and rooms, undergoing repairs, surgeries, and modifications for what seemed an eternity.

When her surroundings and mental awareness came back into focus finally, she stood next to the Guardian in a cavernous launch bay littered with equipment and debris. Otherwise, it was empty except for a small egg-shaped object hovering a few feet above the deck near the center of the huge space. Flitting in the air around it, six Guardians changed positions constantly.

Her companion whispered, "That is the ship that will take you back to Earth. It is very old and the first to use spatial travel technology, which you will need in the future."

Then, just before reaching it, he added, "The leadership sentenced this group of scientists to die with me when the Gargle attack us, so choose your words carefully. They are very upset."

She asked why they had to die.

"It was the best choice of the options they offered."

From many frustrating conversations with Guardians in the past, she knew it would do no good to ask for anything more.

The ship, lovelier and smoother than any object she'd ever before experienced, appeared to be made of greenish-black glass, but her companion said it was metal. But it was ridiculously small, especially if it had to house all the equipment and personnel to keep her alive during spatial travel.

She'd lost track of her guide in the constantly moving group of energy balls and addressed questions to them generally.

A Guardian passing by responded those issues were no problem.

Thanks for nothing, she thought. "How do I get inside?"

A Guardian transformed into the glowing bird shape and pointed to a rickety wooden stepladder fifty feet away on the floor. Mystified why they had a ladder, she retrieved it and, at their prompting, propped it against the side of the ship.

When she hesitated climbing up, they insisted she hurry, but the bottom rung broke, spraining her ankle. Standing on one leg, she demanded to know why they didn't simply transport her.

They told her to try again.

A small round hatch opened when she reached the top, but the hull's surface was so slick she was afraid to move off the shaky ladder. Besides, how did they possibly think she would fit through the small opening, much less inside the tiny pilot's compartment? More concerning, she had suffered acute claustrophobia since childhood, something she was about to discover entities that existed as floating balls of energy could not comprehend.

They became angry when she kept trying to explain the problem and demanded she go inside immediately.

Exasperated, she refused.

A Guardian commented that emergency repairs to her reasoning abilities might be in order. Then they began discussing methods for modifying human brains to achieve better behavior.

Afraid they might harm her, Mercy Ann decided to illustrate the problem. She stuck her legs into the opening and tried to squeeze her hips through. Painfully twisting and cramming, pushing and pulling, and sweating and cursing, she forced her body down into the compartment. No one was more surprised than she was.

A Guardian said her species might eventually evolve into something useful. Another responded that it was doubtful.

Meanwhile, Mercy Ann could hardly move. Controls jabbed and cables entangled. Breathing was difficult. Horrible childhood memories nagged at her. She panicked. She had to get out. Struggling to get her arms over her head to grab the hatch opening, nothing else mattered.

Realizing her intentions, the Guardians started closing the hatch.

Mercy Ann thrust one hand into the opening, forcing the hatch back. She pushed a shoulder up and through, unmindful of jerking out cockpit cables and leaving long strands of hair tangled in instruments. Then a panel box collapsed when she pushed up with all her weight on one foot, wedging the sprained ankle inside. Hurting and frantic, she jerked the foot out and ripped her silver flight boot off her foot. She screamed for them to help her.

A Guardian, glowing dangerously red, flew near her face and lamented the wanton destruction caused by lesser species with corporeal forms. Another warned her to stop kicking and tearing up the inside of the ship or they would jettison her into space.

Mercy Ann shrieked, "You assholes shut your yaps and get me out of here, or I'll blow the whole goddamned place to shit! Get me out! Now!"

Heart pounding and lungs laboring in the thin atmosphere they had created in the bay for no other reason than her, a cable from a robotic crane held her in place on top of the tiny ship. Glaring down at the blood, skin, and hair she'd lost getting out, she demanded to know why they gave her a crappy ladder to use when they had a crane.

They did not respond.

She lowered her voice and spoke more civilly. "Please, I feel I must say something important. Can you hear me?"

A Guardian took the bait. "Yes. Do you wish to apologize for your behavior?"

"Kiss my ass!" she shouted.

They flew around her wildly. One commented that she should be proud they trusted her with this particular ship as though it was a holy relic. Others chastised her crudeness and lack of respect for her betters.

Mercy Ann shrieked and screamed loud as she could until they were silent.

Finally, a Guardian, seeking a compromise, suggested, "We could alter your extremities to fit inside better."

Mercy Ann took deep breaths to calm down, not easy with painful memories of her childhood aroused. "You must change the ship's interior, not my body."

Their glows brightened and darkened in ways she had come to recognize as private communications until a new voice spoke. "We can expand the compartment six inches around by reducing the size of the controls."

She was about to cry. "I must have a chair to sit, room to move my legs, and be able to see outside the ship. I suggest integrating all control functions into a new touch screen monitor and embed everything else into the hull."

"That requires major alterations, and an attack by the Gargle is imminent," one responded testily.

They did not actually use her name for the enemy, but she recognized the unpronounceable sounds that comprised it. "Nonetheless, it has to be done because I have more limitations than you do. You must accommodate them if I'm to use this wonderful ship you so kindly provided."

After another back-and-forth, they agreed.

Mercy Ann never understood how the Guardians' concept of time meshed with hers, but the little ship was ready in less than half an hour even though they said it had taken several Earth days. It was always like that with them.

Trying to work up courage to go inside again, she sat on top with her legs dangling through the hatch. Only one Guardian remained with her. She asked about the cargo he mentioned.

"When you're inside, I will transport a small metallic box to you. It contains several brethren who came onboard while we made the changes you wanted. Fortunately, they did not see the ship I provided you."

More nonsense, she thought. "Why are Guardians going with me?"

He would not say but emphasized she must not open the box until she reached her destination.

"Why not?"

He asked, "Do you recognize the battleship you're on?"

This was the fourth time she had been on one of the big Guardian vessels, which all looked exactly alike to her, same as Guardians did. "No. Should I?"

"It is the one that rescued you from the species collectors."

Instantly, she had tears.

"I am the one who rescued and revived you, and showed you the blue clouds. I am the one who managed your initial reconstruction and repaired you after the malfunction in battle. I am joyful that you experienced survival thus far."

Emotions wrung a loud sob from her. "I did not realize it was you."

"The others can't hear us now. You are a unique being, and powerful brethren factions want to stop Earth's humanoid development. That is why the time has come to take action."

"What do you mean they want to stop Earth's—?"

"You must go! The enemy has begun the attack. Launch quickly or perish with this ship."

He vanished.

Twisting and squeezing her shoulders down through the opening, she dropped onto a hard chair with a low back that did not adjust in any way. After pulling and fastening straps across her, she connected cables from the hull into her wrist ports, and then reached up behind to pull down heavier cables that snapped into plugs on the back of her head.

The hatch closed. The new view screen showed the huge launch door in the bay opening upon a beautiful pink planet with three moons around it.

Then the tiny ship was away, an infinitesimal speck streaking into black infinity. She felt no acceleration, no movement. Had it not been for the rapidly changing display on the screen, she might have thought the ship was still in the launch bay. She wondered if the Guardian battleship was still visible.

The screen responded instantly with a rearview. She choked with emotion as she saw the huge ship surrounded by hundreds of Gargle ships that she must have zipped past. It was in process of exploding, one section at a time.

A beep sounded and the screen flashed red. Two specks enlarged, Gargle cruisers pursuing her. She wondered about her speed and it appeared in the bottom right corner of the screen, a rapidly increasing number that meant nothing without knowing what the units measured.

Were they gaining, she wondered.

More numbers appeared in the left bottom corner showing she was out of range and pulling away. Then messages streamed across the screen in a language she did not understand.

Her Guardian told her the ship was set on course to reach Earth vicinity in the shortest amount of time and she could not take control until arrival. Otherwise, she would never find the way back.

Mercy Ann thought about her situation. Most likely, Earth had failed the Sufficiency Test already. She had asked about it, but the Guardians said they could not monitor events on Earth from so far away. She looked at the small metallic box on top of the monitor. Were there really Guardians inside? Why would they go back with her? She had a bad feeling about all of it.

Soon, however, one concern pushed away all other thoughts. Could this compartment be any smaller?

The hard metal chair prevented standing straight up and made her body ache, especially her tailbone. Her bootless feet were numb with cold. The backs of her legs pressed painfully hard against the chair rail while the knees and toes were tight against the hull in front of her. Leaning back to stretch, her head plugs struck the hull behind her. She could not raise and point her elbows straight out to the sides.

I'm the same as a baby chick imprisoned inside an egg, Mercy Ann thought. Or a young girl locked up in a dark place to force...her...

"Stop it," she rasped, swiping cold tears off her face. "Don't think about that."

Grabbing a tube protruding from the wall, she pulled up the skintight metallic shirt and jammed it into a hidden port on her abdomen. Growing calmer as warmth spread through her body, she sagged forward, resting her head against the screen. She felt at peace, but then, as sleep took hold of her, she realized that the drugs had also removed all defenses against remembering the horrific events leading up to her and her brother's abduction by species collectors. She could not stop it.

The nightmare began as it always did—with her sweating and gasping for air in the dark while straining to hear the sound that meant the beginning of another day.

The little rooster crowed outside Mercy Ann Justice's bedroom window half an hour before time to get up every morning during the hot spring and summer of 1909, but for many days she had been locked up in the tool room where she could barely hear Old Chickenshit—her name for the scraggly, bad-tempered bird. Nor would he hear if she shouted threats to wring his goddamn neck and have him for supper if he didn't shut the fuck up, even if she still had the strength to yell and curse him as she usually did.

When finally Mercy Ann made out his muffled call, it was all she could do to sit up. She needed to go to the outhouse, but couldn't. She had to go on the dirt-packed floor where she slept. She couldn't wash at the well pump, change clothes, do her dawn-to-night chores, or run errands in town. All she could do was despair, suffer, and keep trying to claw her way out, even though she knew it was futile.

Her frazzled mother, known as Miz Edwards since remarrying, had concern etched on her haggard face—which had been pretty and hotly pursued in youth—when she ran out of the clapboard house across the rickety back porch, leaving the warped screen door slap-slapping on a frame it no longer fit.

Jumping two steps into the backyard, her bare feet skidded on patches of dew-wet grass growing around a half-dead tree split in two by winter ice then overgrown by fragrant honeysuckle vines.

Reaching the sagging, ramshackle tobacco curing barn, its large size bespeaking the good days with her first husband, she put her hand into a hole on the scrap-board door, unlatched, and jerked it open, eagerness tearing loose one of the aged leather hinges from the rusty nails holding it to the wall.

She stared at it fearfully, knowing her second husband, Sonny, would be furious.

Dreading what she must do, Miz Edwards pushed into the shadowy drying room filled with rows of tobacco plants hanging upside down by the stems. Dust and acrid odors burned her eyes and coated her sweat-damp skin and hair. Mice and rats skittered, some hitting her feet, but she had long since learned to ignore them.

The tool room was in a dark back corner. Sonny had caulked the gaps so the only opening was the narrow crack where the door scraped on the floorboards. A heavy new hasp with a big bent nail on a chain stapled to the wall held it fastened tightly shut.

Grimacing from arthritis in her hands, Miz Edwards worked the nail free. The door swung inward so she opened it slowly. Used to store tobacco cutting knives, tying string, and tools, it stank of urine and feces.

Miz Edwards crouched and whispered, "Mercy Ann, are you awake?"

Trembling and crying, her daughter scurried on all fours into her mother's arms.

She shushed her. "We don't have much time. I know you're mad at me, but I can't do anything about your stepdaddy right now. He's crazy mean over you defying him. I'm afraid he might kill us all. Please, talk to me, honey."

Her voice was a raspy whisper. "Help me, momma."

"I've been thinking on it. You have to say you're ready to marry."

Expecting her daughter to struggle and pull away, she held tight. "Mercy Ann Justice, you listen to me! You make Sonny believe he broke you. You make him think he's getting what he wants. Then first chance, you take John Junior and skedaddle to where Thomas works on that farm in Level Cross. Your big brother won't take no sass off the likes of Sonny Edwards. You'll be safe with him."

She whimpered. "We can't leave you here alone with him, momma."

"Girl, it was my mistake marrying that piece of shit, and it's up to me to atone for what he's done to my young'uns. It ain't your place or Junior's place. You have to run as if the devil himself is after you, but first you must make Sonny believe you'll marry to get his attention off you. Understand me?"

Mercy Ann stopped crying and was becoming herself again, which meant hard, resolute, and anything but sweet. "Yes, momma."

"I have a dollar squirreled away. You'll need more, but we'll just have to pray the good Lord provides my young'uns Providence or sends angels to watch while you make your way to Thomas."

Mercy Ann had no beliefs that included a good Lord and angels, but she did have an idea to convince her stepdaddy he had broken her.

Her mother did not want to do anything so drastic.

Mercy Ann insisted. "Just make sure you don't hold back. I can take it, momma."

When they came out of the barn, Sonny Edwards was slouched in the kitchen doorway fuming as he waited with the screen door open, but he did not get a chance to unleash the abuse he had ready.

Shoving Mercy Ann to the ground near the honeysuckle, her mother yelled, "Look at you, girl! That dress is ruined! Why are you hiding your hands? Show me what you've done to yourself!"

Hysterical, Mercy Ann scooted away backwards. "I'm sorry! I couldn't help it, momma."

Miz Edwards grabbed her daughter's arm and jerked a hand out to examine. The nails were ragged, split, and bloody with long splinters buried under them in the quick. The knuckles were scraped, bruised, and bleeding. Dragging Mercy Ann to the honeysuckle, she snapped off a handful of willowy branches and held them between her legs to strip leaves off without letting her daughter go.

Mercy Ann jumped up and tried to pull away but could not break her mother's iron grip, so she bent down shielding her scraped, dirty legs, knowing that was where her mother would target.

"Move your arm," Miz Edwards demanded.

Mercy Ann yelled—half-screaming, half-begging. "I couldn't help it, momma! I couldn't stand the dark! I couldn't breathe!"

Miz Edwards switched her daughter's legs mercilessly. "I've had it with you! All this fuss and bother! You're going to get married like your daddy says or I'm going to switch the skin off you!"

Mercy Ann danced around her mother trying to block the stinging boughs until her legs and forearms became streaked and swollen with bloody welts. Then she rolled up into a tight ball on the ground, trembling, moaning, and crying.

Miz Edwards bent down close. "Are you going to mind me?"

Mercy Ann held her breath.

Her mother switched her with the fury of a summertime hailstorm. "I swear, you'll answer me if I have to do this till dark!"

Broken, Mercy Ann surrendered. "I'll marry him, momma. I'll marry him. Just stop. Stop hitting me."

Her mother flung the bundle of bloody switches away and yelled to the house. "Junior Justice, stop peeking around your stepdaddy and get your scrawny butt out here!"

Pushing by Sonny, the boy ran out the door and stopped at the edge of the porch, frightened eyes big as saucers. "Yes, ma'am?"

"Hold your nose and take your sister to the well. Help her strip down and wash the filth off. I'll set out some leftovers and clothes on the porch for her when you finish. Then you come get a needle, dig splinters out of her hands, and dab the wounds with ointment. See to it you do a good job or I'll give you a taste of what she got."

Junior ran to Mercy Ann and tugged at her arms until she stopped pushing him away and stood up.

Meanwhile, Miz Edwards stormed up onto the porch and glared Sonny out of the doorway.

For once, he didn't think it would be a good idea to cuss her, or say anything for that matter. He didn't even go after Junior for shoving him when he came outside. After weeks of aggravation and embarrassment because of his stepdaughter's orneriness, he'd prevailed finally.

Leaving the porch, Sonny walked to the edge of the yard, amused how the little bitch refused to undress when he was around. Well, if he couldn't have her, at least she was going to strip off and open her legs for someone else, whether she wanted it or not. He stared across the field at the stinking hog pen he never went near, imagining all the nights of whoring, drinking, and gambling once he got his hands on that dowry.

Today, Sonny Edwards was a happy man, a happy man, indeed.

Mercy Ann's problems had begun for a ridiculous reason—her mother's insatiable craving for chewing tobacco. If she went more than a couple of hours without a moist chaw tucked in her right cheek, she suffered terrible headaches and became an irritable, nervous wreck. It had been no problem until she remarried and her new husband, Sonny, decided it was unladylike for a wife of his to expectorate black spittle in public. Never mind that most men and women partook. He beat her half to death when he caught her disobeying his rules.

So Miz Edwards began sending her almost twelve-year-old daughter to do most of the errands in town, but because the girl had long blond hair and sultry looks, boys and men who should have known better turned into blithering idiots around her. Even worse, as months added to her age, many of them began flirting as though it was their right, making suggestive comments, lurid propositions, and trying to bully her into giving them what they wanted in spite of her still being on the young side of serious pursuit.

Mercy Ann was coarse, common, and lacked formal education. At the same time, she was highly intelligent, cunning as a fox, and could read and write, unusual even for many males on poor farms in and around Goldsboro, North Carolina. Her real daddy had taught her, and she kept it secret, for the most part, because it would create even more resentment towards her.

Not that she did much else to avoid it. Unflinchingly tough and fast thinking, she employed dismissive stares and a quick tongue to string together obscenities and nasty insults designed to pierce the ego of anyone who messed with her. Very quickly, she earned a reputation for thinking she was too good to associate with the young men of the county though all she'd ever done was react to their churlish behavior and coercion.

By the time Mercy Ann was fourteen going on fifteen, well into marrying age in those parts, hurt feelings, hot passions, and resentment had many lusty young men on the verge of forcing retribution upon her. A tense situation, the smallest thing would push them over the edge.

A boy Mercy Ann hardly knew stopped her in a store one afternoon and blurted out a marriage proposal. Surprised, frightened, and confused, she turned him down with salvos of insults and curses that sent ladies and genteel men hurrying out of earshot. Then she grabbed the bunch of droopy flowers he held out to her and threw them in his face. Since he'd been stupid enough to woo her with people around, he was a laughingstock before the sun went down.

Next day, to salvage his self-respect, he began telling everyone how the "Justice Whore" had asked him to skinny-dip in Neuse River, which ended with him experiencing the dream every lusty male in the county shared about her. Raised in a God-fearing family, he said he wanted to do the honorable thing by her, and she'd treated him like shit for it.

Other spiteful males began bragging how she met them down by the river and did it with them, too. Mercy Ann Justice was nothing but a piece of dirty white trash, they said.

Now, she was fair game in the small minds of cruel, foolish people of every ilk. No longer did they hold back from going after her or calling her a whore to her face.

Even so, Mercy Ann was not easy pickings. She extricated herself from tight situations by outthinking, outtalking, outfighting, and outrunning assailants, but she realized someone would catch and force her into submission eventually. If her father was still alive, she would have gone to her parents for help, but she knew what Sonny would demand in return for his or her mother's protection, so there was no point.

Inevitably, Sonny heard the stories, came home drunk, and whipped Mercy Ann with a leather strap for screwing and ruining the family's reputation. Then he beat his wife for raising a whore and went after John Junior for yelling at him to stop. Fortunately, Sonny was too intoxicated to pull his stepson from under the bed because he never held back when striking a male. He would have killed him that night.

But Mercy Ann had an epiphany. She and John Junior were worth a considerable amount of money to Sonny. A man would pay a fair sum to wed a girl with her looks, even with a loss of virtue bringing the price down. As for John Junior, soon he would be able to do all the farm work, as well as hire out to help on other farms and take odd jobs in town.

So Mercy Ann wasn't surprised next morning when Sonny declared that his wife would go back to doing all the shopping until the uproar about her calmed down. But she was surprised when her mother told him to go to hell and wouldn't back down, even after he kicked her off the back porch. Blows and curses flew for the best part of an hour before they found a compromise.

Junior would accompany Mercy Ann when she went to town. That way, he could keep an eye out to insure she behaved and no one would bother her with him along as a witness.

Mercy Ann earned Sonny's backhand across the face for mouthing off that she could just stay home doing all the goddamned chores while Junior did all the goddamned shopping, if that was the goddamned case.

Sonny ridiculed her for being so stupid. A boy doing women's chores when there were two females in the house was not something any self-respecting man would tolerate. That was the end of the matter.

For a time everything went well, but then two brothers, ages twenty-four and twenty-one, hid in the woods next to the shortcut Mercy Ann and John Junior used to go to town. On the way back, the brothers sprang an ambush.

One punched Junior in the face, and he went down hard. Then the brothers tried forcing Mercy Ann into the bushes for what they called a little kissing, but she was not the same as the girls with whom they had become accustomed to having their evil ways.

She elbowed the younger one in the stomach, doubling him over.

The older brother, holding her other arm with both hands, was confident she couldn't get loose, and laughed at his brother for being a dumbass.

Mercy Ann twisted around, delivered a knee to his scrotum, jerked her arm free, stepped back, and placed two more sharp kicks to the same place. He went to the ground holding his balls and wondering how a girl's small bare foot could inflict so much pain.

Meanwhile, his younger brother went for her again, but Junior smacked him in the face with a broken branch, breaking his nose.

Mercy Ann grabbed the shopping basket off the ground and they ran until the house was in sight. Catching their breath, she reached beneath the cloth covering the shopping and pulled out a curved tobacco knife with a heavy wooden handle. Junior looked from the wicked blade to his sister's determined expression and commented their parents would beat the living daylights out of her if they discovered she had it.

"I know, but I'm afraid."

Startled she would admit such a thing, he put his small hand on hers. "I'll protect you, Mercy Ann."

They exchanged a stare then burst out laughing.

"Well," he said, red-faced, "I'll try anyway."

She embarrassed him with a kiss on the cheek before leading the way home. Rather than rekindle their stepfather's wrath, they made up a story about a group of bullies picking a fight with Junior while Mercy Ann was in a store. The parents were pleased to hear the boy had fought rather than run away because everyone considered him a milquetoast.

During the next trip to town, the younger of the brothers approached Junior, waiting for Mercy Ann at a street corner. Big enough to make two of the boy, the man sneered and warned that his whore sister would get what's coming to her from him and his brother real soon. And when they finished with her, they would deal with him. He punched Junior in the face and stalked off.

Mercy Ann found her brother sitting dazed in the street. Neither said anything on the way home. She kept one hand in the basket gripping the knife, just in case.

A widower, the father of their attackers, owned a prosperous feed store in addition to other valuable properties. He had been to the Justice farm that day to present Sonny with a proposal of marriage for Mercy Ann on behalf of his eldest son, who managed a big farm for him. To show he was well intentioned and to cement ties between the families, the son offered a dowry of two cows, a young mule, and $500, far too generous for a family with the economic and social standing of the Edwards. The only condition was that Mercy Ann had to meet with the son and personally accept the proposal within two weeks.

The excited Sonny insisted his stepdaughter would jump at such an opportunity. "She's not only pretty, she's smart. She says yes."

The man repeated his son's terms and made it clear that he had tried to talk him out of it. "She's the loveliest girl around these parts, but he can marry into any family he wants and do much better. The dowry he's offering is too much, too. No offense intended."

Tactfully, he did not mention the rumors about Mercy Ann.

True to nature, Mercy Ann turned down the offer before hearing Sonny out. He was not surprised because she acted like the Queen of Sheba strutting in the High Court of King Solomon most of the time, but he had no doubt he could make her do as told. After all, she was a weak young girl and he was a strong grownup man with say-so over her.

But after several hours haranguing, he raged angry and out of control while she sat quietly, looking up occasionally, and shaking her head.

Finally, Sonny slapped her so hard she fell off the chair. In case she didn't understand, he did it again with his other hand. He yelled that she would do what she was told and that was all there was to it.

Instead of crying and hiding behind her sobbing momma as a normal girl would, she stood toe-to-toe as if they were in a barroom fight and screamed for him to go fuck himself to death and birth a demon-baby in hell.

In a rage, Sonny drew back to hit her with all the might and fury he could put into his fist, but saw her smug expression and stopped. He was a fool doing exactly what she wanted. He lowered his hands and backed off.

"You want me to mess you up so bad he won't marry you," he declared with a sneer. "Well, I just remembered something about you that I forgot until now."

When Sonny courted her mother, she'd told him a story about Mercy Ann as a little girl trapped in the tobacco tool room. The door had been left ajar, she went in, and ran into the rakes and shovels propped against the back wall. They fell forward against the door, closing and jamming it shut. In the dark, little Mercy Ann did not understand what happened and could not get out.

They had searched miles around for days on end before her father discovered the blocked door, realized what happened, and kicked it in. Fortunately, Mercy Ann was still alive. Since then, she had been terrified of small closed spaces and would not go near the tool room for any reason.

Sonny told what he planned to do and grabbed her. Laughing at her hysterics, he dragged her by the hair kicking and screaming into the backyard.

Junior ran out, tried to block the way, and Sonny kicked him to the ground. His wife shouted and flailed at him. He doubled her over with a punch to the stomach.

Next morning, Sonny sent his wife to let Mercy Ann out to do chores. Noting her bleeding hands and knees, he asked if she was ready to give in then whipped her with a strap when she told him to stick his head up his ass and lick his brains. And so it went for several days, yet she showed no sign of breaking.

After that, Sonny stopped letting her out for any reason until the morning of the thirteenth day. All she'd eaten during that time was water, bread soaked in fat, and raw ears of corn.

He warned his wife that if Mercy Ann didn't give in this time, he'd sell her to one of the brothels near the river and good riddance.

When she screamed she'd go to the law on him, he answered with the quietest words he'd ever uttered to her. "If you don't want this house burned down with you and Junior in it when I take her away, you'll convince the little bitch this is her last chance. Now, go fetch her."

After Mercy Ann agreed to the marriage, Sonny departed for town to set up the meeting with her intended's family.

Miz Edwards came out of the house with more food for her daughter and commented it was a shame she was not up to running away today since Sonny would be away until late that night.

Mercy Ann, sitting on the ground eating while John Junior dug splinters out of the other hand with a big needle, surprised her. "He's hiding in the trees watching because he expects me to do just that. He won't go to the bars tonight, either. We'll have to find a way to stop him worrying about me lighting out so he'll go drinking. Then we can go."

Their mother expressed surprise that Sonny spied on them.

Junior explained they could tell when he actually left for town because he always took the shortest way past the two fishing ponds and disturbed the birds, causing them to fly up above the trees.

She was impressed he had figured that out.

Junior gave credit to Mercy Ann. “She notices everything.”

Sonny returned an hour before dark. He stopped short of getting mean drunk and was in a good mood for a change. He had the biggest kerosene lantern they had ever seen and told how Mercy Ann’s intended made them.

“He’s a regular Thomas Edison, inventing something like this,” he bragged. “His daddy’s thinking of setting up a factory to compete with the Yankees up north getting rich off making lanterns. Reckons four this size will put out enough light to work fields at night. Holds a shit-load of fuel and don’t need filling so much, either. We’re lucky to be joining up with that family.”

A little while later, his wife put a damper on his good mood by insisting he turn off the lantern and take it outside away from the house because it was so leaky and gave off terrible fumes. For once, Sonny did not argue.

During a late supper of fried cornbread, chitlins, and taters, he told how he had been at the feed store with their future in-laws drinking the best moonshine in the county. Mercy Ann’s intended had wanted her brought tomorrow to hear her say yes, but he’d got them to give two extra days by telling how she fell herding hogs and scraped up her hands and knees.

Laughing, he leered at his stepson. “Course, it’s not her hands her intended’s wanting to see, is it?”

Embarrassed for his sister, John Junior got up and went to the counter for the small washtub. He started outside with it.

Sonny barked, “What the hell you doing, boy?”

“Fetching water to wash dishes since Mercy Ann can’t do it.”

Sonny erupted. “No male in my house is doing woman’s work! Put your ass back in that chair until I say you’re excused.”

As Junior hurried to obey, his wife got up do the chore but Sonny hitched a thumb at Mercy Ann. “She messed up her hands and don’t deserve no goddamned help. Get off your lazy ass, girl, and do as I say before I smack you a good one.”

Mercy Ann had not finished eating because it was hard for her and Sonny had objected when her mother tried to help. For a few seconds, it appeared she might badmouth him, but then she pushed the food away, got up, and walked slowly outside holding the tub with her forearms.

Sonny gloated. “Well, well. I should have put her in that goddamned tool room the day I moved in. Would’ve had some peace and quiet.”

Next day, Mercy Ann dragged around the farm looking as if each step might be her last. At first, Sonny watched with an expression of glee and satisfaction, but as the day wore on, it turned to worry. That evening, she began coughing weakly.

Sonny, sitting on the front porch with his wife, threatened, "If the little bitch is too sick to go into town when I said, I'm going to throw both of you down the well."

Wearily, she got up. "I'll put more VapoRub on her chest, but it'd be provident to tell them she's come down with a bad cold and needs another day, just in case."

"Goddamn it, don't give me your bullshit! You go tell her she's going when I told them, no excuses."

Next morning, Mercy Ann came to breakfast with red watery eyes and a snotty nose. Plopping down in a chair, she rested her head on the table in her arms, showing no interest in eating.

Sonny kept looking over at her with growing irritation then warned, "She'd better be ready to go tomorrow, woman!"

"She won't be ready until day after tomorrow, like I said. Anyone with eyes can see that. You go tell them she needs another day, Sonny Edwards."

Watching his stepdaddy across the table, Junior tensed because he thought Sonny was going to strike his mother, but then Mercy Ann distracted him by coughing and sticking her swollen hands out.

Her voice was deep, weak, and phlegmy. "I think they're looking better, don't you?"

Sonny cursed, ordered his stepson to do his sister's chores, and made Mercy Ann go back to bed. Then he spent most of the day chewing tobacco, fidgeting, and pacing everywhere on the farm except the hog pen. He did not speak to his wife again until late in the afternoon when he sent her to check on Mercy Ann again. He did not like the report.

"Her fever broke, but she's too weak to go tomorrow," she said, bone-tired and fed up. "Needs to rest another day or she might come down with pneumonia."

He cursed her.

In spite of her fear, she persisted. "Just go tell them, Sonny. You'll have bigger problems if she doesn't rest a couple more nights. As it is, the girl can hardly move."

"Goddamn you!" he shouted. "She'd better be ready day after tomorrow!"

Sonny rushed off to town to find the groom's father, who everyone knew closed the feed store so he could count the money because he didn't trust anyone else to do it. And, although he hid it, Sonny wanted to avoid dealing with the sons, especially the older one, because there were so many unsavory stories about them. On the other hand, he reckoned an asshole husband who didn't put up with any mess was exactly what Mercy Ann deserved, so it wasn't all bad.

When Sonny went to town that late in the day, he never returned home until after midnight or the next morning, depending on whether he had enough money to pay a whore for the whole night.

Seeing the birds fly above the ponds, John Junior gave the all clear and Mercy Ann ran out to the pump to wash VapoRub from under her eyes and out of her nose. Then she drank from the spout to get it out of her throat, which accounted for the husky voice.

Her mother had sneaked food into her bedroom, so the sickly weakness Sonny had witnessed was an act. Picking at scabs had made the wounds appear worse than they were, too.

Mercy Ann and John Junior had their meager belongings bundled in a blanket each, ready to go. No time for long farewells, their mother kissed and hugged them then they left her standing in front of the house. Junior kept looking back and waving. Mercy Ann blamed her mother and did not look back a single time.

Mercy Ann took a path running through the fields of their farm and the adjacent one then turned onto a seldom-used trail into the woods. Reaching an intersection, she went south, confusing Junior even more.

"This isn't the right way, is it?" he asked.

"We're not going to Level Cross," she answered without looking back or slowing. "That's the first place Sonny will look."

"Thomas won't let him take us."

"Sonny is our legal daddy now. He'll get the sheriff after us. Thomas won't be able to do anything about it. Momma can't either."

"Where are we going then?"

"Our best chance is to take a train to Greensboro and find Aunt Minnie. She and daddy were close. When he died, she gave me her address at the funeral and said to write if I ever needed help."

"You didn't write, did you?"

"No. I was afraid someone would ask Sonny why I was in the post office mailing letters. You know how nosy everyone is."

"What's Aunt Minnie going to say when two runaways show up on her doorstep?"

"Don't know, but it's all I can think to do."

"How are we going to take a train? We only have a dollar. For that matter, how are we going to eat?"

"I have other money. We're on our way to get more."

"How come you have money? No one else does."

"From the first time momma sent me to do errands, I've been putting money aside to run away."

News that she had been thinking of running away did not surprise him, but the money did. "You're talking about pennies. That's not enough money for trains and food, Mercy Ann."

"I have plenty," she said, exasperated. "Guess I better warn you, though. We're going into colored town. You keep your mouth shut and don't be staring."

They came out of the woods and crossed a meadow into a part of Goldsboro Junior had never been. Mercy Ann need not have cautioned him about staring because he was afraid to look anywhere but his sister's back.

She strode down the street as if she owned it and flabbergasted her brother by nodding politely to the colored women they met. She even wished two older ones a good day. She did not speak to the men.

A couple of young, burly farm hands dressed in overalls approached and kept moving subtly to block them when Mercy Ann shifted course to avoid them. Instead of stopping or yielding way as they expected, she speeded up, walking straight at them. They had to hurry out of the way or collide with a young white girl, an offense that would almost certainly result in harsh retribution.

Mercy Ann stopped in front of a small tidy house with a picket fence, opened the gate, and led Junior up onto the porch. The front door opened before they reached it.

A tall black man with graying hair and dressed in a fine suit greeted them. "It is a fine day, Miss Justice, young gentleman."

"Indeed it is, Mr. Parrish," she responded with a respectful nod. "This is my brother, John Junior. May we see Mavis?"

"Welcome, Mr. Junior," he said, stepping back and gesturing grandly for them to go through to the next room.

Heart pounding, gaping at expensive furnishings, and afraid to look back at the big black man behind him, John Junior followed Mercy Ann so closely he stepped on her heels. Then he experienced the most breathtaking sight of his life.

A pretty, youngish woman dressed in red silk finery sat in a yellow brocade chair smoking an ebony pipe, the open window behind her keeping the air in the room tolerable. Cocking her head slightly, she studied him with a somewhat amused expression accented by alluring ruby lips pursed around a shapely mouth.

Realizing he'd never noticed anyone's mouth this way before, John Justice could not stop staring. Then the quiet, gentle way she spoke made him feel warm all over, another startling new experience.

"Are you keeping well, Mercy Ann? This handsome young man must be the wonderful brother you've mentioned so often."

"Yes, thank you. This is Mrs. Mavis Parrish, John Junior, as fine a lady as ever you'll meet."

He was speechless. Half the town was colored, but he'd hardly spoken to any of them his whole life. Moreover, his attitude about coloreds reflected what most white people in those parts thought at the turn of the century, so it was heavy with prejudice and ignorance. More confounding, now he learned his sister did not share those opinions, and he was face-to-face with a woman who did not fit the stereotypes he'd accepted as absolute truth.

Mercy Ann elbowed him. "Mind your manners and say hello."

He stuttered an acceptable greeting.

After that, Mavis turned all her attention to Mercy Ann. "Did you bring something, or is there another reason for the pleasure of your company today?"

"Both." Mercy Ann reached into her blanket of belongings and began pulling out items from stores in town.

Junior stared in amazement as she kept taking merchandise out. He had wondered why her bundle was so much weightier than the one he had.

Mavis examined three sets of fancy hairpins. "How did you get these? They keep them behind the counter."

"Yes, because they're so expensive." She didn't say how she got them.

Mavis gave her a respectful nod and picked up a small box of candy. "I really like these."

"I told Mr. Applewhite they were my favorite and he gave them to me."

Mavis chuckled. "Did you give him something back?"

"I sashayed my butt like you showed me, is all. It's a gift for you."

"So I'll pay more for everything else. Right?"

"Well, I did have a good teacher."

She had a soft laugh. "Are you sure you don't want to come work with me, full partners? We'll both be rich in a year. Then we'll go to France and never look back."

Mercy Ann let out a long sigh in a way her brother had never before heard. "Actually, I have a little problem and need your advice."

She told about the brothers, her stepdaddy, and the marriage proposal. Then she told how she came to be so scraped up and that she and Junior were running away to catch the early morning train out of town.

Taking a draw on the pipe, Mavis turned her head and blew smoke out the window. "I thought your injuries might be from something like that. Hope you don't mind me saying outright, but sounds like you think your fiancé is up to no good."

Mercy Ann looked at John Junior. "Guess you're going to do some growing up tonight. Try not to be too upset." Then to Mavis she said, "He and his brother just want to fuck me. Expect they'll keep me locked up until they're tired of it then arrange an accident. Of course, I'll try to kill them first, but either way, I'm done for if I can't get away from here."

Junior exclaimed, "We can go to the sheriff!"

"Won't do any damn good," Mercy Ann said. "Only tip those shithead brothers off that I know what they're up to. Then I'll end up dead, anyway."

"I'll kill anybody who hurts you!" John Junior swore.

She had never seen him so determined, and it touched her heart. "It's not going to come to that."

"A couple of poor farm girls disappeared after being with those boys," Mavis confided. "They like hurting working girls, too. I don't allow them in my establishments anymore, but others look away because their daddy pays people off. Suppose you know your no-count stepdaddy is in town tonight, too. Did you meet anyone coming here who might tell him they've seen you?"

"Only saw coloreds. Didn't know any of them."

"Everybody knows you, honey," she replied thoughtfully, "and some might work for the brothers' daddy. You best stay here until after dark then go out along the edge of town, wait until daylight, and sneak back on the street running straight to the train station. Less chance of trouble finding you that way."

Mr. Parrish rushed into the room. "You can't send them outside town at night, Mavis. People have been seeing spirit lights again. Preacher says they're restless dead risen from graves looking to drag sinners down to Perdition. They mustn't go out there."

Mavis snorted. "Don't keep repeating everything that comes out of that crazy preacher's mouth. He'll say anything to get more money on the plate."

"Old Moses Miller and his missus witnessed before the congregation how they saw shining spirits in a cornfield," he said. "They were so scared that the preacher offered them to sleep at the church until the dead settle down a mite, but Old Moses said no, he keeps his shotgun next to the bed and reckoned they would be just fine."

"Sounds like they were drinking moonshine, ask me," Mavis responded.

"There's more," he insisted. "I wasn't going to scare you with this, but this morning, Davis, Old Moses' brother, went by to check on them. The front door was wide-open, nary hide or hair of them anywhere. On the floor in the front room was the shotgun, both barrels fired. The spirits done took them, Mavis. There's the proof what's going on staring in your doubting face."

She was curious in spite of herself. "Did the sheriff go out and look around? What'd he say?"

"What he always says to folks like us. Strangers passing through town did it. Davis asked where the bodies were then. Sheriff told him to search the woods for turned ground or go look downriver if he wanted to waste time. Several of us tried telling about the spirit lights, but he wouldn't hear it." He shook his head. "Colored people ain't safe, and the law doesn't care a whit."

Mavis jabbed her pipe at him. "Next time I need you, I'll go look under the bed to see if you're hiding from Haints, but for now, go fry up some fatback and beans. Reckon we don't want to send our guests into the night to face evil spirits on empty stomachs, do we?"

Three hours later, making way in a moonless night along dark streets, Mercy Ann whispered to John Junior how unfair it was that most of colored town didn't have electricity. Then they were cutting across dark farm fields along the town's outskirts, planning to follow Mavis' advice to wait until just before dawn before going to the station. They had about two miles to go before they reached the road they wanted. Progress was slow and plodding.

Junior had been unusually quiet for some time when he asked, "Why are you associating with the coloreds?"

She understood what he meant. "They're no different than you and me except for skin."

"White people are smarter."

"I just told you, except for skin, there's no difference. Do you think you're smarter than Mavis is? I'm not."

Again, he was silent for a while. "She gave you newspapers to read on the train. She can't read, can she?"

"Yes. She even lends me books sometimes."

He thought about that. "Sonny says the reason you're so uppity is because daddy taught you to read and write. Says it's a waste of time, especially for girls."

"Everybody looks uppity to the likes of Sonny Edwards. He's lower than a dog turd mashed into the ground under a shithouse."

"Momma said coloreds can't be trusted and have to be kept in their place. Before he died, daddy said so, too."

"They were raised to believe that way. So were we, but I studied on it, and far as I'm concerned, whites and coloreds both have good and bad, smart and stupid."

"Momma said the reason coloreds can't use the same facilities in town as us is because they aren't clean and give white people diseases."

"Yeah," she replied ruefully, "that's why all the white trash farmers like Sonny stick their business inside black girls at the whorehouses every chance they get."

"Whores are black?"

"Only the ones who aren't white or brown."

"White men do it with all kinds?"

"There's only one kind, Junior. They're called people."

He thought about it. "When the cable car line starts operating next year, coloreds will have to sit on the back benches, if they're allowed to ride at all. If they're good as us, why is that?"

"Because white people treat black people worse than wild animals."

"But momma said it."

"Goddamn it, enough! Use your brain and make up your own mind after you have experience. Don't just believe what anyone tells you, no matter who they are."

"Including you?"

"Goddamn right! Decide things for yourself."

"Why do you always think you know better than everyone else, Mercy Ann?"

"When you're older and smarter, you'll figure out that your big sister is always right."

He laughed a little.

She tripped and almost fell. "Wish we had moonlight."

They walked in silence until he whispered with urgency, "Someone is trailing us with a closed lantern. You can see light from it if you look back carefully."

She glanced back over her shoulder and saw it. She and John Justice were not far from the road that led to the station and had a long lead, but it meant they would have to change their plan and hide in town until daylight.

But then, up ahead, she spotted movement beside the road they wanted. She looked away across the fields at the dark shadows of wooded areas. If they had to go that way to hide, she and Junior had a good head start but were at great disadvantage without a lantern. These fields were unplanted, rough, and uneven. The furrows ran away from town, though, which helped some.

"You see the men up ahead, don't you?" Junior whispered.

"Yes, but keep moving. I'm trying to decide whether to run into town or across the fields to the woods. What do you think?"

"We don't know the streets in town good as them. Let's go across the fields. If we're lucky, they'll come into the field after us. Then we can angle back towards the road going out of town with a good chance reaching it with a lead since men drink and smoke so much. We'll sneak back to catch the train in the morning. Do you feel strong enough to run that far?"

"This shit happened because I'm marrying age and stood up for myself. Wish I could have stayed thirteen forever."

"Wishes don't mean shit, do they?"

"Wishes are another word for hope. If you don't have hope, you might as well be dead."

"Then I have a wish. If we get out of this, stop calling me Junior. Daddy's dead and I'm not a kid anymore."

"Do you want to be called John?"

"Daddy was John. I'll be John Justice."

"Both names?"

"You bet."

She laughed a little to hide her nervousness. "We're a pair, huh? You want to be older and I want to be younger."

The men ahead stood and uncovered a huge lantern that cast so much light they could identify Sonny and the brothers clearly. They just stood there, probably discussing whether to go after them now or wait until they made the first move.

"We have to do something real soon," John Justice warned.

Mercy Ann stopped. "What do you think our chances of getting away are?"

"That lantern is heavy if it's full of kerosene, but they're strong and it won't slow them down enough for us to make up the advantage light gives."

"Wish I'd brought the knife."

He hesitated. "Would you use it on them?"

She wiped away tears with the back of her hand, glad it was dark so he couldn't see how many there were. "I had something else in mind, but yes, I'd use it on them. We'd better get going. Will you lead?"

"Can you keep up?"

"If I leave my bundle and hold my dress up." She gave him all the money to put in his pocket and tossed her belongings away. "Go fast as you can."

The men trailing them uncovered the lantern and turned back toward colored town. Even with the distance, they recognized the two big farmhands they encountered on the way to the Parish house.

Sonny and the brothers did not run into the field, moving parallel to them on the road. John Junior had no choice but to turn away towards the dark woods. The brothers and Sonny ran into the field. Very quickly, the brothers outdistanced him.

John Junior tripped and hurt his knee. He told Mercy Ann to leave him behind, but there was no point since they would catch her regardless. She helped him up and they ran fast as they could. Now, however, a line of strange bobbing lights was in the tree line ahead.

Junior asked over his shoulder what she wanted to do.

"Keep going toward the lights," she said, more afraid of known horrors than evil spirits.

The brothers had almost reached them and were calling out lewd taunts about what they planned to do to Mercy Ann when one stumbled jumping a dry irrigation ditch and collided with his brother, sending both crashing down into it. The lamp broke and kerosene fire engulfed them. The screams were terrible.

Sonny thought the so-called spirit lights ahead were hunters or moonshiners. Besides, they did not seem to be moving in his direction, even with the fire and screams. Ignoring the burning, thrashing brothers, he did not give them a second look when he jumped the ditch because his anger towards Mercy Ann was at the boiling point.

The little bitch's obstinacy had cost him his fortune, and he wanted revenge. He would have some fun then gut her. He'd gut the boy, too. If the brothers were still alive, he'd smother them and leave the bloody knife. They'd been drinking all evening, and with their reputations and the rumors, no one would doubt they raped and killed Mercy Ann, killed her brother, and had a drunken accident.

He would be scot-free because he'd met up with them on the street and learned his stepdaughter was trying to run away. He'd hurry back to the bars, drink, and make sure everyone noticed him. In a few months, his wife would have an accident and he'd find a rich widow worth having, something he should have done long ago.

He caught Mercy Ann and rode her down from behind. Junior ran back yelling to get off her. He poleaxed the boy with his big forearm, and he went down hard, hitting his head on a rock.

Taking his stepdaughter by the shoulders, Sonny twisted her onto her back. Whipping out his knife, he held the flat of the blade against her neck and kissed her. Desire raging, he ripped her dress and underwear off and worked his pants down.

Wide-eyed, Mercy Ann glared up helplessly.

"Say you want it and I'll kill you quick when I'm done, bitch," Sonny said with a sneer that promised otherwise.

Mercy Ann struggled, but he was too strong.

Sonny savored her frightened expression, bent forward, and licked her face. Seeing her revulsion, he threw back his head and laughed. Then he stopped abruptly, his body tensing and raising up slightly off her. His eyes showed fear and bewilderment then went blank. Blood gushed out of his mouth. He fell over sideways.

John Junior was behind Sonny. He stared down at the big curved tobacco knife buried to the handle in the side of his stepdaddy's neck.

Working free of Sonny's legs, Mercy Ann sat up, pulled her brother down, and hugged him against her.

Dazed, John Junior stared over her shoulder at one of the brothers trying to stand, face burned so badly that he couldn't tell which one it was. Facedown half out of the ditch, the other one was still as death. Then he wondered why he could see so well at night and looked up at an enormous glowing light coming down slowly out of the dark sky.

"What is that, Mercy Ann?" he asked in a hushed voice.

Watching tall silver figures gliding fast and soundless across the field towards them, she had no explanation except evil spirits coming to take them to hell. She might have screamed if not for trying to be brave so her brother would not turn around to look.

She patted his back and called him by his new name. "I love you, John Justice."

A weightless, anonymous presence floating in black nothingness, Mercy Ann Justice—designated by the species collectors as a humanoid specimen from the third planet of system 10,971—had no sense of self, recollection of the past, or concept of future. Days became years. Years became decades. She knew nothing else until—

Bright flashing light and jangling bells returned her to reality. Hoses, cables, and wires floated around her in thick, translucent green liquid, entering and exiting her body in numerous places.

She recalled attachments to the back of her head and tried feeling for them, but her arms would not respond. She wanted to move her legs and felt restraints on one of them, triggering a memory of her blood turning the green gel murky orange inside the black, casket-sized box where they kept her because one of the silver creatures had sliced off her leg with a narrow red beam and taken it away.

Soundlessly screaming, she choked on tubes and wires jammed into her nose and mouth, and down her throat. She jerked up, banging her head on the box lid and pulling connections loose inside her. Burning sensations spread through her body then made their way outside, burning the places where she still had skin. Mercifully, her world became black and painless again, but reality remained.

Light returned without upset or pain. The top lifted off. Just above the surface of the gel, a sparkling ball of light moved back and forth slowly, "speaking" in her mind.

It explained that she had been given enough knowledge to understand what it was about to tell her. She must not comment except to answer questions. It asked if she understood.

Although she couldn't speak, she heard her voice. "Yes."

A group of scientists known generally as species collectors had abducted and preserved her and her sibling in medical stasis chambers to determine how susceptible Earth would be to invasion. They removed body parts and caused extensive damage. Her sibling's condition was relatively the same as hers. It asked if she understood.

She was amazed how calm she was. "Yes."

They were collected in Earth year 1909. It was now Earth year 1951. During periods of experimentation outside of stasis, they had aged normally, but unless the collectors' records noted durations of those periods, their exact Earth ages could not be determined. It asked if she understood.

"Yes."

She and her sibling were the only specimens found alive. It was unclear so far why they were preserved. She must listen closely because she had choices to make. They had interviewed her sibling already. He wanted the same fate she chose, so her decision would be for both. It asked if she understood.

"Yes."

She could choose to die peacefully inside the stasis chamber or have her health restored good as new then serve in a fleet manned by surrogate forces protecting the territory where Earth and other planets were located. One condition existed for the second choice. She and her sibling must never divulge their Earth origin. Until now, the beings that controlled the territory allowed no species from the lesser-developed planets to travel in space. Her rescuers did not want to explain reasons for an exception to the more evolved members. It asked if she understood.

"Yes."

Which did she choose?

Mercy Ann's will broke through the strong sedation they had administered. "Two crap-ass choices are all you have?"

Taken aback, the creature explained that returning rescuees to home planets with no memories was an option in some cases, but humanoid repairs required implanting technology too advanced and dangerous to chance Earth discovering it. Then it repeated to hold comments and questions until the interview ended and asked if she understood.

For Mercy Ann, the pain and suffering of her life on Earth ended yesterday, not forty-two years ago. "Just so you know, I hate goddamned Earth and sure as hell don't want to talk about it, but stop telling me to keep my mouth shut as if I'm inferior to you and the other assholes in your fucking fleet. It pisses me off. Do *you* understand?"

A long interval ticked by before the creature asked why she used such crude, insulting language with someone trying to help her.

Mercy Ann realized she should shut up, but anger about the terrors perpetuated against her for no reason raced full-speed in her mind, and she had to express them or burst. "If you wanted a fucking princess with sweet-smelling roses up her ass, you chose the wrong fucking box. They cut my goddamned leg off, and you're worried about cussing. What the hell is wrong with you, you fucking jack-o-lantern?"

The creature remained unmoving and silent as several minutes passed.

Finally, Mercy Ann said, "Sorry. I know I use bad words too much, but that's how I learned to talk. I meant what I said, though."

The creature replied that she still needed to choose whether she wanted to stay in the fucking box or join the fucking fleet.

In her mind, Mercy Ann laughed and wondered if he could tell. "I'll join the fleet."

The creature congratulated her then said a very surprising thing. It liked her more than all other species it had encountered and wanted to give her a special gift to signify her new beginning.

As she tried to think how to respond, everything around her changed.

She floated alone in the vastness of space, no longer inside the box, no longer inside a spaceship. Towering star-embedded blue clouds billowed around her, ranging from dark blue-black tones in thick layers to luminous blue-white wisps at the farthest reaches. Gossamer openings dotted the massive formations with distant stars sparkling through them—as though flickering candles glowed in heavenly windows.

When the box closed around her again, Mercy Ann shook with emotion. "I never expected to see clouds and stars mixed together that way. Was it Heaven? Already, my heart aches to see them again."

The creature explained that the clouds were made of the same matter as the stars, which sometimes formed and died inside the huge formations. In travels with the fleet, she would see star clouds of every hue and color, but blue was the rarest. His species considered this one the most magnificent of them all, yet gave it the simplest name—the Blue Cloud Nebula.

"Thank you for my new life," Mercy Ann said, meaning it with every fiber of her being. "I will try to do better this time."

The little ship awoke Mercy Ann. She yawned, checked the screen, and found the familiar blue dot of Earth, but it grew in size faster than experience taught it should, so she punched on the speed indicator. The numbers didn't make sense no matter how she displayed them. She turned it off.

Time to face facts, she told herself grimly. The Sufficiency Test was surely over. John Justice, Honey Bee, and Miss Flowers would be back with the fleet. When she was closer to Earth, she'd send them a hailing message.

Then she thought better of it. Failing to save Earth would be hard for John Justice, in spite of all his bitching about it. It wouldn't be fair to call and make him give her the bad news. Better to survey the planet to see the condition herself. Later, she would grieve.

The screen flashed red, signifying an enemy sighting, but no readouts she could access indicated how far away or the direction. A cable was in the port on the back of her head, connecting her basic weapons systems to the ship. Until she knew the type of threat, she connected cables to the advanced weapons ports on the insides of both forearms. They were what made her uniquely dangerous.

A formation of ten red blips appeared on the screen near the Moon on Earth-side finally. A long name popped up that she recognized as the Guardian words for Gargle heavy cruisers. Surely, John Justice and Honey Bee were long gone, so she could simply run away. She shook her head. She'd lost Earth and really wanted to fight.

Mercy Ann checked to insure she had full control of the ship then wished she could scan to verify Earth's status before engaging, but the Gargle would detect it. Studying attack and defense possibilities, she no longer felt concern for anything but battle strategy. After all, this was her main purpose in life and she was very good at it.

Changing course to keep the Moon between them, she calculated how fast the ship could whip around it for a surprise attack. She would take out as many as possible in a single pass then use her speed to string out the formation chasing her to Earth, which should present openings to pick off a few more. She'd plunge into the atmosphere and finish the fight there. If she lost, she'd die on the dead planet she failed to save. Yeah, she thought, that's an appropriate end for me.

Nearing the Moon, she synchronized her special weapons to activate simultaneously, opened the ship's external ports, and checked the firing levels on the screen. She had to look a second time to believe her eyes. Her Guardian had not exaggerated about this ship boosting her firepower.

Whizzing behind the Moon, she watched the bright horizon racing towards her. Five minutes more and Earth would rise to meet her. Twenty seconds after that, the enemy would realize the small object streaking towards them was not space debris. They had no idea how fast this ship could move and maneuver, which gave her great advantage, or so she hoped since was uncertain how to use many of the systems.

Almost there, she thought, and began saying a prayer for the people of Earth even though she thought religions were hooey. Then a more appropriate homage occurred to her. Waiting until a few seconds before the enemy detected her, she opened all frequencies and discovered mankind was still alive and well on Earth.

Overjoyed, she shouted, “Houston, you have a problem. Mercy Ann is coming home.”

18

UFO Battle over America

EARLY RISERS ON THE EAST COAST AWOKE TO SHOCKING REPORTS that the White House had been attacked during the night by terrorists. Unofficial accounts indicated the building suffered heavy damage, but authorities would not corroborate and amateur videos taken in the night before placing the National Mall off limits were next to useless due to smoke and heavy rainfall. The government did announce that all attackers were dead and an address by the President to the nation was imminent.

Soon, everyone would learn from the Vice-President, sworn in as President, that terrorists destroyed the White House and, presumably, the First Family. Portions of the East and West Wing's first floor exterior walls and remnants of the North and South Porticos remained, and that was all. Rescuers had dug down to the ultra-secure underground bunker and found no one inside.

Experts combing the site had never seen anything like this. Literally blown to bits, body parts required sorting and testing for identification—a gruesome, painstakingly slow, laboratory process. Weapons and other paraphernalia used by White House security personnel, as well as automatic rifles, bomb vests, and pistols of Middle Eastern origin were bent, twisted, or in pieces, indicating the extraordinary power of the blast. Yet, nothing suggested the kind of explosive that destroyed everything so utterly without collateral damage to surroundings.

Security discovered three passenger vans and a delivery truck abandoned in a nearby underground parking garage with fast food trash, syringes, and tobacco products from the Middle East, predominantly Saudi Arabia. Tightly controlled special passes allowing access to the garage found in the vehicles suggested inside help.

Which made sense because it was already obvious the attackers had the help of White House security personnel. Nothing else explained how they breached one of the most secure areas in the world. At the same time, it appeared all the terrorists and security personnel perished, which raised another confounding question. That the terrorists carried out a suicide mission was a reasonable assumption, but no one believed the entire American security force sacrificed themselves.

Had anyone told the world that in a few hours a second event would occur that wrested everyone's attention away from the White House tragedy, no one would have believed it possible.

Miss Flowers entered the ship's operations room and found John Justice studying dozens of small wall screens displaying e-mails and documents. She asked what he was doing.

"Jared Handley is the leading supplier of weapons and tactical equipment to militaries around the world, including missiles with nuclear warheads. I've found evidence he smuggled twelve to the Middle East. Around the same time, groups of his engineers and technical personnel spent two years working on various projects in the Death Valley region. It seems reasonable to assume that some of them constructed underground launch sites for the missiles, but I can't find evidence of it. Very strange."

She was less than impressed. "What does any of that have to do with us?"

"Just think, Handley, a private citizen, is a nuclear power unto himself and no one on Earth realizes. It's an amazing feat."

She rolled her eyes. "You should be helping us deal with the President's wife, not wasting time with this. All she does is threaten and make demands since you had me place the children in stasis."

"Soon as Honey Bee finishes treating her husband, she'll calm down."

"Honey Bee refuses to administer to the President until she receives an apology from his wife, who called her a shrunken freak. You need to order Honey Bee to help the President before his wife forces one of us to retaliate against her."

John Justice scowled. "That must not happen. I have other important matters to deal with before I waste time with this stupid situation. I'll be back shortly."

The general and sergeant major, stunned by news that the President and his family were dead in the attack on the White House, walked slowly along the inner defense perimeter of the devastation near the smallest pyramid.

The general told his friend that John Justice had warned an incident would occur overnight to keep the three-star from coming to California today, but hadn't specified any details.

The sergeant major reacted with anger because John Justice had not told them so they could warn the White House. The general said they should hear what he had to say before judging too harshly. The sergeant major disagreed, and loudly.

John Justice, behind them, said, "The President and his family are in the house with us unharmed."

After hearing a brief account of the incident, the general responded, "We have to let Washington know he's alive. We swore in a new President a few minutes ago."

John Justice explained that the President had a mental breakdown. The aliens had the means to restore his health, but it would take a week or so. In the meantime, it'd be easier to keep the First Family safe and deal with the conspiracy if everyone thought they were dead.

"You're asking a lot," the general said.

John Justice told him that Abd al-Bensi took orders from Jared Handley, whose objective was to control the biggest oil producing countries in the Middle East in addition to his holdings in the Americas. "We have to consider that, too."

"Mercy Ann didn't say anything about the terrorists and conspirators working together," the general sputtered. "Are you certain?"

"I have tons of evidence I can show you," John Justice responded. "If that doesn't convince you, Handley nearly has control of your country already. Your new President is a member of his conspiracy."

The news staggered the general. "If you have proof, we can have him arrested and tried for treason."

"That route will ignite a civil war that either side could win at the cost of thousands of casualties on both sides. Better to expose the leaders of the conspiracy, separate them from their supporters, and then eliminate the leaders."

"That's a tall order," the general stated, staring down at the slight boy.

"Yes," John Justice agreed with a nod, "but if we work together, we can do it. I apologize, but I just received emergency information that requires me to return to the ship. Alerts from NORAD are on the way to you, too. We'll get back together as soon as this new problem is resolved."

He disappeared.

NORAD, the North American Aerospace Defense Command, had provided the UFO information to the White House the day before then continued tracking the aliens approaching Earth overnight.

Scientists, examining pictures taken by orbiting telescopes, noticed a glimmer ahead of the UFOs and surmised it might be the ship fighting them. Others argued the slight curve suggested a small object that could not possibly have a drive system and weapons to fight the large ships chasing it. They failed to consider that assessing alien capabilities based on Earth's technology was unreliable.

As the UFOs adjusted course to enter Earth's atmosphere, one pulled ahead of the others and exploded. A short time later, the scientists opined that a fiery streak coming down from space over Iran must be the mystery ship until an astrophysicist declared the angle too steep for controlled entry and declared it a meteorite.

Someone else speculated the bigger UFOs might have shot their adversary down, so the object over Iran could be the enemy ship burning up in the atmosphere.

The four star general in charge of NORAD asked where the group of large UFOs were coming down.

"Two hundred miles southwest of Gibraltar," a tracking officer responded, putting an interactive descent graph on the screen that depicted them as blips. "If they remain at the current heading, they're on a direct course for the United States."

Noting that the streaking object over Iran appeared to be pulling out of the descent, the general commented, "That's appears to be a pilot trying to save his ass, but he waited too long."

A satellite photograph of the solitary ship showed on the screen, a blurry image with six enormous, fan-shaped pink appendages extended from a fiery ball, very much resembling an enormous flower. A more precise computer-enhanced picture showed the appendages not attached to the fireball.

The general thought aloud. “Could those function as drag chutes?”

An engineer responded, “Nothing could withstand that much velocity and heat.”

A new picture of the object came up. The appendages were half the former size. The next showed the ball of fire only.

The descent graph reappeared. Now the small ship moved horizontally along the baseline, all but merged with it.

“Goddamn it,” the general exclaimed, “the son of a bitch pulled out in the nick of time!”

Alien or not, it was a hell of a feat. Some of them cheered.

The general ordered, “Show map locations along the baseline.”

Data loaded. The little ship passed over the island of Cyprus at an altitude of one hundred feet on a direct heading to Crete.

A pilot whistled. “Talk about dragging your butt on the ground.”

An enhanced picture of the ship taken by a spy satellite occupied half the screen, eliciting oohs-and-aahs.

The ship was a small, dark green oval viewed through an enormous, semi-transparent pink and blue object tracking above it. As they speculated what it could be, an image taken by a NATO jet fighter as the alien ship passed showed it from the side.

An excited engineer shouted, “It’s a gyroscope! What the hell?”

Many times larger than the ship, the pink of the gyroscope body was the same as the translucent fan-shaped petals had been. The luminous, spinning roto was light blue.

Awe-struck, the general spoke in a hushed voice. “It has an ethereal quality as if made of light. Doesn’t seem attached to the craft, either. I never in my life thought I would see something like this. Remarkable.”

They received reports that the ship’s wake caused major damage and casualties in a half-mile wide corridor across Cyprus. Pictures and videos were popping up all over the internet and would be breaking news on American TV networks shortly.

The small craft passed over Crete at an altitude of one thousand feet and a new course that would take it directly under the group of UFOs coming down over the Atlantic.

Everyone agreed it would be more advantageous for the small ship to attack as the group pulled out of descent. At its present course and speed, it would be in front of them again, as if the pilot wanted to make certain they resumed chase. No one understood why any pilot would consider that a good idea.

As the small ship passed under the group, it destroyed one of the UFOs with something resembling pulsing light flashes. The four remaining ships gave chase.

"Put the graph view back up and show their proximity," the general ordered.

Other than slight course adjustments, both sides seemed content to maintain distance and not fight, puzzling everyone in the room until an air combat specialist pointed out the smaller, faster ship had attacked previously when it could engage one foe at a time. Now, the bigger UFO's stayed in a tight formation and worked together, keeping the smaller ship at bay.

"Took them long enough to figure it out," the general commented critically.

A map appeared on the lower half of the screen showing the new heading was a direct line to Los Angeles. The general ordered a close-up of the city. The course passed directly over the pyramids. No one was surprised, but it raised tensions considerably.

A scientist half-jokingly speculated, "Maybe they're fighting for who gets Earth."

No one thought it was funny.

Standing on a control room console watching the NORAD images of the small UFO, Honey Bee recounted how, in the war-ravaged ruins of a cluster of star systems uninhabited for eons, explorers discovered data crystals that related stories of an ancient humanoid species so technologically advanced that other civilizations considered them gods. Experts concluded the stories had to be fanciful mythologies. Giving credence to that opinion, they found thousands of drawings and paintings depicting the gods' fabulous cities and achievements, but no actual images such as photographs and videos.

John Justice, standing behind the console with Rob, Blake, and Missa, asked, "Why tell us about this now?"

Honey Bee explained that hundreds of images of the small spaceship were on the crystals along with extraordinary accounts about its ability to travel anywhere in what the gods called the Designated Cosmos, by which they meant the entire universe. Some images showed ship functions and systems, including the same giant gyroscope, manifested in clusters of virtual reality fields around the physical craft, which somehow enabled travel between star systems in incredibly short times using something they called spatial-time displacement.

Honey Bee turned to face John Justice and the others. "Do you realize how extraordinary an event the discovery of this ship is?"

"Those ships are on a course straight for us," John Justice replied sternly. "Nothing else matters right now except hiding from them. Blake, please contact the general and tell him we're shutting down communications until the threat is over."

After John Justice and Honey Bee finished powering down everything except outer defenses and flight tracking, Blake quietly informed them that the general said his replacement would arrive tomorrow morning.

"Another problem," John Justice answered, "but it'll have to wait until we're in the clear."

The small ship passed over Myrtle Beach, South Carolina, holding steady at one thousand feet. The four Gargle ships followed thirty seconds behind. High above, USAF fighter jets shadowed them. All were visible from the ground. Since TV networks and cable news tracked their progress live, people everywhere along the route across the United States ran outside to watch them pass over. When the small ship reached Arizona, it began descending.

Suddenly, the monitor screens in the control room flashed red and a map of Southern California replaced the feeds from NORAD and showed two red blips moving fast from the west toward Catalina Island. The ship identified them as Gargle cruisers navigating at a negative altitude.

"They're underwater and not aware of us," John Justice explained to the others. "I think they plan to ambush the small ship."

"Yes," Honey Bee agreed. "That explains why the pursuers haven't attacked. They probably intend trying to disable rather than destroy their adversary, for surely they recognize what that ship is. I recommend we help the small ship fight them."

Her statement surprised John Justice. "Even if we succeed against the attackers, the small ship would likely turn on us."

"Yes," Honey Bee agreed, "but losing Earth is a lesser tragedy than losing that ship. It holds the secrets to travel anywhere in the universe. If Mercy Ann was here, I think that is what she would do."

"She's not here," John Justice answered. "We will remain in hiding."

Honey Bee returned to the matter at hand. "The small ship should have detected the enemy in the water by now, but it is at five hundred feet and continuing to descend. The closer it comes to the planet's surface, the less room it has to maneuver. After the pilot performed so brilliantly coming to Earth, I can't believe this behavior is carelessness, yet I see no way to prevail if it continues this way."

The small craft was at three hundred feet when it passed over Riverside and the pursuing ships shot ahead, attacking. The small ship accelerated, but took no other evasive maneuvers. Two blasts of crackling energy struck as it passed over them. A few seconds later, the Gargle cruisers went by and the ships near Catalina zoomed up out of the ocean.

Suddenly, all systems on their ship went to full power. Alarms warned of systems overload. The ship launched straight up from between the pyramids, tracking systems locking onto the four Gargle cruisers passing over the California coastline. Weapons fired.

Three of the Gargle ships, turning in reaction to warnings of a new enemy behind them, exploded.

The fourth ship had moved to join the attack against the small ship, which unleashed pulsing white beams east and west simultaneously. Enormous explosions indicated complete destruction. Debris showered into the ocean.

The small ship vanished.

John Justice and Honey Bee, with considerable assistance from Rob and Missa, regained control of their ship. A shaken John Justice landed back between the pyramids, powered down, and immediately had everyone working to determine how the small ship wrested control of their locked down systems.

As they worked, Honey Bee communicated with him privately, admitting he had been right about attempting to avoid the conflict. The little ship had taken direct hits that would have destroyed their cruiser, so their weapons would have been ineffective without Mercy Ann's additional firepower.

Several hours later, John Justice had gone to his room exhausted when a very upset Miss Flowers called him with more complaints about the First Lady. He promised to have her and the President put in stasis soon as he determined they no longer had use for the President. In the meantime, she had to deal with the situation since humanoids risked brain damage if they went in and out of stasis for short intervals unless enhanced for deep space travel.

Millions of people witnessed UFOs fly halfway around the world and engage in battle off the California coast, so hardly anyone disputed that aliens were real any longer. Major news networks speculated that John Justice and Mercy Ann must be members of one of the factions fighting. They even pointed out that the government had suggested their appearances as human children might be a façade, which sent social media into a new frenzy guessing about how they really looked, which more and more tended to be monstrous and predatory.

More Americans rushed to buy firearms, but few were available after the events of the last few weeks. At the same time, government controls unraveled. Mobs prowled the streets, fighting with remnants of law enforcement and one another.

Many people simply hid from the turmoil to wait it out, watching through cracks in blinds and curtains of their homes with a weapon of choice ready to defend what was theirs. Increasingly, they lost hope that the situation would get better.

Jared Handley, ensconced in his Colorado mansion-fortress protected by armed security forces that were part of his private worldwide army, was angry. He could not figure out how the White House attack went wrong. His key people were not supposed to die in a blast so powerful it completely destroyed the building and made identifying bodies almost impossible. It threw a monkey wrench into his plans and timetables.

On the other hand, having everyone watching flying saucers all day made it easier for him to tie up loose ends without anyone noticing. Soon, he would have everything back on track.

An encrypted line buzzed and he grabbed it, expecting good news from the lab in charge of identifying bodies taken from the White House. Instead, a pathologist told him the children's remains were not from the President's family and no one had an explanation for them being in the White House.

Handley ordered her to have the tests redone and smashed the phone down when she told him they'd been tested three times already.

How in the hell could they not be the right kids? He called the woman back, made her repeat everything, and slammed the phone down again.

Honey Bee had gone to her room to eat the only food she could consume—a thick green goo from a squeeze bottle. Only Mercy Ann had ever seen her ingest it and confided to John Justice it looked exactly like snot. He'd asked what ingredients Honey Bee used to make it and she had no idea. Then, knowing Mercy Ann as well as he did, he asked how it tasted, and she admitted that it was okay except for the smell and gelatinous bits that stuck between the teeth.

Ashlyn and Miss Flowers were upstairs talking to the First Lady. Everyone else gathered around the dining room table talking about the extraordinary events of the day. Suddenly, without a word to the others, Blake hurried into the kitchen and stopped, listening.

A soft moan come from the parlor then a barely audible voice. "My butt hurts."

Blake, in the doorway, couldn't believe his eyes.

Mercy Ann, standing with the waist of her skintight silver pants rolled down below her butt, gaped at him. "What are you doing in my house?"

He couldn't stop grinning like an idiot.

She thought her tissue-thin underwear and skintight sleeveless top were the reason. Angrily struggling to tug the pants up, her numb fingers refused to hold the slick fabric. Then she lost her balance.

He caught and held her. "My god, is it really you?"

"How long have I been gone?" she asked, aggravated she had to lean against him.

"Eleven days. God, you've lost a lot of weight. Are you hurt?""

"Electromagnetic damage when the Gargle hit my ship."

"That was you fighting them? You were amazing."

Mercy Ann realized finally that his concern for her was genuine and put a hand on his mouth when he started to call for help.

"Will you pull my pants up, please? This is embarrassing."

She liked that he looked away. "Where is John Justice?"

"The dining room. I'll carry you."

"No. I can walk if you help."

The best she could manage was shuffling her numb feet across the kitchen floor. He kept glancing down at the incongruous men's basketball socks tied up with cord around her calves.

She was dizzy and feeling confused. "I tore my boots and only had socks to wear."

Bedlam ensued when they reached the dining room doorway, but didn't last long because Mercy Ann interrupted abruptly. "Why are so many people in my house, John Justice?"

He had remained seated when the others jumped up. Dismayed seeing Blake's arm around her waist, it disturbed him even more that he would no longer be in charge. The way she spoke to him ignited bitter resentment, too.

Not waiting for an answer, she presented another question. "The pyramids? What's that all about?"

He thought of how it was before she disappeared and couldn't help himself. "I blew up the White House, too. Want to make something of it?"

"Are you serious?" she asked. "Why would you do that?"

He shouted, "You don't know anything that's happened, and you're acting all high and mighty. Well, get over yourself, Mercy Ann."

She held tighter to Blake. "I think I should lie down."

John Justice continued. "The President and his wife are in your rooms. You can use a crew room."

She looked around, wanting confirmation. "The President of the United States?"

"I had to make decisions, didn't I?" John Justice yelled. "Well, didn't I?"

Mercy Ann began laughing. She just kept laughing.

"Tell me what's so funny, Mercy Ann!"

"I told you to keep a low profile. Holy shit, John Justice."

If not for Blake, she would have hit the floor hard when she lost consciousness.

19

Silly Word Games

HAD NOT THE SMALL SHIP REACTED AUTOMATICALLY to dissipate the first Gargle energy bombardment that breached the pilot's compartment after Mercy Ann left the external weapons ports open by mistake, she would have been killed and the ship captured. Even so, the blast blew out two plugs on her head and all on the right arm, causing so much pain that she almost lost control and crashed down in Los Angeles.

Everything after that was a confused blur. Fortunately, she'd already planned every step of the attack and executed it without much thought. Taking control of John Justice's cruiser, she launched it straight up and fired on the Gargle ships as they reached the sea. Then she hoped her left arm weapons could take out the remaining enemy with the small ship boosting them. When they exploded, she jammed the feeding tube into her abdomen and administered so much pain medication that it knocked her out instantly.

Mercy Ann came to with ship hovering about halfway between Catalina and Los Angeles. Helicopters and other aircraft circled the wreckage sites waiting for Navy salvage ships to move into position. They didn't notice her ship, which meant it had been set to mask its presence automatically if the pilot became incapacitated. She played with the controls, trying to figure out how to change the settings. Without thinking, she reached to administer more pain medication then stopped as she recognized the familiar desperate cravings. Appalled, she wondered how she could have been so careless.

She became addicted to Guardian pain medications after overdosing on them in the failed attempt to kill herself. Weaning her off had been extremely difficult, even for the Guardians. The drugs were not available on Earth, which was the reason they sent her and John Justice there to recover after the surgeries. Later, they made it their home base for the same reason.

The longings for the drugs remained strong in her over the years, and Honey Bee tried regimens of Earth medicines to help her cope, which caused wild mood swings and chronic insomnia. Then Mercy Ann took matters into her own hands and experimented with all kinds of drugs, including mind-altering substances, until discovering combinations that dulled the need for the Guardian drugs somewhat.

When Honey Bee discovered what she was doing, they had terrible quarrels until Mercy Ann agreed to let her monitor everything she took. In recent years, Mercy Ann often remarked that she owed her well-being to Honey Bee, although she had long since stop being truthful about how much and how often she used concoctions she made herself.

Suddenly, a jet fighter whizzed by dangerously close and snapped Mercy Ann out of her reverie. She flew down close to the water's surface and returned to LA. Not wanting to answer all the questions everyone would have if she called in, she identified herself to the cruiser's security system and ordered no alerts generated about her approach.

The pyramids were amazing, but she couldn't wait to hear why John Justice had done something so ridiculous, not for a second believing he would have valid reasons. Yet, she was ready to forgive him almost anything since no more disasters had occurred. That was a bigger surprise than finding the Giza Plateau in Los Angeles.

The small ship's sensors showed the outline of the cruiser's protective field around the house. Dropping within a few feet, she made a hole in it, turned off door alarms, and opened a storage bay entrance just enough to fly in. Carefully maneuvering through the huge room, she went into the outer hallway and set down near a cargo lift.

She opened the hatch and the fresh air made her recall when Esmé, a junior officer at the time, picked her and John Justice up from Earth in a tiny, four-seat shuttle. They brought along a big supply of nachos, hot sauce, and spicy, honey-baked beans for no other reason than to torment her. As they gulped them down, Esmé complained how foul their food smelled until realizing the fits of giggling and laughing behind her were because they were farting.

That incident marked the beginning of Esmé's love-hate relations with Mercy Ann and contempt for John Justice, who almost everyone considered useless after the accident. Had the Guardians not made Mercy Ann fleet commander over Esmé, she would have removed him from service long ago.

Mercy Ann hesitated, looking at the Guardian box. She was in no mood to deal with them right now and wedged it between the hull and steel chair so the top could not open. Later, she would retrieve it.

Even with the back of the chair to stand on, her injuries made climbing out difficult. Then, because she didn't want to chance someone letting the Guardians out, she added a password to the hatch opening protocol so no one could get in without her.

Mercy Ann thought sliding off the ship to the floor wouldn't be too difficult, but her arms and legs were anything but responsive. She landed on her backside and banged her injured head against the hull. She decided to call for help and discovered her personal transmitters were out, too. She crawled down the hall into the lift, made it upstairs, and Blake found her.

They put her in the grandest bed in the house to recover, displacing Ashlyn, who moved in with Miss Flowers temporarily. Once gracing an English nobleman's bedroom, the bed was so tall that two steps were required to climb up, and so wide that it could accommodate a large family.

Honey Bee's analysis of Mercy Ann's systems showed extensive damage. She performed emergency repairs that would suffice as long as she didn't overdo it.

After that, Mercy Ann's main concern was eating because she'd had no real food since dinner in Blake's apartment, but Honey Bee, John Justice, and Blake insisted she should wait until they discussed everything that transpired since she disappeared. Then she could eat and they could get back to more pressing matters.

Mercy Ann had to admit they were right, but it aggravated her, and she began rushing through an account of her time with the Guardians.

Honey Bee stopped her and wanted to know more about the small ship. "Tell us everything the Guardians told you about it."

"They said it is very old and capable of something they call spatial travel, which must mean travel between galaxies," Mercy Ann responded with considerable glaring to dissuade more questions.

"Do you realize the significance of what you're saying?" Honey Bee asked, astounded. "Until now, that kind of travel has been considered impossible."

Mercy Ann hesitated. "This was the second time the Guardians took me somewhere using it. The first was when they originally installed the advanced weapons."

"Good grief," John Justice said. "Why didn't you tell us?"

"I didn't know it was that big a deal," she answered. "They acted as if it was a routine matter. The Gargle can do it, too. They attacked the Guardian home system while I was there."

"Good grief," he repeated, exasperated.

Honey Bee suggested Mercy Ann finish telling them about her time away.

Mercy Ann described how they changed the little ship's interior to accommodate her then about the Gargle invasion. Then she jumped the narration to discovering ten Gargle cruisers near the Moon and attacking them.

John Justice interrupted. "Why would the almighty Guardians abandon their home system rather than fighting?"

"They decided leading the Gargle across something called a Spatial Divide would result in them being lost forever in something else called the Void, and that was preferable to suffering casualties fighting. Now, where was I?"

"What's a Spatial Divide?" John Justice asked.

"I don't know!" she snapped. "By the way, they gave me a small box containing several Guardians to bring back with me. They didn't say why, so I left it on the ship fixed so they can't get out until I have time to think more about it."

John Justice realized his questions upset her, but this was too much. "You're keeping Guardians prisoner? What are you up to, Mercy Ann?"

"I don't want them interfering with my plans. That's all."

Now, Honey Bee was curious. "What plans?"

"It's no big deal. I want you to analyze the ship I brought back to determine whether we can use the technology to construct more like it, only cruiser size."

John Justice gasped. "The Guardians will wipe out the entire territory before they allow us to have this technology!"

"They probably won't be back anytime soon," she replied as though it wasn't a serious matter. "Anyway, they wouldn't have given me something so advanced unless they expected me to use it. One of them said so."

"Is that really true?" John Justice asked.

She stared. "When we finish up here, I'll have Urlak take the box of Guardians to the Prietus Federation's medical labs. They can help with research and support our missions from there."

"Yeah," he replied sarcastically, "because they can't leave the system except on one of our ships. Are you sure you want to piss them off that much?"

"I'll find a way to un-piss them if it becomes necessary," she replied with false bravado. "Now, tell me what's been going on since I left so I can eat."

John Justice took a deep breath and told her he wanted to recruit Earthlings into the fleet, beginning with the people on board.

Mercy Ann couldn't believe her ears. "You're giving me a hard time for going against Guardian policies and you were planning to do the same thing?"

"It's not as serious as stealing their technology."

"I don't know about that. They're very much against having Earthlings in the fleet. They've made that clear to me on several occasions, but I think it's a great idea, so we'll do it."

John Justice told about Rudy's compatibility and his reasons for deciding against asking him to join. He told how strongly Miss Flowers disagreed.

"He's invaluable if he's compatible with you," Mercy Ann replied. "As much as it pains me to say, I agree with Miss Flowers. Ask the whole family to join. Next subject."

He explained finding Brandi and Sheri and how much he wanted them in the crew, only to discover they'd been involved in the deaths of Missa's parents. He'd decided to tell Ashlyn, Rob, and Missa the truth and give them time to consider whether they could serve with Brandi and Sheri. If not, he'd offer to separate them to work in different quadrants. If that didn't suffice, someone would have to stay behind.

That was the only way to handle it, Mercy Ann thought, but goody-goody John Justice would never have considered professional killers in the crew before she left. Mystified, she wondered what changed him and if he had been this way the whole time.

Blake, who listened in silence until now, spoke up. "From the moment you disappeared, John Justice has been a step ahead of every situation and making sound decisions without regard to his personal opinions."

Mercy Ann communicated silently to Honey Bee that it seemed Blake might know what she was thinking.

Honey Bee told how he'd insisted she wasn't dead and that he was compatible with her.

Until that very moment, Mercy Ann had attributed her feelings about Blake to physical attraction. Now, thinking it over, she suspected a much more significant connection might exist. If so, it was far more important than what Rudy and John Justice experienced because Blake might have some of her abilities to interface with advanced Guardian systems and weapons. As fantastic as it seemed, she had a strong hunch that it was true. She communicated with Honey Bee again.

She jumped off Mercy Ann's lap, ran across the bed, and reached up for Blake. Surprised, he took hold of her waist to lift her up then jerked his hands away, examining the palms. Both had bloody punctures.

"What the hell was that for?" he demanded as Honey Bee ran back across the bed.

Mercy Ann laughed. "Sorry about that. She does the craziest shit sometimes."

John Justice told her about Handley's LA boss picking up the new general at the airport at this very moment. They planned to stop somewhere on the way to the site to discuss working together before the general reported for duty. His first action would be to launch an attack against them, but Brandi and Sheri were tailing them, looking for a chance to kill the boss. The general might get in the way and become a casualty, if they were lucky.

"You didn't tell them to kill him, did you?" Mercy Ann asked.

"That would be a violation of the Sufficiency Test," he replied, irked she felt it necessary to ask.

She hesitated, knowing what she was about to say would upset him. "Since the conspirators seem determined to keep attacking us, I will return to Death Valley and finish what I started with al-Bensi's army. Everyone on Earth needs to understand what we can do."

John Justice was incredulous. "The repairs to your systems and ports are temporary fixes. Until we get you to a reconstruction facility, you should avoid using weapons. Besides, if destroying ten Gargle cruisers didn't convince them, nothing will."

"They didn't know that was me. Seeing a lone girl defeat an army is much more effective, anyway. If I use low power attacks, my circuits will be fine. No need to worry."

He was not ready to drop it. "It's too late. Al-Bensi's armies are not in Death Valley any longer. They're fighting in Iraq and preparing to take Bagdad."

"That's even better," she answered. "Now, have the food brought up, wait thirty minutes, and then send the First Lady to me."

"What do you want her for?" John Justice stammered.

"You'll listen to everything we say, so why waste time telling you? Time to eat." She clapped her hands. "Chop, chop."

Mercy Ann sat on the huge bed with a wooden tray across her lap. Spearing a fat kosher dill pickle, she jerked it out of a big jar, sending juice flying everywhere. She bit off a piece and scooped a sticky handful of buttered popcorn off the bedcovers where she'd dumped it out of a large plastic bowl. Chewing ferociously, she gulped everything down and chased it with steaming Earl Grey tea, sloshing a good amount on the bedcovers when she set the cup back on the tray.

She surveyed the mess then grabbed a cheese, bacon, lettuce, and tomato sandwich, took a big bite and bit off another chunk of pickle. Yellow mustard and pickle juice dribbled down her chin onto the gown. She wiped it off with the bedspread.

The whole time, she used infrared vision in one eye to watch John Justice lurking in the dark hallway, spying on her and shaking his head. She'd expected he'd come back alone to try talking her out of facing the al-Bensi army and knew he wouldn't be able to stomach being in the room with her eating this way. He often criticized her bad table manners and the food she ate, especially yellow mustard, which he swore was the most disgusting substance in the universe.

Nor could he understand her love for kosher dill pickles with popcorn. Once she had convinced him to taste them together and he ran from the room to spit it out. Unbeknownst to him, she'd dipped the pickles in habanero sauce.

Mercy Ann leaned back and belched monumentally. Then she almost choked laughing when John Justice scurried away.

He wasn't the main reason she did this, however. She wiped her face on a pillowcase, looked at the mess around her, and smeared more mustard on the bedcovers. Now, she was ready for the First Lady.

Fuming from the lack of respect and decorum shown her and her husband, the First Lady marched resolutely to meet with the leader of the aliens finally. No one told her who it was.

Entering the room under a full head of steam prepared to demand and threaten, incredulity stopped her dead in her tracks when she saw Mercy Ann sitting on a big filthy bed in a dirty nightgown sucking a pickle.

"Y-you're the alien girl killed by al-Bensi's army."

Mercy Ann stopped a handful of popcorn on the way to her mouth. "You're wrong."

"I saw the classified report and pictures. It was you."

"Obviously, I meant the dead part."

The First Lady was capable of monumental glares. "I demanded to meet the person in charge, not another nasty child."

Digging a popcorn hull from her teeth with the nail of her little finger, Mercy Ann wiped it off on the bedcovers. "Did you order them to take you to their leader? I always get a kick out of that in movies—don't you?"

The First Lady looked as if she might rush the bed flailing her clenched fists.

"Guess it's funnier from my perspective," Mercy Ann said with a shrug.

"I demand to speak to the adult in charge of this madhouse!"

"I'm older than you."

"The boy said you're thirteen!"

"Yeah, I've told him that so long he believes it. Truth be told, I don't know my age exactly, but I'm certainly older than you."

"That's ridiculous."

"It's complicated."

"Just what in the hell are you then?"

"A human augmented by technology. To avoid constant surgeries and implants, our bodies don't change much over the years."

"So you're a cyborg, a machine, a thing!"

Mercy Ann hated words that described people based on differences because invariably someone used them to discriminate. "I can restore your husband's health, expose the conspirators, and help him resume the Presidency."

"Can you really do all that?" she asked with much less contempt now that Mercy Ann offered something she wanted.

"Show her the information, John Justice."

Twelve screens lit on the walls streaming documents, videos, and transcripts of phone calls between conspirators. A video made in Jared Handley's Colorado home had sound as he presented the details of his plan for the White House attack.

Astounded, the First Lady demanded, "How did you get all this?"

Mercy Ann lifted Honey Bee from under the covers. "John Justice told you that she is a lifeform, but you were too pig-headed to listen. If you hold her to your husband's chest for an hour, he'll regain control of his emotions and health. Just go do it, please."

The First Lady did a double take. "Where are you from? Really?"

Mercy Ann realized she had been careless. "A blue nebula. Do you know what that is?"

"You sound like a Tar Heel," the first lady said, baiting a trap.

"You think I have a North Carolina accent? How droll."

"Most Americans don't know what a Tar Heel is. Why do you?"

"I have internal data processors and looked it up on the internet. Oh, I see you grew up on a farm near Greenville, North Carolina. Sounds idyllic."

"It was anything but," the First Lady replied then lapsed into a mostly fictional campaign story about the hardships growing up youngest of six children on a poor farm.

Mercy Ann skimmed a blog by the First Lady's oldest brother. Their parents' dairy farm had been prosperous by the time she was born. They had two farm hands, a housekeeper, and five children helping with chores. The brother called his youngest sister a spoiled brat.

"It was a long, hard climb from that little farm to the White House," the First Lady said, concluding her story. "It shows anything is possible in America."

Mercy Ann was tired of listening to her. "Ashlyn is waiting outside your room. Take Honey Bee and go. Treat her well or she may hurt you in a permanent way. We'll talk more after the President recovers."

"What if I refuse?"

"I'll barter you and hubby to aliens who consider unenhanced human organs to be gastronomical delicacies," Mercy Ann replied. "I'll even give them some special mouthwash to get rid of the shit aftertaste."

After the First Lady stormed out, John Justice's voice sounded in the room. "Good grief. What was all that about?"

"I made this mess to disrespect the bitch. You and the others saved her family from dying, for God's sake. Have they thanked you or even said a civil word? Their asses would be dead and gone except for you. To hell with them. Nobody treats my people that way."

John Justice laughed. "I'll tell the others. They'll appreciate it."

"No big deal. Hey, can you find someone with high rank in the government loyal to the President? I've decided to make a video with him and want someone who will prove conclusively it was made after you demolished the White House."

"I'll find someone. By the way, I asked Miss Flowers to send up clean bedclothes since your bed looks as if hogs rooted slops out of a trough on it. Some of us will come tidy up for you, so you just rest."

That really surprised her. "Thank you, John Justice. I appreciate it."

She leaned back against the pillows, thinking over her meeting with the First Lady and everything John Justice said. She kept coming back to the hog reference. That sounded strange coming from her former commander. He was as citified and proper as anyone she'd ever met. She shrugged it off. He probably saw it on TV.

Brandi followed the boss man's black Mercedes. He was in the backseat with the lieutenant general. Two big thugs in expensive suits were in front.

As dawn brightened the city, they sped along a highway. Sheri, scrunching down in the passenger seat wearing a baseball cap so she looked from the outside like a kid, wrote a text to John Justice.

Brandi said, "Ask if he wants us to get rid of the new general."

"His previous message said not to ask him for instructions."

"Ask anyway."

A reply came back in seconds. "Do not ask him for instructions."

Exiting onto an eastbound freeway, the Mercedes pulled away from a group of cars they followed.

Sheri glanced at the GPS and thought the Mercedes would take one of three exits into the Glenwood Heights area. "Just work your way up to the front of these cars and keep them in sight."

Sheri climbed into the back seat, folded part of it down to access the trunk, and grabbed their military gear. Changing clothes in a car was an art, and she had it mastered, doing most of it on her back and kicking her legs in the air. Tossing her boots over the seat, she returned headfirst, somehow making twisting around in the seat look easy.

"Sometimes, I think you're half monkey," Brandi said.

Sheri made a cute face. "I bet that's the part you like best."

The Mercedes moved into the HOV lane and accelerated. Sheri instructed Brandi to move to the right lane and turn on the signal to take the next exit. They had just gotten into position when the Mercedes whipped across traffic and took the exit.

Yawning, Sheri said, "Nothing like telegraphing your intentions, dumbass."

But the exit road dropped down out of sight quickly and they were behind a slow moving vehicle. When they reached the cross street into neighborhoods both ways, the Mercedes was gone.

"Any ideas?" Brandi asked.

Sheri pulled on an MP armband. "Turn on the flashers and lean on the horn!"

She leaped out of the car leaving the door open, ran into the street, and waved to stop traffic coming from the left way. Horns blared, windows went down, and people yelled while she bent down examining layers of tire marks. Sniffing close to the pavement, she motioned Brandi to turn right.

Jumping back in as the car rolled by, she whipped out her cellphone, called John Justice, and asked if he could locate the Mercedes. He said he'd call back.

"How could you tell which tire marks belonged to them?" Brandi asked.

"Educated guess. A heavy vehicle with rear wheel drive left tire marks on top of the others and there was a fresh burnt rubber smell."

"The whole city has that smell. Maybe you're more bloodhound than monkey."

"Arf."

A sign warned of a military checkpoint ahead so Brandi stopped in a side street, jumped out, and stripped. Her black panty briefs exposed most of her backside when she reached into the backseat for her uniform.

Sheri was not one to let such a moment pass. "You're about to give an old dude on the porch a heart attack. Me, too."

John Justice called back. He'd found the Mercedes parked in front of a neighborhood playground not far inside the buffer zone. The general and boss had just sat down at a picnic table with a bag of fast food while the hired help stood eating off the car trunk. The boss man had two king-size coffees, so they probably would be there a while.

"God," Sheri said after clicking off the phone, "we've got to find out how he knows so much."

After they passed through the checkpoint, Brandi parked around the corner from the playground. "Did John Justice say anything about the general this time?"

"Not a peep, so he must be fair game. We'll be up to our necks in Army if there's gunfire, though."

"We won't get a better chance," Brandi replied. "The boss usually has more men around him."

"Let's wear the special security armbands. We'll walk up and ask for IDs. Only downside is that it'll be a straight-on fight with us outnumbered two-to-one."

"I'll take the men with the car since they're professional muscle," Brandi said. "You lag back a little and deal with the primary target."

Sheri slung a rifle carelessly over the right shoulder so she could discard it easily and pulled her shirttail out more. These kind of people would not take someone who looked so sloppy seriously.

Brandi, on the other hand, was the perfect recruiting poster. The set of her chin and glint in her eyes declared confident authority. No one could doubt she knew how to use the rifle slung tightly over her right shoulder. A small two-way radio clipped to her web vest droned reports from other patrols in the area and she carried a clipboard attached to a small metal forms case with pens dangling on short chains tucked under one arm, adding to her authenticity as a seasoned sergeant with authority.

They rounded the corner at a brisk pace, pretended to spot the men standing next to the Mercedes, and made a beeline for them. About halfway, Brandi stopped, pointed to the other men at the table in the playground, popped open the metal case, and handed Sheri two forms and a pen. Then they split up.

As Brandi neared the two men at the car, she opened the case and reached in again. One man put his hand inside his jacket near a gun and it earned him the first bullet from Brandi's silenced pistol. The next two went into the heart of the other man. The forth went into the head of the first.

The boss man had turned as Sheri approached, gave her a cursory glance, and then left it to the general to take care of his inept soldier while he continued eating. When the general made a choking noise, the startled boss looked up to see him grabbing at two small knives stuck in his throat as a bigger one struck his chest.

The boss was a brilliant, well-informed criminal with a nimble mind. He reacted to dangerous situations lightning fast.

He realized several things simultaneously. The soldier behind him must be the mysterious young woman with knives he'd heard about for years. Which meant her companion was the beauty who could snap men's necks with her bare hands. They had access to the restricted area, so they must be the Cowboy team that he'd ordered killed without taking time to find out more about them. He'd fucked up.

But he'd also spent years perfecting skills that gave him a better than even chance of surviving impossible situations. Too disciplined to waste time turning around, his hand automatically went to the shoulder holster as he threw himself sideways onto the bench, intending to roll off under the table and use the bench as a shield while he got a shot off.

Sheri, obsessively calculating probabilities based on keen observation, experience, and endless practice, anticipated his going left because he ate with his right hand and would need it free to pull a gun. She dove sideways down to the left an instant before he did, grabbed him around the neck, rode him down, and plunged a commando knife up through his ribs into the heart.

Brandi and Sheri worked fast, propping one of the gunmen in the front passenger seat of the Mercedes and setting up the general next to the boss in back. They took the shirt and sunglasses off the last man and put him in the trunk.

Sheri cleaned up trash and kicked dirt on blood while Brandi ran to get the other car. Putting on the gunman's shirt, tie, and sunglasses, Sheri wrapped her uniform t-shirt tight around her head to hide her hair. Then she pulled on thin cloth gloves she always carried and jumped into the driver's seat.

Brandi arrived with the rental car and yelled, "Give me one minute then do your thing."

Sheri gulped the boss man's coffee and found a metal music station while the seconds ticked by. Then she sped back to the checkpoint.

Brandy had stopped in the single lane, flirting and joking with the soldiers. Barreling up the road behind her, Sheri flashed lights and held the horn down.

Frantic not to get on the bad side of the new commander, the soldiers yelled and waved for Brandi to get moving.

Sheri rolled past the guards with the driver's window half down and made her voice deep as she could. "The general will return at noon."

Glancing in the rearview mirror at the soldiers holding salutes, including the sergeant speaking emphatically into a vest mic, Sheri smiled. He was no doubt repeating to the command post that he did not know why the new commander left the site.

All that remained was to get rid of the bodies and the car. She turned up the radio and accelerated to catch up to Brandi, thinking what she wanted to eat.

John Justice was in a women's bathroom in the DHS Headquarters building in Washington checking his hair in a big mirror when Dr. Helen Rogers of Intelligence and Analysis came out of a toilet stall adjusting her skirt. Astounded, she stopped, stared, and pretended not to know who he was.

"The men's bathroom is on the other side of the hall, young man," she said, hiding her fear.

He faced her with a smile. "You get high marks for a fast response and low marks because this is a high security area that no one can enter without a security badge. Not a place where you'd find kids."

"Then you know you're breaking the law," she replied with all the authority she could muster. "Go outside and wait while I wash my hands then you can explain how you got by security."

John Justice pantomimed applauding. "Give it up. You have big pictures of Mercy Ann and me all over the walls of your office. The San Francisco hippie photos are your favorites even though you believe they're fakes. They're not, by the way. You've told your staff on several occasions you'd love to meet with us and discuss what we want rather than keep trying to kill us. Well, Dr. Helen, I've come to grant your wish, in exchange for a small favor."

Helen Rogers had been an officer in the Marines. She was in tiptop shape and could subdue someone twice her size in a matter of seconds, but her intelligence and respect for science argued against attempting anything against this alien boy. If he could fly through space, possess technology to hold off the Army, and materialize wherever he wanted, he could surely deal with a physical attack, regardless how weak and puny his appearance.

"What do you want?" she asked, dropping all pretenses of threat.

"I thought you might be interested to know the reason you can't find the bodies of the President and his family is that we rescued them before the terrorists reached their living quarters."

"Why should I believe you?"

"You think that the Deputy Secretary is involved in a conspiracy to overthrow your government. You're suspicious that the new President is, too, but you're afraid to tell anyone outside a small circle of confidants. If you'll help me, I'll provide all the evidence you need to prove it."

"I can't make a deal with you. You're an enemy of America."

"You should reconsider. You're third on a list of government officials the conspirators plan to eliminate in two days. I'll show you proof if you'll go with me. Otherwise, your fate is sealed, I'm afraid."

She leaned heavily on the counter. "God help us all."

He reached into his shirt, pulled out a copy of the Sufficiency Test notice, and gave it to her.

Sufficiency Test Site for Humankind

You must solve the riddle:

This is an alien facility with capabilities vastly superior to yours
Destroy it and pass the test without further evaluation
Each unsuccessful attack doubles the area of devastation and increases chances of failure
As the situation evolves, you must take the most intelligent actions or fail the test

Sufficiency judged at the end of Day 30

Pass — Humankind continues on present course
Fail — Humankind purged from Earth

This is Test Day 24

"Yes, I've seen it. So what?"

"You were one of the few people to whom the President might have listened. Why didn't you tell him you didn't think attacking us was the correct action?"

"I'm too weak politically to go over the heads of my superiors."

"I don't understand how your government gets anything done, but no matter. I want you to go with me to the President's hiding place. It'll save your life and give the President the upper hand against the people trying to overthrow the government."

"If the President and his family are where I think, you need to get them out of there. A new general is taking over today with orders to destroy the house."

"You already know the general is missing and there won't be an attack today."

"You killed him?"

He shook his head. "We had no reason to do anything to stop him. The coil cannons won't hurt us."

"That's ridiculous. They destroyed the female alien."

"If I can prove it conclusively they won't hurt us, will you do as I ask?"

"I don't see how you can possibly do that."

John Justice looked up at the ceiling. "Can you join me for a minute, please? No, that's not necessary. Come as you are."

Mercy Ann appeared sitting on the counter in a nightgown. "A women's restroom? You're a weird guy, John Justice."

"This is Dr. Helen of Homeland Security. She's going to help the President soon as you give her your personal assessment of coil cannons."

"Nice to meet you, Dr. Helen. Coil technology is obsolete crap." She vanished.

Aggravated having to negotiate with Mercy Ann and John Justice, the President and Dr. Rogers nonetheless agreed to remain with them incommunicado until the Sufficiency Test ended in return for evidence against the conspirators.

So Mercy Ann and John Justice told them the truth about the Sufficiency Test, hostile alien threats to Earth, and the conspiracy. All went well until John Justice mentioned Jared Handley had long-range nuclear missiles in the Middle East.

The President declared all deals off and demanded immediate release because only the American government and military could deal with nuclear threats.

Coolly, Mercy Ann replied, "That isn't your biggest problem—the Sufficiency Test is."

"The conspiracy has nuclear weapons, a terrorist army, and an illegitimate President colluding with them. I don't think a young girl can understand the complexity of this situation."

"My plan begins with you announcing to the world that you're alive," Mercy Ann answered. "Then we..."

"Only the threat of nuclear retaliation can deter nuclear aggression!" the President asserted loudly.

"It can kill everyone and destroy the planet, too," John Justice answered.

"Exactly," Mercy Ann agreed. "My plan is much easier and less likely to kill innocent people."

He was President of the United States and expected people to listen to him, not the other way around. "How long will your plan take to reach fruition? Time is of the essence. We can't dilly-dally with a nuclear threat."

Mercy Ann and John Justice had not discussed time specifically, but it only took a few seconds for her to answer. "If there are complications, it could stretch out as long as two days. Otherwise, it'll be over in one."

John Justice agreed. "Yeah, around twelve hours."

The President was incredulous. "My wife said you have a fleet of spaceships. Do you plan to use them?"

"Don't need them," Mercy Ann replied.

"What will you do if they launch nuclear missiles?"

"Deal with it."

The President sagged back in his chair. "You have no idea what you're talking about."

"You have no idea what we can do." Mercy Ann replied. "Anything else?"

"I don't really have a choice, do I?"

"No," she answered, tired of wasting time, "you don't."

John Justice broke the awkward silence that followed. "I hear Miss Flowers in the kitchen. Let's have dinner. I'm hungry."

Demoralized and aggravated, the President and Dr. Rogers ate with the First Lady in the upstairs study.

Mercy Ann tiptoed down the quiet dark hall and tapped on a bedroom door with light shining under it.

If Blake was surprised seeing her in a robe, nightclothes, and barefoot, he did not show it. "Please come in. Should I leave the door open?"

"Close it."

He followed her to a small table with four chairs, where she stood beside one and waited until he pulled it out for her. "Would you like more light?"

"The bed light is plenty. Please sit down and stop fidgeting."

Blake was not fidgeting at all, so he smiled and sat opposite her, immediately wishing he could see her face better because her back was to the light.

She had chosen that seat intentionally. "I have something important to discuss."

"So this isn't a midnight tryst?"

"No. It is after 2 a.m."

"You're quick."

"But not fast."

"Ouch."

"Enough silly word games," she answered. "While I was gone, you insisted that we're compatible."

"Oh, yes."

He'd said it in a suggestive, exaggerated way. "Stop screwing around, Blake. This is a serious matter."

"Yes, my lady."

She made an exasperated noise.

"Just being polite to my elders. The First Lady said you claimed to be older than her."

"I am."

"It's hard to believe."

He looked good in the dim light, making her doubly glad he couldn't see her face, which was hot and flushed. "You don't know who your father was, do you?"

That got his attention. "No. Why do you ask?"

"To explain, I must tell you secrets about myself. Promise you'll not divulge them or ask questions. One day, I will tell you everything, but not now."

He could feel how difficult this was for her. "You have my word."

She liked that he made no provisions. "I was born on Earth in 1894, where I lived until my younger brother, the original John Justice, and me were abducted by aliens in 1909. The John Justice you know doesn't remember any of this, and I want to keep it that way."

That she was from Earth so long ago amazed him, but it wasn't his foremost thought. "To be taken that way must have been awful for both of you."

"You have no idea. Until now, Honey Bee was the only one who knew."

Her uneasiness transferred to him, making him feel the same. "Why are you telling me this?"

"I asked Honey Bee to sample your DNA and research ancestry. You're a direct descendant of my older brother, Thomas. That makes me your aunt, many times removed, of course. Small world, isn't it, nephew?"

He was silent for a time. "Guess that explains where I got such a bad personality."

"If you want to know about your father and relatives, Honey Bee will answer all your questions."

"That won't be necessary, but I do have a question for you."

She knew what it was because she'd asked herself the same thing. "Ask away."

"Will this make a difference with things between us?"

She let out a long breath. "To answer, I have to tell you more of my secrets. Close relationships are impossible for me. Soon as I begin feeling too much for someone, I get crazy and push him or her away. Someone once called me a nasty bitch. That was uncomfortably close to the mark. Sorry, but that's just the way I am."

"Does this mean you're pushing me away?"

"Unless we stop, I will, and I value your friendship too much to put it in jeopardy."

He took her hands. "You're just afraid of getting hurt."

"You don't need Sigmund Freud to figure that out. I know that I'm an emotional mess. I know why. I've tried to deal with it. So far, I can't."

"Maybe I can help somehow."

"You've got a bigger problem. Compatibility with me means feeling everything I feel. You must already realize you'd be smart to run away fast as you can. A lot of angst and pain is coming your way."

"Yeah, I can already tell," he answered, very serious, "but I'm not going anywhere."

She sighed and stood to go. "Yeah, I already knew that. On the other hand, I know better than most that everything in life can change in a minute, so who knows?"

He walked her across the room, grabbed, and hugged her to him. Then he let go and opened the door.

"Go get some sleep, Mercy Ann," he said with quiet strength underscoring every word. "You can count on me."

"Yes I know." She turned and walked down the dark hall. "Good night, gangster."

20

Man-Boy, Rambo, and the Bunny

CONFIDENCE IN GOVERNMENTS COLLAPSED WORLDWIDE. Police and military everywhere fought rioters and disorder, increasing the numbers of people hurt and killed to extraordinary levels. Many people clung tighter to their religious beliefs while others lost faith altogether. Despair, desperation, confusion, and hopelessness pervaded.

Which was ideal for Jared Handley, working furiously to find out why his plans to attack the White House had gone wrong and his LA boss and new disaster site commander disappeared without a trace. In the latter case, he had suspicions that people in his West Coast organization might be involved, so he dispatched two top operatives from his Colorado headquarters to investigate.

They were foremost on his mind when he arrived at the office before dawn wearing basketball shorts, tank top, and running shoes. One of his secretaries brought in a message from them with a cup of coffee.

They'd arrived at LAX shortly before midnight and were on the way to the hotel where the organization's top people stayed. They planned to surprise and question them individually then compare accounts to determine everyone's whereabouts when the boss and general disappeared. Then they would work their way down through the ranks, compiling information. They promised Handley a progress report in the morning.

As far as Handley was concerned, morning was now. He touched his computer screen to connect to one of them on an encrypted line. A popup informed that the number was unavailable. Scowling, he received the same message with the other man's number.

He buzzed Miss Noto and told her he suspected the men had disappeared same as the new boss and the general. Call their people in LA to find out if they arrived at the hotel as they said. He expected the answer would be no.

Miss Noto buzzed him back and confirmed that was the case. She had the President holding to speak with him, too.

Handley picked up his direct line to the new leader of the free world. "Good morning, Paul. What can I do...?"

"Oh shit, got to go!" the President blurted and hung up.

Before Handley could react, Miss Noto hurried in and turned on the television. "You need to see this, Jared. It's on every channel."

The former President sat behind a grand desk displaying the Presidential Seal. Standing next to him, hand on his shoulder, was the First Lady. On his other side stood Dr. Helen Rogers, head of DHS Intelligence and Analysis. Across the bottom of the screen, a message scrolled: Standby for a statement from the Legitimate President of the United States at 8 p.m., EST.

Miss Noto paused to see if Handley wanted to discuss anything, but he motioned her out and called the Deputy Director of Homeland Security. He asked what intelligence they had about the transmission.

Stammering, he said the message was on TVs worldwide. They could not tell where the transmissions originated. They could not jam it because, well, the signals were everywhere and extremely strong. As for Dr. Rogers being with the President, she had vanished from DHS headquarters yesterday. Nothing showed she ever left the building. They'd even searched with dogs. He had not told Handley about her disappearance because—

Handley slammed the phone down and jogged down a long hall to his gym. Forty-five minutes later, he ended a grueling run on a treadmill, stripped down, and walked into a circular shower-steam room with a round, waterproof bed barely visible through clouds of steam.

Stretched out naked, Miss Noto sat up. He shook his head. She departed.

Handley pushed buttons on a remote. Pastel lights illuminated the misty interior. Atmospheric music played. He stretched out on the bed and relaxed while he thought through recent events.

The former President and his wife were impetuous, conceited ninnies incapable of effective planning and had a habit of bulling into every situation headlong, so someone very powerful must be forcing them to build suspense by waiting until tonight to speak.

Someone helped the First Family escape the White House even though he had every exit secured before al-Bensi's soldiers attacked. There had been no way out.

His people in California disappeared into thin air with no clues. They were topnotch professionals, used to taking care of themselves in the direst situations.

Someone hijacked television communications worldwide and the best security analysts in the world couldn't figure out how to get it off the air.

A department head disappeared from DHS Headquarters in spite of guards and cameras covering every point of egress. Now, she was with the missing President.

Cadavers vanished in Canada then searchers pulled them out of the White House rubble. Never mind why, it was more important to know who could do it.

Handley jumped off the bed. Stinging jets of cold water and pounding rock music assaulted his senses. Exiting through a state of the art drying room, he jogged into his elaborate dressing room.

There was only one possible answer, of course—the aliens. Had they found out he planned to destroy them with his coil cannons? Did it have something to do with his people trying to dissect the boy in Death Valley? More likely, it was the alien girl's death.

He laughed. He'd certainly given them more than enough reasons to come after him, but they had no way to know about the conspiracy or the people involved, so he didn't much care.

Back at his desk in black jeans, a dress shirt, and tie, he called the Chairman of the Joint Chiefs, demanded an immediate attack on the alien site, and lost his temper when informed that the coil cannons' controller system had malfunctioned. The site commander had even called Handley's plant, but the parts were not in stock, and manufacturing more would take two days.

"All this because you recommended sending the backups to al-Bensi," Handley growled.

The Chairman was through taking the blame. "We discussed it and you agreed."

Bristling, Handley demanded to know if the Chairman thought the site commander might be helping the aliens.

The Chairman didn't like the man, but defended a brother-in-arms. "He has a distinguished service record. He's overly cautious, but would never disobey orders or commit treason."

Handley noted the Chairman's hypocrisy with heavy sarcasm. "So do you, but you don't seem to have problems doing it."

The Chairman erupted, "If you want, I'll fly to California and take charge of the site personally. Or would you rather I fly to Colorado and kiss your butt first? Awaiting orders, sir."

A rift with the Chairman at this stage did him no good, Handley realized, forcing himself to calm down. He apologized then shared his thoughts about the aliens being responsible for all their recent setbacks in hopes the Chairman would find flaws with his reasoning.

But the Chairman agreed. "Maybe I really should fly to California, take command, and use the missiles against them."

It was a tempting proposal, but Handley experienced a sinking feeling. "No. I can't afford to lose you, too. Before we make firm plans, let's hear what our lily-livered President has to say tonight. Just hang tight. I'll call you back in a little while."

After Mercy Ann left Blake's room, she had gone to the dark parlor to calm down because the drugs Honey Bee administered to ease the pain of repairs to her ports and circuits made cravings for the Guardian drugs worse. To get her mind off them, she decided to call Esmé and get it over with finally.

Esmé did nothing to hide her aggravation. "There must be a big emergency for you to waste time talking to me, commander."

Mercy Ann acted as if she didn't understand. "Is something wrong? Have I done something to upset you?"

"What can I do for you?"

She decided to end the conversation fast as possible. "Have Urlak leave immediately for Earth with the flagship and six cruisers then redeploy the fleet to resume regular patrols."

"Since we haven't encountered the enemy forces you predicted in this quadrant, I already sent Urlak and his escort back to cover your activities. You should hear from him in the next twelve hours."

Esmé was the better fleet commander and Mercy Ann knew it, not that she would ever admit it to her. "The Gargle withdrew from the territory, but a few squadrons are still be around, so stay sharp. We've destroyed twelve heavy cruisers in the last two days. Six were in battle inside Earth's atmosphere."

The news excited Esmé and made her forget her pique temporarily. "That's great news, but it must mean you left the test site and Earth's population perished. I'm sorry things didn't work out the way you wanted, Mercy Ann."

She did not usually make those kind of slips, but talking to Esmé flustered her. "No, Esmé, Earth is okay. We, uh, acquired a one-person fighter before the test started. I used it to intercept the Gargle near the Moon then drew the rest into range of our cruiser at the site for an ambush. Since the battle occurred over a city, Earth's governments have publicly acknowledged the existence of aliens, which is causing turmoil, but it couldn't be helped."

"I hope none of you were hurt."

The praise and concern were genuine, causing Mercy Ann to feel pangs of guilt for the way she treated her. "No. We were lucky."

"I'm sending the news out to the fleet. It will give them a much needed morale boost. You're fantastic, Mercy Ann." Her voice caught. "I can't wait to see you again. I've missed you so much."

It was exactly what Mercy Ann didn't want to hear. "It wasn't just me that fought them, Esmé."

"Well, it certainly wasn't John Justice."

Mercy Ann's mind raced as she considered where to send Esmé to avoid facing her. "Uh, please call when you're underway, and we'll talk about getting together."

"I will! Give my regards to Miss Flowers and Honey Bee. Esmé offline."

John Justice heard it all. "You really should meet with her and smooth things out. It'd be better for everyone, don't you think?"

She was too tired to discuss it again. "Whatever. I'm going to sleep now. Goodnight."

She lay down on the settee and shoved a small pillow under her head. Why hadn't she secured the communication? John Justice badgering her about making up with Esmé was the last thing she needed.

Meanwhile, other significant news could not get on the air because of John Justice's transmissions blocking everything else. Many of the stories could have dominated the day's news.

The al-Bensi armies massed north of Bagdad had been poised to attack since dawn and analysts could not understand why they waited all day then camped in place. They had no way of knowing Jared Handley had become concerned the aliens might have more surprises in store for him and ordered them to wait in case he needed a diversion away from his activities. After all, postponing the attack another day or two wouldn't change the outcome.

In Egypt, rumors of a massive object in the ground at the site of the Great Pyramid resulted in frenzied crowds rushing to dig for treasure. Police tried to make them leave so the government could benefit directly from any discoveries. Emboldened by their massive numbers, the crowds refused to budge. Soldiers joined the police. Fighting broke out. A bloodbath ensued.

In Washington, DC, the new President took a helicopter to Andrews AFB and boarded Air Force One. No one knew the purpose of the trip until a terse comment by the President to reporters that it was a matter of national security for him to have a meeting with Jared Handley in Colorado. They asked why Handley wasn't coming to Washington instead. The President yelled at them to mind their own business.

In darkness off Catalina Island, a boat crammed with journalists moved close to a brightly illuminated salvage ship lifting part of a flying saucer from the water. Navy patrol boats asked if they should detain them and confiscate their camera equipment. The command ordered them to stand down since the President had announced the presence of aliens on Earth and pictures of their craft had circulated around the globe already.

In Los Angeles, a well-organized group of heavily armed vigilantes from Arizona had become frustrated with the government's inability to get rid of the aliens in LA. In a caravan of ten trucks and vans, they tried to crash through a military checkpoint into the buffer zone. They killed one soldier and wounded four others before reinforcements intercepted them. In less than three minutes, nine vigilantes were dead, an unreported number wounded, and the remainder under arrest.

They were not the first group of vigilantes that had tried to get into the area, but it had been the first that posed a serious threat with automatic weapons. The other attempts were hushed up until the threat was past. This one was too big to keep under wraps completely, but initial reports downplayed it by stating it was a few drunken hotheads being stupid.

Searches through the remains of the White House continued around the clock, adding to the number of questions while providing few answers. Media had not succeeded getting access yet, but reported the severity of the destruction as fact. Authorities realized all hell would break loose when the public tired of the endless psychobabble about aliens in the news and started paying attention to the White House attack again, increasing pressure to find answers.

John Justice had tipped Brandi and Sheri that Handley sent two assistants to LA. They intercepted them in the parking lot of the hotel where Handley's people stayed. With the heavy military presence in the area, two female soldiers getting out of a car and walking past the men as they took bags out of the trunk raised no concerns. Ninety minutes later, with the bodies incinerated and a rental car reduced to a block of scrap, Brandi drove back into central LA.

Sheri complained in her whiny-kid-about-to-throw-a-tantrum voice. "I want to take a hot shower to get the dead body stink off. Can't you drive faster?"

Brandi looked at her sidelong and turned up the radio.

"This uniform is hot. My armpits smell like sewers."

Brandi turned up the air conditioner fan. "I've been driving for two days and you've been asleep most of the time. You don't have anything to complain about."

"Yes, but you're a big strong Rambo and I'm a snuggly bunny."

"Some bunny. You've killed four people in the last twenty-four hours."

"Yeah, but I did it hand-to-hand, not with a big pistol. You only had to move one finger. I jump around all over the place like Jackie Chan. That's why I need more energy food and rest than you."

"I assume you'd rather eat before getting cleaned up?"

"What a great idea. Long as it's not another bag of greasy fast food."

"I'll find a restaurant."

Sheri smiled. "Since you brought it up, there are two nice places at the next exit. Sorry for calling you a Rambo, you gorgeous doll you."

"You could have just said you had a place picked out without all the drama," Brandi replied, shaking her head.

"And have you criticize how much I eat again?"

"God, you're a nutjob. Good thing you're pretty."

During lunch, John Justice voiced a frustration. "I've gone through all the ship's systems and programs trying to determine what triggers Sufficiency Test responses but haven't found anything out of the ordinary. There ought to be something."

Across the table, Mercy Ann looked up. "That's a dumb thing to do. You might trigger a response. Even if you found how it was done, we couldn't do anything about it."

"If I figured it out, maybe I could," he snapped back.

"No more fiddling with the ship without telling me what you're doing."

He agreed, but didn't sound convincing.

Across the table, Blake sensed again how much the changes in John Justice troubled Mercy Ann.

She caught him staring, realized why, and said she had to go discuss something with Honey Bee.

John Justice's demeanor changed immediately. He was more confident and outgoing with the others. He smiled and joked. He led conversations.

Blake was alone when Mercy Ann returned. He chanced irritating her by asking if he could do anything to help ease the situation with John Justice.

She nodded. "It baffles me how he managed against the Sufficiency Test while I was gone. Was it just dumb luck or did he really seem to know what he was doing?"

"He told us that as long as we did the unexpected and kept everyone confused, they'd delay decisions and make mistakes, giving us opportunities to influence them without interfering with the test."

"Really? How did he come up with something crazy like that, I wonder?"

"He said it was your idea."

She hesitated, thinking. "Oh, the Chaos Theory. That's right. I didn't think he understood what I meant. I must say that I'm surprised. Good for him. By the way, I discussed an idea with Honey Bee that might relieve the tension between John Justice and me, but I need more time to think about it. We'll get back together and finish discussing things later."

John Justice appeared on the sidewalk in front of the Johnson house in Redlands dressed like a neighborhood kid. He was nervous at the prospect of facing Elena even if Rudy was with her.

Before he rang the bell, she threw the front door open. "Boy, Rudy isn't home, but you can come in and talk to me."

John Justice considered transporting but decided it would just make him look foolish. He tried to hurry, but dread slowed his legs.

Elena led the way into the kitchen where John Justice stopped and waited, expecting her to tell him to sit down at the table. Instead, she hugged the air out of him.

"I can't tell you how happy we were to find out Mercy Ann is alive. Rudy sobbed like a baby."

John Justice had called Rudy with the news but not given any details.

"Thank you for saving Zach. Tell Mercy Ann and Honey Bee thanks, too."

John Justice was so relieved he couldn't do more than nod.

"You and Mercy Ann are all Zach talks about. He's keeping his word not to tell anyone about you. Did you need to discuss something with Rudy? He won't be back until tonight. He took Zach camping at Big Bear."

Finding out on the internet that Big Bear was a nearby mountain and lake resort area, John Justice asked, "Why didn't you go with them?"

"I love my husband. I love my son. But I don't love anyone enough to sleep in a tent."

"That's not something I like, either," John Justice replied, happy they had something in common. "Did Rudy say anything about us being compatible and what it means?"

She had gone to the fridge, taken out two soft drinks. "He told me all about it. Would I be wrong thinking you want him to leave with you?"

John Justice was impressed she dealt with the subject head on. "Yes. Of course, we want you and Zach to go as well. Many people in our crews have families. Some serve together on ships. Kids have good lives and endless opportunities, to say the least."

"Rudy always underestimates himself. Would I be of any real use, though?"

"Your work as a school teacher and administrator is invaluable," John Justice replied, "but I must point out that while ours is an amazing way to live, it can be dangerous, too."

Elena related how a young couple a few blocks away had become radicalized followers of General al-Bensi and murdered seventeen people in a church last year. "It's not safe anywhere. How soon do you need an answer?"

"Sorry, but it must be in the next three days."

"We'll talk and will probably have questions, especially about Zach and the kind of home life to expect. Can we get in touch with you somehow?"

"Send texts addressed to John Justice.

"Your name only?"

"Yes. I must go. Tell Rudi I'm sorry I missed him."

Stretched out face down on a chaise lounge sunning next to the pool of a seedy hotel while Brandi swam laps, Sheri heard the slight creak of the chair next to her. Making soft snoring noises, she turned onto her side and slipped a hand into a rolled up towel under her head.

"Don't shoot," John Justice said. "I'm just admiring your bikini butt."

Little Bitch in hand, she propped up on her elbows and squinted. "Aren't there any schoolgirls for you to harass?"

"I like big girls."

"Act your age, kid."

"I'm a man in a boy's body."

"Keep it up and I'm going to cut your nose off."

"That's not what you started to say, is it?"

Shaking her head, Sheri put Little Bitch back in the towel and sat up as Brandi left the pool and wrung water from her hair. Her bathing suit consisted of three yellow triangles of fabric connected by black cords, covering just enough skin to argue she wasn't nude, but it wouldn't stand up in most courts of opinion.

"I can't believe you're wearing that in public," Sheri said, dead serious. "Wrap a towel around you. You're about to give John Justice a stroke."

Brandi turned her backside to them and stuck it out. A small dagger tattoo on the right butt cheek had "Sheri" printed on the blade.

"If you don't like the scenery," she said, twisting to look back at them, "go diddle yourself, honey."

"If you wanted to tan naked," Sheri fired back, "you can go to a salon."

"I wondered how you managed such a great tan all over your body," John Justice said with a grin.

Brandi faced Sheri. "At least he's not criticizing every little thing."

"Yeah, well," she answered with a snort, "he claims to be a man trapped in a boy's body. You shouldn't confuse him more. He has too many issues already."

Brandi sat on the chaise and pushed Sheri over with her hip. "Most males act like boys in men's bodies, so what is the big deal?"

"We saw how you dealt with the boss man and the general," John Justice interrupted, wanting to get to the reason he came. "Mercy Ann said it was like watching a scene in a movie. High praise, coming from her."

"We thought she died," Sheri said.

"No, turns out she's alive. You'll hear all about it when you move to the ship. For the time being, though, it's more useful having you in the city."

"We haven't said we'll join you, yet," Brandi answered.

He cocked his head slightly, listening to internal communications. "We'll talk more about it, but I have to go now. See you later."

Soon as he was gone, Sheri asked, "Did you put together the comments about how he knew you were tanned all over and how they watched us take out the boss man. How can they do that?"

"We should just ask him."

"I doubt he trusts us enough to tell us."

John Justice reappeared on the chair and handed the surprised Sheri a small round cylinder with a glass lens at each end. "Look through it at your arm. Twist to focus."

"I have tiny silver specks all over me."

"They indicate the saturation level of micro-machines we released over the city. Air currents distribute them same as dust particles, but we can order them to fly where we want, too. They replicate until millions saturate an area. That's how we gather information, eavesdrop, make videos, transmit information, and so on. After a specified time, they dissolve."

Sheri did not like that one bit. "They go inside buildings? Bedrooms? Bathrooms?"

"They go everywhere."

Sheri's mouth dropped open. "People walk around with cameras and microphones stuck to them? You can watch everything we do!"

"We don't have the capacity to watch everything all the time. No one does."

Brandi squeezed Sheri's leg to stop her launching into a tirade. "We breathe in dust, so couldn't these little machines be used as biological weapons?"

John Justice expected those kind of questions from Sheri, but Brandi surprised him. "Ours are programmed not to go inside living creatures, but they could. Anyone capable of deep space travel has protections against that kind of biological attack, however. Not that anyone would use them for that purpose."

"Why not?" Sheri asked, almost afraid to hear the answer.

"Other means are more efficient, sorry to say. Mercy Ann just called again. I really have to go this time."

John Justice appeared in the dining room where Mercy Ann, Blake, and Tom sat watching Brandi and Sheri on the big monitor.

Mercy Ann said, "One is butt-naked, and the other doesn't have on much more. Are you certain it was their skills that peaked your interest?"

He hoped they hadn't been listening, too.

She persisted. “They’re going to cause quite a stir with the crew.”

“I’m sure, but don’t forget they’re a devoted couple and not interested in men,” John Justice answered.

“I wasn’t just referring to men,” she said.

He almost responded then didn’t.

“Just say it,” Mercy Ann snapped.

He shrugged. “Obviously.”

She stiffened. “What does that mean?”

“Brandi and Sheri did a great job extracting the President and his family from the White House,” Tom offered, trying to change the subject. “They were very professional and cool under fire.”

Mercy Ann started to retort that men’s opinions had more to do with curves and eyelashes than fighting skills, but stopped herself. She was in a bad mood and taking it out on them.

“Sorry for being a pain, everyone,” she said. “I’m still shaky from the battle. You did well recruiting Brandi and Sheri, John Justice. I look forward to meeting them.”

A smile lit his face. “Maybe I should windup Jared Handley now.”

“If you’re ready, go ahead.”

John Justice sat down, picked up notes they had gone over earlier, and skimmed through them a last time.

Handley hung up from a conversation with the new President, holed up at his estate. He’d shouted at the nincompoop for running away from Washington without calling him beforehand to put a cover story in place. He shook his head at the man’s stupidity.

One of his secretaries buzzed and said someone claiming to be the alien John Justice had been holding until he finished with the President. He jotted a note to Miss Noto to fire the man for not realizing the alien took precedent over their idiot President.

“This is Handley. Can you prove you’re John Justice?”

“Never would have thought you and I enjoyed the same kinds of music,” he replied.

“What does that mean?”

“You listened to ambient music followed by some great rock during your shower. The naked truth is, we have the same tastes in personal assistants, too. Very nice, indeed.”

He sat straight up in the chair. “How the hell do you know all that?”

“Not just anyone can wear a yellow silk tie and overpriced jeans together. I admire your unconcern for the opinions of people with good taste.”

Handley's had his offices checked twice a week by the best security experts money could buy and his communications systems were amongst the best in the world.

He raised his arm and stuck up his middle finger. "What am I doing now, you sarcastic asshole?"

"Shooting me the bird. By the way, you might want to stop banging that cute secretary in the outer office. She and your Assistant Chief of Security are shacked up together plotting to sell information to a Chinese company about your acquisition plans for Delta Ray Communications. It's going to cost you millions extra."

Handley wanted to stop looking around the room for some indication how John Justice could see him in spite of knowing there was nothing to find, but he couldn't. Fighting to calm himself, he jotted down the names of the secretary and security guy.

John Justice laughed. "Can't trust anyone these days, can you?"

"What do you want?"

"To give you a heads-up about what the President will say to the world tonight."

"Why would you do that?"

"Maybe I feel sorry for all the shit that's going to hit you. Or perhaps, I just want to watch you squirm because you're such a prick."

"You have the President and his family, don't you?"

"No."

"But you do know where he is?"

"Yes."

"You took them out of the White House, didn't you?"

"Why would I do that?"

"You won't be so smug when my people blow you away with coil cannons, same as we did with your pretty companion."

Mercy Ann wanted to keep the fact she was alive a secret from Handley, so John Justice responded, "The new team of technicians and thugs you had Miss Noto send to the site an hour ago disappeared, same as the others."

"Screw you!"

"We gave the legitimate President copies of e-mails and recordings of calls between you and your top conspirators. We have videos of the White House attack, private conversations, meetings, and details of your plans to topple the government. More evidence is being compiled as we speak."

"The cameras in the White House were offline and our encryption is the best on Earth," Handley said, laying down a challenge for John Justice to prove his claims.

"You must realize by now that we have our own means of gathering information that has nothing to do with your technology, not that we can't access it at will, too. As for encryption, I've taken over the internal communications of your headquarters complex and activated the TV in your office to show you the proof. The program lasts thirty minutes. Enjoy."

John Justice broke off communications and sat back in this chair. "How was that?"

"Great," Mercy Ann answered, very impressed. "It will send the rats scurrying to their hidey-holes the way we want."

Sure enough, when the President's TV address aired that evening, Handley, the Chairman, the new President, and dozens more conspirators were already on private jets headed for the Middle East.

Mercy Ann would not allow the President to deliver his message to the world live. She did not trust him to stay on script, although she did not say that to him exactly.

The President and First Lady wanted the presentation to last at least an hour, seeing it as a historical moment that would bolster his prestige and insure his chances for reelection. Mercy Ann insisted it be less than twenty minutes because her only purpose was to stampede the conspirators. The actual length ended up being forty minutes because the President kept adlibbing. Mercy Ann had John Justice edit it by more than half.

The telecast opened with the President and his wife together. John Justice had removed comments about how they and their children escaped the assassination attempt. Then the First Lady went off camera.

The President explained the attack had been part of a grand conspiracy to seize control of the government. The ringleaders included his traitorous Vice President and the Deputy Secretary of Homeland Security, who had fled the country this very night.

The President also named the Chairman of the Joint Chiefs, Jared Handley, and many other well-known people, but Mercy Ann had John Justice cut those parts. She wanted to be certain the top conspirators reached al-Bensi in Death Valley on the chance they might give away the missile locations.

The President promised to send the names of everyone involved in the conspiracy to federal investigatory and prosecutorial agencies as well as major news outlets by noon tomorrow, followed by evidence against every person named over the next few days.

He introduced Dr. Helen Rogers from DHS as conclusive evidence he'd recorded the video after the attack on the White House. His first act upon return to Washington would be to nominate Dr. Rogers to head DHS.

The presentation closed with the President saying a prayer for the American heroes who died in the White House attack. At no time did he bow his head, a requirement imposed by Mercy Ann. When he finished, a muted version of the "Battle Hymn of the Republic" played as the screen showed the President's face frozen with a fierce, determined stare.

Thirty minutes passed before John Justice relinquished control of Earth's communications.

The President and First Lady raged at Mercy Ann for editing his speech.

She let it go on for a while before turning to John Justice. "Tell them the reason you saved him and his wife."

"You don't mean the real one, do you?"

"Yes, John Justice, the real one."

He stood and faced them. "I wanted to save your children and thought they needed their parents."

"Exactly," Mercy Ann said, eyeing them. "They needed you, not us, so quit being pains in the butt. Miss Flowers will show you to your rooms. Stay in them. Have a good night."

21

Romance, Panic, and Hard Lessons

SGT. AASIM LOVED HIS COMMANDER. Loved General Abd al-Bensi. Loved his men. Loved his life. Only not as much as twenty-four hours ago, when at dawn thirty thousand of al-Bensi's finest warriors prepared to begin a glorious final assault to take Bagdad then waited all day for an order to attack that never came.

Late in the afternoon, a large convoy of new troops arrived, causing a stir since they had clean uniforms and newer weapons. They made no secret that they belonged to al-Bensi's elite guard, sent to insure the general received his fair share of spoils from the soldiers, which meant they would be stopping soldiers in the streets and confiscating their loot.

Cursing under his breath, Aasim sneaked away from his unit and hid so he could come up with a scheme to give better odds for safeguarding his loot as well as help him desert without creating too much fuss. A seasoned schemer, it did not take him long.

Soldiers carried a large woven bag for personal belongings they also used to gather valuables after battles. Aasim acquired a second bag then returned to the ranks bragging loud and long to anyone who would listen that he planned to separate loot fifty-fifty between the two bags. If stopped by agents, he would claim one was for al-Bensi's share. That would give him a better chance to keep his fair share.

The men reacted with ridicule and scorn because everyone knew al-Bensi agents would take all the loot you had, no matter the number of bags. The only thing that worked was avoiding them.

Aasim argued they were missing the point. If he demonstrated he played by the rules, he would get fair treatment. He'd even allow the agents to choose the bag they wanted and praise them for letting him keep the other one.

Everyone howled with laughter. Finally, feigning hurt feelings, he sulked off to find another group to tell his story.

Those who didn't know Aasim expressed surprise a seasoned soldier could be so naïve. Some even speculated he might be suffering from battle fatigue. Men who did know him assumed it was a con, but everyone was too busy to try figuring it out.

That night, the youngest member of his unit came to Aasim and showed he had gotten a second bag, too. It made Aasim feel warm inside, but not enough to tell the youngster that the real purpose of two bags was to keep agents from discovering the third one. Made of lightweight cloth, it was not very big and hung inside the front of his pants by the waistband so it was easy to slip in jewelry and cash, the most valuable loot by far.

If stopped, he'd keep declaring loyalty to al-Bensi, keep explaining his two bag theory, and keep expressing moral outrage—maybe even crying if they took both bags They'd ridicule and give him beatings perhaps, but he would have wasted so much of their time, they would not waste more searching a pathetic fool's pants. After all, they knew that when it came to looting, it paid to get there first.

Aasim was kept awake that night by everyone talking about the former President of the United States being alive. The al-Bensi army had been proud their fighters killed the leader of the free world and many felt their hero martyrs severely diminished by the news. Loud arguments ensued.

Aasim still thought the martyrs were amazing heroes. Destroying the White House was an incredible feat. That the President escaped was a shame, but not a reason to say the attackers failed to carry out the mission. With those thoughts in mind, he dozed off.

An hour before dawn, the men were still at it and woke him up. Cold lying on the ground, he crawled into the back of a small pickup truck he and his men had commandeered from a foolish farmer who died defending it. They took turns sleeping in it, and it aggravated him all of them were up, in the groups making so much noise, apparently.

Aasim felt exhausted, but no matter. He lay back and marveled at the serene beauty of the starry sky as daylight chased it away. Then he gathered his men for the dawn prayer. Later he'd sneak away to catch up his sleep. Then he would continue haranguing everyone to carry two bags and acting as if something was wrong with his mind. That way, no one would care very much when he disappeared with his loot.

The conspirators were in frenzied panic after the President's address. News programs ran continuous live reports speculating who other than the former Vice-President and DHS Secretary might be involved. They argued whether imposing the death penalty was the right thing. A prominent talk radio host proposed firing squads or hanging for everyone involved with the attack on the White House, something listeners favored by more than ninety percent. Such was the mood of the country.

Ignoring instructions not to discuss their activities on unsecured communications systems, desperate conspirators contacted each other by every possible mean as they tried to decide what to do. The firebrands remained defiant and unbowed, telling anyone who would listen they should fight to the death if necessary. Cooler heads counseled to wait and see if their names were on the lists before doing anything drastic because the President couldn't possibly know everyone involved. He would have to have evidence against all of them, too, which simply wasn't possible.

John Justice, even as he released the information promised by the President, had most of the ship's resources busy recording, sorting, and compiling everything new the conspirators discussed.

All was not peaches and cream in the romance of Rob and Missa. That didn't mean they had doubts or misgivings about loving each other, but it seemed to Missa that Rob was more interested in learning about the technological mysteries of the spacecraft than exploring the biological wonders of his girlfriend. Ironically, Rob had similar concerns about Missa, only with a significant twist. He couldn't understand why she spent so much time with his mother studying how aliens improved humans with technology and alterations to biology rather than with him learning about the ship.

They had been in the dining room with the others to watch the President's address and witnessed the altercation between Mercy Ann and the Presidential couple. Later, while snuggling and watching a movie in Missa's room, Rob commented Mercy Ann should have been more considerate of them. Missa said they deserved her harsh rebuke and more. They argued until Missa said he was just upset being away from the love of his life, the ship's control room. He said she was right and stormed out.

Missa was not a crier. She stared at the television for a time without seeing the show then switched it off, jumped out of bed, and tugged on her short exercise tights, sports bra, and running shoes. She jogged silently through the house, opened the passageway to the ship, and took the elevator down to the hallway that ran around the circumference of the outer hull.

Light in the corridor was dimmer than usual but adequate. Passing Mercy Ann's small egg-shaped craft, she marveled at its cool beauty and wondered how it looked inside. John Justice was peeved she hadn't given him or Honey Bee access yet.

From what little she'd seen of Mercy Ann, the girl was imperious, self-centered, and resentful that John Justice brought others onboard. Ashlyn insisted she would like Mercy Ann once they were better acquainted, but Missa didn't think so. She had done everything possible to avoid her and intended to continue.

So when Missa saw a brighter area ahead with Mercy Ann sitting on two bed pillows and slouched back against a wall reading from a messy pile of papers on her lap with Heath Bars, a big bag of potato chips, and bottles of cola were on the floor beside her, she stopped. Disappointed having to stop her run, she turned to tiptoe away.

Mercy Ann called out to her.

Missa thought of Mercy Ann as being excessively prim and proper because mostly she'd seen her in Victorian clothes on the internet. Now, she found her wearing a huge pair of ragged cargo shorts with frayed rope holding the bunched waistband around her. A stretched-out-of-shape, men's sleeveless t-shirt hung off her slim shoulders, so big that she kept lifting her arms to prevent it falling down. Men's white cotton socks consumed her feet and legs loosely halfway to the knees.

Missa tried not to stare, but it was difficult with the shirt's big neck and armholes showing Mercy Ann naked otherwise. Not having seen her close up in good light until now, she realized how strikingly attractive the girl was. Her heart beat faster as surprising feelings sprang to life. Swallowing hard, she forced her gaze out of the shirt so she could gather her thoughts.

"Sorry to disturb you," she said, not quite stammering.

"Please, have a seat," Mercy Ann replied, pulling one of pillows from under her for Missa, causing the pile of papers to slide off her lap and spread across the floor.

Missa bent down to pick them up at the same time Mercy Ann leaned and reached out for them. They bumped heads. It didn't seem that much of a blow but it staggered Missa, who sat down hard on the pillow and leaned back against the wall holding her head.

Mercy Ann was flustered. "Our skulls are made stronger to protect the brain better. Sorry, I know that hurts."

Mostly, Missa was glad for something to say. "I read in the medical files how cartilage and bones are strengthened for space travel."

"I didn't realize biology and medicine interested you. Oh, please forgive my atrocious appearance, but I felt compelled to wear as little as possible after being cooped up in a small ship so long."

Surprised by how nice and polite she was, Missa answered, "No, you're fine. Really."

"Medicine is what I did before...before they discovered I could use advanced weapons."

"Yes, John Justice told us."

Her demeanor changed in a nanosecond. "What did he say?"

Missa felt as though she had strolled into a conversational minefield. "Just that you loved medicine and were very good with it."

"Did he explain I had no choice but to accept the weapons?"

Missa was afraid where this conversation might go. "Yes."

"Did he tell you what I did to my brother and commander?"

"Yes, but he was upset because he thought you were dead."

"I realize that, but even after all the awful stuff I did, I still want to slap the little shit senseless sometimes for the stuff he blabs. I just can't help myself."

Missa was very uncomfortable. "Maybe I should just go."

Mercy Ann shrugged then leaned forward on one hand and began picking the papers up. Missa hesitated, wondering if injuries were the reason she moved so slowly. Then she saw wet spots appearing on papers Mercy Ann bent over. Carefully looking away from her, she scooted forward to help.

Brittle and discolored from age, black ink faded to translucent in places, small lines of handwritten cursive filled every page. Mistakes were marked out and corrections squeezed in; even so, the preciseness of every page was a marvel.

Missa could not help reading a few lines then blurting, "This is a story about chopping the heads off a family of giants."

"They're *Jack Tales,*" Mercy Ann replied quietly, keeping her head down. "Are you familiar with them?"

"No. Sorry."

Mercy Ann's father had told some of the stories to her when she was little, and they provided one of her warmest memories because he used silly voices for the characters, making her laugh. After he died, she'd taught them to her brother. Of course, she couldn't tell Missa or anyone about it without admitting she was from Earth.

Picking up the last of the papers, Mercy Ann sat back, took Missa's stack, and sorted them in order.

"*Jack and the Beanstalk* was a *Jack Tale,*" she explained. "*Jack and Jill* was another. They're folk tales, nursery rhymes, and poems about a clever rascal named Jack passed down through the generations by families retelling them to children, mostly. They're outdated and no one cares about them anymore."

Missa saw no evidence Mercy Ann had been crying, although her gloomy expression did nothing to repudiate the possibility. She could not help feeling concerned for her.

Pointing, she asked, "Did you make those notes?"

She nodded. "Collecting them became kind of a hobby for my brother and me when we came to Earth. We'd read them to each other during long trips in space. The new John Justice thinks they're stupid. I still like to read them and remember my brother, though."

Missa struggled for something to change the subject. "May I have one of your candy bars?"

Mercy Ann was genuinely surprised. "I would have offered but noticed you're careful what you eat. Do you want a cola? They're the ones full of sugar."

Missa grabbed a bottle and twisted off the cap. "Right now, I wouldn't care if I gained fifty pounds."

Mercy Ann eyed her. "Having problems with the boy friend?"

Missa never thought she would share her personal feelings so easily but went on for several minutes describing her frustrating relationship with Rob. Then she realized Mercy Ann had become silent and staring again. This time it seemed different, though.

"Is something wrong?" she asked, hoping it didn't cause another mood change.

"I just realized how much I need someone to talk to."

"You and Ashlyn talk, don't you?"

"I need someone more like you."

She was so shy about it that Missa could not help smiling. "You mean girl talk?"

Mercy Ann nodded. "I've never had a close female friend; at least, not one that's human. I don't relate to others very well, and my cussing puts people off, even though I do try to watch it. I'm not exactly warm to be around, I guess."

"Actually, I've never had a close girlfriend, either," Missa admitted.

Mercy Ann was surprised. "But you're so pretty and intelligent. Blake says you're skilled at athletics, too. I thought you'd have loads of friends."

Missa explained she'd spent all her time growing up with Rob and studying until high school when her parents and career counselors insisted she participate in social activities to prepare for college. She related how she became a cheerleader and it led to the football boyfriend fiasco.

Mercy Ann thought Missa fighting off two young men trying to hurt her was great and said so. Then she almost said she had been in a similar, but much worse situation. Almost.

Ashlyn was right, Missa realized. She liked Mercy Ann. Too much, perhaps. The feelings confused her.

Then, more girly than Missa thought possible, Mercy Ann swore her to secrecy and told how Blake could tell what she was thinking and sometimes it was about him.

"Oh my god! How utterly awful!"

Words gushed from both of them for half an hour before Mercy Ann returned to the subject most on her mind recently. "Did John Justice tell you how the Guardians combined the former fleet commander and my brother into the way he is now? I promise not to freak out this time so don't worry."

She certainly seemed able to deal with the subject now, but Missa was cautious. "Yes, but only because he missed you so much."

Mercy Ann took Missa's hand and held it. "The commander was in love with me. Then, after I went crazy in battle, everyone said I was a monster, so it was just me and the new John Justice recuperating on Earth while the Guardians tried to come up with a solution for all of us to work together again. It was a very difficult time. I had to learn how to cope with the commander expressing his feelings through my dead brother's eyes while he had to convince himself to trust me again."

Shaken as you thought about it, Missa managed, "I can't imagine how difficult all that was, but I assume they found a way to get the others to accept you."

"Yeah," she answered with a sour expression. "They installed new emotional programs in me, announced my abnormalities corrected, and named me new fleet commander. Everyone was pissed and complained, no one more than me, but the Guardians refused to reconsider."

"That's crazy!"

She shrugged. "Looking back, everything worked out except the problems with the new John Justice. For a long time, he was terribly forgetful and unable to make even the simplest decisions. His behavior was childish and petulant. Not that I'm complaining. I made him that way, after all. It was my obligation to help him."

The more Missa looked at Mercy Ann, the harder her heart pounded. She breathed deeper, trying to calm down as they continued talking.

"Slowly but surely, though, John Justice improved enough to not be a constant burden. We even had fun together sometimes. He learned to do his new job with communications and became an expert. But now, since I returned, he's changing again, and I don't understand why or whether he's getting better or worse. He makes no secret that he would be happier if I hadn't come back. I don't know how to act or what to do about it. It's driving me crazy."

Missa had to speak, but it was difficult to find something to say. "I wish I could help somehow."

Mercy Ann slid against her. "You can hold me."

Arms hugged around each other, for a time the corridor was a shared secret world with beating hearts and quiet breathing the only sounds. Then Mercy Ann moved away just enough so they no longer touched.

"I'm way more frayed than I realized," she said, shaking her head. "Sorry."

Shaken by emotions, Missa blurted, "May I ask you something? You can tell me if it's out of line. No, on second thought, forget it."

Unexpected, Mercy Ann thought, recognizing the meaning behind Missa's red flushed face and frightened, confused expression. "Just say what's on your mind. It's okay."

Missa took a deep breath. "Would you... Uh, could I..." She cleared her throat. "Have you ever...been with a guy?"

Mercy Ann sighed. "Only two. The first was in San Francisco. It was the Summer of Love. Flowers in my hair. Tall and good-looking, he played bass in a dynamite band. We nibbled purple sugar cubes and smoked pipes filled with rainbow dreams. It was the perfect setting, the perfect time, and the perfect disappointment."

"Why?"

"I didn't like the sex."

"Was it because you didn't love him enough?"

"You don't have to be in love to take your pants off for someone."

Missa turned even redder. "I don't...haven't... Other than Rob, I mean."

Mercy Ann refrained from saying, no kidding. "The second guy was more recent and on a dreamy planet with lovely seas, two moons, and a sun similar to Earth's. Handsome and debonair as a leading man in a romantic movie, I was attracted to him bigtime."

"What happened?"

"The same bad feelings about sex, but we had a great time otherwise until he bragged in a crowded restaurant that he'd been sent by the government to debunk UFO sightings in the area. People around us paid attention then he began preaching to the whole room that only stupid people believed life on other planets existed. The irony of the situation tickled me, and I joked that he'd better not let an alien hear him say that. Well, he became downright mean, declared I'd offended the state religion, and demanded I beg forgiveness on my knees. It became quite a scene, especially after I said how amazing it was that he could get his fat head so far up his asshole."

"Good for you!"

Mercy Ann shook her head. "The prick officially denounced me as a heretic and ordered the restaurant staff to hold me until he returned with the church police or whatever they were. Fortunately, the restaurant owner had strong connections politically and only cared about having the bill paid. I literally ran out the back door as the cops came in the front. I had to leave all my shopping in the room and skedaddle to the shuttle, which pissed me off even more."

"Did you ever see him again?"

"Oh, you bet I did. He frequented a nude beach near the resort, which was a violation of his precious state religion, by the way. I chased the buck-naked jerk up and down it with the shuttlecraft while sending live feeds to their equivalent of television networks. I didn't realize he was a famous guy until then."

Missa clapped her hands.

Mercy Ann stood suddenly, grabbing the shorts to keep them from falling down. "To say the least, the Guardians were not happy. They said I should've known government officials on that planet lorded it over regular citizens and insulting one in public would have dire consequences. Turned out they were right. After my little stunt, enough people challenged church doctrine that the government cracked down hard, forcing everyone to follow dictates of the church or suffer serious consequences. The Guardians forbade anyone in the fleet returning to that planet except on official business. Since it was one of John Justice's favorite places, he complained to them. They told him it was my fault and to have me explain what I'd done. I wouldn't tell him, and he's been pissed about it ever since."

"You'd do it all again, wouldn't you?" Missa asked.

"Oh hell yes, but it'd still be wrong."

"Does John Justice know about the men you slept with?"

"He suspected the first one and followed us everywhere until I had some of the hippie chicks stuff him with trippy brownies. The San Francisco pics that turned up a few days ago were of me walking him around the city trying to sober up enough to remember where he left the shuttle. Finding it was the biggest pain in the butt ever."

"Don't you worry he might hear us talking? He listens to everyone."

She smirked. "We're in one of the communications dead zones caused by the Sufficiency Test programming. I call them Cones of Silence after a gizmo on an old TV show named *Get Smart*. Have you ever seen it? It's really funny."

Missa had never heard of it, so Mercy Ann asked that she not tell anyone about their discussions then vanished back to her bedroom, taking all the goodies with her.

Mulling over the encounter, Missy blushed thinking how she had started to ask Mercy Ann for a kiss before chickening out and asking about men instead. Never having even considered doing anything like that before, she ran until exhaustion forced her to stop. She didn't think Mercy Ann had noticed.

The sergeant major was in front of the command post talking to a group of his sergeants under a streetlight when a truck jumped the curb and ran over Bongo, curled up asleep next to the road. The dog was still alive but no one gave him a chance of surviving. The general called John Justice to see if the aliens could do anything.

Following Miss Flower's instructions, the general ordered the men to return to their duties so the sergeant major and he could spend Bongo's last minutes alone with him. Then they crouched so shadows fell across the poor animal. No one saw Honey Bee whisk him away.

A short time later, Mercy Ann contacted the general and informed him that Honey Bee could save Bongo. Then, because she wanted time to figure out how to keep Blake from knowing all her thoughts, she asked if he could use any of the people staying with them since he couldn't get more soldiers until the turmoil died down. Other than Blake and Tom, she offered two women he didn't know, explaining that they were professional assassins and were already posing as soldiers at the site.

The general hadn't thought anything else could surprise him, but news of two professional killers operating under his nose did the trick. "That's not possible. Where did they get passes and credentials?"

"Probably from Handley's people. They hired them to gather information about John Justice. Instead, they became friends. They helped him get the President out of the White House. He asked them to join us, but it's not a settled matter yet."

"Good Lord. Are you sure you can trust them?"

"I haven't met them, but I have to say yes based on what everyone told me. Your people are used to seeing them around so they'll blend in without any problems."

The general made a mental note to review his internal security procedures again. "Well, I can definitely use the help. Thanks."

The line went dead and Mercy Ann asked, "Did you get all that, John Justice?"

It took several seconds before he responded. "Yes. And I have some bad news. The Chairman called conspirators in the Pentagon a few minutes ago. Handley wants another attack launched against us using missiles, but frankly, everything is such a mess that I don't know if they can pull it off. I'll keep you advised."

She wanted to discuss it more but John Justice insisted he was too busy. Irritated, she went to talk to Tom and Blake.

Tom was happy to help the military since he had little to do except receive treatments from Honey Bee and babysit the First Family. Blake didn't like it but didn't fuss. He even volunteered to contact Sheri and Brandi so Mercy Ann didn't have to bother.

After that, she wandered aimlessly through the house for a time wondering if Blake realized how hard it had been for her to send him away. Then she transported to the control room and found John Justice hunched over a console. He had all his personal ports plugged in for full interface with the ship's computers.

Rob and Missa sat at two of the information consoles watching data flashing across large screens and did not notice her. Each of them had a cable plugged into the right wrist. John Justice must have had Honey Bee install temporary interface ports and brainwave transfer devices in them, a radical departure from established Guardian protocols concerning unapproved humanoids.

Breaking the rules didn't bother her, but the fact John Justice and Honey Bee had not mentioned it infuriated her. She started to demand an explanation but stopped herself. It wasn't his fault they'd used her brother's body. On the other hand, she was the fleet commander and he should keep her informed. Realizing she was about to start yelling, she rushed into the corridor and kicked a wall.

She'd forgotten she wasn't wearing shoes. Swearing under her breath, she hopped on one foot holding her throbbing toes.

Rudy had not been surprised the aliens wanted him, but never in a million years thought Elena would want to go.

They had discussed it all night by the shimmering light of the pool. As the sun came up, they sent a list of questions, most of them concerning Zach, to John Justice.

Minutes later, Mercy Ann and Ashlyn, wearing bathing suits, scared them half to death by appearing next to the table. After introductions, Mercy Ann gave them a computer tablet containing pictures and extensive information about the two planets where most people in the fleet lived. She explained that she couldn't leave it with them and they had to look it over now. If they had any questions, she'd be in the pool.

Mercy Ann performed a clumsy belly flop. Ashlyn executed a graceful dive.

Elena had managed to mumble her way through niceties when Rudy introduced Mercy Ann, but could not stop gawking at her. "God, Rudy, the internet doesn't do justice to that girl. She's a real eyeful. Why didn't you tell me?"

"I hadn't noticed."

Elena punched him in the arm. "Don't give me that!"

"A wise man knows some things in marriage are best left unsaid, honey bunch."

She chuckled. "Did you notice that she's limping? Wonder what happened?"

Floating on her back far enough away that a normal person would not have heard, Mercy Ann called to them. "Broke a toe. It's almost better, though."

John Justice sent out the names of conspirators as the President promised. Jared Handley and the Chairman of the Joint Chiefs were at the top of the lists. The first reaction by news media was surprise at how many prominent people were involved. Nor had they expected short synopses of each person's involvement to be included, allowing them to broadcast the information within minutes.

Almost as quickly, legal experts and attorneys began releasing statements rebutting the accusations and claiming clients' rights violated.

John Justice, aggravated Mercy Ann had on her Victorian clothes, confronted her when she entered the operations room. "Is it true the government could dismiss our evidence because they don't understand how it was gathered? If that's the case, why waste time doing all this? I have other work I could do."

"Doesn't matter. Just keep the information going out on schedule."

"There is so much that it will take several days to send all of it using their systems."

"You have faster ways, don't you?"

John Justice was snide. "I decided this is the best way. Anything else?"

Rob saw her flinch and said, "It will keep everyone's attention away from us if we stretch it out."

She glanced at the other console where Missa had her head down asleep and decided to try making peace. "Yeah, that makes good sense. You've all done a great job."

John Justice wouldn't leave it alone. "Why are you wearing that ridiculous outfit again? Wear your protective flight suit if you're determined to go into battle."

She held her temper in check. "I have it on underneath. Seeing this dress will make them realize instantly that they didn't kill me last time. The effect will be devastating to their confidence."

"Life isn't a movie, Mercy Ann."

"Why must you argue about every little thing?" she demanded irritably. "I told you that I'm going to fight them, so just accept it."

"That's not the problem. Your brother is waking up inside me. You need to accept that."

All expression left her face. "You think being him will make us closer. It won't. Your snide claims make you even creepier than usual."

"I don't expect you to feel that way about me anymore, so get over yourself," he retorted. "Your brother is waking up inside me. You have to deal with it."

"Shut up!"

"Why won't you listen?"

"Why won't you do what I tell you?"

"I'm not wearing those stupid clothes!

"I haven't asked you to!"

"You have a spaceship you won't let anyone near. Why don't you use it to fight instead of playing dress-up in your little fantasy world?"

Her reply was quiet but with unmistakable danger in every syllable. "If you want the goddamned ship so bad, take the goddamned ship. The password to open the hatch is my brother's name, John Justice. When you go inside, fasten bands around the metal box holding the Guardians before you move it. If they get out, I'll kick your ass over the Moon and you'll never be seen again, former commander without a name of your own."

He twisted around ready to fight, but she was gone.

Rob said, "You need to discuss this matter reasonably with her rather than picking an argument then using it as a club to hit her."

"I just learned that she told her brother how much she cared for me. Yet, she never stopped pushing me away. What kind of sick game was that?"

Rob had never seen him this upset. "Do you want me to talk to her about it?"

"No! Her brother's memories are reaching farther back every day. Soon I'll learn something from before they went into space. Then she'll have to admit part of him is alive in me."

"Then what? You've told me that she won't discuss anything before they joined the fleet. She must have good reasons. Are you sure you want to go there?"

"I don't have a choice, do I?"

"I just want to help you, John Justice."

"I know, but you can't. That goes for Missa, too. Mercy Ann and I have to resolve this matter ourselves."

Just before sunset, the general came out of the mess tent and looked around for the two women Blake and Tom said were outside. He saw a soldier he recognized and asked if she'd seen anyone else waiting around.

Snapping to attention, she gave a perfect salute. "I'm one of the people you're looking for, sir. Sergeant Brandi Collins."

Someone tapped him on the shoulder and he turned to find a small slouching soldier he had pointed out to the sergeant major several days before as needing special attention. She had been nowhere in sight when he came out of the tent.

"Hi," she said, chewing a big wad of gum. "I'm Sheri."

The general stared down at her. She certainly didn't look like a lethal killer. Hell, she didn't even look like an adult.

"Stand at attention," Brandi hissed.

Sheri did her best.

The general decided the ill-fitting uniform caused most of the bad impression. "Couldn't you find a smaller size?"

"I'd have to ditch the stubby shotgun on my back and a few other goodies if I did that. I'm not dressed to pass muster. My job is to deal with problems without too much fuss, if you get my meaning."

The general had known many trained killers. This young woman looked like a kid playing dress up. Even so, something made her the scarier of the two by far.

"You're fine the way you are," he said. "Have you eaten? This is the mess tent."

Brandi answered, "We've eaten here several times, sir. Good chow and great camaraderie."

"Brings back memories of her younger days in the military," Sheri added.

He studied Brandi with interest. "Where did you serve?"

"I'm not at liberty to say, sir."

That was not surprising considering what he knew of her, but it didn't occur to him that it was in another country's army. "Understood. Wish all my soldiers had your bearing and professionalism, Sergeant Collins. When you finish eating, we'll meet in my tent to discuss the best ways to use you."

As they hurried into the tent, Sheri elbowed Brandi in the ribs. "That made your day, didn't it, soldier girl? Well, come on, didn't it?"

Governments and news agencies all over the world tried to determine the origin of the data transmissions proving information about the conspirators, thinking it might help determine the President's location. Several actually came up with the right answer. The transmissions originated out of empty sky above the United States and Middle East, but everyone discounted those as false readings since the aliens' micro-machines were undetectable.

Otherwise, close examinations of the video showed the President's big wooden desk subtly changed appearance three times and a subliminal message that "Minnesota lakes have the answers" flashed across the bottom of the screen twice. Both had been Rob's suggestions and had no purpose other than confounding analysts.

As night grew late, media sources reported nonstop about the rollout of conspiracy evidence. TV news concentrated coverage on evidence against Jared Handley and the Chairman of the Joint Chiefs. Speculating about their whereabouts dominated the airways until the blockbuster release of information about Handley funding Dictator General Abd al-Bensi. Someone speculated that was probably where the conspirators had gone. Quickly, it became the consensus opinion.

22

Prepping for Battle

DICTATOR GENERAL ABD AL-BENSI WATCHED from the tarmac of Death Valley Airport as Jared Handley, the Chairman of the Joint Chiefs, and the President, respectively, deplaned from Handley's lush jet. Behind his hand, al-Bensi told an aide to change the President's suite at the palace to the smaller one they had prepared for the Chairman then rushed forward to greet them.

Having knowledge of the aliens' surveillance abilities, Handley had sent word to al-Bensi to assume they could see and hear everything they did, so no one was to mention the missiles under any circumstances. Al-Bensi thought Handley was overcautious bordering on paranoia, but did as told because he learned long ago that disobeying Handley could be fatal.

He'd been the leader of a radical militia group on the verge of takeover by larger factions when approached by a Handley operative with a proposal he could not refuse. Taking the great man's money, he did his bidding with the assumption his growing power and prominence would result in better offers of partnership, ultimately allowing him to slip from under Handley's thumb and be in charge of his own destiny.

Al-Bensi, as did nearly everyone who dealt with the young Handley, underestimated his financial reach and ruthlessness. The secret tendrils of his burgeoning financial empire ran through so many businesses and countries that it was impossible to negotiate with other major money brokers without him knowing, a fact al-Bensi learned the hard way after months of surreptitious wheeling and dealing with powerful group of oligarchs in Russia.

On a peaceful moonlit night, black-hooded commandos wearing military uniforms without insignia or other designation dragged al-Bensi out of bed. They spoke English, and he thought they were American military.

Marched into the courtyard with arms tied behind him, he was astounded to see a black helicopter idling silently and no evidence of his guards or staff anywhere. Bagging his head, they shoved him inside the aircraft and pulled a wide strap tight around his chest and arms.

His stomach knotted with fear as the craft zoomed straight up, cold wind roaring through the open side doors. Someone jerked the bag off his head. He was face-to-face with a hooded soldier whose iron grip dug painfully into his arms then twisted him around with startling strength. A pinpoint light illuminated a man's face, seated and staring up at him.

"I thought we had an agreement," Handley said, voice the calm at the center of violent winds churning through the cabin.

"We do! Why are you doing this?"

Handley said he knew about al-Bensi's dealings with the Russians.

He dropped to his knees. "It won't happen again! You have my word! Please!"

"You can't get that kind of money without me knowing it," Handley responded, giving a slight sideways nod.

The hands gripped al-Bensi in the armpits from behind and flung him out the door. He plummeted twenty feet before a cable fastened to the chest strap stopped him with a hard jerk. A winch returned him to the craft. The steel-vise hands pulled him inside and held him on tiptoes from behind facing Handley.

Al-Bensi begged and groveled every way he knew.

"As a rule, I don't give second chances, so this is your lucky night," Handley decided finally. "Release him, soldier."

A loud metallic click and the chest restraint dropped off him.

"I created Dictator General Abd al-Bensi," Handley said. "I can create another one as easily. Do you understand?"

Before al-Bensi could answer, the hands threw him out the door again. He fell fifty feet before a bungee cord around his ankle jerked and yo-yoed him up and down. Hanging motionless finally, the winch pulled him up, much slower this time, affording plenty of time for an upside-down look at the Moon, the stars, and his compound lights far below.

Lifted inside the craft, the hands body-slammed al-Bensi onto his back. A heavy boot kicked him in the face then in the stomach.

"What's that stink?" Handley demanded.

Al-Bensi managed to get onto his side, pulled his knees up to his chest, and bawled. "I shit myself. Just kill me! Please!"

"Soldier, remove your hood and show this traitor the face of his executioner before you cut his throat," Handley ordered.

The hands jerked al-Bensi off the floor and gripped him by the neck so tightly he could scarcely breathe. His eyes widened with surprise and fear.

She was the kind woman he'd only seen on western fashion magazine covers. Young. Tall. White-blond hair buzzed-cut on the back and sides, spiked on top. Pale, perfect skin and a smooth sculpted face. Crystalline blue eyes. And strangely, a strong sweet scent of peppermint.

But al-Bensi also recognized a demon lurking behind her façade of female perfection. A demon that could inflict pain and torment until he screamed for the only salvation possible dealing with someone such as this—death, which surely she would withhold until he no longer cared.

"Cross me again," Handley warned, "and she'll come for you. Do you understand?"

His terror was genuine. "Yes! Yes!"

Holding him by the throat with one hand, the demon punched him in the face with a sledgehammer fist.

Next morning, al-Bensi woke up in his bed with wounds cleaned, set, and bandaged. The guards, personal staff, and wives talked about his car accident while they fussed over him. Later, he would see the remains of his prized red Ferrari and agree with his aides and generals that he was lucky to be alive, for he understood now that nothing he had was really his.

But it was the memory of Handley's blond demon with peppermint breath that kept al-Bensi in line for the many years afterward. Every single night when he turned off the lights for bed, he saw her face when he closed his eyes.

During the flight to the Middle East, the President had complained about having to leave the most powerful job in the world until Handley lost his temper and told him that people with salaries don't have true power, even the President of the United States. If he didn't find ways to make himself useful, he'd be expendable.

When they landed, the combination of too much alcohol and extreme heat caused the President to almost faint on the steep metal stairs leaving the plane. Only the Chairman's quickness saved him from a nasty fall. Later, Handley commented it was too bad the moron hadn't broken his damn fool neck.

Private jets arrived one after the other in the hours that followed. Limos and vans took more than a hundred conspirators to al-Bensi's luxurious palace. When the last arrived, Handley convened a meeting in the ballroom.

"We can still win this thing," he announced. "The fact the former President wasn't killed is only a setback."

An egocentric international real estate developer spoke up. "I thought the purpose of flying halfway around the world was to plan a united defense against the charges. At least, that's what we were led to believe."

"They have too much evidence to do that," Handley answered, looking around the room. "Better that we continue with our plans to take control of—"

"Bullshit!" the real estate developer bellowed. "It would be smarter to hotfoot it back home, lawyer up, and deny, deny, deny. They will presume everyone who fled to be guilty. They can't have evidence against everyone. Most of us will get off scot-free."

"They do have evidence against everyone," Handley insisted, "and it is irrefutable. Now, let's get back to the plan."

"Who made you the goddamned king?" the developer demanded. "If you have information we don't, then tell us."

Handley had decided not to say anything about his discussion with John Justice until he rid the group of members he considered lily-livered hangers-on. "You'll just have to take my word for it. Everyone came into the cause knowing the risks, but the game is not over by a long shot. We can still win."

The room was uncomfortably quiet while everyone looked around, trying to decide who was right and what to do.

The real estate developer, who had never liked Handley, said, "I'm leaving, and you're not going to stop me."

Handley shrugged. "Anyone else who wants to leave, best do it now. A powerful haboob will close the airport soon. We'll let everyone know what those of us staying behind plan to do tomorrow. Good luck, everyone."

Roughly half departed, the President and Deputy Secretary of DHS leading the stampede.

The Chairman stood, signaled the staff to close the big double doors, opened his briefcase, and removed a stack of handouts that he passed around the room. It was Handley's assessment of the situation and actions he proposed.

One after another, people finished reading, stood, and applauded.

Handley motioned for silence. "I apologize for all the melodrama, but I wanted to give the weak-kneed cowards a last chance to prove wrong my doubts about their dedication to the cause."

"Won't they sell us all down the river and tell where we are?" a CEO asked. "We should have discussed this before—"

Bursts of machinegun fire, yelling, and screaming came from outside, followed by a series of single pistol shots. Several people jumped up to look out the front windows then realized no one else left their seats or seemed in the least surprised. Sheepishly, they returned and sat down.

The Chairman informed that they spared the President, who would be held in Death Valley Prison for the time being. Everyone else was dead.

Handley discussed the call he'd received from John Justice and showed examples of damning evidence against them. Nonetheless, they thought his plan had a good chance of succeeding. He did not mention the nuclear missiles he had as an ace in the hole. Even some of his most loyal supporters would choose to give up rather than use them. So would he, but as a bluff, nothing spoke louder.

His plan began with a video showing the Chairman of the Joint Chiefs in full dress uniform declaring his candidacy for President. He reminded how dangerously weak and indecisive the President had been. How he refused to heed the advice of the military, Homeland Security, and top law enforcement agencies to quell the alien threat in Los Angeles. How allies around the world lost all respect for America and laughed at the weakest Commander-in-Chief in history while terrorists and enemies of America ran amok. How his policies benefited the rich and screwed the American middle class. And now, he planned to waltz back into office and give them more of the same.

The Chairman insisted these were special times and circumstances. The Constitutional remedy for excising a failed leader was impeachment, but the backroom shenanigans and payoffs to corrupt legislators who cared more for themselves than their constituents had thwarted that course of action.

Everyone should consider that what began as a small group of patriots' whispered worries about a corrupt President had grown into a nationwide movement numbering millions who wanted nothing more than secure futures for their families. He challenged everyone to look at the names and occupations on the lists of the so-called conspirators the former President released. Could anyone who loved this country not imagine his or her name beside those brave Americans?

John Justice summoned Mercy Ann to the operations room and explained what Handley had done in the Middle East, including a video showing the machine-gunning of conspirators hurrying out of al-Bensi's palace.

She glanced at Missa and Rob, grim and ashen-faced in front of ship scanners. "What else do you have?"

He showed her the Chairman's speech.

Mercy Ann was impressed with it. "Having the Chairman act as the face of the conspiracy while Handley stays in the background is a great idea. He's a tough, intelligent adversary."

"Indeed," John Justice agreed.

Mercy Ann tapped a forefinger on her chin, thinking. "Do you think maybe Earth would be better off with Handley in charge of the whole she-bang?"

"No, it would be impossible to control him with so much power, but he might be a useful tool on another planet. Specifically, I'm thinking of the Squarles Alliance. Perhaps he could discover whether Honey Bee's suspicions about them are correct."

Rob interrupted, "You've got to be kidding! The man's a mass murderer."

Mercy Ann regarded him curiously. "Yes, but he's also close to establishing rule over an entire planet. He's quite remarkable, and might be useful somewhere else."

"You shouldn't consider using someone like him for anything," Rob insisted.

Missa chimed in. "From what little I've seen and heard, Mercy Ann and John Justice need all the help they can get right now, Rob. Hard times require hard choices."

Taken aback that Missa saw it that way, Rob started to argue, but Mercy Ann ended the discussion. "We'll wait and see what happens then decide later. Everyone get back to work."

Again, Mercy Ann had been surprised John Justice considered using someone so extremely unsavory, but she was more interested in

Missa's quickness to see the reasoning behind the idea. Her working with the two female killers might not be as unlikely as she thought. Rob, on the other hand, had a moral compass that he would follow no matter what. While that made him difficult in some situations, it was invaluable in others.

The President insisted he and Dr. Rogers had something important to discuss with Mercy Ann and John Justice. To their surprise, he brought the First Lady.

Soon as he sat down, Mercy Ann slid a book across the dining room table. The subject was Bonobo Apes.

"Enough about peaceful apes!" the President erupted. "You keep insisting aliens altered the DNA in animals back before who gives a damn and they evolved into mankind. So what? Who cares? Stop talking nonsense and allow me to respond to Handley and the Chairman."

"We've already discussed this," Mercy Ann said.

The First Lady acted condescending. "You don't understand how politics work. We must respond quickly to refute the Chairman's accusations to win back the news cycle. If we don't, they'll just keep replaying his lies."

John Justice glanced at Mercy Ann and could tell she was not going to answer. "We're only interested in provoking Handley into activating his nuclear missiles so we can pinpoint their locations."

The President half-stood and leaned across the table menacingly. "That's crazy! What happens if he launches them?"

"We'll deal with it," John Justice answered.

"How?" the President demanded.

He turned to Mercy Ann. "That's up to her."

"I insist that you allow me to deal with this," the President responded.

Mercy Ann slid a copy of the Sufficiency Test Notice across the table. "Until this is over, we can't allow you to communicate with anyone."

He wadded it up and threw it on the floor.

The First Lady took up the argument. "What if Handley sends more videos castigating my husband? Are you really so dense you can't understand why we must respond?"

"In a few days," Mercy Ann said, "the conspiracy will no longer exist. You'll be back in Washington in charge of the country. We'll be back in space protecting you. Unless you fail the Sufficiency Test. In which case, you'll be dead, and we'll be back in space protecting an unpopulated planet. Are you so dense, you can't understand that?"

"You're going to cause a nuclear holocaust!" the President shouted, slamming the table with both fists.

"You made stupid weapons that endanger everyone on Earth, not us," Mercy Ann responded.

The President, followed closely by Dr. Rogers and the First Lady, stormed back upstairs.

Mercy Ann called into the kitchen and asked if they had any apple cupcakes left.

Miss Flowers appeared in the doorway frowning because Mercy Ann had eaten all of them before anyone else had a chance. "Only the one I saved for John Justice."

Rather than endure Mercy Ann's ire, John Justice said to give it to her.

In the kitchen, Miss Flowers slammed drawers and set a plate on the counter hard enough to break, judging by the sound. Then she rushed in, thrust it down in front of Mercy Ann, and went back into the kitchen murmuring under her breath.

Stuck straight up in the center, a big fork had all but split the cupcake in two. Mercy Ann leaned forward, looking closer.

"I think she spat on it," she whispered.

John Justice had already noticed and expected an explosion of anger. "Please, just let it go."

Mercy Ann jammed a finger into the icing, lifted off the spit-glob, and studied it. Then she stuck it in her mouth and smacked her lips when she swallowed.

John Justice snickered. "Oh, gross."

Licking the finger, she surprised him again. "Do you want half?"

"Are you certain?"

"It was yours. I only asked for it to piss her off."

"Okay, since you've eaten the poison part already."

She divided it with the fork, making an intentional mess for Miss Flowers to clean up. Neither spoke while they nibbled, not wanting to disrupt their only friendly time together since she returned. Unfortunately, it was not a big cupcake.

Mercy Ann asked, "Did you inform the American government to keep their surveillance aircraft away from Bagdad when I engage al-Bensi's military?"

"Several times, but they haven't made a decision yet. Too bad we can't have the President tell them to stay away."

"That'd be the same as saying where he is. I saw on the log that you talked to Urlak."

"I told him where salvage warehoused the Gargle wreckage and gave him the coordinates where they crashed in the ocean. He'll destroy everything."

"The navy could move it somewhere else before he arrives, couldn't they?"

"I'm monitoring them."

"Did you tell Urlak to move the pyramids back after the test?"

"Of course," he answered, growing irritable with her checking every little thing. "What do you want done about the old Guardian facility that was under the Great Pyramid?"

"Have him destroy it before he puts the pyramids back."

"What do you want to do about people at the site?"

"Warn them to get out of the goddamned way or spend eternity there," she snapped, irritated now that he asked her the same kinds of questions. "You don't need to ask me every little thing."

"You'll jump all over me if I do anything you don't like. Even when I ask, you always find something wrong, even if it was your idea."

Here we go again, Mercy Ann thought, then checked herself. She took a deep breath. "You know how much I suck when it comes to other people's feelings, especially yours. I'm trying to change, but I'm still my usual bitchy self sometimes. Sorry."

He stared. "Do you have some sort of terminal disease that you've been keeping secret?"

He'd made her smile. "Uh, the thing is, I'm nervous because I want to take you and some of our people to deal with al-Bensi and Handley in Death Valley while Honey Bee and stop armies in Iraq."

John Justice was too astounded to respond.

"I envision Honey Bee and me transporting our people over while you take the small ship and stash it somewhere near the palace in case they launch missiles that get by us. Have you had time to look the controls over, yet?"

"Yes, but I didn't try them out. The pilot's compartment was so tiny I could barely move. How did you manage such a long trip in that thing? You get antsy on shuttles."

Mercy Ann did not want to discuss that. "There's no time to practice so you'll have to learn on the job, so to speak. After this is over, you can teach me how to use all the controls. You know how dense I am about stuff like that. So you'll do it?"

His emotions gave way. "Thank you for trusting me, Mercy Ann. Of course I will."

It was the kind of thing her brother might have blurted out, and nothing at all like the commander's whiney digs about their relationship. It made her feel good that asking him to go was the right thing to do.

"Let's go to the Middle East today and get it over with," Mercy Ann said, making an instant decision. "Ask the general if we can meet in his quarters in a few minutes. I just want Brandi, Sheri, Blake, and you. If the general has time, I'd like him to sit in and learn how we do things. Oh, and tell everyone the meeting can't last more than an hour."

"Are you sure you can explain everything so quickly?"

"My part will take ten minutes at most. You and the others can have the rest to discuss whatever. Honey Bee and I will leave three hours before the attack starts, which means at five this evening. That'll give you plenty of time to go ahead in the ship to prepare the area outside Bagdad the way I want. Then you'll join Sheri, Brandi, and Blake at the palace in Death Valley and take care of business there."

"Good grief, this is so quick. Exactly what do you want prepared outside Bagdad? It isn't anything complicated, is it?"

"I'll cover that first thing in the meeting. Call me soon as everyone is assembled."

John Justice stopped her leaving and asked with a big grin, "Do I have to wear those silly knee pants?"

She actually laughed. "You'll be in an al-Bensi army uniform."

"That'll look ridiculous on me, too."

"Yes, but Sheri will be wearing one so you won't be the only dork in the group."

Aasim had not managed to sneak away to sleep during the day after being kept awake all night. Uncharacteristically, he had not seen his commander going by while touting the advantages of his two-bag theory with another unit. The commander admonished Aasim for wasting time then sent him to head a work detail loading trucks since he had nothing better to do.

He had just gotten started when word came that the attack on Bagdad would commence tomorrow morning. He needed to get back to his men but could not leave until the work was finished. Making matters worse, a senior sergeant came by and took men for another job. Then a captain yelled at him because the work was behind and took down his name.

Bone-weary, he did not return to his unit until after dark, only to find the truck and his men gone. It had been his plan to sneak away and move closer to Bagdad before the attack, and now they'd left without him.

He could do nothing about it. Reporting them would reflect badly on him so he had to cover up their desertion until he could say they were missing in action. Meanwhile, he'd be stuck on foot, arriving in Bagdad with the main force too late for looting.

But first, he had to deal with exhaustion and hunger. His men had taken the food, his blanket, and extra clothes, so he found a sergeant friend and received the favor of a meal. Then he wandered off, found a depression in the ground, rolled up a loot bag under his head, and used the other as cover against night's coolness. His last thoughts before succumbing to sleep were of the money and jewelry in the lining of his coat. This would have been a complete disaster if he had not worn it today.

Suddenly, a young man's voice blared so loudly that it hurt Aasim's ears and woke him. He sat up, flipping the safety off his rifle automatically. Around him, all was bedlam as soldiers jumped up confused and shouting. Someone started firing. Others joined in.

Aasim hunkered down in the depression until they stopped. The whole time, the voice boomed. Badly distorted initially, it was distinct now, repeating two messages continuously in Arabic.

The alien Mercy Ann stands vigil before the gates of Bagdad.
If you want to die, attack.
If you want to live, throw down your weapons and run away.

Abd al-Bensi will die today in Death Valley.
His American masters will die with him.
If you want to live, throw down your weapons and run away.

Aasim had no idea how a voice came out of clear sky, but assumed it must be some new Western technology. As for threatening them, everyone had seen the videos of al-Bensi's powerful new weapons killing the alien Mercy Ann. The enemy must think them superstitious fools who didn't know how to use smartphones and the internet. Shivering from the cold of a desert night, he stuffed his ears with paper wads and went back to sleep.

Honey Bee sat on the big bed enthralled with a TV reality show about people living in a swamp. Mercy Ann sat on the couch splitting a soft drink while Missa, who had shown up unexpectedly wanting to discuss how she was tired of being left behind and wanted to get back at those bastards in Death Valley for what they'd done to her and Rob.

Mercy Ann had not known how bad the torture had been for them and felt guilty for not asking. Nor had she realized Missa and Rob were so mentally tough, but no way would she allow them to work with Brandi and Sheri until they knew everything about how her parents died, and now was not the time.

"We need you and Rob in the operations center," she said quietly.

Missa responded that Rob could be fitted with a second cable port and have his brainwave transfer device boosted to handle everything without her.

"You're not ready for an operation like this. If anything bad happened to you, I wouldn't be able to...I couldn't bear losing someone else who I..." Mercy Ann stopped, angry with herself for becoming emotional.

Missa reached across the table and took her hand. "I understand. Just promise you'll come back without getting hurt again."

Mercy Ann watched her run from the room, beating herself up mentally for allowing everything to get so complicated. What was she thinking? Then she saw Honey Bee staring at her. Could this get any worse?

"Well, that was a surprise," John Justice said out of nowhere.

"I told you to stop eavesdropping on me."

"I didn't realize how much you liked her."

"I like everyone you recruited. What's up?"

Even he knew not to push this any farther. "The Americans agreed not fly spy planes in Iraq after hearing our warnings to al-Bensi's soldiers. I don't understand why that decided them, but it did. They're mystified by your name in the warnings."

"What else?"

"Tom agrees that he should stay behind to help Miss Flowers with the First Family. His treatments have made him weak and shaky, as Honey Bee predicted."

"In a few weeks, we'll have him at a good hospital that can repair the damage. Did the sergeant major say anything about being excluded?"

"He didn't expect to go since they're so shorthanded. Having Bongo back is keeping him busy, too."

"I didn't think he sounded all that thrilled to hear his dog would live a hundred years or more," Mercy Ann said, making an obvious understatement.

John Justice chuckled. "If Bongo gets to be too much trouble, he could simply forget to take him in for tune-ups."

Mercy Ann smiled. "That's mean, John Justice."

Jared Handley thought the threats of Mercy Ann defending Bagdad and John Justice coming to kill al-Bensi were nothing more than ploys to unnerve the soldiers. The aliens might be technologically superior, he told al-Bensi and the Chairman, but they gave away their advantage with poor planning and undisciplined behavior. Even so, coming up with a strategy was difficult since they had no idea what to expect.

Al-Bensi expressed concerns about UFOs showing up at Bagdad. Handley and the Chairman expressed confidence the coil cannons could destroy them and that led to wanting them in the front ranks, the most likely place the enemy would attack. Al-Bensi argued against it because that also made them too easy to target.

After much back and forth, they decided to have fourteen flatbed trucks follow close behind the four carrying coil cannons in the front rank. They'd cover all of them with identical canvas. Additionally, they'd handpick two hundred troops from other units to accompany the cannon flatbeds in small trucks. Then, as a final measure, they'd use al-Bensi's fighter-bombers to provide air coverage.

Al-Bensi still did not like the plan, but he could do nothing about it.

Handley saw the aliens as his last obstacle to ruling Earth and wanted to leave nothing to chance. The coil cannons had been fitted with new adjustable barrels that could fire wider beams, ideal for bringing down squadrons of aircraft and killing soldiers across a broad expanse of battlefield. New coils carried twice the charge as the ones that killed the alien girl. Half a dozen missiles of the type used in LA were ready to fire from a site south of Tikrit. The fighter-bombers would carry new rockets based on coil technology.

As for the nuclear missiles, his research scientists had adapted coil beam technology to power small, lightweight missiles years ago. They were capable of delivering nuclear warheads to targets anywhere in the world and did not require special launch pads, silos, combustible fuel, or extra personnel. Housed inside insulated metal cylinders, he incorporated ten of the missiles into the construction of hotels, casinos, and resort complexes at various locations in the Middle East. The final two, which al-Bensi knew about, were in Death Valley—one inside the prison, the other in the palace.

The Chairman knew all the sites, but only Handley had control of them. Firing his nuclear weapons was as simple as entering codes into his special smartphone.

Aasim cried tears of joy after his unit commander ordered him to report to an officer with the new cannons in the front ranks to help guard them during the attack. Then, primarily because of his sharp appearance, the cannon commander presented him with a new automatic rifle and assigned him to ride shotgun in the lead truck.

Rather than suffering thick dust and insufferable heat in one of the smaller vehicles, he would be high up in a truck cab, affording him the opportunity to watch for his treacherous comrades. Even if he failed to find them, he would still have the opportunity to be amongst the first groups to reach the city. Hurrying toward the truck's big shiny cab, he thought it might even have air conditioning.

23

The Battle for Bagdad

THE MORNING SKY WAS BRIGHT BLUE after a freakish dust storm whipped across the battlefield. Having expected it to delay the attack on Bagdad another day, al-Bensi soldiers discussed how unnatural it was that no dust remained in the air after such violent winds before word came to move out in one hour.

Aasim was so excited being in the Abd al-Bensi army about to take possession of the capital of Iraq that he could not sit still while waiting to get underway, causing the Iraqi driver to rebuke him for bouncing in the seat as a child would. Because he was a sergeant, Aasim responded by criticizing the driver for not understanding the momentous importance of the occasion and his eagerness to see the famous city for the first time.

Aasim did not realize this was only the fifth time the man had driven this rig and how nervous he was transporting an important weapon and the personnel responsible for operating it on the big trailer behind them.

The vertical exhausts mounted on either side of the cab came to life, deep-throated roars that prompted soldiers on the trucks around them to fire weapons into the sky, cheer, and shout. Up and down the front lines, others mimicked the behavior. Continuing for several minutes, the activity calmed and steeled nerves. Then the soldiers laughed and shouted insults at any enemy foolish enough to stand in the way of Abd al-Bensi's mighty armies.

Near the front of the line, the big truck jerked forward. In spite of strict orders not to exceed a safe limit, everyone knew looters would begin recklessly passing and racing ahead when they neared the outskirts of the city, forcing everyone else to try keeping up with them.

On narrow roads laughingly called highways, they passed through miles of irrigated fields abundant with crops of grains and vegetables. Small towns, villages, clusters of houses, and small businesses hugged the roads tightly. Booby traps and ambushes were concerns despite reports that inhabitants had fled into the city despite most of the defenders having abandoned it already.

Aasim had imagined this attack with al-Bensi forces charging forward on wide modern highways at dramatic speeds, but the reality was too many vehicles making agonizingly slow process.

In spite of the air conditioning, Aasim and the driver were sweat-soaked under the brutal late morning sun. His legs ached from bracing against sudden stops. The noise of the truck and booming warnings to run away forced him to slouch down, fingers stuck in his ears. He wondered how the driver could stand the racket, never considering that he should offer him something to stuff in his ears.

Several hours later, after the first looters' vehicles squeezed by, traffic in front of them sped up and opened a wide gap. Vehicles behind blew horns to speed up. Aasim assailed the driver to go faster.

The driver shouted that he had orders to maintain enough room from the vehicles ahead to pull off the road and position the cannon if they encountered the aliens.

Aasim scoffed and declared the aliens were nothing more than American propaganda and trickery, utter nonsense. Then he told the driver he should be less uptight and speed up, which he did immediately.

Finally, Aasim realized the man was intimidated having a seasoned sergeant riding with him. Now he liked him, smiled encouragement frequently, and urged him on.

In much better spirits, the driver shouted they would reach the outskirts of Bagdad in a matter of minutes. Then they passed through a small village of one and two-story buildings. As they emerged on the other side, Aasim commented about the strangeness of a high cone-shaped hill straight ahead of them.

The driver, concentrating on the traffic ahead, looked up and gasped. "Where did that come from?"

Suddenly, a chain reaction of vehicles screeching to a stop came down the line. The driver stood on the brakes with both feet but the heavy truck plowed into a pickup packed with troops and pushed it into the car in front of it. Behind them, the sounds of more collisions, screaming, and yelling.

Aasim began climbing out to help the injured but the commander of the coil cannons ran back from one of the lead vehicles yelling and gesturing to move the truck into a side road to hide it behind a building with the cannon pointed towards the mysterious mound.

As he scrambled back into the cab, Aasim yelled at the men around the pickup to move the injured out of the way. They ignored him. He shouted at the driver, staring down at the accident in terror, to go. The commander pulled up on Aasim's side of the cab yelling to run over the men ahead if necessary. Aasim slapped the driver in the face.

The driver snapped out of it. He gunned the engine.

The big rig jerked forward, crashed into the pickup, and knocked the commander off into the road. The driver kept going.

The truck cab's rear wheels ran over the commander's legs. The thunderous exhaust pipes masked his and others' screams.

Leaning far out the window, Aasim motioned for the driver to keep going until they pushed the vehicles in front of them far enough to back up and make the turn. The technicians and guards riding on the big trailer held on for their lives.

A colonel near the front of the column stood on the hood of his car and witnessed Aasim's actions. Called by the general in charge of the attack to move the lead cannon in position to fire immediately or suffer the consequences, he resolved to seek the sergeant out later to determine if he would make a good officer.

Meanwhile, soldiers spread out across fields either side of the road and took firing positions facing the mound. They knew it would not be long before al-Bensi's helicopter gunships and fighter-bombers arrived.

Meanwhile, atop the high hill, Mercy Ann looked to the right at the Tigris River and recalled a TV program about satellites detecting two ancient riverbeds in this area that once joined with the Tigris and Euphrates, matching descriptions of four rivers mentioned in the Bible near the Garden of Eden. The show said the garden site would be offshore now because of higher sea levels. Fascinated, she'd taken a shuttle and gone underwater to look. Turned out to be a waste of time because she found nothing any different from the rest of the seafloor.

John Justice laughed when she told him about it, pointing out that thousands of years had passed and the Garden of Eden didn't have monuments and buildings, just a couple of people, a big snake, and an apple tree in a paradise setting, presumably. Then he said she shouldn't disturb holy places, even fictitious ones, regardless.

She remembered thinking at the time that John Justice was full of interesting bullshit that didn't make any sense.

Mercy Ann checked the readouts in her right eye again. John Justice had made the hill perfectly symmetrical and fifty feet high precisely, a masterpiece construction of dirt. He'd probably taken care to be so exact just to see if she noticed.

Her purpose for wanting higher ground was so enemy fire would pass over the city instead of destroying heavily populated areas behind her. John Justice reported there was not enough time to evacuate people from the neighborhoods where he placed the hill. He'd selected the area with the least number of homes, but that was all he could do.

Mercy Ann felt bad about the deaths, in spite of knowing the hill would save many more lives.

Twisting around, she looked behind her. Nothing moved in the city streets that she could see without zooming in. No boats were on the river nor traffic on the highways and streets either side except for al-Bensi's approaching army. The outlying areas to the west of her were quiet, too.

But she knew if she used infrared scanners, she'd find hundreds of people hiding in buildings where they worked, lived, and worshipped. Always it was the same, no matter the planet or species where battles were about to be waged.

Mercy Ann glanced down at her prim Victorian outfit, so out of place in this sunbaked country, but it made her easy-to-spot atop the barren hill. She wanted her face clearly seen and wore nothing on her head. She'd braided and tied back her hair out of the way so her weapons didn't damage it, making her look older than when wearing it down.

Hidden under a short cape, Honey Bee clung to her back with cables from the back of Mercy Ann's head plugged into a panel on her chest. Connected, they were a diabolical fighting unit.

Mercy Ann kicked dirt with one of her high button shoes. It was no good trying to think of anything other than the people she was about to kill, no good at all. She hoped that the soldiers heeded the warnings to run away. Otherwise...

Sensing her need for distraction, John Justice reported, "We're inside al-Bensi's palace."

When she didn't respond right away, he asked, "You haven't fallen off your silly mountain, have you?"

He made her smile, for which she was grateful. "You created a work of art out of a pile of dirt. It's amazing."

"It's not that big a deal."

She could tell how pleased he was. "Did you have a chance to evaluate the saturation levels of communications devices in the area?"

"I reseeded both areas of operation when I arrived. We can transmit as much high quality video as we want."

"Have you located the coil cannons? Are they charging?"

Obviously, she wasn't scanning the battlefield because she didn't want to know how many potential casualties there were. He decided to leave the subject alone for now.

"Three are in position," John Justice reported as though normal for him to provide this kind of information, "but the fourth has vehicles jammed around it and can't move. It has the controller unit, so none of the cannons can operate until it is situated. It's going to take a while, I'm afraid."

Mercy Ann wanted this over quickly. "Feed the visual and location data for the vehicles blocking the control unit transport to me, and I'll clear the road. Do not begin media transmissions until they're in position."

If she had reservations about taking decisive action, John Justice did not hear it in her voice. "Sending requested information to your external panel display."

A semi-transparent screen showing the traffic scene appeared in the air before her.

John Justice assigned numbers to the vehicles that she could read with the targeting camera in her left eye, which flashed red as she locked on each target. A popup menu listing weapons appeared in her right eye.

Mercy Ann held her arms straight out to the sides. "Activate Lime Sparklers, level one."

A glowing green mass materialized above her. Staccato bursts of emerald, star-shaped lights streaked from it to the vehicles around the big truck, reducing them to molten puddles in seconds.

Shocked, John Justice asked, "What was that?"

She had just killed a large number of people and couldn't pretend it didn't bother her any longer. "The Guardians fitted me with a new battery of weapons. As if I wasn't horrible enough already."

Her tone concerned him. "If you want, we can abandon this and find another way to demonstrate our superiority."

She didn't sound at all confident. "No, I'm fine."

"Take deep breaths and remember they are bad people, Mercy Ann."

"I killed them for nothing more than being in the way."

John Justice knew he had to make her think about something else and fast. "You will be live on TV in ten seconds, nine, eight, seven, six..."

A long, cinematic shot of Mercy Ann on top of a high hill watching the approach of al-Bensi's armies appeared on TVs and personal media devices carried by al-Bensi soldiers massed to attack Bagdad, in the Pentagon's National Military Command Center, the Death Valley palace, and the Los Angeles disaster command post. Devices came on at full volume, demanding instant attention. Then picture zoomed in slowly until it showed Mercy Ann from the waist up.

To the al-Bensi soldiers, most of whom had no knowledge of the Victorian Age, her short cape and black and white clothes simply appeared foreign and upper class. Then word spread that she was the alien, Mercy Ann, who supposedly died in the Death Valley battle, confounding and frightening them.

Mercy Ann spoke to the al-Bensi soldiers. "I won't retaliate until you strike me with everything you have. Then I will use my least powerful weapons against you, but do not take comfort in that fact. Nothing about this battle will be fair to you. Save your lives. Drop your weapons and run."

John Justice relayed a comment made in the Pentagon Command Center to Mercy Ann.

She turned her head slightly, staring through the camera. "Yes, talk is cheap, General Haymeyer, especially when you're sitting inside an underground bunker eating jelly donuts in Washington, DC. If you keep making ignorant comments, I'll transport you here with me to watch."

John Justice communicated privately. "Two cannons are charged. The others are almost ready."

She sighed. "Idiots."

Handley was the only one who did not lose composure when Mercy Ann appeared on the big wall screen in the palace's main meeting room. He wondered if her image was a John Justice fabrication or if she survived the previous coil cannon onslaught somehow. While it did plant a small seed of doubt, he still thought he had the upper hand.

The aliens were unaware how much stronger the cannons' were now. Nor did they expect six missiles of the same type used against them in LA to strike her. If those weren't enough, new rockets powered by coil beam technology would rain down from fighter-bombers, already on the way.

"Help yourselves to refreshments, my friends," he announced. "I think you'll find the show entertaining, to say the least."

John Justice had left the little spaceship burrowed into the side of a hill not far from Death Valley and transported to the coordinates where Mercy Ann and Honey Bee dropped off Blake, Sheri, and Brandi. He didn't really think he needed them, but Mercy Ann cautioned that even the best plans go awry and wanted people who could improvise, just in case.

He transported with them into a spacious bedroom in an empty wing of the palace where they watched Mercy Ann on television while he periodically checked the conspirators' activities in the big meeting room. All they could do now was stay out of sight and wait.

Their job was to corner Handley, al-Bensi and the Chairman inside until Mercy Ann arrived. Handley would have no recourse but to threaten them with nuclear missiles. They would refuse to believe he had any. He'd have to begin launch preparations to prove it, allowing them to pinpoint and destroy them.

The aliens did not know Handley had found ways to manufacture smaller missiles based on coil technology that he could launch remotely from tubes without additional personnel. Nor that he deployed them throughout the Middle East, not just in territories under al-Bensi's control, which made stopping all of them after launch impossible.

Crouched in a ditch behind the trailer with the driver and other soldiers as the big cannon revved up power, Aasim watched crackling energy pulsing up and down the big glassy coils, turning the barrel white-hot. Only the driver had witnessed test firings and knew what to expect. Everyone else shivered from fright.

Raising up to see over the trailer, Aasim could just make out the tiny figure on top of the hill. He looked down at the image on his cellphone again. Could this pretty girl really be an alien from outer space? She looked more like an actress on a TV drama.

He'd missed hearing her speak a few minutes earlier because he helped remove the canvas from the big gun. The men said she'd spoken Arabic and promised to take no action until they hit her with all their weapons. He shook his head. No way would she survive, no way at all.

An officer came and made the other men spread out along the ditch in fighting positions. Now Aasim and the driver were alone behind the cannon. Without realizing, fear moved them closer to each other.

Looking around at troops arrayed behind them, Aasim saw that everyone still had their phones out watching the girl rather than the battlefield. No one would notice him sneaking away if he went now. It would be simple to steal a vehicle, drive a few miles east, and slip into the outskirts of Bagdad.

He decided to wait because he wanted to see what happened when the big gun opened fire, and no place was better than this. Slouching down, he rested his back against the bank and cupped his hands around the screen to see it better.

The coil cannon screeched with the fury of a wild beast when it fired. Its crackling beam converged with three others at the top of the hill, forming a huge, kinetic energy ball that consumed Mercy Ann.

At the same instant, John Justice cut off transmissions to the battlefield, so al-Bensi soldiers did not witness her standing inside a membranous sphere resembling a flimsy soap bubble. Yet, it withstood the onslaught of energy, the shape fluctuating with the intense attacks on its surface, but never yielding.

Meanwhile, the Pentagon received an urgent alert that a satellite showed al-Bensi's army had just fired six of America's new top-secret missiles.

General Haymeyer erupted, "He gave those away, too! That goddamned traitor, Handley!"

Mercy Ann turned and asked, "What's more important, general, your weapons, or the people they kill?"

"How the hell can she hear us?" he thundered. "And how can she transmit through all the interference around her?"

Mercy Ann smiled and pulled a pair of red-framed sunglasses from a pocket and slid them on to shield her eyes from the brightness. Then, sighing frequently, she tapped one foot then the other while crossing and uncrossing arms, apparently not concerned about anything other than having her time wasted.

In truth, every second shut away inside the protective field unable to see anything but raw energy dancing on the bubble's surface caused Mercy Ann extreme anguish. The real purpose of the sunglasses was so no one could see her tightly closed eyes.

Aasim and the driver scooted farther down the ditch because the cannon's cooling system exhausted blistering hot air back towards them. That was when Aasim decided he might as well leave since the girl was surely dead already. He yelled to the driver that he would be right back, jumped up, and looked around for the best way to go.

The driver grabbed his arm and pointed to missiles streaking down out of the sky. They dived face down in the ditch as huge explosions erupted. High velocity outflows of wind, dirt, and debris roiled down the hill across the battlefield. Only the fact they were in a ditch prevented the blasts sweeping them away as other soldiers were. Then something struck Aasim in the head.

Dust hung thick in the air, limiting visibility to a few feet. Aasim's throat was so dry he choked and couldn't swallow. The driver helped him sit up and gave him a mouthful of water. He hacked up muddy phlegm then laid back in the ditch gasping. The driver put a wet cloth over his mouth and nose.

All this to kill one girl, Aasim thought. Has everyone gone mad?

His phone, in the dirt next to him, came back to life. He wiped it off and gestured for the driver to hurry and check his, too.

The girl was alive on top of the hill with no damage or dust around her at all. Aasim didn't think about that, instead wondering why she looked so worried and unhappy after the miracle of living through all that. He'd be overjoyed and down on his knees giving thanks.

The cannons began revving to fire again, making it more difficult for him to unscramble his thoughts. More than anything, he wanted to leave, but stumbling around choking and unable to see more than a few feet made no sense. He had to stay put for now.

The picture on the phone showed the girl talking. He held it to his ear.

"In the front ranks," she said, "one in five bearing weapons will die. Activate Cotton Candy, level one."

Frantic, Aasim discarded his weapons then watched as pink specks of light materialized and spun above the girl's head, forming a growing mass of tumbling clouds. She lowered her arms, and they flew out from the hill to the army.

Frenetic pink specks flitted around Aasim and the driver. They scarcely dared to move or breathe for fear of inhaling them. Then

Aasim saw one land and disappear into the skin of the driver's cheek, leaving a minuscule drop of blood.

Aasim asked if he felt anything.

The terrified man answered through clenched lips. "Same as a fly biting, brother."

Aasim smiled to assure him and started to say not to worry.

The driver's head exploded, not loudly, more as if a paper bag full of air popped softly. More of the muted sounds came from all directions. Aasim added his screams to others and scooted away from the body wiping bloody mess off his face and swiping pink specks away hysterically.

When he regained his senses, he was still in the ditch. The beam cannons revved and glowed white-hot, casting freakish shadows of soldiers running past toward the rear ranks. That kind of behavior was likely to end with an injury or death, he thought. Better to catch his breath and calm down first.

Dust settled. Fewer specks were in the air. He saw his phone near his feet but fought the urge to pick it up. The last thing he wanted was to see the alien girl ever again.

Taking a deep breath, Aasim stood slowly. He began jogging away from the hill. It felt liberating. Then he tripped and sprawled over a body with a cavity where the abdomen had been. The gore didn't bother him so much now, but as he scraped muck off with the side of his hand, he realized the coat with his wealth was in the cab of the coil cannon truck.

He looked back. Strangely, the coils continued revving and brightening, but not firing. Was something wrong? Was it worth risking his life to go back for the coat?

Aasim cursed himself for being foolish. Without money, he'd be the same worthless schmuck as before leaving home to join al-Bensi. Four years it had taken him to accumulate that money. He ran back, dodging soldiers running the other way.

In spite of John Justice's telling Mercy Ann that he could no longer monitor the battlefield, his concern for her made him continue doing just that.

"The cannons are dangerously overheating," he warned. "The crews abandoned them and ran when they realized you were unharmed. You have to destroy them."

"They left them charging?" she asked, surprised to hear from him.

He did not want to upset her but had to say something. "Please turn on your scanners so you know what's going on, Mercy Ann. You can't keep operating blind."

She turned them on and mumbled, "Sorry."

She sounded so rattled that he had trouble keeping his voice under control. "Can you destroy the cannons without discharging the energy they've built up?"

There was a short delay before she answered. "All but the one with the controller. I'll make it explode then I can take out the others without collateral damage. Target acquired. Activating Lightning, level one."

Above Mercy Ann, a crackling sphere the size of a volleyball appeared then streaked to the target. An enormous explosion rocked the battlefield. Unleashed coil energy burned soldiers and equipment massed around the truck. The remainder of the energy dispersed as raging flames and smoke shooting more than a mile into the sky.

Mercy Ann said, "Activate Green Sparklers, level three."

The same star-shaped lights she used to clear the road earlier formed in front of her in a much bigger mass, divided into three streams, and streaked to the cannon trucks. They melted.

"You said you wouldn't use anything above level one," John Justice said.

"It was necessary to consume the pent up coil energy quickly to avoid more explosions."

"But your ports can't handle more stress."

"They're okay. Oops, hold on a sec."

A new targeting grid had appeared in her eye showing dozens of red and black blips approaching in the sky. The black ones were helicopter gunships. The red, fighter-bombers.

"What if I send Honey Bee to deal with the jets?" she asked John Justice. "Seeing her in action ought to cause quite a stir and take some of the load off me."

"Good idea."

Mercy Ann reached back and lifted the cape, revealing Honey Bee dressed in tight metallic silver pants, silver boots, and a matching jacket with a hood pulled tight around the head so only her face showed through a protective glass faceplate. Unplugged from Mercy Ann's cables, she climbed onto her shoulder. Mercy Ann lifted her off and flung her underhanded into the air.

A large backswept fin snapped out of each side of her body, reaching far beyond her feet. A smaller one came out of her back. Between the tips of the big fins, pale blue flames ignited.

Honey Bee shot into the air with tremendous acceleration, an arcing vapor trail showing an intercept course with the largest formation of jets. She streaked past them, and they exploded.

Mercy Ann detected more aircraft approaching as two groups of fighters swooping down to engage her. No time left for finesse, she ordered Honey Bee out of the battle area.

She held her arms straight out in front of her. “Activate Snaky Whips, level six.”

A huge glowing black globe materialized high above her. Dozens of writhing, tentacle-like beams radiated miles from it in an instant, snapping missiles, rockets, and aircraft out of the air. Fiery, exploding debris crashed down. In less than a minute, no airborne threats remained nearby. She told Honey Bee to take care of the ones farther away.

Mercy Ann deactivated the whips and cut the TV feeds so no one could see her. “The soldiers are regrouping in the rear ranks, John Justice. They all should be running away. What’s wrong?”

“Uh, I’m moving through the palace with Brandi, Sheri, and Blake. Unless you want to change the plan, you’ll have to determine that yourself. If you want, maybe I can...”

“No. I’ll deal with it.”

Mercy Ann sunk down to her knees, pulled a vial from her pocket, and drank it empty. Then she scanned and discovered Al-Bensi fanatics in the back ranks machine-gunning retreating soldiers unless they rejoined the fight. She scanned al-Bensi’s forces farther north and found them moving to join the attack on Bagdad. Instead of the situation getting better, it was getting worse.

Mercy Ann stood and looked out across the battlefield. From this vantage point, it seemed she’d won, but it simply wasn’t so. She had to break the back of the attack across the entire battlefield.

She expanded the area of the next attack twenty miles northward. It meant large numbers of civilians would die, but she couldn’t do anything about it. Finally, she looked at the data details then suffered a panic attack, gasping for air more than two minutes before calming down enough to do what she must.

Mercy Ann re-enabled the TV transmissions. “From my position to a point twenty-one miles north, thirty-one thousand, five hundred, and eleven al-Bensi soldiers are moving to attack Bagdad. Since they haven't heeded warnings, half will die now. Activate Cotton Candy, level nine."

As gigantic pink clouds expanded across the sky above the hill, she issued a warning. "Next, I will go to Death Valley and render justice to Jared Handley, Abd al-Bensi, and anyone else stupid enough to be with them. You have twenty minutes to say your prayers."

Pandemonium erupted in the palace. Except for al-Bensi, the Chairman, and Handley, the Westerners ran outside and yelled at confused drivers to get them away from the palace fast as possible. Meanwhile, Al-Bensi marveled at the calm exhibited by Handley, assuming he had a solution for the alien girl's threats.

Then the great man turned to the Chairman. "Guess a palace isn't the worst place a man can die."

The Chairman responded hotly. "What the hell are you talking about? Launch a nuclear missile at the bitch! She won't survive that."

"From what we've seen, a missile won't get anywhere near her."

"We won't know for certain unless we try. Hurry. Do it before she leaves Iraq."

Handley's demeanor hardened. "Better to use the missiles to negotiate. The last thing we want to do is fire them."

"No! First, kill her. Show them we mean business."

Handley had enough. "Just shut up and let me handle it. First, we need to—"

The Chairman whipped out a pistol. "Give me your goddamned phone if you're too chickenshit to do anything."

Caught by surprise, Handley reached for his gun. Three shots struck him in the chest. He was dead before he hit the floor.

The Chairman turned Handley onto his back and pulled his phone and wallet from inside jacket pockets. He took out a photograph of Handley's mother. On the back were twelve lines of telephone numbers with a name beside each one. After holding the phone to Handley's left eye to unlock it, he pressed two travel apps simultaneously to open a map of the Middle East with locations of the missiles, each with a numbered white space next to it.

He glanced up at al-Bensi, watching over his shoulder. "The smug jerk thought he was so clever. Used to leave his wallet in the office when he worked out in the mornings. I went through it looking for the launch codes for cities he'd pre-targeted in case he'd been stupid enough to write them down. He'd already showed me missile app on his phone. It only took a day or so to figure out after that."

"He was careless to underestimate you, my friend," al-Bensi said, expressing admiration for the Chairman's intelligence just before he cut his throat. He took the phone from his hand as he fell on top of Handley.

"Now, you shits will pay," he swore, studying the phone. "Obviously, you count down the phone numbers and match them to the numbers on the blank spaces beside the missile locations. The area code tells you the city targeted. The rest of the phone number goes in the blank space to activate the missile. Hmm, if you press this symbol, you can select different cities or simply blow missiles up. It took you a day to figure this out?"

Al-Bensi's fingers had been broken when he was young, so he was slow and clumsy with touchscreens. The big TV showing Mercy Ann and his soldiers kept distracting him, too.

Meanwhile, worried about Mercy Ann, John Justice had only checked on the conspirators at intervals, so when soldiers began running helter-skelter through hallways looking into every room for valuables to steal, they caught his team by surprise. But while seeing Western male and female non-Arabs in al-Bensi uniforms was unusual, the first two groups they encountered assumed they were with the other Westerners visiting al-Bensi. The third team recognized John Justice and attacked. They died quickly.

When it was over, John Justice checked video feed to the meeting room again and witnessed Abd al-Bensi standing over the bodies of Handley and the Chairman laboriously entering information into a phone. He realized immediately what he intended to do.

Al-Bensi sobbed while watching Mercy Ann on the big TV killing his soldiers. Then the survivors threw down their weapons and ran. Trembling with rage, he wiped his runny nose with the back of his hand and resumed inputting numbers into the phone. When he finished the last entry, he peed on Handley and the Chairman's bodies.

Then he gloated because millions of his enemies would join these assholes in hell when Mercy Ann arrived and he gave her the surprise he had prepared. The missiles in his palace and prison would detonate when the others launched to destroy America cities. He would be martyred and have the greatest revenge in the history of the world.

Suddenly, al-Bensi heard a slight noise behind him. He spun around, gripping the phone tightly with the index finger of his other hand poised to tap the flashing button on the screen. He expected to see the alien girl. He froze in shocked disbelief.

It was Handley's demon of death, standing as close as the night on the helicopter. The same peppermint breath, short blond hair, and cold blue eyes. But the powerful hands were to her sides, doing nothing to hide her nakedness from the waist up, which consumed his attention for precious seconds.

Sheri and Blake appeared behind al-Bensi. Sheri, taut as an overwound spring, wore nothing but a sports bra and panties to insure silence. A Japanese wakizashi short sword gripped in both hands next to her right cheek pointed straight up. Blake held a pistol aimed at the back of al-Bensi's head. Sheri gave a quick nod, took three fast steps forward, pivoted, and slashed down as Blake fired.

Brandi had grabbed, bent back, and broken al-Bensi's index finger with one hand while taking hold of the phone hand with the other. When the body dropped to the floor, she still held his severed hand with the phone, in spite of Sheri cutting off two of her fingers below the second knuckle. Even so, Brandi did not move until Blake carefully took the phone.

Sheri was frantic. "Oh, honey, I'm so sorry."

Brandi sank to the floor and held the hand up over her head while gripping the wrist to slow blood loss. "Goddamn it, Sheri, stop blubbering. Pick up my fingers and put them on ice."

John Justice had transported to the ship in case the missiles launched. Now, he flew to the palace, crashed through the roof of the main hall, and left the ship hovering twenty feet in the air where no one could reach it.

Mercy Ann and Honey Bee appeared in the meeting room. Honey Bee injected Brandi with micro-machines to stop pain and stem bleeding. Then she made the first jump back to Los Angeles with Brandi and the fingers. Mercy Ann sat off to one side eating pastries and drinking tea while John Justice deactivated the missiles with Handley's phone.

When he finished, Mercy Ann said, "From the expression on your face, we almost had a disaster."

"Handley created missiles using coil propulsion that are small and launch remotely," he explained. "He deployed them all over the Middle East, including one in this building and one in the prison that al-Bensi set to explode when the others launched."

"Shit," Mercy Ann said.

"Yes, shit," he agreed.

"Honey Bee and I have to share the blame," she responded tiredly. "We should've realized he could apply coil technology to propulsion systems. The rockets his fighters used against me were coil-driven, too. Those suckers were really zipping. Nearly got one up the old wazoo before I realized."

"Could have been painful," he said half-heartedly.

She held up her right arm, showing the blood-soaked sleeve of her dress. "Actually, it was. I blew out a port again. Honey Bee checked it out before she left, so don't make a big deal about it. Just another repair."

It wasn't meant to be critical. "I knew you'd overo it."

"Let's just be thankful we had such good people with us," she answered, looking across the room at them. "They were incredible."

24

Respite

MISSA EXPLAINED, "The First Lady confronted Miss Flowers, Ashlyn, and me with a butcher knife. Miss Flowers surprised me by asking if I could subdue her. Before I had a chance to answer, the First Lady ran at me. I reacted automatically, I'm afraid. She hit the wall hard and ended up with a swollen face, black eye, and nasty cut on her arm."

Blake laughed.

"Then I certainly can't blame Miss Flowers for putting them in stasis boxes," John Justice said, doing his best not to laugh, too. "I thought about doing it before we left, but was too busy. Mercy Ann is going love you for subduing the First Lady."

Missa blushed.

Blake glanced at John Justice, wondering if he'd chosen those words intentionally to get a reaction out of her but couldn't tell. Rob, monitoring long-range scanners, was oblivious.

"Funny thing was," Missa continued, "the President didn't seem to mind stasis. Ashlyn thought he was glad to get away from his wife's nagging. Wish I hadn't punched her in the face, though."

"If Miss Flowers had dealt with her," John Justice replied, "the First Lady might be dead and Mercy Ann would be going crazy about it. I'm just glad she showed restraint for a change."

Blake was surprised. “That nice old lady would do something like that?”

“She’s responsible for taking care of the ship when we’re away and doesn’t put up with nonsense.”

“By which,” Blake realized, “you mean the housekeeper is weaponized?”

“She has a basic array that is defensive for the most part. Nothing more was required on this mission since the Sufficiency Test handles responses to external attacks on the ship.”

John Justice went with Sheri and Blake to see Brandi, who Honey Bee had in induced sleep because she wouldn’t stay still. Encased in a clear substance, her hand had tubes running into it from a quietly humming machine.

Ashlyn, watching a display of pulsing lights and symbols on a handheld device, explained that Honey Bee, standing on top of the machine, was teaching her how to program microscopic machines performing surgery.

Looking at her unconscious friend, Sheri’s emotions gave way. “Every time I see those scars I’ll be reminded what I did to her.”

Ashlyn tried to assure her there would be no scars or problems using the fingers, but Sheri was too upset to listen. Then John Justice touched Sheri’s arm and she disappeared.

Sheri stammered a hello to Mercy Ann, sitting on the edge of the high bed in a white nightgown with her feet dangling over steps. She hitched the nightgown up, displaying her legs to the tops of the thighs.

“One of my legs was replaced,” she said. “Come see if you can tell the difference.”

Sheri stood on the steps, studying her legs. “May I touch?”

“Yes.”

With no shyness whatever, Sheri poked, probed, and ran fingers over them. She took the lamp from the bedside table and held it close, peering intently. Finally, she shook her head.

“One of these is artificial?” she asked doubtfully.

“The right one is a biological regeneration created from my tissues in a process called accelerated replication. It has artificial bones, but otherwise, it’s identical to the one it replaced except I had scars on the knee of the original.”

“That’s incredible.”

“Reattaching parts that don’t require replication is easy-peasy in comparison, so Brandi’s hand will be good as new in a few days. You won’t be able to tell she was ever injured.”

"How long did it take for your leg to be fully functional?"

"A full regeneration requires a month or so. Of course, I'm talking about humanoids. Every species is different."

Sheri's mouth dropped open. "I hadn't really thought about that."

"It was attached halfway above the knee."

Shaking her head, Sheri asked, "How did it happen?"

The last thing Mercy Ann wanted to discuss was going crazy and nearly killing herself and the commander again. "Everyone downstairs knows the story, if you're interested. Did my sharing this with you help your concerns?"

"Very much. Thank you."

Mercy Ann nodded and touched her.

Back in the infirmary, John Justice asked Sheri how Mercy Ann seemed to her.

She knew exactly what he meant. "Something is eating her up inside."

Reluctantly, John Justice turned to Blake. "Please go to her. She's upset about killing those soldiers."

"She's not ready to discuss it, yet."

"I realize you sense her thoughts and feelings, but she'll just keep getting worse unless she's forced to deal with it," John Justice answered quietly. "Doing it at the onset is much easier than waiting. I've had a lot of experience with this."

"Okay, but mightn't Missa get through to her easier than anyone else?"

It had not occurred to John Justice that Blake knew about that, but realized he should have. "It might complicate things too much. It's better for her that you do it."

Ashlyn was puzzled. "What's Missa got to do with all this? She and Mercy Ann hardly know each other."

Blake felt like an idiot mentioning it in front of her. "I thought since they were close in age Mercy Ann might feel more at ease, but John Justice is right. I should do it."

When Blake appeared in the open doorway, Mercy Ann ran and clung to him, crying uncontrollably. Then she yelled, beat her fists on him for coming to her room unbidden, and for intruding into her personal thoughts. Eventually, she fell into exhausted sleep in his arms. He put her in bed, pulled up the covers, and turned out the light.

He had not uttered a single word.

Returning to the infirmary, he and John Justice exchanged nods then awkwardly ignored each other.

Sheri guessed the reason and exchanged a knowing stare with Ashlyn. Honey Bee made a nasty private comment to the two women about where males did most of their thinking, causing them to laugh suddenly.

Although suspecting the joke was about them, John Justice and Blake asked no questions.

On the twenty-eighth day of the Sufficiency Test, the media concentrated coverage on three subjects: the government's ugly internal clashes over what to do about the Presidency and the conspiracy, the incredible videos of Mercy Ann in battle, and live feeds from the Middle East showing al-Bensi's tattered forces leaving Iraq.

Nearly all the al-Bensi soldiers were unarmed, dressed in whatever clothes they found after shedding uniforms, and on foot. Most had their faces covered and claimed to be refugees. When pressed, they walked away from cameras, refused to talk, and pretended not to understand languages spoken to them.

One man was a notable exception. Covered head to toe in soot, he wore a burned and tattered al-Bensi uniform jacket with no shirt underneath as well as two big handwoven bags tied skirt-like around his waist. Interviewed on numerous programs, he mugged for cameras and told how the alien girl blew his pants off because she heard he had handsome legs and wanted to see them. If reporters gave him something to eat or a little cash, he pulled the bags up and showed his legs off.

Around noon, Mercy Ann appeared in the ship's control room with two pastries and orange juice that she shared with John Justice, who had not slept since returning from Iraq.

They didn't speak to each other while they ate until she said, "Sending Blake to me couldn't have been easy for you. Go get some sleep. I'll keep watch."

Without a word, he vanished.

Mercy Ann whiled away time scanning for intruders in near space and wondering why John Justice thought her brother's consciousness had awoken more than fifty years after the incident. Why couldn't he understand that it was crazy to think two people could coexist inside one body, especially him and her brother, who never got along, and that was before the commander developed romantic feelings for her?

She recalled a campy old movie starring Ray Milland, a famous movie actor playing a rich, dying white racist, and Rosie Greer, a black football star portraying an athlete down on his luck and money. The white guy ended up having his head implanted as a second head on the body of the black athlete in a radical procedure that preserved their separate personas. It saved the rich racist's life, but he freaked out because he was part of a black man now.

It was a ridiculous movie but made its point. It was the same for her brother and the commander except neither would ever accept the other.

She checked the buffer zone perimeter cameras. Could anything be more boring than this kind of work? She almost called Missa to come relieve her then decided it wouldn't be fair to wake her up. But if Rob was with her, she probably wasn't sleeping, anyway. She stopped, irritated how that made her feel.

She decided to watch a movie since all the TV feeds kept showing news about her killing soldiers, but then Rob came in and said he would take over. He'd slept in the control room before everyone returned from the Middle East and was concerned he would wake up Missa if he stayed in the room with her.

Mercy Ann was glad for the chance to leave but had nothing to do. She wandered aimlessly through the house straightening and rearranging rooms for no reason until she found herself going down the hall toward Missa's room a second time. She made herself stop then spent several minutes trying to decide whether to wake her or not.

The general hurried into his tent to take a quick shower only to find Mercy Ann stretched out on his bed eating his potato chips and surfing the internet on his laptop.

Embarrassed, she jumped up and brushed crumbs off the bed with her hands. "Sorry, I needed to get out of the house for a while and came over here. Didn't expect you'd be back until evening."

"You're welcome anytime. Have a problem?"

"Just killing time. Hope you don't mind me using your computer."

"It's fine, but do you really need one?"

"No, but it's more relaxing than viewing internally. I'll straighten your bed and go."

"Don't hurry off. I'm glad to see you, but you seem a little down."

She nodded. "Aren't you afraid after watching me kill all those people?"

He bent down and hugged the air out of her. "I'm just glad you're okay."

She had tears in her eyes. "You shouldn't grab me. My defense systems could have given you a severe jolt."

He pulled a couple of tissues from a box on the dresser and handed them to her.

She dried her eyes and blew her nose. "Those soldiers didn't have a chance."

"The people they killed didn't have a chance, either. Stop beating yourself up."

"I'm a monster."

"No, you're not. Sit down and let's talk a bit. Want a cola to wash down my bag of chips?"

"Yes, please."

He stayed away from discussing the battle until she told him about the nuclear missiles and that Blake, Sheri, and Brandi saved them from disaster.

"And to think, I wondered why you wanted them with you."

"I'd like you and the sergeant major to join us, too. I'd planned to bring it up after the Sufficiency Test ended, but there shouldn't be any possibility you'll be ordered to attack us now."

"Why do you want two old farts like us? We're well past our sell-by dates and will just get in your way."

"I want you to replace me as commander of the fleet or possibly serve as second to my current vice commander. She should have gotten the job when they chose me for it. The two of you can work it out if it comes to that, but I imagine she'll defer to you. We need real military leadership, especially when it comes to developing battle strategies and deploying our defenses. Those will be big deficiencies now that the Guardians are gone. Mostly, we just did what they said."

"That's not your only reason, is it?"

She shook her head. "Making all the decisions about who and how we fight as well as being the main option in every battle is too much for me."

"The sergeant major and I don't understand your technology, not to mention leaving Earth and adapting what we know to fighting in space."

"Science and technical matters can be downloaded into your internal computers when they're installed. That doesn't mean you'll understand automatically, but accessing information instantly is the next best thing and speeds up the learning process. I call it our Second Brain system. There's a real name, but it's about a hundred unpronounceable words long."

"What about our ages, the physical demands?"

"Once your body is ready for deep space travel, you'll feel as if you bathed in the Fountain of Youth. You'll live a lot longer, assuming you don't become fatalities in battle or have an accident. Space is a dangerous place."

"Out of curiosity, how many in your fleet are from Earth?"

She considered telling him the truth about her origin but now wasn't the time to deal with all the questions it would raise. "Only one, a brilliant man named Urlak, who is the oldest member of the crew. He's from the Neanderthal species, however."

The general did a double take. "You're joking."

"Urlak's not at all the way your science says. He's very charming, quite the ladies' man, in fact. Everyone says he's on a personal mission to resurrect the species since he leaves children nearly everywhere he visits."

The general laughed then turned serious. "From the first, you and John Justice shared information with me that could have triggered a failure with the Sufficiency Test or jeopardized your safety. Why?"

"Several reasons. I wanted you with us from the moment you visited me. Then again, we knew Washington wouldn't listen to your recommendations since everyone in your chain of command was committed to the conspiracy's agenda. And, of course, John Justice monitored everything you and the sergeant major did. I regret spying on you, but it was necessary."

"What would you have done if we'd tried to trap or kill one of you?"

"I don't want to sound arrogant, but no one on Earth is capable of that unless we're careless, such as John Justice was in the Death Valley Prison. That was a really stupid mistake he made."

"Is your science really that far ahead of us?"

She shrugged and stood. "I need to go somewhere else before it gets too late. Please discuss joining us with the sergeant major. Thank you for an enjoyable visit."

Mercy Ann appeared on a quiet street on small, horseshoe-shaped Linda Island in the Newport Beach Harbor, California. Close to the mainland, the only vehicle access a short bridge with a gate and security, every house in the nosebleed expensive Linda Isle neighborhood had a private dock, and nearly every dock had a big expensive boat alongside.

Legendary movie star, John Wayne, lived on the island until his death in 1979. Because John Justice loved his movies so much, Mercy Ann had surprised him during one of their stays on Earth by suggesting they go visit his house while everyone was away, something they did frequently to famous people.

The visit was a bust far as John Justice was concerned. He'd expected something akin to a western ranch house stuffed with cowboy paraphernalia, not a modern home with breathtaking harbor views, yachts, expensive furnishings, and displays of mementoes from all over the world. He did like Mr. Wayne's office, the biggest room in the house, because it had manly, wood-paneled walls, but that was all. After making a couple of disparaging remarks about what he characterized as two frou-frou chandeliers hanging over a big but unremarkable dining room table, he left Mercy Ann standing alone in the house. Far as she knew, he'd never been back to the area.

But she'd loved Newport Beach Harbor and found it intriguing that so many people bought fine houses as convenient places to keep large boats and for entertaining away from primary residences. That made finding empty houses easy when she wanted to be alone and relax in beautiful surroundings. Of course, most houses had sophisticated alarm systems, but they were no challenge for her.

Usually, people kept the homes well stocked with food and drinks, too. Some even had indoor pools, incredible entertainment systems, and great selections of music, books, and movies—not surprising since many of the inhabitants were in the entertainment industry or rubbed up against people who were.

Mercy Ann loved watching boats glide by the island on glorious California sunshine days while rummaging through fabulous people's fabulous stuff. It gave her tremendous guilty pleasure, but she never took anything from the Newport Beach Harbor homes, unlike most other places she visited. They provided her sanctuary too special to violate.

As she scanned residences to determine which were empty, the sun and salt air revitalized her energy and assuaged the dark cloud of guilt drowning her. Only a few houses had anyone in them, which meant she could walk around outside looking at boats in the harbor without much chance of anyone recognizing her, especially if she borrowed the right hats. She might even have time to go see a couple of places on nearby Balboa Island if she wanted. She picked a recently renovated home and transported inside to see what they'd done with the place since she was last there.

As afternoon wore to evening, the sergeant major stood at the base of the Great Pyramid staring up at it. The general, Blake, and Tom, out for a walk, asked what he was doing.

"Damn fool dog," he growled, pointing to the top of the huge structure. "This is his third trip to the top. If he slips, he's going to break his neck."

Watching the dog leaping, Tom whistled. "Don't think you need to worry. He looks as sure-footed as a mountain goat."

"Ain't natural," the sergeant major declared.

"We'll have to ask Honey Bee what she did to him," Blake said. "Never seen a dog climb that fast."

The general had something else on his mind. "Has anyone seen Mercy Ann? She stopped by earlier, and I'm a little concerned about her."

Blake answered, "John Justice said she probably won't be back until after dark and not to worry. She does this occasionally when she wants some alone time."

They returned to watching Bongo coming down the pyramid at breakneck speed. Jumping the equivalent of two stories to the ground, he ran past them towards the mess tent. The sergeant major followed his dog, waiting impatiently for him at the entrance.

Honey Bee communicated with Miss Flowers, expressing how pleased she was with Brandi's progress. The patient was up and in such good spirits that she had taken her to visit Rob and Missa in the control room.

Miss Flowers agreed that Brandi was a much stronger specimen than most humans she had encountered, so maybe there was hope one or two of these backward humans might survive long term in the fleet.

Honey Bee noted that Mercy Ann, who both of them had initially thought wouldn't last a year when she joined, had a natural knack of overcoming challenges, which was unusual for most human species.

John Justice cut in. "The humans on my planet were an old species before your ancestors evolved intelligence, half-pint."

Honey Bee made a noise that was her equivalent to laughing. "Just wanted to make sure you were spying on us as usual, John Justice."

"I'm not spying! Communications is my job."

"You seem to monitor females more than males, John Justice," Miss Flowers commented drily. "Why is that?"

He switched off loudly.

She chortled.

"My sensors indicate he's still listening on another channel," Honey Bee said then laughed when they heard another loud click. "That was just a guess."

That night, everyone was in the dining room when Mercy Ann appeared with two grocery sacks filled with fast food. She told everyone to take what he or she wanted.

Brandi, seated next to Sheri, had her arm propped up on the table.

Mercy Ann went to her. "Can you manage with one hand or do you want me to feed you?"

Brandi swallowed a retort when she looked up and realized Mercy Ann had been joking. "You almost got me."

Mercy Ann bent down close to Missa. "I brought you a Greek salad if you would rather not pig out on junk like the rest of us."

She accepted with gratitude.

While they ate, Mercy Ann causally mentioned, "We've asked some of you to join the fleet. I don't think it will come as a surprise to anyone that I'm extending the offer to everyone onboard. We'll discuss it with each of you over the next few days. In the meantime, just think about it and hold your questions. I'm too tired to think straight."

John Justice sat next to Mercy Ann, "Did you go somewhere special today?"

She nodded.

"An amusement park?"

"No, but I thought about it."

Rob overheard. "Tom told me how you took him on a roller coaster, Mercy Ann."

John Justice hadn't heard about it. "When was this?"

Tom told the story, making it funnier that it was at the time.

After that, talk flowed freely for more than an hour.

Brandi kept stealing glances at Mercy Ann, trying to understand how a pretty teenager could have so much weaponry with absolutely no evidence that she was extraordinary.

Mercy Ann noticed her looking and understood why. After all, she'd received those kinds of questioning stares for decades. She used to resent them and feel angry and hurt. Now, she accepted her differences and realized it was only natural to be curious. It still hurt that some people considered her a freak, though.

25

Sentries, Miss Noto, and Bongo

JOHN JUSTICE, WEARING PAJAMAS AND BEDROOM SLIPPERS, appeared in the kitchen and was surprised to find Mercy Ann fiddling with the toaster. More surprising, she had on shorts, a t-shirt, and sneakers, unusual for her so early in the morning.

Irritated because he valued his early mornings alone, he asked, "Why are you up already?"

"I woke up and couldn't go back to sleep. Thought I'd eat then walk around the pyramids and watch the sun come up. Want to go with me?"

"I have too much work to do."

"You can spare a few minutes. It'd be nice to spend some time together."

"Ask Missa. I'm sure she'll do anything you want."

Mercy Ann thought things between them would be better after the Middle East trip, but he'd tried to talk about her brother again last night and gotten upset when she refused, which was why she didn't sleep well.

"Or you could ask Blake," John Justice suggest, rather strident. "He and Tom are patrolling around the pyramids for the general. I'm sure he'll drop everything to follow you around."

The last thing Mercy Ann wanted was to get into an argument that John Justice would doubtless steer back to the subject of her brother. Then the toaster popped up.

Taking out a waffle, she asked, “Want some? I found a case we missed in the big freezer.”

“Those kind taste like cardboard.”

“Not if you pile on strawberry jam and vanilla ice cream. I picked up some yesterday.”

For the most part of an hour, they pigged out, but Mercy Ann couldn’t get John Justice into a conversation. They went their separate ways just before dawn.

Miss Flowers found the half-empty two-gallon container of ice cream melting on the counter. Sticking out of it, a steel scoop had the name of a national chain embossed on the handle. A messy quart jar of jam stood open next to a stack of empty toaster waffle packages. Waffles were cold in the toaster.

For Mercy Ann, this was a minor mess. She created disasters everywhere she went in the house, particularly the kitchen. In fact, the stove was off-limits to her except for heating water, a restriction she agreed to after causing a fire that burned down the first Earth house she brought onboard.

The ship had a modern computerized food preparation area capable of turning out good meals in minutes, but Mercy Ann, John Justice, and Miss Flowers had learned to love having an Earth house and preparing meals, even though it required more work and took up half the ship’s cargo space.

They welcomed the sense of family the house created. Even the bickering and disagreements between Miss Flowers and Mercy Ann were easier to tolerate inside the house than in the austere rooms of warships, something they could not explain but felt deeply.

Miss Flowers pushed toasted the waffles just long enough to reheat then helped herself to jam and ice cream. In spite of her animosity for Mercy Ann, she had to admit the girl was never dull and provided occasional happy surprises.

Honey Bee ordered Brandi to rest and not move her arm any more than necessary. She did her best to lie on a couch watching TV without fidgeting, squirming, and getting up every few minutes, but failed miserably. Honey Bee became exasperated and threatened to put her in stasis. They had a hot argument.

Ashlyn played peacemaker, suggesting they brace the arm against Brandi’s body and administer painkillers but otherwise allow her to move around some. Honey Bee assumed that meant Brandi would try to rest and agreed. A short time later, she discovered Brandi had left the ship to find Sheri, who was helping the general.

Honey Bee contacted Brandi and told her she could live without fingers if she damaged the repairs. Brandi told her not to get her underwear in a knot and broke off the communication. Honey Bee didn't have underwear and didn't understand the comment. Ashlyn tried to explain without giving offense.

Honey Bee surprised her, thinking it was funny. "She's telling me to go to hell and leave her alone. We're more alike than I realized."

Ashlyn had already reached that conclusion and wondered how difficult it would be living and working with this contrary group of beings, unaware they had the same concerns about her.

Brandi caught up with Sheri around four in the afternoon. They had a good laugh because Brandi had her arm braced and was very much under the influence of drugs, same as Sheri had been. The situation went downhill from there, however.

Brandi refused to stay behind while Sheri went on patrol. Sheri thought her friend would cope with no problem. After all, Brandi was as close to indestructible as anyone could be. Once, four thugs had beaten her for two days then left her staked out in the desert to die. Several days later, a room attendant found them dead in their Vegas hotel rooms, each with a metal stake attached to a broken chain driven through his heart.

So it surprised Sheri having to help Brandi into and out of the back of an Army truck, which was almost more than she could handle. Then she explained three times that their patrol duties consisted of nothing more than walking a quarter mile back and forth next to a busy road between two guard posts before Brandi understood.

But Sheri saw a bright side to the situation. The aliens must have hellacious drugs.

Miss Noto had been Handley's business and personal confidant, bodyguard, and closest thing to a wife a self-centered, distrusting man such as him could have. They never lived together officially, but were very close, even during his involvements with other women, none of which lasted long.

She respected that Handley had much more important matters on his mind than the demands of personal relationships. She had grown up in a strict Japanese household ruled by a philandering father. But now, the aliens took the one thing that gave her life meaning away, and she decided to sacrifice her life in exchange for revenge.

As the last light of day waned, Miss Noto sat on the outdoor patio of a fast food place looking across a busy street bordering the outer perimeter of the buffer zone at two female sentries ambling back and forth the three blocks between two gated guard stations. The big soldier had an injured arm and other incapacities, judging by the laborious way she moved.

Even so, she appeared more a danger than the small sentry did. She was one of those people who could not talk without using hands, and they were in constant motion. Same for her feet, dancing around her big companion, walking backwards in front of her, and skipping along like a little girl. Contemptuous of useless people, she would take pleasure killing her if it came to that.

A man walked out of the restaurant with a tray and looked around the patio. He was exactly what she expected, a crass, money-grubbing lowlife. He sat down across from her, placed an elbow on the small plastic table, and leaned forward, chin resting on a fist that showed a lot of use.

"Wasn't expecting a woman, especially a hottie like you," he said, leering and flirting as though expecting to have his way with her.

She needed help to reach the aliens so only gave him a warning stare when she asked, "What's your name?"

Experienced enough to recognize danger when it stared him in the face, he took his elbow off the table and sat up straighter in the chair. "Larry Stanton. Call me Larry."

Although surprised he read the situation so well, she showed nothing. "I understand you worked at the alien site until recently, Mr. Stanton. I need you to help me evade patrols."

"Yeah, but like I told the guy who called, security has tightened bigtime since they put me on admin leave. Even if we get past the perimeter guards, we can't go anywhere except main roads without setting off electronic surveillance. They'll catch us in minutes. He said you'd pay if I just showed up and explained the situation. You'd better not try to welch on the deal."

She wondered if he really expected pay for doing nothing. "What if I can make it so the surveillance devices don't detect us? I work for the company that makes them." She took out a small round object slightly larger than a shirt button and slid it across the table. "Just carry that in your pocket."

He considered her with more interest. "It's still too risky for the kind of money you're offering."

She would have said the same thing. "I'll double it."

He picked up the disk. "Lady, for twenty thousand dollars, I'm all yours."

It was easy for Sheri to divert attention from fact she constantly checked out people on the other side of the road, especially in and around fast food restaurants, where it was natural to sit and stare at the surroundings while eating. When she wanted to observe someone closely, she used an electronic telescope small enough to hide in her palm. It zoomed, changed to night vision, and took pictures automatically sent to their cellphones.

She had taken a quick look at the prim Japanese woman sitting alone at a burger joint facing the road just after she sat down. Nothing was unusual except for a short executive hairdo that looked too expensive for this seedy area. Probably drove by and stopped in for a quick bite, she thought, moving on.

Sheri had worked in fast food and been promoted to shift manager, where she learned the basics of the business. Failure to meet service time requirements could cost a shift manager the job. The tables and chairs were hard, small, and uncomfortable to encourage customers to eat and go. Interior lighting was harsh and too bright at night for the same reason.

So when the Japanese woman continued nibbling cold fries and her small burger fifteen minutes later, Sheri wanted to stop and examine her more closely, but a quick look with the scope showed her staring straight at them. Streetlights were coming on, so she decided waiting until the next go-round made the most sense.

A man sat with the woman, his back to the street. Sheri dropped to the ground and Brandi kept going. It wasn't quite dark, but it was improbable anyone across the street would notice with traffic whizzing by.

Sheri could tell the man and woman were strangers, but nothing made her think they were up to anything. Then they left, going separate ways. Sheri had taken their pictures as a matter of routine.

Two monotonous hours later, Brandi and Sheri were turning back at a guard station when a car flew by, jumped the curb, and sped across the grassy expanse to the fence running behind houses. Two people dressed in black jumped out and went over it into the buffer zone.

Brandi emptied her pistol through the fence hoping to get lucky while Sheri examined new pictures she'd just taken with the night scope. It was the Japanese woman and the guy. She went after them.

Brandi sent the pictures to the command post and John Justice while watching Sheri discard her Army rifle, pistol belt, and uniform shirt at a full run. Then she went over the fence as quick and graceful as a cat, the curved wooden grip of the sawed-off shotgun on her back catching light before she disappeared into darkness.

Angry that she was not able to go with her, Brandi listened to soldiers discussing the intruders on her vest radio then called the general on their private line and told him Sheri was in pursuit. He expressed concern troops might mistake her for the enemy because detection devices had begun going off.

John Justice broke in. “Sheri is tripping the devices, not the intruders, who have a way to pass through without detection.”

The general sputtered, “That’s impossible.”

“She was Jared Handley’s assistant,” John Justice explained. “It’s not impossible at all. It is interfering with my monitoring devices, too. I expect to have everything working again shortly, but for now, we’re blind to everyone in the restricted area.”

Sheri, breathing heavily, interrupted. “General, can you turn off the surveillance devices in this area? They’re serving no purpose except giving away my location to the intruders.”

The general did as she asked. Then he told them he had ordered helicopters into the area to provide more light on the east side of the pyramids and to illuminate the way for troops sweeping up from the south. The plan was to drive the intruders around the north side of the Great Pyramid, where he had the sergeant major leading a unit to intercept.

Suddenly, all communications went out.

Mercy Ann materialized in the ship’s control room where John Justice, Rob, and Missa worked frantically. “Why didn’t you tell me all our surveillance and communications systems stopped working, John Justice?”

He didn’t look up. “I’ll have them up and running in a few minutes.”

“How’s it possible that something interferes with us? Is it more alien technology Handley acquired?”

“I don’t have time to waste discussing it with you!” he shouted.

Mercy Ann realized it was no good trying to talk with him now. “I’ll be outside with Honey Bee helping search for Handley’s assistant.”

“Your scanners aren’t working and communications are out, so you won’t be...”

John Justice had not realized she was gone.

Sheri checked a dark alleyway behind houses with the night scope and spotted two solders on the ground. Hurrying to them, she confirmed they were dead. Too bad, she thought, but it confirmed she was going the right direction.

She ran between two houses to the next street, brightly lit by streetlights. She hesitated. This was the perfect place for an ambush.

Suddenly, three helicopters flew over, searchlights sweeping back and forth along the east sides of the two big pyramids, concentrating on areas not lit by spotlights. Then she saw the helicopters to the south, casting a wall of light for soldiers moving through neighborhoods.

Surely, Sheri thought, the intruders hotfooted it out of here with the helicopters and soldiers hurrying this way. Zigzagging into the road holding the shotgun ready to fire, she held her breath. Sometimes you had to play percentages and hope your opponents weren't too stupid to do the same thing.

Heavy gunfire from north of the Great Pyramid stopped her. She dropped to one knee and grabbed the phone in hopes the jamming had stopped. If anything, it was worse.

More gunfire came from another area to the east, behind her. That couldn't possibly be her quarry. Furiously thinking, she decided the best course was to continue to the north side of the Great Pyramid, but at this rate, she would never close the gap between them.

Jumping up and sprinting down the middle of the street, Sheri whispered, "This is Brandi's kind of macho shit, not mine."

Heavy gunfire and small explosions erupted to the north, so far away that it must be at the outer boundary of the new buffer zone. Two of the three helicopters helping light the east sides of the pyramids sped off in that direction, dropping down to fly just above the rooftops.

A series of explosions and gunfire erupted a few blocks northeast of her. That was where the military maintained a compound housing all the generators supplying extra power for the huge spotlights in the disaster area. She experienced a sinking feeling in the pit of her stomach as she realized what was about to happen.

Running full speed, she turned west onto a wide boulevard just as the spotlights went dark, leaving a single helicopter spotlight sweeping the east side of the Great Pyramid. Then automatic weapons fire and explosions came from numerous locations in surrounding neighborhoods.

Two helicopters sped away from the soldiers moving up from the south to join the one next to the Great Pyramid. Streaks of fire roared into the sky from outside the buffer zone to the east. Sheri recognized shoulder-fired missiles. They blew the three helicopters near the pyramids out of the sky.

Dodging flaming debris crashing into the street, Sheri surmised this had to be more al-Bensi soldiers smuggled into the country with the ones who attacked the White House. They had the same devices to avoid detection as the couple she was after.

Running full speed toward the dark pyramid, she did not like the odds against her making it through the night. She thought of the last time she embraced Brandi, smiled, and cleared her mind of everything except staying alive and completing the mission at hand.

Sheri reasoned that her quarry was more likely to go up the north face instead of the east because of the approaching soldiers and helicopters to the south. At the same time, the sergeant major's troops were northwest of the Great Pyramid and she'd heard no firing from there. If she was right, they climbed up near the northeast corner and intended to move around it until they were above the alien house. What they would do then, she had no idea.

Sheri spotted them with the night scope about two hundred feet up using a small, direct beam flashlight to pick their way west across the face of the pyramid. Considering the amount of technology Handley's assistant had available, this act struck her as hare-brained and born out of desperation. She let out a deep breath. None of that mattered. Nothing to do now but go after them.

An experienced climber, Sheri progressed quickly. She had a small light, but used her hands to feel the way, pausing occasionally to use the night scope to insure she stayed on course.

When the lights illuminating the pyramids went out, Mercy Ann and Honey Bee transported two hundred feet up onto the east side of the Great Pyramid and tried to scan for the intruders again, but to no avail. Honey Bee expressed surprise John Justice had not gotten the system working yet.

Then rockets blew up the helicopters, peppering their defensive shields with shrapnel. Eyes unaffected by the fireballs, Honey Bee used the light to perform visual searches of this side of the pyramid and confirmed to Mercy Ann that no one else was on it.

At the same time, the remaining helicopters pinpointed where the rockets originated and destroyed two panel trucks speeding out of a warehouse parking lot. Then the general ordered all aircraft out of the area until they could be certain there were no more missiles.

Mercy Ann picked up Honey Bee and transported to the north face, materializing in an area with badly deteriorated stone blocks. She could not get her footing and began sliding down the steep slope. Transporting again, she found a better spot about three-quarters up near where the north and west sides intersected. Setting Honey Bee down, they found it difficult to see with bright city lights playing tricks with shadows and hard to hear because of wind.

Honey Bee suggested disconnecting their infrared vision from scanning systems in case the infrared worked on its own. It did.

They saw Sheri coming up fast below the intruders. Then Honey Bee pointed out something unexpected—Bongo, crouched on an outcropping above Miss Noto and the man.

"He was not very useful so I gave him upgrades," Honey Bee communicated. "He can see in the dark now, amongst other things. His expression indicates concern about their intentions."

It was such a strange statement that Mercy Ann started to ask about it, but directly below Miss Noto, Sheri had positioned her feet on a jutting stone and taken the shotgun off her back. Then she must have made noise because the man twisted around and fired several pistol shots in her direction.

Bongo leaped, knocking Miss Noto and the man off the ledge. They tumbled into Sheri, firing the shotgun as she fell backwards with them.

Mercy Ann shouted for Honey Bee to save Bongo and leapt. Rockets ablaze, Honey Bee roared by as Mercy Ann transported into the tangle of bodies, grabbed onto someone with each hand, and hoped they were all touching. She transported again.

They crashed hard onto the gray metal floor of the ship. Without time to shield them, only Mercy Ann did not suffer from the impact.

Sheri's shotgun blast had hit the guy in the stomach. Mercy Ann recognized that he was the man who shot her on the porch and felt a little guilty because she was not sorry he was dead. She extricated his body from the others, all of whom were unconscious.

Miss Noto had a concussion and buckshot wounds. Sheri had a bullet in the thigh. Their injuries were minor considering everything.

Mercy Ann had a bigger concern—small disks found in Miss Noto and the man's pockets. They came from aliens that attacked the territory more than a decade ago. The fleet had run them off, but it had been difficult. Discovering Earthlings had dealings with them was bad news. She called John Justice using the ship's internal comm system.

"Omarkian jamming devices are the reason our scanning and comm systems aren't working. I'll send one to you in a few minutes so you can determine the frequencies and help the general locate the remaining terrorists. Handley's assistant had an Omarkian explosive device in her backpack. Guess she thought it might blow us up if she could get close enough."

"You have Miss Noto? Why didn't you tell me, Mercy Ann? We're going crazy in the control room. Exactly where are you, anyway?"

As much as she didn't want to lose her cool, that question was too much to let slide. "You've got to be shitting me, John Justice. Obviously, I'm in the ship since external communications aren't possible. I transported Noto, Sheri, and the dead male intruder into a confinement room two doors down the hall from you. I didn't turn off security so the operations room must have received notification that I returned with three people. How can you not know that?"

"I'm busy trying to repair scanners and external communications."

"So no one is monitoring ship security? For that matter, why didn't you know about Noto's attack beforehand? She's an obvious threat. Everything indicates she threw it together after Handley died. I doubt she did anything to keep it secret. Do your job!"

"That's not fair, Mercy Ann."

"Not fucking fair?" she demanded, raising her voice. "You're running the control room, aren't you? Can you tell where Honey Bee is?"

"She isn't with you?"

"I just told you that I returned with three people. If you can't understand that, look at the ship security log!"

"And I told you, I don't have time—"

Mercy Ann appeared in the control room, thrust the Omarkian jamming devices into John Justice's hand, and transported back to take care of the wounded until Honey Bee returned.

Miss Noto woke up wondering why she was alive. Stretched out on a futon in a dim room, she did nothing to indicate consciousness until certain she was alone.

Her clothes were men's pajamas, socks, boxer shorts, and no bra. Tiny holes dotted a flat metallic ceiling eight feet above her. The smooth metal walls and floor had no discernable openings. A black, box-shaped toilet occupied one corner with a roll of toilet paper mounted on one side, paper towels on the other.

She sat up and executed a graceful, quarter-spin up onto her knees without using her hands.

She remembered a shotgun blast pelting her and hitting her head when she fell, but the rest was blank. Feeling for wounds, she discovered tender skin all but healed, yet felt certain no more than a few hours had passed.

Miss Noto moved around the room. The lid over the toilet disappeared into the wall when she approached. The same gray floor was inside, no water or chemicals. She sat, peed, and then looked. Nothing was different. She tossed in a wad of toilet paper. It disintegrated, leaving no residue.

She'd try throwing something more substantial into the toilet when they fed her. Then maybe she could convert the toilet mechanism into a weapon of some kind. She examined the walls for a hidden opening but found no indications of one.

Miss Noto exercised, doing a combination of tai chi and Taikiken hand movements for an hour. Then she sat on the futon to wait.

A rectangular screen appeared on a wall showing a video of Handley, al-Bensi, and the Chairman in a room Miss Noto recognized from visits to Death Valley. She watched how they died. Even though it upset her, she admired the skills of the two women and man who averted nuclear disaster by killing al-Bensi. She grieved for Jared Handley, but it didn't show.

Sensing someone behind her, she scooted around slowly.

Mercy Ann, dressed in a gray t-shirt, black cargo shorts, and big white socks, seemed unconcerned being alone with her. Miss Noto was disappointed she looked so unremarkable and frail close up. She decided to attack her.

"I'm sorry Handley died," Mercy Ann said. "That was not what I wanted."

Miss Noto could kill from a sitting position faster than most people could react, but when she thrust out a hand to crush Mercy Ann's windpipe, an unseen force slammed her backwards into the wall across the room.

Mercy Ann crouched over her. "Are you conscious?"

Numb and hurting all over, Miss Noto could barely speak. "Go to hell."

Mercy Ann dropped a translating device into her ear. "Someone will come to help you in a few minutes. If you're polite, she'll show you how to work the TV, use the room furniture, the kitchen, and the shower. If you try anything, she won't kill you, but you'll suffer a great deal for years to come. By the way, there are no doors or windows. We don't need them."

She vanished.

Late that night, Mercy Ann answered soft knocking on her door.

John Justice asked, "Can we discuss wrapping up our business here?"

Reluctantly, she stepped back for him to come in. "Just don't bring up the subject of my brother."

He sat across the table, not looking at her directly. "The general finished rounding up the terrorists. The media made a hero of him again."

A TV was on, reporting that very thing, so she didn't answer.

"What do you want to say to Earth when we release the First Family after the Sufficiency Test?"

"Nothing."

"You don't want to warn Earth about its future?"

"No."

"I thought that was one of the reasons we came."

"I've changed my mind."

He didn't think that would be her final decision. "How long do you plan to hold Miss Noto?"

"Until we know the extent of Earth's involvement with the Omarkians. We'll take her with us."

"Might she be a recruit?"

"Maybe. In the meantime, she's Honey Bee's prisoner."

John Justice was surprised. "You think Miss Noto is that tough?"

"Guess we're going to find out."

"Urlak will be in Earth orbit in a few hours. I told him to confiscate the Gargle wreckage from the Navy. I provided a list of Handley's operations so he can scan them for alien technology and take it, too."

"Good."

"In Egypt, I've begun broadcasting that the object in the ground will be destroyed and the pyramids returned. If anyone interferes, it will mean instant death. That's just to scare them since I assume you don't want us to hurt anyone else."

"I don't care. Just get it done."

He looked at her finally. "I've already instructed Urlak not to kill anyone unnecessarily, Mercy Ann. You'll be sorry if he does. You know you will."

"Fine. Have it your way."

"Are you feeling okay?"

Mercy Ann had taken a large dose of Guardian drugs just before he showed up and suspected his main reason for coming was to discuss her brother again.

She just wanted to get it over with and go to bed. "Yes."

"Do you want me to talk to Rob, Missa, and Ashlyn about Missa's parents?"

"I'll talk to them tomorrow."

"Rudy and his family will come onboard in the morning."

"A kid on board. What was I thinking?"

He had rehearsed with Rob, yet stumbled over the words. "I'm remembering things about your brother that only you and he could possibly know. I promise that I'll never mention him again if you'll listen to me for five minutes. Just five minutes, Mercy Ann. Please?"

To get him to leave, she agreed, but not until after the Sufficiency Test.

26

No Pain in My World, Baby!

MERCY ANN WANDERED INTO THE DINING ROOM, having just gotten up judging by her rumpled, ankle-length nightgown, tangled bed hair, and bleary-eyed expression. So out of it she did not notice Blake and Brandi at the far end of the long table, she sat down with a soft moan and rested her face in her hands.

"I need coffee," she called out weakly to the kitchen.

"It's on table," Miss Flowers shouted back.

Mercy Ann looked up and saw Blake pouring a cup for her. "Oh, I should have worn a robe."

"Cream and sugar?" he asked with an amused smile that normally would have elicited a sharp comment from her.

Putting her face back in her hands, all she could manage was, "God, no."

Brandi was not one for beating around the bush. "Are you hung over?"

"I had a glass of wine because I couldn't sleep."

Blake set the cup down in front of her. "How big was the glass?"

"If you must know, I used one of those long plastic straws because I didn't have a glass," she replied then made herself sit up straighter.

Miss Flowers appeared in the doorway. "She doesn't have straws, either. Drinks from the bottle. Probably find it empty under the bed. That's where she usually puts them."

If looks could kill, the old woman would have been dead.

"Let me know when you want your spicy sausage and pepper sauce grits," Miss Flowers said, then returned to the kitchen chortling.

Mercy Ann gulped down the coffee and motioned Blake for a refill. "Could you put some bread in the toaster? Burned black with a little butter."

After three cups of coffee and four slices of toast, Mercy Ann looked down the table at Brandi. "I'd planned to talk to you and Sheri about Missa later, but this feels like the right time."

"Is it about her parents' deaths?"

"Yes."

"Considering John Justice's capabilities, Sheri and I thought you might know our part in it. Do you want us to leave?"

"Would you blame us?"

"No, but we'd be sorry to go."

"I'll get everyone involved together before we leave Earth to see if we can work something out. In the meantime, why don't you go discuss it with Sheri?"

After she left, Blake asked, "What will you say to them?"

"Nothing, if everything works out."

"What do you mean?"

With a loud moan, she put her head on the table. "I feel like shit."

"You shouldn't drink so much."

"Leave me alone, please."

He was enjoying the situation entirely too much. "What if there was an emergency? Could you handle it the way you are right now?"

She raised her head and stared. "I want you to go somewhere with me. Change into jeans and sturdy, hard-soled shoes. Meet me back here in twenty minutes."

Mercy Ann reappeared wearing a shoulder-length brown wig with eyebrows darkened to match. Worn, faded jeans, a flannel long sleeve shirt, and hiking boots completed the transformation.

Blake couldn't help himself. "That's a good look for you."

"Thank you. May I hold your hand?"

Blake gasped as suddenly they stood on the narrow, topmost point of a rock spire towering out of a jagged stone ridge already hundreds of feet above the floor of a desert canyon, its colorful layered walls stretched even higher around them.

Fighting not to sway and lose his balance, Blake gripped her hand harder and tried to keep his gaze fixed on a rock spur jutting from the high canyon wall straight ahead.

"If you could have one wish right now, what would it be?" Mercy Ann asked.

"To be an eagle," he replied, not daring look down at her.

She snickered. "Five years ago, a young woman climbed this formation and stood on this very spot. Can you imagine how remarkable that was?"

"Is she still alive?

"Why yes, she is. A tour helicopter spotted her climbing then more came to gawk until she went down. Pictures ended up all over the internet, ruining what was supposed to be her perfect moment of solitude. Why couldn't they have left her alone?"

He had closed his eyes. "You can't expect people to ignore something like that."

"They filmed her scratching initials where we're standing. She received all sorts of criticism and authorities issued a fine for defacing the park, not that anyone could find her. How messed up was that?"

"She should have come forward and denied it. The only way they could prove it would be to climb up here."

"She didn't hear about it until a long time after. If you move over a little, you can see her initials. Go ahead, check them out."

He didn't open his eyes. "I'll take your word for it."

"After I brought you all this way, you really should look."

"No way."

She was silent for a few seconds. "In that case, we'll have to test Newton's law of gravity. Since I don't have an apple..."

She let go of his hand and gave him a nudge. Horrified, he opened his eyes and discovered they were in a mostly empty tourist area overlooking the stone spire where they'd been.

"You scared the hell out of me," he said, more relieved than angry, which was considerable.

She sat down at the end of a long bench and motioned him to join her.

He sat at the other end, far away as possible.

"I thought it would be funny to tell you a story about some wonder woman climbing up, putting her initials on top, and then show you they were mine. Of course, I can't climb ten feet without falling on my butt. I'm pretty pathetic at those kinds of things."

In spite of everything, he felt bad for her. "Transporting onto something that small is pretty impressive, too."

"My computers calculate jumps to anything within sight, allowing me to move point-to-point very quickly. It's a Guardian battle tactic."

He could tell she wanted to talk about something else and didn't comment.

Sudden tears ran down her cheeks. "I never believed Earth would pass the Sufficiency Test, especially after it was up to John Justice to make decisions. I'm glad things worked out, yet I feel sad. How messed up is that?"

"You've been under incredible stress."

"But I should be happy now."

"Maybe it's because of John Justice changing. Or maybe it's because of your indecision about Missa and me."

She was silent for a time then stood up. "Next time you have a crying girl on a bench, dumbass, you might want to put an arm around her or something."

He came and hugged her to him. "Something else has you worried, doesn't it? What's wrong?"

She moved away. "They have drinks in the building across the parking lot. Let's go get something then hike along the rim for a little while."

As they crossed the lot, John Justice called wanting to know where she was because sensors couldn't locate her.

"Everything's fine. Be back soon."

"Any ideas where we should put Rudy, Elena, and Zach? All the bedrooms in the house are taken."

"Give them mine. Zach can sleep on the sitting room couch. Most of my clothes are still in the crew quarters so it won't take but a few minutes to move me out. I'll sleep there or with Ashlyn and Honey Bee. Anything else?"

"I can't locate Blake. Is he with you?"

"You know he is, John Justice."

He clicked off.

She responded to Blake's questioning stare. "Nothing important."

Blake had never been to the Grand Canyon. Mercy Ann had seen it countless times. Yet, both thought it would never again be as beautiful. Neither shared that thought with the other. They spoke very little and lost track of time until John Justice called again.

He was crying.

"What happened?" she demanded.

His sentences came out in gasps. "We received a Guardian warning. Earth failed the Sufficiency Test. We must leave before midnight. Or perish with humankind."

Mercy Ann fell to her knees. When Blake tried to help, she pushed him away then stood up on her own, a scowl of fierce determination and anger on her face.

Mercy Ann appeared and interrupted John Justice in mid-sentence giving directions to Honey Bee, Rob, and Missa. "Could a system malfunction be responsible for an erroneous message?"

"We're checking that possibility now," he replied, irritated by what he saw as a needless question. "I'll let you know if we find anything."

He'd started turning away and she stopped him. "Listen to me, John Justice. I smell a rat. I'm going to confront the Guardians. They'll tell me what's going on or suffer the consequences."

He was incredulous. "They won't stand for you threatening them."

"I'm much stronger than I used to be. They fear me."

Usually he could tell if her bravado was an act, but not this time. "The ports in your right arm are jury-rigged so you can't use them at full power. And if you're correct about the Guardians fearing you, won't they simply hide? If they do, there's nothing we can do about it."

She concentrated, thinking. "What if we set up another containment room and use energy disrupters around the exterior after I take the box with them inside? If they're hostile and more than I can handle, I can transport out and they can't follow. The disrupters will tear their little energy butts to smithereens."

He wondered how she always knew just enough science to theorize somewhat feasible solutions that were incredibly dangerous and unproven. "That's too reckless. We won't be able to communicate with each other or turn the disrupters off to check if you don't come out. We'll have to assume you're...well, you know."

"Yeah, but we don't have time to do anything else," she answered. "I need your support to make this work, Commander Justice. Do I have it?"

That was the first time she officially addressed him as a senior commander since the incident, and it produced the result she wanted. He snapped to attention and agreed with confidence he did not feel one bit.

Listening closely, Blake experienced feelings of trepidation and foreboding. Although he didn't think he would be any help, he offered to go inside with her, which prompted Missa, Brandi, Sheri, and Tom to volunteer, too. Then Honey Bee said she was better equipped to fight the Guardians than the others were.

Mercy Ann answered with cold candor. Only her weapons would be effective against them. If she didn't come out, they must assume she failed. Then they had to abandon Earth and jettison the containment room in space before rejoining the fleet.

"Do you have any questions, John Justice?" she asked in conclusion.

He shook his head.

Standing in the hallway outside the containment room wearing tight flight clothes and boots, Mercy Ann took the metal box John Justice handed her. She transported inside.

John Justice transmitted they were turning on the disrupters and wished her good luck.

Hoping the Guardians were in the mood to negotiate, Mercy Ann burned off metal bands Honey Bee placed around the box. Expecting three, maybe four Guardians, she released the lid.

Two dozen glowing balls of energy swirled around the room firing pulsing blasts that struck with such rapidity and power that Mercy Ann's defensive bubble tumbled and bounced off the walls, ceiling, and floor at high velocity, disorienting her. She tried firing back, but none of her weapons worked. Then she experienced a numbing jolt.

Mercy Ann woke up on her stomach puking her guts out. A dense yellow haze and vile odors filled the room. All her defensives were off. She activated them.

Recovering quickly, she was confused and worried. The only access to her system controls were inside the defensive bubble. She rolled over and stood up, close range weapons ready to fire. Nothing happened.

She had no idea how long she'd been in the room. The haze reduced visibility to half an arm's length. Scanning, she discovered other life in the room, but no other information. Normally, she would see numbers and pinpointed locations. A quick check indicated the scanner was fully functional, but she couldn't get more information.

Having no choice, she transmitted, "Who's in here?"

"The one who rescued you from collectors."

"I thought you died with your ship."

Silence.

"Are you near a wall?"

Silence.

"Are you hurt?"

Silence.

Even if it was her Guardian, where were the others?

She "felt" her way to a wall then followed it to a corner, all the while looking for telltale glows in the haze. Moving along the next wall, her foot struck something.

Kneeling, she found a golden man on his side in a pool of sticky yellow substance. He was naked. He had no hair. No ears or ear passages. Depressions where eyes should be. Yet, his beauty made her gasp with wonder.

Scanning, she received no readings until touching the body. He was alive, but the vital signs did not conform to any lifeforms in her systems.

Then she heard his whisper. "No time. Leave me."

She threw herself onto his back, wrapped defenses around him, and hoped the disrupters didn't rip them apart.

They materialized in the hall outside the containment room, knocking Brandi to the floor. Left to keep watch while the others prepared the ship for departure, she jumped up to help Mercy Ann.

Two and a half hours remained before the end of mankind.

Helping Mercy Ann inject the golden man with powerful stimulants, Honey Bee said he matched images from the same ancient records that depicted Mercy Ann's little ship. She speculated this might be the Guardians' true appearance.

Mercy Ann asked him what kinds of facilities the Sufficiency Test required for a cleansing not originating from space.

He understood the need to hurry and kept responses short. "A cluster of huge facilities packed with micro-projectiles that launch into a planet's stratosphere. They will be hidden in ways that reduce the possibility of discovery for thousands of years."

John Justice was first to think of the object beneath the Great Pyramid in Egypt. He described it.

The golden man affirmed that was it.

John Justice accessed airborne sensors over Cairo and verified two more objects in the ground where the other pyramids had been located.

The golden man told Mercy Ann, "Only you can destroy them using the small ship to amplify the weapon you call Lime Sparklers at full power, but I fear not enough time remains."

Mercy Ann transported to the top of the little ship, jammed herself inside, and opened the storage bay. John Justice fed the shortest route to Egypt into her computers as she launched, piling on as much acceleration as the ship allowed. People in a high-rise downtown described its departure as a wrong-way meteorite shrieking into the night sky.

Honey Bee warned John Justice she did not think Mercy Ann's circuits and ports would hold up.

Mercy Ann heard through John Justice's comm system. "Guess we're going to find out."

Watching the ship's progress on a big screen, John Justice asked Miss Flowers to take the others to the flagship in a shuttle.

Miss Flowers pointed out he did not need to stay since they could communicate with Mercy Ann from space.

He wanted to stay anyway. The others, including the golden man, said the same. Then Miss Flowers stayed, too.

John Justice called Urlak and warned to stay away from Earth.

"I understand how you feel," he replied. "Good luck."

Moving into position over Giza with an hour and fifteen minutes remaining, Mercy Ann unleashed a frightening web of lightning above the crowds. Some people ran. Dazzled by the possibility of treasure, more didn't.

Mercy Ann had no time for more warnings. Unleashing barrage after barrage of Lime Sparklers, she layered the site with bubbling molten goo that ate into the earth.

She switched off monitoring equipment for her systems. She had enough to worry about without John Justice warning her about matters she'd know before him.

The clock counting down showed she did not have enough time. She turned it off and concentrated on keeping firepower at maximum.

She reset the airborne micro-machines in the area to project images of the underground objects onto her ship's screen. The upper portions of the huge structures were dissolving, but too slowly. She increased firepower.

She tried to think of other things and succeeded for longer than she'd thought possible.

Pain in her right arm indicated circuits overheating. The standard remedy was turning them off for two minutes. She checked the countdown clock then switched it off again. Forty minutes to go and two-thirds of the structures remained. She could not spare two minutes.

Mercy Ann reached into a small pouch of drugs she had taken to the confinement room battle, took out a vial, and sucked it dry. The pain faded somewhat.

Ground-to-air missiles, rockets, and small arms fire from inside the city began hitting the ship's defensive barrier, which posed no danger other than disrupting the shower of Sparklers. She had the ship calculate whether it would be more beneficial timewise to destroy the attackers or ignore them. She did not like the answer, especially after killing so many people on the site already.

Mercy Ann blew away entire areas of the city then disbursed Sparklers at an even faster rate. Soon the pain in her arm became unbearable. She drank two more vials.

Warnings flashed in her eye that the right arm was close to critical failure. She'd hoped to avoid taking Guardian pain medicine. Then she messed up and took so much she felt herself blacking out. To counter, she administered an emergency dose of stimulants.

She suffered a mild seizure and pounding chest pain.

John Justice transmitted, "What are you doing, Mercy Ann? Dosages that size can kill or cause brain damage."

She cursed under her breath for not turning off those readings. On the other hand, she didn't much care anymore.

"I soak this stuff up like a sponge," she said, speaking faster than usual. "Don't worry your pretty little head so much."

"Those were Guardian drugs, weren't they?"

She ignored him. "Hey, golden guy, will my other weapons work on the projectiles if they launch?"

"No, but you've destroyed enough for mankind to survive without too many setbacks. You can leave now."

"Millions will die if any get airborne, though. Right?"

"Depends on where they're programmed to go."

"I'll stay another minute or two then," she said, slurring words badly.

John Justice knew she wouldn't leave without destroying all of them. "The territory will be lost if something happens to you, Mercy Ann."

"The others will help you find it," she replied, giggling.

"Don't take anymore drugs," he warned.

She kept giggling. "Feels like the night I tripped to Trans-Love Airways at Fillmore West. Do you remember how we danced?"

"That wasn't me, Mercy Ann. Please try to focus."

She sang, "La-la-la. Sis-boom-bah. John-Boy's bra. Ha, ha, ha."

He yelled to get through to her. "What if you die? What will we do?"

"Blake will be able to use my weapons. I can tell."

John Justice was silent for a few seconds. "Will you share control of the ship with me? I promise not to do anything until you finish."

"I already set my little shippy to return, but I'm more than splendid with letting you ride along. There, all set. Satisfied?"

The monitor in front of him flashed red. "Mercy Ann, your firing output just declined by sixty percent. Do you have a malfunction?"

"John-Boy doesn't miss a frigging thing, does he? Right arm, kaput."

"What do you mean?"

She laughed. "Burned that sucker up, but no worry. I'm on Misty Mountain tripping with the policeman. Remember the fun we had back then?"

John Justice choked off a sob. "How's your left arm?"

Her words were thicker and harder to understand. "Smoking, but no pain in my world, baby!"

"Please give me full control now, Mercy Ann."

"A minute and a half more melty Sparklys, then you can take me back to the farm where I belong, John-Boy-O."

That was her last transmission.

The Sufficiency Test ended. Mankind survived. Other than the handful of people close to the aliens, no one realized.

27

The Most Important Thing

TOM AND BLAKE PULLED MERCY ANN UP through the hatch of the ship. John Justice transported them to the infirmary. The others crowded around while Honey Bee and Ashlyn worked frantically to connect her to medical consoles, not an easy task with the appalling damage to her arms, ports, and circuits.

Ashlyn, who thought she had seen every kind of horror as an emergency room nurse, felt sick examining the charred remains of her right arm.

The whole time Mercy Ann stared up at the ceiling, showing no indication she knew where she was or what they were doing.

Ashlyn diagnosed, “She’s in shock.”

Honey Bee, standing on the gurney frame, watched scan results on a handheld monitor. Suddenly, she jumped onto Mercy Ann’s chest and bent over her face.

“You took huge doses of Guardian pain medications, Earth hallucinogenics, and dangerous stimulants. What the hell is wrong with you?”

Ashlyn reached to pull Honey Bee away. “I just told you she’s in shock.”

Mercy Ann raised her head, looking at Honey Bee. “It was a one-time-only kind of thing so I could destroy the site.”

“Liar!” Honey Bee accused. “How long have you been taking them?”

Mercy Ann did not answer.

"I'll filter as much as I can out of your system then run a full scan to assess how much damage you've done," Honey Bee said.

Mercy Ann rolled her eyes. "Just patch me up and start preparations to replace the arm. You can complete a full assessment after we leave Earth."

"Your system health is marginal and unstable. You should go into stasis so I can begin emergency repairs immediately."

Mercy Ann's scowl showed that was not going to happen.

Honey Bee stung her with a crackling spark.

"What the hell was that for?" Mercy Ann yelled.

Honey Bee looked back at John Justice. "Take command and order her to stand down."

Mercy Ann wasn't having it. "I'm the ranking medical officer, ship captain, and fleet commander. Seeing this mission through to the end is the most important thing in my whole life. Sorry, but that's the way it is."

Mercy Ann sat up on the gurney-bed encased from waist to neck in a layer of gel except for the left arm, which was bandaged but usable. Cables and tubes connected her to medical equipment and a stasis box, synchronizing to her body.

She had called a meeting with the golden man, upsetting John Justice by excluding everyone but Honey Bee at the beginning. She even had Honey Bee transmit waves of white noise in case he tried to eavesdrop because she had many questions that related specifically to her, her brother, and the new John Justice.

First thing, the golden man surprised them by asking that they call him George, an Earth name he had chosen to make interaction simpler. Then Mercy Ann began asking her questions.

George explained how shocked the Guardians had been to find two Earth specimens kept alive so long until studying the collectors' science logs. She and her brother were mutants, considerably more advanced mentally and physically than other human samples from Earth. The news concerned Guardian leaders, who ordered more samples and tests to determine how widespread the mutations were. They also directed George, chief scientist for the territory's humanoid experiments, to convince Mercy Ann and her brother to join the territory protection force to study them further. He had not been completely truthful with her at the time, for which he was sorry.

When the Guardians discovered Mercy Ann could interface with their advanced technologies, it caused such strong disagreements about whether to discard her and her sibling that it brought about a change in leadership. The new rulers supported giving her limited use of advanced weapons. To placate dissenting factions, they agreed to integrating safeguards to insure she never used the weapons against her benefactors. Unfortunately, the safeguards were not adequately tested and caused her to go berserk in battle. He was the one responsible for installation and subsequent removal of the safeguards, for which he was sorry.

After the incident, the leaders decided to repair and rehabilitate Mercy Ann, but gave in to demands by dissenting factions that her brother and the commander were expendable. George and other scientists argued that allowing her budding love interest and sibling to die would crush her emotionally, rendering her useless. The only way to save them was by combining both existences inside her brother's body. He planned to make her brother dominant, but dissenting factions demanded his subjugation in favor of the commander. George was the one who directed the changes, for which he was very sorry.

"Stop saying you're sorry about every goddamned thing," Mercy Ann snapped. "It's pissing me off."

The dissenting factions had one last demand. She and the new John Justice must not be able to produce children lest they contaminate other humanoid planets in the territory with mutant genes. He had disagreed, but supervised the alterations, for which he was very sorry.

Mercy Ann shouted, "Why wasn't I told about this?"

Genuinely perplexed by the question, he asked, "For what purpose?"

She hadn't wanted children, but that wasn't the issue. "What about Urlak? He's fathering kids all over the universe."

The Guardians took Urlak from Earth before his species merged with hers. Otherwise, they would have hunted down and culled all branches of his progeny when they discovered the mutations.

"That's atrocious," Mercy Ann responded. "You assholes should be the ones culled."

"I don't disagree, which is why I'm here," George answered. "I have much worse things to tell you. Do you wish me to continue?"

She nodded.

Preliminary studies had shown Earth's mutations accelerating and becoming a threat to stability in the territory in less than ten generations. In forty generations, Earth might even threaten Guardian rule, which was why the leadership made the decision to wipe out humanoid life on Earth.

But the leadership found themselves in a conundrum. Mercy Ann was the only way to protect the territory when the Guardians executed its plan to evacuate because of the Gargle invasion. To preserve her loyalty, they moved Earth's next Sufficiency Test forward six hundred years and told her the program was automatic, outside their control.

They had not realized how much her feelings for Earth had changed since joining the fleet. When she demanded a chance to help Earth pass the test, they scrambled to impose restrictions to insure she failed without becoming overly suspicious. He had been surprised she did not object more at the time because the restrictions were arbitrary, obvious fabrications.

He paused, expecting a reaction.

"Go on," she said.

Yet, Earth did better than expected. Gargle attack was imminent. The leadership was out of time. They took drastic action, removing Mercy Ann from Earth after probability models indicated swift test failure with John Justice in charge.

By then, George opposed the leadership openly and was onboard the ship that took her from Earth. He downloaded his original programs to make her brother the dominant personality into John Justice at the same instant he transported her from the Death Valley battle. Although it would take months for the changes to manifest completely, John Justice experienced spikes in intelligence immediately, greatly improving his decision-making and odds of helping humankind survive.

Mercy Ann asked that he not to tell the others about any of this, especially about her being from Earth. She wanted to see if the new John Justice remembered it first.

He didn't see why it mattered.

"You owe me for all the shit you've done, so just do it."

He agreed after saying he was sorry again.

It amused Mercy Ann the different ways everyone reacted seeing the distorted image of her naked chest through the gel. Then Missa ran up and kissed her hard on the cheek. The gesture touched Mercy Ann deeply, but she didn't show it.

George explained how the Guardians developed the ability to compress their physical forms into balls of pure energy over eons of existence. As Honey Bee had surmised, the gold-skinned humanoid form was their true evolutionary appearance, but they lived much longer in energy form.

The leadership had sentenced him to remain behind with other dissidents to get Mercy Ann underway then perish with the battleship. Doing so would give their families assured futures without the stigma of disloyal ancestors, which would forever relegate them to the lower levels of Guardian society.

George fully intended to sacrifice himself until they gave him the container of Guardians to send back to Earth with orders to kill Mercy Ann and her crew if Earthlings survived to the last day of the Sufficiency Test. That would trigger an automatic failure and Mercy Ann would realize the test was bogus. The last thing they wanted was to wipe out the Earthlings and leave her behind in charge of a powerful fleet of ships. Better to lose the territory altogether and begin anew when they returned.

So George decided to leave with her. He compressed to pinpoint size, entered Mercy Ann's ship as the hatch closed, and stowed away under the chair. He had to maintain a deep dormant state or the other Guardians would detect his presence in such a confined area. Later, when she removed the box from the ship, he flew up into her hair and resumed dormancy hoping the others would not sense his activity with the sudden inundation of new readings from outside the ship.

He waited until the Guardians attacked then rendered her unconscious and took over her systems. His brethren did not expect to face the new weapons he had given her. Even so, they managed to penetrate all the defenses, requiring George to shield her with his body until wiping them out.

"Why did you decide to help us against your own kind?" Mercy Ann asked.

George explained that the leadership had become more interested in power and ruling than protecting and helping other civilizations. They had such a strong grip on all facets of Guardian society that the only way to oppose them was from the outside. Of all species he had encountered, Earthlings had the best chance against them—given enough time.

Miss Noto paced back and forth in the containment room, stopping frequently to stretch and exercise. A big television screen embedded in a wall showed the President walking beside people carrying his injured wife to an ambulance.

Miss Noto looked up and cursed them. The President was useless and his wife the biggest bitch she'd ever met. She genuinely regretted they survived the terrorist attack.

She touched the TV screen, a menu popped up, and she selected a local channel. A report was on about damage caused by an alien ship leaving the disaster area last night. Asked for comments, the military commander, Major General Wainwright, responded that the alien threat would end within the next twenty-four hours then refused to comment further.

Miss Noto took that to mean the aliens were leaving. She wondered what would happen to her.

Touching a spot above the toilet, a door in the wall slid open, revealing a shower. She stripped and stood under cold water for a long time.

Naked and wet, she came out and selected a meal from a different TV menu. In a few minutes, a compartment would open with the food, which was surprisingly good. Movies, TV shows, and e-books were available, too. She'd spent several hours trying to search for something they didn't have. So far, they had everything.

No one had visited since the weird little alien healed her wounds and showed how the room worked. She found clean bath towels and clothes folded next to the futon when she finished bathing. Toilet dispensers were always full. Dirty clothes vanished if she left them on the floor, but never with her watching.

That they could keep her from seeing how they maintained the room did not surprise her, but the fact they bothered with something so trivial was. She was determined to see items removed and replenished, but never would. The ship's computers controlled Honey Bee's mind games and had only just begun.

Final preparations for the ship to depart Earth were underway.

Honey Bee transported the First Family and Dr. Helen to the White House south lawn. It should have been without incident, but the First Lady tried to kick Honey Bee and had her ankle snapped for the trouble. Mercy Ann told Honey Bee she'd done a good job when she returned.

Miss Flowers, Tom, Rudy, and Sheri stayed busy shopping and transporting supplies for the trip. The flagship, in orbit around Earth, had sent a few crewmembers to go with them to replenish items they needed. Tom, Rudy, and Sheri were disappointed that all were humans, identical to them for the most part.

Miss Flowers laughed. "What do you think would happen if non-humans brought a cart full of groceries to the checkout?"

Brandi, Elena, and the sergeant major reorganized the ship's storage areas. With so many people onboard, Mercy Ann's tendency to put things anywhere they fit wouldn't work any longer.

Zach was with them, playing with a robot toy that belonged to John Justice. Resembling an octopus, it climbed walls and scurried across ceilings. He had a great time but looked forward to playing with other children soon.

The general, inspecting troops and site security with his officers, heard breaking news that the President was back in Washington. He witnessed an immediate change in his men's morale and felt more at ease about leaving them. He planned to vanish without explanation or goodbyes, an old soldier soon forgotten. He had no way of knowing his departure would create a worldwide sensation.

Urlak filled the huge chasm created by Mercy Ann's Sparklers. Soon as her cruiser departed Earth, he would return the pyramids to Egypt then wait for word to destroy Handley's alien technology hidden around the world. Neither he nor John Justice knew why she wanted him to wait since it delayed him departing to rejoin Esmé.

George was in the infirmary with Mercy Ann, John Justice, Honey Bee, Ashlyn, and Blake discussing the planet they would visit next. That was where new crewmembers would begin having their bodies strengthened and fitted with enhancements for deep space travel.

Ashlyn, working at a control panel directing micro-machines to repair Mercy Ann's circuits, only half-listened to George, Mercy Ann, John Justice, Honey Bee, and Blake discussing final plans. Missa was on her mind. She'd seemed deeply upset last she saw her but wouldn't talk about it. On the wall, a muted television kept showing the fantastic sight of the alien ship leaving LA then wreaking havoc in Cairo. Mercy Ann kept glancing at it, concerned by the amount of damage she did to the Egyptian city.

Rob and Missa were in the operations room monitoring site security while the general and sergeant major prepared for transport to the ship from the general's tent. Rob was in charge of the control room and communications with the flagship while John Justice coordinated preparations for departure. He didn't notice how quiet and troubled Missa was.

Honey Bee transported the general, sergeant major, and Bongo onboard. John Justice announced on the intercom that he wanted to show everyone something interesting. All floors except in Miss Noto's room appeared to become transparent. They were in space orbit over the west coast of North America. No one had felt anything to indicate the ship moved.

Most of them freaked out and grabbed for something to hold onto before Justice explained, "All walls, floors, and ceilings can show images from external cameras or any other video source. That's why we can have monitor screens any size and anywhere we want them, so relax. Welcome aboard."

Propped up on the gurney bed, Mercy Ann was at the end of a long meeting table brought into the infirmary. Blake stood behind Ashlyn, Rob, and Missa, seated on one side. The general stood behind Sheri and Brandi, seated on the other.

Before Mercy Ann said anything, a grim-faced Missa stood and took a tiny pistol from her pocket. "Brandi and Sheri came to my room, gave me this, and told me they had been part of a team paid to murder my parents. Then they said I could kill them if I wanted."

"Did they make any conditions?" Mercy Ann asked.

"Only that I kill both if that was what I chose, because neither wants to live without the other. I couldn't do it."

Rob jumped up and grabbed for the gun. "Then give it to me!"

Roughly knocking his arm to the side, she shoved him back into the chair. "I don't need anyone making decisions for me."

He started to say more then swallowed his words. As his face reddened, Ashlyn put an arm around him.

Missa leveled a cold stare at Brandi and Sheri. "I accepted that you killed people for money and thought you were two of the coolest people I ever met before you told me about my parents. Now, part of me wants to kill you and part argues that I don't have the right, especially after being so goddamned unconcerned about other people's lives."

She slid the pistol across the table at Sheri so fast and unexpectedly that she nearly missed catching it.

"I will never forgive you," Missa continued, "but taking your lives doesn't help. I will learn to live with it, but hurt me or mine again, and I will kill you."

"That's not good enough!" Rob shouted as she ran from the room. Then he glared at Mercy Ann. "How can let them get away with this?"

"It was Missa's decision to make. The matter is closed."

"This is insane!" he yelled, out of control. "No way would they have allowed her to kill them!"

"We meant it," Sheri said, putting her hands over Little Bitch then raising them to show the pistol gone. "It was a fair way to resolve the matter."

Brandi added, “But the offer was for her, not you. Now, we have to learn to get along and work together. You, too.”

Rob stormed from the room. Ashlyn went after him.

“Missa is a lot like Sheri and me, and I don’t mean it as a compliment,” Brandi commented, leaving with Sheri.

The general turned to Mercy Ann. “I’m surprised everyone agreed to leave Earth with you. You’re not subjecting us to some sort of brainwashing, are you?”

She smiled weakly. “We enter identifying information of people we want into the ship’s computers and out pops everything it can find about them along with the probability they will join. We don’t know how it works. It’s a Guardian program.”

“Rob needs to be separated from Brandi and Sheri or he may get hurt,” Blake said.

Mercy Ann nodded. “John Justice listened in and suggested sending him to train with Urlak. I’ll send Ashlyn with him. She’ll be useful working in the flagship hospital.”

“What about Missa?” the general asked.

Mercy Ann’s reply was thoughtful. “She is qualified to work in numerous positions, including ship pilot. Blake, Sheri, and Brandi can enhance her fighting skills. Everything else she can learn from John Justice, Honey Bee, you, and me, but I’ll leave it to her whether wants to go to the flagship with Rob and Ashlyn. My guess is she won’t.”

“You don’t think she’ll object to being trained by Brandi and Sheri?” the general asked.

“Not after a little time passes,” Mercy Ann answered. “Brandi nailed it. They’re three uniquely talented women with more similarities than differences.”

Thinking the aliens were gone, the President addressed the world, telling lies to make everyone think that the Mercy Ann and John Justice had worked with Handley’s conspiracy. He depicted himself fighting the terrorists during the White House raid, pledged to manufacture more of Handley’s cutting-edge weapons, and to fund research to make them more powerful. If aliens ever dared return to Earth, they would regret it.

“I knew he would do something like that soon as he thought we were gone,” Mercy Ann said. “Now, we’ll return and show what a liar he is. At the same time, have Urlak destroy the site housing Handley’s alien technology then leave Earth to rejoin Esmé. Now, we’ll start by piecing together a video showing us saving his family while he cowered in his bedroom under the covers.”

John Justice corrected, “He wasn’t cowering. We kept him there.”

She was undeterred. “Along with the video, we’ll say the Sufficiency Test was a fiction and create a new scenario to explain our actions that will win people to our side while discrediting the President so he loses the election.”

“You mean we’ll make up lies,” John Justice sputtered. "You always said we should be honest and not interfere in the affairs of planets.”

“That was Guardian policy that I had to carry out. When you finish editing the video, we’ll send it out to the media. Then we’ll return to Earth.” She turned to the general. “I want to create a *Day the Earth Stood Still* moment in front of the Capitol building tomorrow. You’ll be cast in the Michael Rennie role speaking from the ship’s ramp.”

“Good grief, Mercy Ann,” John Justice said. “We can’t be ready to do all that by tomorrow.”

“Sure we can. Think of the visuals, the stir having an American military hero dissing the President and presenting our story before going into space to defend Planet Earth. Pretty good, if you ask me. But to have proper impact, it needs to be soon, and by soon, I mean tomorrow.”

The general shook his head. “The public resents generals making derogatory comments about the Commander-in-Chief, even if he’s incompetent. And landing the ship near the Capitol building right after the White House attack guarantees them attacking us. Crowds of tourists will be present, too. We can’t be responsible for more casualties.”

Crestfallen, she had to admit he was right.

The sergeant major suggested they land on the lawn of the Washington Monument away from government buildings full of people. It would be less a threat yet close enough for people to come to them.

“Won’t they be frightened and run away?” Blake asked. “Nothing to keep security from attacking, either.”

Realizing how determined Mercy Ann was, John Justice contributed grudgingly. “Politicians are unhappy the President is back, even his own party. They’ll be in the Capitol building in the morning. I will contact the leaders before we land and tell them we come in peace with important information refuting the President’s account of events that will open up the election for new, stronger leadership. We’ll also tell them we have information concerning the well-being of the planet.”

“What if I introduce the crew?” the general suggested. “Having such a diverse cross-section of people will resonate.”

"Identify them by professions, not actual names," Tom suggested. "It'll take the press longer to ferret out details of their lives and keep the public's interest longer, taking airtime from the President."

"In which case, Brandi, Sheri, and I had best stay out of sight," Blake said. "Knowing about us won't help."

The plan came together fast, and everyone was pleased.

Honey Bee had waited to speak. "You don't look well, Mercy Ann. Let me induce sleep for a few hours. You can review what we put together when you wake up."

Her terse response surprised everyone. "Give me some credit, you little twerp. If I let you have control, I'll wake up in that infernal stasis box on another planet."

"It's for your own good."

"It won't be much longer," Mercy Ann answered, moderating her tone. "Please stop worrying so much."

Honey Bee gave in, but next morning transported into the clinic and found Mercy Ann staring at her diagnostic readings, many of which were flashing red. "How bad is it?"

Mercy Ann had not realized anyone was behind her and knew there was no point trying to lie to Honey Bee. "I burned out all my core power units except one after I drained them to increase my firepower. I thought it would be sufficient to maintain my systems for a few weeks, but now it failed, too. My systems are shutting down, diverting energy to biological functions."

Fighting to keep her emotions in check, Honey Bee said, "That's why those units were sealed, Mercy Ann. The nearest replacements are three weeks away. What were you thinking?"

"That I couldn't let all those people die. Anyway, the most important thing now is seeing this mission through to the end. Then I want you to put me in the box and do what you can. Don't tell the others until it's over. I can't handle all the maudlin crap that goes with these kinds of things."

"Very well. I will do my best for you."

"I know. Now let's get to work."

According to press reports, the saucer-shaped UFO dropped out of the morning sky and set down on tall tripod legs next to the Washington Monument across Constitution Avenue from the Ellipse. A section of the ship's midsection slid open. A wide ramp with ten people standing shoulder-to-shoulder extended towards the ground.

Senators, House Members, military, security personnel, office workers, and press corps ran from Capitol buildings and down the

Mall. Tourists, initially panicked by the spacecraft, joined the mad rush to the Washington Monument.

The ramp stopped eight feet from the ground. Surprised murmurs and scattered applause rippled through the gathering crowds as people recognized Major General Harry Wainwright, the LA disaster site hero.

General Wainwright introduced John Justice, his sergeant major, a police lieutenant, a nurse with her teenage son and his girlfriend, and a fireman with his wife and young son. He said John Justice would explain why Earthlings were on the ship when he finished telling them the truth about events in Los Angeles and other locations during the last month.

While the general spoke, the girl took dozens of selfies and pictures of the event. The fireman's son grinned and waved. The others gawked, pointed, and acted same as the tourists visiting the National Mall. Their behavior took the apprehension out of the situation, exactly as Mercy Ann said it would.

The general explained that Earth was in a territory of space protected from hostile intruders and natural disasters by fleets of spaceships from neighboring systems. They kept their existence secret from the less technologically advanced planets except in direst circumstances, which was now the case with Earth.

Then he told how, long before mankind existed, a confederation of planets governed this area of space until imploding due to horrible civil wars. One faction left behind doomsday devices on several planets that had the capability to wipe out all life. Earth was one of them.

No one in the territory knew about any of this until an enemy somehow obtained ancient accounts disclosing locations of the devices. They secretly infiltrated Earth and offered advanced technology and rule of our planet as the newest member of their military empire to Jared Handley, deceased head of Handley Industries. The fool didn't realize the real plan was to activate the doomsday devices and use our dead planet as a base to launch all-out war against the territory.

Fortunately, a territory cruiser on patrol detected an enemy ship in Earth's solar system last month and followed it to the Glenwood Heights area of Los Angeles, where they discovered aliens using a tunnel to access something deep underground. After a surprise attack, a few survivors fled, leaving behind a dying soldier who divulged their plan. The patrol crew went into the tunnel to verify his story and discovered two huge devices counting down.

Mercy Ann was in charge of the crew with John Justice second-in-command. They only had two other crewmembers and no reinforcements available due to enemy attacks in other quadrants, plus an enemy squadron of twelve ships was speeding towards Earth. The territory's central command advised Mercy Ann to leave the planet to its fate and flee, although the chances of escaping so many enemy ships were not good.

The patrol crew chose to stay and fight, beginning with destroying the LA devices. Then they discovered Handley's plot and rescued the First Family before his terrorists killed them. They defended Bagdad against al-Bensi's armies and defeated the squadron of enemy UFOs in spectacular battles that ranged from the Moon to the coast of California. Finally, they located the remaining doomsday devices in Cairo, Egypt, and destroyed them.

The general removed his cap. "During the course of events, Mercy Ann suffered grave injuries which require us to take her to another planet for emergency treatment, which is why she isn't standing here with us."

John Justice, small and unimpressive next to the general, stepped forward and read from a sheet of paper. "Mercy Ann asked me to speak for her. The people with us will be the first Earthlings to serve in the forces protecting the territory. I'm certain more of you will join this endeavor very soon. Earth's participation in the fleet is long overdue."

Applause startled him.

"We thought telling you about doomsday devices and hostile aliens would cause panic, but the story we made up about testing mankind's sufficiency was just as bad. We're sorry for causing so much confusion and worry."

More applause.

"Many actions we took killed innocent people. It is never sufficient to say some had to die so more may live, but that is all we can do. We are very sorry. Every life is precious, something the people of Earth need to realize if you want to take your place amongst other societies and species in the stars. You must first respect and hold dear everyone on your planet. Otherwise, you won't be welcome anywhere else."

"One last matter," he said, looking around. "The President and his wife are fine people, but when it comes to leading you into a better future, you can do much better. Of course, that's up to you. We are happy to help and advise you, but you must make your own decisions then accept the fate you earn. Please remember Mercy Ann in your prayers."

Shouted questions went unanswered. The ramp disappeared into the ship. The big doors closed. The ship rose slowly then shot straight up and out of sight in seconds.

Honey Bee had administered drugs to put Mercy Ann in stasis while the others were outside. Blake and George watched from chairs in the corner. John Justice appeared in the doorway with Ashlyn and realized she was going under already.

He rushed to her side. "You promised we could talk."

She looked up with droopy eyes. "Too late."

"I remembered! We're from Earth!"

She fought to keep her eyes open. Failed.

"I killed our daddy! You were there! I don't know why!"

It took everything she had to whisper, "It was...our stepdaddy...raping me. You...saved us."

The panels on the stasis box lit, indicating full control. John Justice staggered out into the hall.

Ashlyn helped George lower Mercy Ann into the box and removed the gurney frame. They started setting the lid in place.

Blake jumped up and yelled at Honey Bee. "She's dying, isn't she?"

The others coming into the room stopped in stunned silence.

John Justice transported past them to Honey Bee. "Is it true?"

She sank down on her stubby legs. "All we can do is make sure she doesn't suffer."

"Why?" John Justice cried out. "Why?"

Miss Flowers transported in and looked down at Mercy Ann's still form. Tears filled her eyes.

The others moved closer around, a silent vigil.

An unexpected voice came from the hall—Rudy. "Uh, since they're compatible, would it help any to connect Blake to her?"

George responded quietly. "Plugging into someone this powerful experiencing a system crash will drain a life force in seconds."

"Won't she sense who it is and hold back?" Rudy asked doggedly.

"He'll be dead before she knows who it is," George answered.

Blake said, "I'll chance it. Stick one of those temporary ports in my arm and hook us up."

Honey Bee was stern. "No. If we lose both of you, it is certain we can't defend the territory."

"I think we should go all or nothing," Blake argued. "She's much more than a bunch of weapons. We need her."

Missa held up her arm and flipped open the wrist port. "What if another person connected at the same time? Wouldn't it reduce how fast she drained them?"

Pandemonium broke out as everyone volunteered.

"All of us together will not be enough," George said over the hubbub, bringing silence back to the room.

Then Rob asked, "Is there a mechanism that could act as a transformer or resistor to regulate the amount of energy going to her?"

"That might work," John Justice answered glumly, "if we had time to construct something."

"I'll go into the box, have the energy pass through me, and control the flow," George said. "Yes, that is worth a try."

Honey Bee objected. "Guardian or not, she will burn through you to get to the others."

George's answer was solemn. "I can last long enough for her to realize who we are. All of you are willing to risk lives for her. I'm honored to do the same."

Honey Bee asked, "Do you think it will work?"

"It is feasible," George answered then transformed into golden ball of light, and sank slowly into the green gel with Mercy Ann.

Honey Bee looked at readings then connected Blake to the box. He felt a slight jolt and that was all. Then she connected Missa, who experienced agonizing pain that abated before it did damage to her.

Honey Bee added John Justice and had Rudy rest his hands on him. Mercy Ann's shutdown rate slowed to a crawl.

She added more people until Mercy Ann's levels began inching up. She experimented, noting the numbers for each member of the crew. When she had all the readings, she made shift schedules except for Blake, Missa, and George, who had to remain in place until they reached their destination.

It remained touch and go until the fifth day when one of Mercy Ann's systems sputtered back to life. The next day, two more came on.

Midway through the ninth day, those lucky enough to be connected heard Mercy Ann's first conscious communication transmitted from the box: "Was there ever any doubt?"

Then came the unmistakable sound of laughing.

END

ABOUT THE AUTHOR

Growing up in Greensboro, North Carolina, B. C. Howell was an avid reader of fantasy and science fiction. After joining the Air Force and serving in Vietnam, he worked as a civilian manager in an agency of the Department of Defense. His career allowed him to meet many great people and live in numerous states, as well as Germany and Korea. Currently residing in Arizona with his wife, Jill, he enjoys writing the kinds of books he always loved.

Also available by B C Howell on Amazon.com: *Maidservant the God*

Please take the time to review this book on Amazon. It helps improve future works.

Made in the USA
Middletown, DE
19 December 2018